CW01626876

"There will inevitably be comparisons to *The Da Vinci Code* and the *National Treasure* movies with Neville's latest, but it's a poor comparison. This book lords it over most recent historical thrillers with its sharp research and a story that doesn't hit its reader over the head with that research. It's been nearly ten years since Neville put out a book. It was worth the wait."

—*Rocky Mountain News*

"Katherine Neville has a remarkable ability to weave strands of history into one vivid tale. Readers who love culture, travel, and, of course, the detective work of research will delight in this work."

—ELIZABETH KOSTOVA, author of *The Historian*

"Four stars. Intrigue and mystery fill the sequel to Neville's popular 1988 novel, *The Eight*. In this detailed, engrossing follow-up, Neville's globe-spanning descriptions of Russia, the Middle East and the United States are vivid, her characters unusual and the plot intricately woven."

—*Romantic Times Bookreviews*

"Stellar . . . Despite the staggering amount and quality of the research, nothing feels shoehorned or extraneous. The story's relentless pace is matched by characters both sympathetic and real. In the end, readers will be heartened to find signs pointing to the continuation of the Game in future novels."

—*Publishers Weekly* (starred review)

"*The Fire* by Katherine Neville has got to be one of the best novels I've read this year, a masterpiece of riveting suspense, evocative history, exotic international settings, and beautifully crafted characters. *The Fire* is a compulsively readable novel for *Da Vinci Code* fans who want to graduate to a real writer, as brilliantly complex as a grand-master chess match. A bravura performance from a major talent, who keeps the excitement at a high pitch from beginning to end. I could *not* put this book down."

—DOUGLAS PRESTON, *New York Times* bestselling author of *The Monster of Florence*

"I've been waiting for this book for twenty years, and it still blew me away. Katherine Neville's long-anticipated book, *The Fire,* proves once again that she is the true grand master of international intrigue and historical mystery. From the palaces of a lost Arabia to the halls of Washington, D.C., here is a story that twines the past and future into a complex game, played across millennia yet resting on the shoulders of a young woman with a destiny like no other. Relentless, gripping, convoluted, and grand, this is a classic for the new millennium."

—JAMES ROLLINS, *New York Times* bestselling author of *The Last Oracle*

"Neville deftly employs time-shifting storytelling and casts historical figures in her story with such dexterity that you are sure all these people must really have known one another. Ingenious puzzles, enthralling historical ambience, and masterful plot twists abound. More please!"

—*Library Journal*

"Fans of *The Eight* who have long awaited the rest of the story will be delighted with this entrancing blend of history, chess, and high adventure."

—*Booklist*

"The thriller for people who don't read thrillers . . . A great read."

—*The Bethel Beacon*

"Just as ambitious as its predecessor, Neville's latest recreates her fresh approach to storytelling. . . . A chess set has never been more exciting than this one."

—*The Hartford Courant*

"Fans of *The Eight* will enjoy this long-awaited sequel, with its abundant ciphers, intrigues and a splash of romance."

—*The Free Lance-Star*

"Fans of Dan Brown's *The Da Vinci Code* likely will find this book difficult to put down."

—*Wisconsin State Journal*

Also by Katherine Neville

THE EIGHT
A CALCULATED RISK
THE MAGIC CIRCLE

Books published by The Random House Publishing Group are available at quantity discounts on bulk purchases for premium, educational, fund-raising, and special sales use. For details, please call 1-800-733-3000.

THE FIRE

A NOVEL

KATHERINE NEVILLE

BALLANTINE BOOKS • NEW YORK

Sale of this book without a front cover may be unauthorized. If this book is coverless, it may have been reported to the publisher as "unsold or destroyed" and neither the author nor the publisher may have received payment for it.

The Fire is a work of fiction. Names, characters, places, and incidents are the products of the author's imagination or are used fictitiously. Any resemblance to actual events, locales, or persons, living or dead, is entirely coincidental.

2009 Ballantine Books International Edition

Copyright © 2008 by Katherine Neville

All rights reserved.

Published in the United States by Ballantine Books, an imprint of The Random House Publishing Group, a division of Random House, Inc., New York.

BALLANTINE and colophon are registered trademarks of Random House, Inc.

Originally published in hardcover in the United States by Ballantine Books, an imprint of The Random House Publishing Group, a division of Random House, Inc., in 2008.

ISBN 978-0-345-51730-2

Cover design: Marc Cohen
Cover illustrations: © Stuart Abraham/Alamy (fire), © David Muir/ Getty Images (chess piece), © James Porto/Getty Images (phoenix)

Printed in the United States of America

www.ballantinebooks.com

OPM 9 8 7 6 5 4 3 2 1

To Solano

In AD 782, the emperor Charlemagne received a fabulous gift from Ibn al-Arabi, the Moorish governor of Barcelona: a gold and silver, bejeweled chess set that today we know as the Montglane Service. The service was rumored to contain a secret of dark, mysterious power. All those obsessed with power were determined to obtain the pieces. In order to prevent this, the Montglane Service was buried for nearly a thousand years.

In 1790, at the dawn of the French Revolution, the chess set was exhumed from its hiding place, Montglane Abbey in the Basque Pyrenees, and the pieces were scattered across the globe.

This move launched a new round in a deadly game, a game that threatens—even today—to light the match that will set the world aflame . . .

END GAME

The only goal in chess is to prove your superiority over the other guy. And the most important superiority, the most total one, is the superiority of the mind. I mean, your opponent must be destroyed. Fully destroyed.

—GRANDMASTER GARRY KASPAROV,
WORLD CHESS CHAMPION

ZAGORSK MONASTERY, RUSSIA
AUTUMN 1993

SOLARIN GRIPPED HIS LITTLE DAUGHTER'S MITtened hand firmly in his own. He could hear the snow crunch beneath his boots and see their breath rise in silvery puffs, as together they crossed the impregnable walled park of Zagorsk: Troitse-Sergiev Lavra, the Exalted Trinity Monastery of Saint Sergius of Radonezh, the patron saint of Russia. They were both bundled to the teeth in clothes they'd managed to forage—thick wool scarves, fur cossack caps, greatcoats—against this unexpected onslaught of winter in the midst of what should have been *Zhensheena Lieta:* the Women's Summer. But the biting wind penetrated to the core.

Why had he brought her here to Russia, a land that held so many bitter memories from his past? When he was just a child himself, when Stalin had reigned, hadn't he witnessed the destruction of his own family in the dead of night? He'd survived the cruel disciplines of the orphanage where he'd been left in the Republic of Georgia, and those long, bleak years at the Palace of Young

Pioneers, only because they'd learned how very well the young boy, Aleksandr Solarin, could play chess.

Cat had begged him not to risk coming here, not to risk bringing their child here. Russia was dangerous, she'd insisted, and Solarin himself had not been back to his homeland in twenty years. But his wife's biggest fear had always been not of Russia but of the game—the game that had cost them both so much. The game that, more than once, had nearly destroyed their life together.

Solarin was here for a game of chess, a critical game, the last game of the weeklong competition. And he knew it did not bode well that this, the final game, had suddenly been relocated to this particular location, so far from town.

Zagorsk, still called by its Soviet name, was the oldest of the *lavras,* or exalted monasteries, forming a ring of fortress-monasteries that had defended Moscow for six hundred years, since the Middle Ages, when, with the blessing of Saint Sergius, they had driven back the Mongol hordes. But today it was richer and more powerful than ever: Its museums and churches were packed with rare icons and bejeweled reliquaries, its coffers stuffed with gold. Despite its wealth, or perhaps because of it, the Moscow church seemed to have enemies everywhere.

It was only two years since the bleak, gray Soviet Empire had collapsed with a *pouf*—two years of glasnost and perestroika and turmoil. But the Moscow Orthodox Church, as if born again, had risen like a phoenix from the ashes. *Bogoiskatelstvo*—"the Search for God"—was on everyone's lips. A medieval chant. All the cathedrals, churches, and basilikas around Moscow had been granted new life, lavished with money and a fresh coat of paint.

Even sixty kilometers out here in rural Sergiev Posad, Zagorsk's vast park was a sea of newly refurbished edifices, their turrets and onion domes lacquered in rich, jewel-like colors: blue and cranberry and green, all splashed with gold stars. It was, thought Solarin, as if seventy-five years of repression could no longer be contained and had suddenly exploded in a confetti of feverish color. But inside the walls of these bastions, he knew, the darkness remained.

It was a darkness Solarin was all too familiar with, even if it had changed its hue. As if to reinforce this truth, guards were stationed every few yards along the high parapets and the interior perimeter of the wall, each wearing a black leather jacket with high collar and mirrored sunglasses, each with a bulging gun strapped beneath his arm and a walkie-talkie in hand. Such men were always the same, regardless of the era: like the ever-present KGB who'd escorted Solarin everywhere, back in the days when he himself had been one of the greatest of Soviet grandmasters.

But the men here, Solarin knew, were the infamous Secret Service belonging to the "Mafia Monks of Moscow," as they were called throughout Russia. It was rumored that the Russian church had formed a less-than-holy alliance with disaffected members of the KGB, Red Army, and other "nationalist" movements. Indeed, that was Solarin's very fear: It was the monks of Zagorsk who had arranged for today's game.

As they passed the Church of the Holy Spirit and headed across the open court toward the Vestry, where the game would soon take place, Solarin glanced down at his daughter, Alexandra—little Xie—her small hand still grasping his. She smiled up at him, her green eyes filled with confidence, and his heart nearly broke with the beauty of her. How could he and Cat have created such a creature?

Solarin had never known fear—real fear—until he had a child of his own. Right now, he tried not to think of the armed and thuglike guards glaring down at them from atop each wall. He knew he was walking with his child into the lion's den and he was sick at heart at the thought of it—but he knew it was inevitable.

Chess was everything to his daughter. Without it, she was a fish taken out of the water. Perhaps this was his fault, too—perhaps it was in her genes. And though everyone had opposed it—most especially her mother—he knew this would surely be the most important tournament of Xie's young life.

Through it all, and through a week of abysmal cold, snow, and sleet, the awful tournament food—black bread, black tea, and gruel—Xie had remained undaunted. She seemed not to notice anything outside the domain of the chessboard itself. All week, she'd played like a *Stakhanoviste,* raking in point after point in game after game, a hod carrier stacking up bricks. In the week, she'd lost only one game. They both knew she must not lose another.

He'd had to bring her here, hadn't he? It was only at this tournament—here at Zagorsk today, where the last game would take place—where his young daughter's future would be decided. She must win today, this last game at Zagorsk. For they both knew that this was the game that could make Alexandra "Xie" Solarin—who was not yet twelve—the youngest grandmaster of chess, male or female, in the history of the game.

Xie tugged her father's hand and unwrapped her muffler so she could speak. "Don't worry, Papa. I'll beat him this time."

THE ONE SHE REFERRED to was Vartan Azov, the young chess wizard from Ukraine, only a year older than Xie and the only player in the tournament so far to have defeated her. But he hadn't really defeated Xie; Xie had lost on her own.

Against young Azov, she had played the King's Indian Defense—one of her favorites, Solarin knew, for it allowed the valiant Black Knight (in the guise of her father and tutor) to leap to the front over the heads of the other pieces, and take charge. After a daring Queen sacrifice that brought murmurs from the crowd and gave her the center board, it appeared that Solarin's fearlessly aggressive little warrior would—at the very least—go over the Reichenbach Falls and take young Professor Azov with her in a deathlike embrace. But it wasn't to be.

There was a name for it: *Amaurosis Scacchistica.* Chess blindness. Every player had experienced it at one time in his career. They preferred to call it a "blunder"—the failure to spot a truly obvious danger. Solarin had experienced it once, when really young. As he recalled, it felt like falling down a well, tumbling in free fall with no sense of which end was up.

In all the games Xie had ever played, it had happened to her only once. But *twice,* Solarin knew, was one time too many for a mistake like this. It could not happen again today.

BEFORE THEY REACHED the Vestry where the game would take place, Solarin and Xie encountered an unexpected human barricade: a long line of drab women in threadbare overclothes and babushkas, who had queued up in the snow awaiting the perpetual daily memorial services, outside the charnel house of the famous Troitsky Sobor—the Trinity Church of Saint Sergius, where the saint's bones were buried. These pitiful creatures—there must have been fifty or sixty of them—were all crossing themselves in the compulsive Orthodox fashion, as if seized by a mass religious frenzy, as they gazed up at the portrait of Our Savior high on the outer church wall.

These women, as they moaned and prayed in the whirling snow, formed a barrier nearly as impenetrable as the armed guards posted high on the parapets. And in the old Soviet tradition, they refused to budge or part ranks to let anyone pass through their queue. Solarin could scarcely wait to get past them.

As he picked up his pace to skirt the long queue, over the women's heads Solarin glimpsed the facade of the Art Museum, and just beyond, the Vestry and treasury, where they were headed for the game.

The museum's facade had been festooned with a large, colorful banner displaying a painting and hand-printed words that announced, in Cyrillic and English: *SEVENTY-FIVE YEARS OF SOVIET PALEKH ART.*

Palekh art were those lacquered paintings that often depicted scenes from fairy tales and other peasant themes. They'd long been the only primitive or "superstitious" art acceptable to the Communist regime and they adorned everything in Russia, from miniature papier-mâché boxes to the walls of the Pioneers' Palace itself, where Solarin—with fifty other boys—had practiced his defenses and counterattacks for more than twelve years. As he had had no access all that time to storybooks, cartoons, or films, the Palekh illustrations of these ancient tales had been young Aleksandr's only access to the realm of fantasy.

The painting on this banner was one with which he was well acquainted, a famous one. It seemed to remind him of something important. He studied it carefully as he and Xie picked their way around the long line of zealously praying women.

It was a rendering of the most famous Russian fairy tale, the story of the Firebird. There were many versions that had inspired great art, literature, and music, from

Pushkin to Stravinsky. This picture on the banner was the scene where Prince Ivan, hiding in his father the tsar's gardens all night, finally sights the luminous bird that had been eating his father's golden apples, and he tries to capture her. The Firebird escapes, leaving just one of her fabulous magical feathers in Ivan's grasp.

This was the well-known work of Alexander Kotukhin that hung in the Pioneers' Palace. He was one of the first generation of Palekh artists from the 1930s, who was said to have hidden secret messages within the symbols he used in his paintings that the State censors couldn't always easily interpret—though the illiterate peasantry could. Solarin wondered what this decades-old message had meant, and to whom.

At last they reached the end of the long line of waiting women. As Solarin and Xie curved back to head toward the Vestry, a stooped old woman in a babushka and threadbare sweater and carrying a tin pail left her place in the queue and brushed past them—still crossing herself fervently. She bumped into Xie, bowed an apology, and continued across the yard.

When she'd passed, Solarin felt Xie tugging his hand. He glanced down to see his daughter extracting a small embossed cardboard placard from her pocket—a ticket or pass to the Palekh exhibit, for it bore the same picture as the banner.

"Where did this come from?" he asked, although he was afraid he knew. He glanced after the woman, but she'd vanished across the park.

"That lady put it into my pocket," Xie was saying.

When he looked down again, his daughter had flipped over the card, and Solarin snatched it away. On the back was pasted a small illustration of a flying bird set inside an Islamic eight-pointed star, and three words were printed in Russian:

опáсно берéчься пожáр

Reading these words, Solarin felt the blood pulsing in his temples. He glanced quickly in the direction the old woman had gone, but she seemed to have vanished. Then he saw something flicker at the far periphery of the walled fortress; emerging from the copse of trees, she was vanishing again around the far corner of the Tsar's Chambers—a distance of more than one hundred paces.

Just before she disappeared, she turned to glance over her shoulder directly at Solarin, and he—who had been about to follow her—halted in shock. Even at this distance, he could make out those pale blue eyes, the wisp of silvery-blond hair escaping from her scarf. This was no old crone, but a woman of great beauty and infinite mystery.

And more. It was a face he knew. A face he had imagined he would never see again in this life.

Then she was gone.

He heard himself speak. "It cannot be."

How *could* it be? People do not rise from the dead. And if they did, they would not look the same after fifty years.

"Do you know that lady, Papa?" Xie asked in a whisper so no one could hear.

Solarin dropped to one knee in the snow beside his daughter and tossed his arms about her, burying his face in her muffler. He felt like weeping.

"For a moment she looked familiar," he said to Xie. "But I'm sure I do not."

He squeezed her harder, as if he could wring her out. In all these years, he had never lied to his daughter. Not until now. But what could he tell her?

"And what does her card say?" Xie whispered in his ear. "The one with the flying bird?"

"*Apahsnah*—it means 'danger,' " Solarin told her, trying to pull himself together.

For God's sake, what was he thinking? This was a fantasy brought on by a week of stress and bad food and miserable cold. He must be strong. He got to his feet and pressed his daughter's shoulder between his fingers. "But perhaps the only danger here is of *you* forgetting your practice!" He gave a smile that Xie did not return.

"What do the other words say?" she asked.

"*Byrihgyees pahzhar,*" he told her. "I think it's just a reference to the firebird or phoenix in this picture here." Solarin paused and looked at her. "In English, it means, 'Beware the fire.' " He took a deep breath. "Now let's go inside," he said, "so you can beat the pants off of that Ukrainian *patzer*!"

FROM THE MOMENT they entered the Vestry of Sergiev Lavra, Solarin knew something was wrong. The walls were cold and damp, depressing like everything else in the so-called Women's Summer. He thought of the woman's message. What did it mean?

Taras Petrossian, the dashing nouveau capitalist tournament organizer, in his expensive Italian suit, was handing a large wad of rubles as a pourboire to a skinny monk with a big ring of keys, who'd unlocked the building for the game. Petrossian, it was said, had made his fortune through under-the-table dealings in the several designer restaurants and nightclubs he owned. There was a colloquial word for it in Russian: *blat.* Connections.

The armed thugs had already penetrated the inner sanctum—they lurked everywhere in the Vestry, leaning conspicuously against the walls, and not just for warmth. Among other things, this low, squat, unobtrusive building served as the monastery's treasury.

The glut of the medieval church's gold and jewels were displayed on pedestals in brightly lit glass cases scattered around the floor. It would be hard to concentrate on chess, thought Solarin, with all this blinding glitter—but there was the young Vartan Azov, already seated beside the chessboard, his large dark eyes focused upon them as they entered the room. Xie left her father and went to greet him. Solarin thought—not for the first time—that he would like to watch Xie wipe the board with the arrogant brat.

He had to wipe that message from his mind. What did the woman mean? Danger? Beware the fire? And that face he could never forget, a face from his darkest dreams, his nightmares, his worst horrors—

And then he saw it. In a glass display case far across the room.

Solarin walked as in a dream across the wide-open floor of the Vestry and he stood looking down at the large glass case.

Within was a sculpture he had also thought he would never see again—something as impossible and as dangerous as the face of that woman he'd glimpsed outside. Something that had been buried, something long ago and far away. Yet here it was before him.

It was a heavy gold carving, caked with jewels. It portrayed a figure dressed in long robes and seated in a small pavilion with the draperies drawn back.

"The Black Queen," whispered a voice just beside him. Solarin looked down to see the dark eyes and tousled hair of Vartan Azov.

"Discovered only recently," the boy went on, "in the cellar of the Hermitage in Petersburg—along with Schliemann's treasures of Troy. They say this once belonged to Charlemagne and was hidden—perhaps since the French Revolution. It may have been in possession of Catherine the Great of Russia. This is the first time it has been shown in public since it was found." Vartan paused. "It was brought here for this game."

Solarin was blinded by terror. He could hear nothing further. They had to depart at once. For this piece was theirs—the most important piece of all those they had captured and buried. How could it be surfacing here in Russia, when they had buried it twenty years ago, thousands of miles away?

Danger, beware the fire? Solarin had to get out of this place and get some air, he had to escape with Xie right now, the game be damned. Cat had been right all along, but he couldn't see the whole picture yet—he couldn't see the board for the pieces.

Solarin nodded politely to Vartan Azov and crossed the room in a few swift strides. He took Xie by the hand and headed for the door.

"Papa," said Xie in confusion, "where are we going?"

"To see that lady," he said cryptically, "the lady who gave you the card."

"But what about the game?"

She would forfeit if she wasn't there when they started the clocks. She would lose everything they had worked so long and hard for. But he had to know. He stepped outside, holding her hand.

From the top of the Vestry steps, he saw her across the park. The woman was standing at the gates, looking across the space at Solarin with love and understanding. He had been right about her. But then her look changed to one of fear, as she glanced up toward the parapet.

It was only another instant before Solarin followed her gaze and saw the guard, perched on the parapet high above, the gun in his hand. Without thinking, Solarin shoved Xie behind him for protection and glanced back at the woman.

"Mother," he said.

And the next thing he saw was the fire in his head.

PART ONE

Albedo

At the beginning of every spiritual realization stands death, in the form of "dying to the world." . . . At the beginning of the work ["The Albedo" or "Whitening"] the most precious material which the alchemist produces is the ash.

—TITUS BURCKHARDT, *Alchemy*

You must consume yourself in your own flame; how could you wish to become new unless you had first become ashes!

—FRIEDRICH NIETZSCHE,
Thus Spake Zarathustra (Kaufmann translation)

THE WHITE LAND

Pray to Allah, but hobble your camel.
—SUFI SAYING

JANINA, ALBANIA
JANUARY 1822

THE ODALISQUES, CHAMBERMAIDS OF ALI PASHA'S harem, were crossing the icy footbridge through the marsh when they heard the first screams.

Haidée, the pasha's twelve-year-old daughter, clutched the hand of the nearest of her three escorts—none of them older than fifteen—and together they peered into the darkness, afraid to speak or breathe. Across vast Lake Pambotis, they could make out the torches that flickered along the far shore, but that was all.

The screams came faster, harsher now—hoarse, panting cries, like wild animals barking to one another in the forest. But these were the cries of humans—and not those of hunters, but of the hunted. Male voices, raised in fear, blowing across the lake.

Without warning, a lone kestrel flapped up from the stiff cattails before the clustered girls, winging past them in silence, hunting its prey in the predawn light, and then the cries and the torches vanished as if swallowed by the fog. The dark lake lay in silvery silence—a silence more ominous than the cries that had gone before.

Had it begun?

Here on their floating wooden bridge, protected only

by the thick marsh grasses that surrounded them, the odalisques and their young ward were unsure what to do: retrace their steps back to the harem on its tiny isle, or continue across the marsh to the steamy *hamam,* the bathhouse at the edge of the shore, where they'd been ordered—urgently, under pain of severe punishment—to deliver the pasha's daughter before dawn. An escort would be waiting near the *hamam,* to bring her—on horseback, under cover of darkness—to her father.

The pasha had never issued such a command before. It could not be disobeyed. Haidée was dressed for the trek, in thick kashimir pantaloons and fur-lined boots. But her odalisques—frozen here in indecision upon the bridge—were trembling more from fear than from the cold, unable to move. Sheltered as she'd been in her twelve years, it was clear to young Haidée that these ignorant country girls would prefer the warmth and relative safety of their harem, surrounded by fellow slaves and concubines, to the icy winter lake with its dark and unknown dangers. In truth, she'd prefer it herself.

Haidée silently prayed for a sign of what those terrified screams had meant.

Then, as if in answer to her unspoken request, through the dark morning mist across the lake she could make out the fire that had flamed up like a beacon, illuminating the massive form of the pasha's palace. Projecting into the lake on its spit of land, its crenellated white granite walls and pointed minarets shimmering in the mist, it seemed to rise from the waters: Demir Kule, the Iron Castle. It was part of a walled fortress, the Castro, at the entrance to the six-kilometer lake and it had been built to withstand the onslaught of ten thousand troops. In these past two years of armed siege by the Ottoman Turks, it had proven impregnable.

Just as impregnable was this strip of craggy, mountainous terrain—Shquiperia, the Eagle's Country—a wild, unconquerable place ruled by a wild, unconquerable people who called themselves Toska—"coarse"—after the rough, volcanic pumice that had formed this land. The Turks and Greeks called it Albania—the White Land—for those rugged, snowcapped mountains that protected it from attack by land or sea. Its inhabitants, the most ancient race in southeastern Europe, still spoke the ancient tongue—older by far than Illyrian, Macedonian, or Greek: Chimaera, a language comprehended by no one else on earth.

And the wildest and most chimaerical of these was Haidée's father, red-haired Ali Pasha—Arslan, "the Lion," as he was called from the age of fourteen, when, alongside his mother and her band of brigands, he'd avenged his father's death in a *ghak*, a blood feud, to recover the town of Tebelen. It would be the first of many such ruthless victories.

Now, nearly seventy years later, Ali Tebeleni—Vali of Rumelia, Pasha of Janina—had formed a sea power to rival Algiers and captured all the coastal towns down to Parga, once possessions of the Venetian Empire. He feared no power, east or west. He himself was the most powerful force in the far-flung Ottoman Empire, after the sultan in Constantinople. *Too* powerful, in fact. That was the trouble.

For weeks now, Ali Pasha had been sequestered, along with a small retinue—twelve of his closest supporters and Haidée's mother, Vasiliki, the pasha's favorite wife—in a monastery at the middle of the enormous lake. He was awaiting his pardon from the sultan, Mahmud II, in Constantinople—a pardon now eight days overdue. The only insurance against the pasha's life was the hard, stony fact of Demir Kule itself. The fortress, defended by six batteries of British mortar, was also packed with twenty thousand pounds of French explosives. The pasha had threatened to destroy it, to blow it to the skies—along with all the treasures and lives within its walls—if the sultan's promised pardon was not forthcoming.

Haidée understood that it must be for this very reason the pasha had ordered her to be brought to him, under cover of darkness, at this final hour. Her father needed her. She vowed to quell any fears.

But then in the deathly silence Haidée and her chambermaids heard a sound. It was a soft sound, but infinitely terrifying. A sound borne very close by, only meters from where they stood, sheltered here among the high grasses.

The sound of oars, dipping into the water.

As if with one thought, the young girls held their breath and focused upon that lapping sound. They could nearly touch its source.

Through the dense, silvery fog, they could just make out three longboats slipping past them in the waters. Each slender caique was rowed by shadowy oarsmen—perhaps ten or twelve shadows per boat, more than thirty men in all. Their silhouettes swayed rhythmically.

In horror, Haidée knew there could be no mistake where these boats were headed. There was only one thing that lay beyond the marsh—out there in the middle of the vast lake. These boats and their clandestine oarsmen were headed for the Isle of Pines, where the monastery lay: the island refuge of Ali Pasha.

She knew she must reach the *hamam* at once—she must reach the shore, where the pasha's horseman was waiting. She knew just what those terrified screams had meant—what the silence, and the small beacon fire that followed it, must signify. They were warnings to those awaiting the dawn, those who were waiting on that isle across the lake. Warnings by those who must have risked their lives just to light such a fire. Warnings to her father.

It meant that the impregnable Demir Kule had been taken without a single shot. The brave Albanian defenders who had held out for two long years had been defeated, by stealth or treachery, in the dead of night.

And Haidée understood what that meant: These boats slipping past her were no ordinary ships.

These were Turkish ships.

Someone had betrayed her father, Ali Pasha.

MEHMET EFFENDI STOOD in darkness, high in the bell tower of the St. Pantaleon monastery on the Isle of Pines. He held his spyglass, awaiting his first glimpse of dawn with uncustomary anxiety and trepidation.

Such anxiety was uncustomary to Mehmet Effendi due to the fact that he had always known what each next dawn, in a long succession of dawns, was going to bring. He knew such things—the unfolding of future events—with a sharp precision. Indeed, ordinarily he could time them to within the fragment of a moment. This was because Mehmet Effendi was not only—in his civil role—Ali Pasha's chief minister, he was also the pasha's chief astrologer. Mehmet Effendi had never been wrong in predicting the outcome of a maneuver or a battle.

The stars had not been out last night, and there'd been no moon to go by, but he hardly needed such things. For in these past few weeks and days, the omens had never been clearer. It was only their interpretation, right now, that still gave him pause. Though why should it? he chastened himself. After all, it was all in place, wasn't it? Everything that had been foretold was coming to pass.

The twelve were here, weren't they? All of them—not just the general, but the shaikhs, the Mürsits of the order—even the great Baba himself, who'd been brought here from his near-death bed, by litter-bearers, over the Pindus range of mountains, to arrive just in time for this event. This was the event that had been awaited for more than one thousand years, since the days of the caliphs al-Mahdi and Harun al-Rashid. All the right people were in place—and the omens, too. How could it possibly go wrong?

Waiting beside Effendi in silence was the general: Athanasi Vaya, head of the pasha's armies, whose brilliant strategies had held the Ottoman armies of Sultan Mahmud II at bay these past two years.

To accomplish this, Vaya had employed the freebooting Klepht banditti to guard the high mountain passes against intrusion. Then he'd deployed Ali Pasha's crack Albanian Palikhari troops, in Frankish-style guerrilla warfare and sabotage. At the end of last Ramadan, for instance, when Sultan Mahmud's officers were inside Janina's White Mosque at their *Bairam* prayers, Vaya had ordered the Palikhari to demolish the place by cannonade. The Ottoman officers, along with the mosque, had been reduced to charcoal. But Vaya's real stroke of genius involved the sultan's own troops: the Janissaries.

The degenerate Ottoman sultans—ensconced in their harems in the "Golden Cage" of the Topkapi Palace at Constantinople—had always raised armies by imposing upon their outlying Christian provinces a levee called the *Devishirme*—the "Tax of Children." Each year, one in every five Christian boys was removed from his village, then taken to Constantinople, converted to Islam, and enrolled in the sultan's armies. Despite the injunctions of the Qur'an against forcible conversion to Islam, or against selling Muslims into slavery, the *Devishirme* had existed for five hundred years.

These boys, their successors, and their descendants had grown into a powerful, implacable force that even the Sublime Porte at Constantinople could not control. The Janissary troops, when not otherwise employed, did not blanch at setting the capital city aflame, robbing civilians in the streets—nor even removing sultans from their thrones. The sultan Mahmud II had lost his own two predecessors to such Janissary predations. He'd decided it was time to put a stop to it.

But there was a twist to the plot—and it lay right here in the White Land. That problem was precisely why Sultan Mahmud had sent his armies here over the mountains, why they had laid siege to these lands for the past two years. Why their vast armies had been waiting outside the Castro to bombard the fortress of Demir Kule. But this problem also explained why they had not yet been successful—why the Janissaries had not demolished the fortress. And it was this problem that gave Chief Minister Mehmet Effendi and his companion more than a small bit of confidence tonight, as they stood here now, watching, in the bell tower of St. Pantaleon, in the predawn light.

There was only one thing on earth that the all-powerful Janissaries truly venerated—something they had continued to revere, over all the past five hundred years of their military corps' existence. This was the memory of Haji Bektash Veli—the thirteenth-century founder of the mystical Bektashi order of Sufi dervishes. Haji Bektash was the *Pir* of the Janissaries—their patron saint.

This was, in truth, why the sultan feared his own army so. Why he'd had to replenish the forces fighting here with mercenaries drawn from other pashiliks, elsewhere throughout his far-flung empire.

The Janissaries had become a true menace to the empire itself. Like religious zealots, they swore an oath of allegiance drenched with secret mystical codes. Worse, they swore allegiance only to their *Pir*—not to the house of Osman or its sultan, trapped in his Golden Cage on the Golden Horn.

I have trusted in God . . . (so began the Janissaries' oath)

> *We are believers of old. We have confessed the unity of Reality. We have offered our head on this way. We have a prophet. Since the time of the Mystic Saints we have been the intoxicated ones. We are the moths in the divine fire. We are a company of wandering dervishes in this world. We cannot be counted on the fingers; we cannot be finished by defeat. No one outside of us knows our state.*
>
> *The Twelve Imams, the Twelve Ways, we have affirmed them all: the Three, the Seven, the Forty, the light of the Prophet, the Beneficence of Ali, our Pir—the head sultan, Haji Bektash Veli . . .*

It gave Mehmet Effendi and General Vaya relief to know that the greatest Bektashi representative here on earth—the *Dede,* the oldest Baba—had traveled over the mountains to be here tonight. To be present for the event they had all awaited. The Baba, who alone knew the true mysteries and what the omens might portend.

But despite all the omens, it seemed something may have gone wrong.

Chief Minister Effendi turned to General Vaya in the darkened bell tower of the monastery. "This is an omen I do not understand," he told the general.

"You mean, something in the stars?" General Vaya objected. "But my friend, you've assured us that all is well in that department. We've followed your astrological injunctions to the closest. It's as you always say: *Con-sider* means '*with* the stars'; *dis-aster* means '*against* them'!

"Furthermore," the general continued, "even if your

predictions are completely wrong—if the Castro is destroyed, with its millions in jewels and thousands of barrels of powder—as you know, we are all Bektashis here, including the pasha! They may have replaced their leaders with the sultan's men, but even they haven't dared to destroy us yet, nor will they attempt it, as long as the pasha holds the 'key' that they all covet. And do not forget—we also have an exit strategy!"

"I fear not," said Mehmet Effendi, handing his spyglass to the general. "I cannot explain it, but something seems to have happened. There has been no explosion. The dawn is nearly here. And a small bonfire is burning, like a beacon, across the lake."

"ARSLAN" ALI PASHA, the Lion of Janina, paced the cold, tiled floor of his monastery chambers. He'd never been so terrified in all his life—though not for himself, of course. He had no illusions about what would soon become of him. After all, there were Turks at the other side of the lake. He knew their methods all too well.

Well, he knew what would happen—his head on a pike, like his two poor sons who'd been foolish enough to trust the sultan. His head would be packed in salt for the long sea voyage, then brought to Constantinople, as a warning to other pashas who'd got themselves too far above their station. His head, like theirs, would be stuck on the iron prongs, high on the gates of the Topkapi Palace—the High Gate, the "Sublime Porte"—to dissuade other infidels from rebellion.

But he was no infidel. Far from it, though his wife was a Christian. He was terrified for his beloved Vasiliki, and for little Haidée. He could not even bring himself to think of what would happen to them the very moment that he was dead. His favorite wife and her daughter—

now there was something the Turks could torture him with—perhaps even in the afterlife.

He remembered the day he and Vasiliki had met—it was the subject of many a legend. She had been the same age then as Haidée was now—twelve years old. The pasha had ridden into her town that day, years ago, on his prancing, caparisoned Albanian stallion, Dervish. Ali had been surrounded by his broad-chested, long-haired, gray-eyed Palikhari troops from the mountains, in their colorful embroidered waistcoats, shaggy sheepskin capotes, armed with daggers and inlaid pistols tucked in their waist sashes. They were there for a punitive mission against the village, under orders from the Porte.

The sixty-four-year-old pasha himself had cut a dashing figure, with his ruby-studded scimitar in hand and, slung on his back, that famous musket inlaid with mother-of-pearl and silver—a gift of the emperor Napoleon. That was the day—was it seventeen years ago already?—when young Vasiliki had begged the pasha to spare her life and her family's. He'd adopted her and brought her here to Janina.

She'd grown up in splendor in his many palaces, their courtyards replete with splashing marble fountains, shady parks of plane trees, oranges, pomegranates, lemons, and figs, luxurious rooms filled with Gobelin carpets, Sevres porcelains, and Venetian glass chandeliers. He'd raised Vasiliki as his own daughter and loved her better than any of his own children. When Vasiliki was eighteen, and already pregnant with Haidée, Ali Pasha had married her. He'd never regretted that choice—until today.

But today, at last, he would have to tell the truth.

Vasia. Vasia. How could he have made such a mistake? It must be his age that explained it. What was he?

He didn't even know. Eighty something? His leonine days were over. He would not live to be much older. Of that, he was sure. It was too late to save himself, or even his beloved wife.

But there was something else—something that must not fall into the clutches of the Turks, something critical: something more important than life and death. That was why the Baba had come all this long, long way.

And that was why Ali Pasha had sent the boy to the *hamam* to collect Haidée. The young boy Kauri, the Janissary—a πε∝πτοσ, a *pemptos,* a "fifth"—one of those boys of the *Devishirme,* those one in every five Christian boys who'd been collected each year, over these past five hundred years, to replenish the Janissary ranks.

But Kauri was no Christian: He was Islamic from birth. Indeed, according to Mehmet Effendi, Kauri himself might be a part of the omen—perhaps the only one upon whom they could rely to complete this desperate and dangerous mission.

Ali Pasha only hoped to Allah that they were not too late.

KAURI, IN A PANIC, hoped precisely the same.

He lashed the great black stallion ahead along the darkened lake shore, as Haidée clung to him tightly from behind. His instructions had been to bring her to the isle with as little fanfare as possible, under cover of darkness.

But when the pasha's young daughter and her frightened maidservants arrived at the *hamam* and told him of the ships that were already rowing across the lake—Turkish ships—Kauri threw such precautions to the wind. He quickly understood, regardless of what his orders might have been, that as of this moment the rules had certainly changed.

The intruders were moving slowly, trying to remain silent, the girls had told him. Just to reach the isle, the Turks would have to cross a good four miles of water, Kauri knew. By circumventing the lake on horseback himself, to where Kauri had lashed down the small boat among the rushes at the far end, it would cut their own travel time in half—just what they needed.

Kauri had to reach the monastery first, before the Turks, to warn Ali Pasha.

AT THE FAR END of the enormous monastery kitchens, the coals blazed in the *oçak,* the ritual hearth beneath the sacred soup cauldron of the order. On the altar to the right the twelve candles had been lit—and, at center, the secret candle. Each person who entered the room stepped across the sacred threshold without touching the pillars or the floor.

At the room's center, Ali Pasha, the most powerful ruler in the Ottoman Empire, lay prostrate, facedown upon his prayer rug, spread upon the cold stone floor. Before him on a pile of cushions sat the great Shemimi Baba, who had initiated the pasha so many years ago: He was the *Pirimugan,* the Perfect Guide of all Bektashis throughout the world. The Baba's wizened face, brown and wrinkled as a dried berry, was suffused with an ancient wisdom attained through years of following the Way. It was said that Shemimi Baba was more than one hundred years old.

The Baba, still swathed in his *hirka* for warmth, was plumped upon his pile of cushions like a frail, dry leaf that had just floated down from the skies. He wore the ancient *elifi tac,* the twelve-pleated headdress given to the order, it was said, by Haji Bektashi Veli himself, five hundred years ago. In his left hand, the Baba held his ritual staff of mulberry, topped with the *palihenk,* the sacred twelve-part stone. His right hand rested upon the recumbent pasha's head.

The Baba looked about the room at those who were kneeling on the floor around him: General Vaya, Minister Effendi, and Vasiliki, the soldiers, shaikhs and Mürsits of the Bektashi Sufi order, as well as several monks of the Greek Orthodox Church, who were the pasha's friends, Vasiliki's spiritual guides—as well as their hosts, these many weeks, here upon the isle.

To one side sat the young boy, Kauri, and the pasha's daughter, Haidée, who had brought the news that had prompted the Baba's call for this meeting. They'd stripped off their muddy riding cloaks and, like the others, performed their ritual ablutions before entering the sacred space near the holy Baba.

The Baba removed his hand from Ali Pasha's head, completing the blessing, and the pasha arose, bowed low, and kissed the hem of the Baba's cloak. Then he knelt along with the others in the circle surrounding the great saint. Everyone understood the severity of their situation, and all strained to hear Shemimi Baba's critical next words:

"*Nice sirlar vardir sirlardan içli,*" began the Baba. There are many mysteries, mysteries within mysteries.

This was the well-known Doctrine of the Mürsit—the concept that one must possess not just a shaikh or teacher of the law—but also a *mürshid* or human guide through the *nasip,* the initiation, and through the following "four gateways" to Reality.

But, Kauri thought in confusion, how could anyone imagine such things at this moment, with the Turks perhaps only moments away from the isle? Kauri glanced surreptitiously at Haidée, just beside him.

Then, as if the Baba had read these private thoughts,

the old man suddenly laughed aloud: a cackle. All those in the circle looked up, surprised, but another surprise was just to come: The Baba, with much effort, had planted his mulberry stick in the pile of pillows and hoisted himself ably to his feet. Ali Pasha leapt up at once and was rushing to help his aged mentor, but he was whisked away with a flutter of the old man's hand.

"Perhaps you wonder why we are speaking of mysteries like this, when we have infidels and wolves nearly at our door!" he exclaimed. "There is only one *mystery* we need speak of at this moment, just before dawn. It is the mystery that Ali Pasha has guarded for us so well for so long. It is the mystery that itself has now placed our pasha here on this rock, the very mystery that brings the wolfish ones here. It is my duty to tell you what it is—and why it must be defended by all of us here, at any cost. Though those of us in this room may find different fates before this day is over—some of us may fight to the death or be captured by the Turks for a fate that may prove worse than death—there is only one person, here in this room, who is in a position to rescue this mystery. And thanks to our young fighter, Kauri, she has arrived here just in time."

The Baba nodded with a smile at Haidée, as the others all turned to look at her. All but her mother, Vasiliki, that is—who was looking across at Ali Pasha with an expression that seemed to mingle love, trepidation, and fear.

"I have something to tell you all," Shemimi Baba went on. "It is a mystery that has been handed down and protected for centuries. I am the last guide in the long, long chain of guides who have passed this mystery on to their successors. I must tell the story swiftly and succinctly, but tell it I *must*—before the sultan's assassins arrive. You must all understand the importance of what we are fighting for, and why it must be protected, even unto our deaths.

"You all know one of the famous *hadis* or reputed sayings of Muhammad," the Baba told them. "These famous lines are carved above the threshold of many Bektashi halls—words that are attributed to Allah Himself:

I was a Hidden Treasure, therefore was I fain to be known,
therefore I created creation, in order that I should be known . . .

"The tale that I am about to tell you involves another hidden treasure, a treasure of great value, but also great danger—a treasure that has been sought for more than one thousand years. Only the guides, over the years, have known the true source and meaning of this treasure. Now I share this with you."

Everyone in the room nodded: They understood the importance of the message that the Baba was about to impart to them, the very importance of his being here. No one spoke as the old man removed the sacred *elifi tac* from his head, set it down in the pillows, and shed his long sheepskin cloak. He stood there amid the cushions dressed only in his simple woolen kaftan. And leaning upon his mulberry staff, the Baba began his tale . . .

THE TALE OF THE GUIDE

In the year of the Hegira 138—or by the Christian calendar, AD 755—there lived, at Kufa, near Baghdad, the great Sufi mathematician and scientist, al-Jabir ibn Hayyan of Khurasan.

During Jabir's long residence in Kufa, he wrote many scholarly scientific treatises. These included his work

The Books of the Balance, the work that established Jabir's great reputation as the father of Islamic alchemy.

Less known is the fact that our friend Jabir was also the dedicated disciple of another resident of Kufa, Ja'far al-Sadiq, the sixth imam of the Shi'a branch of Islam since the death of the Prophet and a direct descendant of Muhammad, through the Prophet's daughter, Fatima.

The Shi'as of that sect did not then accept any more than they do today the legitimacy of the line of caliphs forming the Sunni Islamic sect—that is, those who were friends, companions, or relatives, but not direct descendants, of the Prophet.

The town of Kufa itself had remained, for hundreds of years since the Prophet's death, a hotbed of unrest and rebellion against the two successive Sunni dynasties that had meanwhile conquered much of the world.

Despite the fact that the caliphs of nearby Baghdad themselves were all Sunnis, al-Jabir openly and fearlessly—some say foolishly—dedicated his mystical alchemical treatise, *The Books of the Balance,* to his famous guide: the sixth imam, Ja'far al-Sadiq. Jabir went even further than that! In the book's dedication, he expressed that he was only a spokesperson for al-Sadiq's wisdom—that he had learned from his Mürsit all the *ta'wil*—the spiritual hermeneutics involved in the symbolic interpretation of hidden meaning within the Qur'an.

This admission in itself was enough to have destroyed Jabir, in the eyes of the established orthodoxy of his day. But ten years later, in AD 765, something even more dangerous happened: the sixth imam, al-Sadiq, died. Jabir, as a noted scientist, was brought to the court at Baghdad to be official court chemist—first under the caliph al-Mansur, then his successors, al-Mahdi and Harun al-Rashid, famous for the role he played in *The Thousand and One Nights.*

The orthodox Sunni caliphate was noted for rounding

up and destroying all texts of any sort that might ever suggest to anyone that there was another interpretation of the law—that there might be a separate, mystical descent of meaning or interpretation of the sayings of the Prophet and of the Qur'an.

As a scientist and Sufi, al-Jabir ibn Hayyan, from the moment of his arrival at Baghdad, lived in fear that his secret knowledge would vanish once he was no longer alive to protect and share it. He thrashed about for a more permanent solution—some impermeable way to pass on the ancient wisdom in a form that could neither be easily interpreted by the uninitiated nor easily destroyed.

The famous scientist soon found exactly what he was seeking—in a most uncanny and unexpected fashion.

The caliph al-Mansur had a favorite pastime: something that had been brought to the Arab world during the Islamic conquest of Persia a century earlier. It was the game of chess.

Al-Mansur called for his noted alchemist to create a chess service forged from uniquely created metals and compounds that could only be produced through the mysteries of alchemical science, and to fill this set with stones and symbols that would be meaningful to those acquainted with his art.

This command was like a gift to al-Jabir, directly from the archangel Gabriel himself—for it would permit him to fulfill the request of his caliph and at the same time to pass on the ancient and forbidden wisdom—right beneath the noses of the caliphate.

The chess service—which took ten years and the help of hundreds of skilled artisans to produce—was completed and presented to the caliph at the Festival of Bairam, in AH 158—or AD 775, ten years after the death of the imam who had inspired its meaning.

The service was magnificent: It measured a full meter

on each side, the squares comprised of what appeared to be a shimmering, untarnishable gold and silver, all studded with jewels, some the size of quails' eggs. All those in the court of the 'Abbasid dynasty at Baghdad were astonished by the marvels before their eyes. But unknown to them, their court chemist had encoded a great secret—one that would remain secret, even down until today.

Among these mysteries that al-Jabir had encoded into the chess set, for example, were the sacred numbers thirty-two and twenty-eight.

Thirty-two represents the number of letters in the Persian alphabet—these were codes that Jabir had embedded in the thirty-two silver and gold pawns and pieces of the service. Twenty-eight, the number of letters in the Arabic alphabet, was represented by codes that were carved into the twenty-eight squares around the circumference of the board. These were two of the many keys used by the father of alchemy, to pass on to initiates in every subsequent age. And each such clue represented a key to a part of the mystery.

Al-Jabir gave his masterful creation a name: he called it the Service of the *Tarik'at*—that is, it was the key to the Secret Way.

THE BABA SEEMED weary when he completed his story, but he was unbowed.

"The chess set I have spoken of still exists today. The caliph al-Mansur soon realized that it contained some sort of mysterious power, for many battles broke out surrounding the service—some within the 'Abbasid court itself, at Baghdad. Over the next twenty years, it changed hands several times—but that is another, and longer, story. Its secret was at last protected—for until recent times, it had lain buried for one thousand years.

"Then, only thirty years ago, at the dawn of the French Revolution, the service surfaced in the Basque Pyrenees. It has now been scattered abroad in the world, and its secrets are exposed. It is our mission, my children, to return this great masterpiece of initiation to its rightful owners: to those for whom it was initially designed, and for whom its secrets were intended. This service was designed for the Sufis, for we alone are the keepers of the flame."

Ali Pasha stood and helped the Baba to his seat in the deep cushions.

"The Baba has spoken, but he is weary," the pasha told the group. Then he held out his hands, for little Haidée and for Kauri, who sat beside her. The two young people came to stand before the Baba, who motioned them to kneel. Then he blew upon their heads, one after the other: "Hu-Hu-Hu." The *üfürük cülük*—the blessing of the breath.

"In Jabir's day," said the Baba, "those who were engaged in alchemical research called themselves the Blowers and the Charcoal Burners, for these were secret parts of their sacred art. That is where many of our terms come from, in our sacred art today. We are sending you, by a secret route, to our friends in another land—they are also known as the Charcoal Burners. But now, time is of the essence, and we have something of value to send with you, which Ali Pasha has protected for thirty years—"

He paused, for there were shouts from above, coming from the sealed upper rooms of the monastery. General Vaya and the soldiers raced toward the door to the steps.

"But I see," said the Baba, "that we have no more time."

The pasha had reached within his robes in haste, and now he handed the Baba something that looked like a large, heavy black lump of coal. The Baba handed this to Haidée, but he addressed himself to Kauri, his young disciple.

"There is an underground route out of this building, which will deliver you near to your skiff," the Baba told him. "You may be detected by others, but as children you will be unlikely to be apprehended. You are going to cross the mountains by a special route, to the coast, where a ship will be awaiting your arrival. You will travel north by directions I give you—you will seek a man who will lead you to those who will protect you. He knows the pasha well, from many years past, and he will trust you—that is, once you have given him the secret code that he alone will understand."

"And what is the code?" asked Kauri, anxious to take off quickly, as the sounds of hammering and splintering wood proceeded from the floors above.

But the pasha interrupted. He had pulled Vasiliki to his side, with one arm protectively around her shoulders. Vasiliki had tears in her eyes.

"Haidée must reveal to this man who she really is," the pasha told them.

"Who *I* am?" said Haidée, glancing in confusion at her parents.

Vasiliki spoke for the first time—she seemed in some sort of pain. She now took both of her daughter's hands in her own, as they still held the large lump of coal.

"My child," she addressed Haidée, "we have kept this secret for many years, but now, as the Baba has explained, it is our only hope, as well as yours." She paused, for her throat had choked on the final words. It seemed she could not go on, so the pasha intervened once more.

"What Vasia means, my darling, is that I am not your true father." When he saw the look of horror on Haidée's face, he added quickly, "I married your mother out of my great love for her, almost as a daughter, for I am greatly her senior in years. But when we married, Vasia was already expecting you—by another man. It was impossible for him to marry her, as it still remains. I know this man. I love him and trust him, and so does your mother, as well as the Baba. It has been a secret, kept in agreement by all of us—against this day when it might be necessary to reveal it at last."

Kauri had grasped Haidée's arm with great strength, for it appeared that she might faint.

"Your true father is a man who possesses both wealth and power," the pasha went on. "He will protect you—and will protect this as well, when you show him what you bring."

Haidée felt a dozen emotions warring within her. The pasha not her father? How could this be? She wanted to scream, tear her hair, cry—but her mother, weeping over her hands, was also shaking her head.

"The pasha is right. You must go," Vasiliki told her daughter. "Your life is at risk if you remain longer—and it is too dangerous for any but the boy to go with you."

"But if the pasha is not—then who is my father? And *where* is he? And what is this object we are bringing to him?" Sudden anger was helping her to recover a bit of her strength.

"Your father is a great English lord," said Vasiliki. "I knew him well, and I loved him—he lived here with us at Janina, in the year before your birth."

She could not go on, so the pasha continued.

"As the Baba said, he is our friend and is connected with those who are our friends. He lives on the great canal at Venice. You can reach him by boat within a few days. You can easily find his palazzo—his name is George Gordon, Lord Byron.

"You will bring him the object you hold in your hands, and he will protect it with his life, if necessary. It is disguised in carbon, but beneath is the most valuable chess piece from the ancient Service of the *Tarik'at* created by al-Jabir ibn Hayyan. This special piece is the veritable key to the Secret Path. It is the piece we know today as the Black Queen."

THE BLACK LAND

Wyrd oft nereth unfaegne eorl, þonne his ellen deah.
(Unless he is already doomed, fortune is apt to favor the man who keeps his nerve.)

—*Beowulf*

MESA VERDE, COLORADO
SPRING 2003

BEFORE I'D EVEN REACHED THE HOUSE, I KNEW something was wrong. Very wrong. Even though on the surface it all seemed picture-perfect.

The steep, sweeping curve of drive was blanketed deep in snow and lined with stately rows of towering Colorado blue spruce. Their snow-covered branches sparkled like rose quartz in the early-morning light. Atop the hill, where the driveway flattened and spread out for parking, I pulled up my rented Land Rover in front of the lodge.

A lazy curl of blue-gray smoke rose from the moss rock chimney that formed the center of the building. The rich scent of pine smoke pervaded the air, which meant that—although I might not be warmly welcomed after all this time—at least I was expected.

To confirm this, I saw that my mother's truck and jeep were sitting side by side in the former horse stable at the edge of the parking area. I did find it odd, though, that the drive had not yet been plowed and there were no tracks. If I were expected, wouldn't someone have cleared a path?

Now that I was here at last, in the only place I'd ever called home, you would think I could finally relax. But I couldn't shake the sense that something was wrong.

Our family lodge had been built at about this same period in the prior century by neighboring tribes, for my great-great-grandmother, a pioneering mountain lass. Constructed of hand-hewn rock and massive tree trunks chinked together, it was a huge log cabin that was shaped like an octagon—patterned after a hogan or sweat lodge—with many-paned windows facing in each cardinal direction, like a vast, architectural compass rose.

Each female descendant had lived here at one time or another, including my mother and me. So what was wrong with me? Why couldn't I ever come here without this sense of impending doom? I knew why, of course. And so did my mother. It was the thing we never spoke about. That's why—when I had finally left home for good—my mother understood. She'd never insisted, like other mothers, that I come back for familial visits.

That is, not until today.

But then, my presence today hadn't exactly been by invitation—it was more of a summons, a cryptic message that Mother had left on my home phone back in Washington, D.C., when she knew very well I'd be off at work.

She was inviting me, she said, to her birthday party. And that, of course, was a big part of the problem.

You see, my mother didn't *have* birthdays. She'd *never* had birthdays.

I don't mean she was concerned about her youth or appearance or wished to lie about her age—in fact, she looked more youthful each year.

But the strange truth was, she didn't want anyone outside our family even to know when her birthday *was*.

This secrecy, combined with a few other idiosyncrasies—

like the fact that she'd been in hermetic retreat up on top of this mountain for the past ten years—ever since . . . the thing we never spoke about—all went far to explain why there were those who may have perceived my mother, Catherine Velis, as a pretty eccentric duck.

The other part of my current problem was that I hadn't been able to contact my mother for an explanation of her sudden revelation. She'd answered neither her phone nor the messages I'd left for her here at the lodge. The alternate number she'd given me was clearly not right—it was missing some final digits.

With my first true inkling that something was really wrong, I took a few days off work, bought a ticket, caught the last flight into Cortez, Colorado, in a tizzy, and rented the last four-wheel-drive vehicle in the airport lot.

Now, I left the engine running as I sat here for a moment, letting my eyes graze over the breathtaking panoramic view. I hadn't been home in more than four years. And each time I saw it afresh, it smacked the wind out of me.

I got out of the Rover in knee-deep snow and let the engine run.

From here on the mountaintop, fourteen thousand feet atop the Colorado Plateau, I could see the vast, billowing sea of three-mile-high mountain peaks, licked by the rosy morning light. On a clear day like this, I could see all the way to Mount Hesperus, which the Diné call Dibé Nitsaa: Black Mountain, one of the four sacred mountains created by "First Man" and "First Woman."

Together with Sisnaajinii (white mountain, or Mount Blanca) in the east, Tsoodzil (blue mountain, or Mount Taylor) in the south, and Dook'o'osliid (yellow mountain, or San Francisco Peaks) in the west, these four marked out the four corners of Dinétah—"Home of the Diné," as the Navajo call themselves.

And they pointed as well to the high plateau I was standing on: "Four Corners," the only place in the United States where four states—Colorado, Utah, New Mexico, and Arizona—come together at right angles to form a cross.

Long before anyone ever thought to draw dotted lines on a map, this land was sacred to everyone who ever walked across it. If my mother was going to have her first-ever birthday party in the nearly twenty-two years I had known her, I could understand why she wanted to have it here. Regardless of how many years she had lived abroad or away, like all the women in our family she was part of this land.

For some reason, I knew that this connection with the land was somehow important. I knew that was why she had left a message so strange to bring me to this spot.

And I knew something else, even if no one else did. I knew why she'd insisted I come here today. For today—April fourth—actually was my mother, Cat Velis's, birthday.

I YANKED MY KEYS from the ignition, grabbed my hastily packed duffel bag from the passenger seat, and plowed my way through the snow to our hundred-year-old front doors. These huge doors—two massive slabs of heart pine ten feet high, cut from ancient trees—were carved in bas-relief with two animals that seemed to be coming right at you. On the left, a golden eagle soared straight at your face. And from the right door burst an angry, upright female bear.

Despite the weathering of these carvings, they were fairly realistic-looking—with glass eyes and real talons and claws. The early twentieth century had loved clever inventions, and this one was a doozy: If you pulled the bear's paw, her jaw dropped open to reveal very real and frightening teeth. If you had the nerve to stick your hand into her mouth, you could twist the old-fashioned door chime, to alert those within.

I did both, and waited. But even after a few moments, there was no response. Someone must have been inside—the chimney was active. And I knew from practice that stoking that fire pit took hours of tending and a Herculean effort to haul the wood. But with our hearth, which was capable of receiving a log of fifty caliper inches, a fire could have been laid days ago and still be burning.

My situation suddenly dawned upon me: Having flown and driven a few thousand miles, I was standing in the snow on top of a mountain, trying to get access to my own house, desperate to know if anyone was inside. But I didn't have a key.

My alternative—wading through acres of deep snow to peep through a window—seemed a poor idea. What would I do if I got wetter than I already was and still couldn't get inside? What if I got inside and no one was there? There were no car tracks, ski tracks—not even deer tracks—anywhere near the house.

So I did the only intelligent thing I could think of: I yanked my cell phone out of my pocket and dialed Mother's number, right here at the lodge. I was relieved when her message machine picked up after six rings, thinking she might have left some clue as to her whereabouts. But when her recorded voice came on, my heart sank:

"I can be reached at . . ." and she rattled off the same number she'd left on my D.C. phone—still missing the very last digits! I stood before the door, wet and cold, and fuming with confusion and frustration. Where did one go from here?

And then I remembered the game.

My favorite uncle, Slava, was famed throughout the

world as the noted technocrat and author, Ladislaus Nim. He'd been my best friend in my childhood, and though I hadn't seen him in years, I felt he still was. Slava hated telephones. He vowed he would never have one in his house. Telephones, no—but Uncle Slava loved puzzles. He'd written several books on the topic. Through my childhood, if anyone received a message from Slava with a phone number where you could reach him, they always knew it wasn't real—it must be some kind of encrypted message. That was his delight.

It seemed unlikely, though, that my mother would use such a technique to communicate with me. For one thing, she wasn't even good at deciphering such messages herself, and she couldn't invent a puzzle if her life depended upon it.

More unlikely still was the idea that Slava had created a message for her. As far as I knew, she hadn't talked to my uncle in years, not since . . . the thing we never spoke about.

Yet I was sure, somehow, that this was a message.

I jumped back up into the Land Rover and switched on the engine. Decrypting puzzles to locate my mother sure beat all hell out of the alternatives: breaking into an abandoned house, or flying back to D.C. and never learning where she'd gone.

I phoned her machine again: I jotted down the phone number she'd left there, for all the world to hear. If she was in real trouble of some kind and trying to contact only me, I prayed that I would decipher it first.

"I can be reached at 615-263-94. . . ." my mother's recorded voice said.

My hand was shaking as I wrote out the numbers on a pad.

I'd been provided eight numbers, rather than the ten numbers required to make a long-distance call. But as with Uncle Slava's puzzles, I suspected this had nothing to do with phones. Here was a ten-digit code, of which the final two numbers were missing. Those two numbers themselves were my hidden message.

It took about ten minutes to figure it out—much longer than when I was running neck and neck with my crazy but wonderful uncle. If you divided the string of numbers into twos (hint: we were missing the last two digits), then you ended up with: 61–52–63–94.

If you reversed those numbers, as I quickly saw, you ended up with each two-digit square number, starting with the square of four. That is, the product of four, five, six, and seven, when multiplied by themselves, resulted as follows: 16–25–36–49.

The next number in the sequence—and the missing number—was *8*. So the missing last two digits of the series were the square of 8—that is, 64. In the real puzzle, of course, if you reversed the number, the answer would have been 46—but that wasn't it.

I knew—and so did my mother—that 64 had another meaning for me. It was the number of squares on a chessboard, with eight squares on each side.

In a nutshell—*that* was the thing we never talked about.

My distraught and intractable mother had refused ever to speak of the game of chess—even to permit it into her house. Since my father's death (the other thing that we never talked about), I was forbidden to play the game—the only thing I'd ever known how to do, the only thing that helped me connect with the world around me. I might as well have been ordered, at the age of twelve, to become autistic.

My mother was so opposed, in every way imaginable, to the idea of chess. Though I'd never been able to follow her logic—if indeed, it *was* logic—to my mother's mind, chess would prove as dangerous to me as it had been to my father.

But now it seemed that by bringing me here on her birthday, by leaving that cryptic phrase with its encrypted message, she was welcoming me back to the game.

I TIMED IT: It took me twenty-seven minutes and—since I'd left the engine running—a gallon of hog-guzzling gas until I had figured out how to get inside.

By now, anyone with half a brain would have guessed that those two-digit numbers were also combinations on a tumbler. But there were no locks on the house. Except there *was* one in the barn. On a lockbox. The keys to the cars were kept there.

Would I be justified in saying "Duh"?

I switched off the Rover, plowed through the snow to the barn—and voilà!—a few tumblers dropped, the door to the lockbox opened, and the door key appeared on a chain. Back at the house, it took a moment to recall that the key was inserted into the eagle's left claw. Then the ancient doors groaned open a crack.

I scraped my boots on the rusty old fireplace grille we kept beside the entrance, shoved open the heavy front doors of the lodge, and slammed them shut behind me, causing a flurry of sparkling snowflakes to sift through the slanted morning light.

Within the dim interior light of the mudroom—an entry not much bigger than a confessional that kept the cold winds out—I kicked off my dripping boots and pulled on a pair of the fuzzy sheepskin aprés-ski booties that always sat there atop our frozen-food locker. When I'd hung up my parka, I opened the inner doors and stepped into the vast octagon, warmed by the giant log that was burning in the central hearth.

The octagon was a room perhaps one hundred feet across and thirty feet high. The fire pit took up the center, with a copper hood above it, hung with pots, rising to the moss rock chimney that pulled smoke upward to the sky. It was like an enormous teepee, except for the massive furniture scattered everywhere. My mother had always been averse to things one might actually *sit* on—but there was our ebony parlor grand piano, a sideboard, an assortment of desks, library tables, and revolving bookcases, and a billiard table that no one ever played on.

The upper floor was an octagonal balcony that overhung the room. There were small chambers there where people could sleep and even, sometimes, bathe.

Molten light poured through the lower windows at every side, glittering across the dust that draped the mahogany. From the ceiling skylights, rosy morning light sifted down, picking out the features of the colorfully painted heads of animal totems that were carved into the enormous beams supporting the balcony: bear, wolf, eagle, stag, buffalo, goat, cougar, ram. From their lofty perspective, nearly twenty feet high, they seemed to be floating timelessly in space. Everything seemed to be frozen in time. The only sound was the occasional cracking of fire from the log.

I walked around the perimeter, from one window to another, looking out at the snow: except for mine, there was not one print to be seen anywhere. I went up the spiral stairs to the balcony and checked each partitioned sleeping space. Not the slightest trace.

But how had she done it?

It appeared that my mother, Cat Velis, had vanished into thin air.

A jarring noise broke the silence: A telephone was ringing. I dashed down the steep, twisted stair and snatched the receiver from atop Mother's British campaign desk, just before the machine kicked in.

"Good *Lord*, what *were* you thinking, darling, choosing this godforsaken spot?" came the throaty voice, tinted with a bit of British accent, of a woman I knew only too well. "And for that matter, where on earth *are* you? We've been driving around this wilderness for what seems *days*!" There was a pause, when she seemed to be speaking aside to someone else.

"Aunt Lily?" I said.

For it was surely she—my aunt, Lily Rad—my first chess mentor and still one of the top women grandmasters in the game. Once, she'd been my mother's best friend, though they hadn't touched base in years. But what was she doing calling here now? And driving around—what on earth did that mean?

"Alexandra?" said Lily, confused. "I thought I was phoning your mother. What are *you* doing there? I thought you and she weren't . . . on the best of terms."

"We've reconciled," I said hastily, not wanting to open that can of worms again. "But Mother doesn't seem to be here right now. And where exactly are you?"

"She's not *there*?! You can't be serious," Lily said, fuming. "I've come all the way from London just to see her. She insisted! Something about a birthday party—God knows what that means. As for where I am right now, it is anyone's guess! The satellite positioning system on my automobile keeps insisting that I'm in Purgatory—and I'm fully able to accept that judgment. We haven't seen anything resembling civilization for hours."

"You're here? In Purgatory?" I said. "That's a ski area—it's less than an hour from here." But it seemed crazy: The top female British-American chess champion came from London to Purgatory, Colorado, to attend a birthday party? "When did mother invite you?"

"It wasn't so much an invitation as an edict," Lily admitted. "She left the news on my cell phone, with no means to reply." There was a pause. Then Lily added, "I adore your mother—you know that, Alexandra. But I could never accept—"

"Neither could I," I said. "Let's drop it. So how did you know how to find her?"

"*I didn't! Good God, I STILL DON'T!* My car's by the road someplace near a town that promotes itself as the next stop from Hell; there's no edible food; my driver refuses to budge without being given a pint of vodka; my dog has disappeared into some . . . *dune* of snow—chasing some local *rodent* . . . *AND*—I might add—I have had more trouble locating your mother by *phone,* this past week, than the Mossad had in tracking down Dr. Mengele in South America!"

She was hyperventilating. I considered it was time to intervene.

"It's okay, Aunt Lily," I told her. "We'll get you here. As for food, you know I can whip something up. There's always plenty of tinned food here and vodka for your driver—we can put him up, too, if you like. I'm too far away, it would take too long to reach you. But if you'll give me your satellite coordinates, I've a friend quite near there who can escort you here to the lodge."

"Whomever he may be, bless him," said my aunt Lily, not a person normally given to gratitude.

"It's a she," I said. "And her name is Key. She'll be there in half an hour." I took down Lily's mobile number and left a message at the airstrip to arrange for Key to pick her up. Key had been my best friend since childhood, but she'd be more than surprised to learn that I'd turned up here with no warning after all this time.

As I hung up the phone, I saw something across the room that I hadn't noticed before. The top of Mother's parlor grand piano—which was always raised, in case she got the urge to play—had been lowered flat. Atop was a piece of paper with a round, dark weight set upon it. I went over to look, and I felt the blood flooding into my brain.

The paperweight was overt enough: Propped on a metal key ring, to keep it from rolling, was the eight ball from our billard table. The note itself was definitely from my mother; the code was so simplistic that no one else could have invented it. I saw how hard she'd worked to communicate cryptically, clearly with no help.

The note, in large print, read:

WASHINGTON
LUXURY CAR
VIRGIN ISLES
ELVIS LIVES

AS ABOVE, SO BELOW

The Elvis part was simple: my mother's last name—Velis—was spelled two different ways to show it was from her. As if I needed that helpful clue. The rest was a lot more upsetting. And not because of the code.

Washington was, of course, "DC"; Luxury Car was "LX"; Virgin Isles was "VI." Together, in Roman numerals (as they clearly were), their numeric value was:

D = 500
C = 100
L = 50
X = 10
V = 5
I = 1

Tally them up, and it's "666"—the Number of the Beast from the apocalypse.

I wasn't worried about that Beast—we had plenty of

those protecting us, scattered about the lodge as our animal totems. But for the first time, I *was* truly worried about my mother. Why had she used this hackneyed pseudomillennial ruse to grab my attention? What about the paperweight on top—another standard bunkum, *"Behind the eight ball"*—what on earth did *that* mean?

And what should one make of that old alchemical drivel, *"As above, so below"*?

Then, of course, I got it. I removed the eight ball and the bit of paper, setting them on the keyboard music stand, and I opened the piano. Before I could set the strut in place, I nearly dropped the lid.

There, inside the hollow body of the instrument, I saw something I thought I would never, ever see again inside my mother's house as long as she lived.

A chess set.

Not *just* a chess set—but a chess set with a game set up, a game that had been partially in play. There were pieces here that had been removed from the field of play and were set out upon the keyboard strings at either side—black or white.

The first thing I noticed was that the Black Queen was missing. I glanced over at the billiard table—good heavens, Mother, really!—and saw that the missing queen had been placed in the rack where the eight ball was supposed to be.

It was something like being drawn into a vortex. I began to feel the game in play. Good Lord, how I had missed this. How had I been able to leave it behind me? It was nothing like a drug at all, as people sometimes said. It was an infusion of life.

I forgot the pieces that were off the board or behind the eight ball; I could reconstruct everything from the patterns that were still there. For several long moments, I forgot my missing mother, my aunt Lily lost in Purgatory with her chauffeur, her dog, and her car. I forgot what I'd sacrificed—what my life had become against my will. I forgot everything except the game before me—the game cached away like a dark secret, in the belly of that piano.

But as I reconstructed the moves, the dawn arose through the high glass windows—just as a sobering realization dawned within my mind. I could not stop the horror of this game. How could I stop it, when I had replayed it over and over again in my mind these past ten years?

For I knew this game quite well.

It was the game that had killed my father.

THE PIT

Mozart: Confutatus Maledictum—*how would you translate that?*
Salieri: "Consigned to the flames of woe."
Mozart: Do you believe in it?
Salieri: What?
Mozart: The fire that never dies, burning you forever.
Salieri: Oh, yes . . .

—PETER SHAFFER, *Amadeus*

DEEP IN THE PIT OF THE HEARTH, THE FIRE spilled over the sides of the giant log like liquid heat. I sat on the moss rock fireplace ledge, and I gazed down mindlessly. I was lost in a daze, trying hard not to remember.

But how could I forget?

Ten years. Ten years had passed—ten years during which I'd believed I had managed to repress, to camouflage, to bury a feeling that had nearly buried *me*, a feeling that emerged in that splinter of a second just before it happened. That frozen fragment of a moment when you still think that you have all of your life, your future, your promise before you, when you can still imagine—how would my friend Key put it?—that "the world is your oyster." And that it will never snap shut.

But then you see the hand with the gun. Then it happens. Then it's finished. Then there is no present anymore—only the past and future, only before and after. Only the "then," and . . . then what?

This was the thing we never spoke of. This was the thing I never thought about. Now that my mother, Cat, had vanished, now that she'd left that murderous message lodged in the bowels of her favorite piano, I understood her unspoken language, loud and clear: You *must* think about it.

But here was my question: How do you think of your own small, eleven-year-old self, standing there on those cold, hard marble steps in that cold, hard foreign land? How do you think of yourself, trapped inside the stone walls of a Russian monastery, miles from Moscow and thousands of miles from anyplace or anyone you know? How do you think of your father, killed by a sniper's bullet? A bullet that may have been intended for *you*? A bullet that your mother always believed was intended for you?

How do you think of your father, collapsing in a pool of blood—blood that you watch in a kind of horror, as it soaks into and mingles with the dirty Russian snow? How do you think of the body lying on the steps—the body of your father as his life slips away—with his gloved fingers still clinging to your own small, mittened hand?

The truth of the matter was, my father wasn't the only one who had lost his future and his life that day, ten years ago, on those steps in Russia. The truth was, I had lost mine, too. At the age of eleven, I'd been blindsided by life: *Amaurosis Scacchistica*—an occupational hazard.

And now, I had to admit what that truth really was: It wasn't my father's death or my mother's fears that had caused me to give up the game. The truth was—

Okay. Reality check!

The truth was, I didn't need the truth. The truth was, I couldn't afford this self-examination right now. I tried to squash that instant rush of adrenaline that had always accompanied any glimpse, however brief, into my own past. The truth was: My father was dead and my mother was missing and a chess game that someone had set up inside our piano suggested it all had plenty to do with *me*.

I knew this lethal game that still lurked there, still ticking away, was more than a gaggle of pawns and pieces. This was *the* game. The *last* game. The game that had killed my father.

Whatever the implications of its mysterious appearance here today, this game would always remain etched with acid in my mind. If I'd won this game, back in Moscow, ten years ago, the Russian tournament would have been mine, I'd have made the grade, I would have been the youngest grandmaster in history—just as my father had always wanted. Just as he'd always expected of me.

If I had won this Moscow game, we'd never have gone to Zagorsk for that one final round, that "overtime" game—a game that, due to "tragic circumstances," was destined never to be played at all.

Its presence here clearly carried some message, like my mother's other clues, a message that I knew I must decipher before anyone else did.

But there was one thing I knew, above all: Whatever this was, it was no game.

I TOOK A DEEP BREATH and stood up from the hearth, nearly conking my head on a hanging copper pot. I yanked it down and slapped it atop the nearby sideboard. Then I went to the parlor grand, unzipped the bench cushion, gathered all the pieces and pawns from the piano strings, and dumped them into the pillow sack along with the board. I left the piano lid propped open as it usually was kept. I zipped up the lumpy pillow and shoved it into the sideboard.

I'd nearly forgotten the "missing" Black Queen. Plucking her from the triangular rack of balls on the billiard table, I put the eight ball back in its proper place. The pyramid of colored balls reminded me of something, but at the moment I couldn't think what. And perhaps it was my imagination, but the queen seemed slightly weightier than the other pieces, though the circle of felt on the base seemed solid enough. But just as I thought to scratch it off with my thumbnail, the phone started ringing. Recalling that my aunt Lily was about to descend, with chauffeur and yappy dog in tow, I shoved the queen in my pocket along with the bit of paper containing my mother's "encryption," dashed to the desk, and caught the phone on the third ring.

"You've been keeping secrets from me" came the liquid voice of Nokomis Key, my best friend since our youth.

Relief flooded through me. Though we hadn't spoken in several years, Key was the only person I could think of who might actually figure out a way to solve the quandary I found myself in at this moment. Nothing ever seemed to ruffle Key's feathers. She'd always been able to solve problems with that same ingenious and ironic detachment in a crisis that Br'er Rabbit possessed. Right now, I hoped she could pull this particular rabbit out of the hat—or in my case, the briar patch—one more time. That's why I'd asked her to meet Lily and bring her here to the house.

"Where are you?" I asked Key. "Did you get my message?"

"You never told me you had an auntie," Key said in reply. "And what a babe! I found her along the roadside, accompanied by a dog of unidentifiable genetic origin, surrounded by stacks of designer luggage, and plowed into a snowdrift in a quarter-million-dollar car that would do James Bond proud. Not to mention the younger 'companion' who looks like he could pull down that much cash each week himself, just by sauntering along the Lido clad in a thong bathing suit."

"You're referring to Lily's chauffeur?" I said, astonished.

"Is that what they call them these days?" Key laughed.

"A gigolo? That doesn't sound much like Lily to me," I said.

Nor did it sound like any of a long procession of rigidly formal drivers that my aunt had always employed. Not to mention that the Lily Rad I'd known since my infancy was far too preoccupied with her international image as the Queen of Chess to waste her time, her energy, or her wads of cash on keeping a man. Though I admit, the rest of the Lily scenario—the car, the dog, and the luggage—all rang true.

"Believe me," Key was saying with customary assurance. "This guy's so steamy, he has smoke coming out of his nostrils. 'Where there's smoke there's fire.' And your auntie sure looks like she's been 'rode hard and put away wet.' "

Key's addiction to slogans and colloquialisms was exceeded only by her favorite topic: heavy metal, the kind you drive.

"But that car in the snowdrift," she informed me, practically panting, "it's a *Vanquish*—Aston Martin's flagship limited edition." She began rattling off numbers, weights, gears, and valves until she caught herself and realized just whom she was talking to. Simplifying it for the mechanically impaired, she added: "That monster cruises at a hundred and ninety miles per hour! Enough horses to pull Ophelia from here to China!"

That would be Ophelia Otter—Key's favorite bush plane, and the only machine she trusted to get into those remote sites where she did her work. But knowing Key, if unfettered, she could go on talking horsepower for hours. I had to rein her in, and fast.

"So where are they now, the motley crew and their car?" I pressed, with no small amount of urgency. "When I last heard from Lily, she was on her way here for a party—that must've been an hour ago. Where is she?"

"They were hungry. So while my crew's digging out the car, your aunt and her sidekick are watering and foddering at the Mother Lode," Key said.

She meant a restaurant just off the track, which specialized in wild game, and I knew the place well. They had so many horns, antlers, and other cartilaginous display on the walls there that walking through the room without paying attention was as dangerous as running with the bulls at Pamplona.

"For God's sake," I said, my impatience bubbling over. "Just get her here."

"I'll have them at your place within the hour," Key assured me. "They're just watering the dog now, and finishing their drinks. The car's another matter, though: It'll have to be shipped to Denver for repairs. Right now, I'm at the bar, and they're still at the table, thick as thieves, whispering and sipping vodkas." Key snorted a laugh into the phone.

"What's so funny?" I said, in irritation at this further delay.

Why did Lily—never a drinker—require a booze infusion at ten in the morning? And what about her chauffeur? Though, in fairness to him, it appeared he wouldn't have much left to be chauffeuring around, if the car was that badly damaged. I confess, I had trouble visualizing my flamboyant, chess-playing aunt, with her de rigueur flawless manicure and exotic clothes—brunching atop the peanut-shell-and-beer-encrusted floors of the Mother Lode, nibbling away at their trademark fare of possum stew, rattlesnake steak, and Rocky

Mountain Oysters—the Colorado euphemism for deep-fried bulls' balls. The image boggled the brain.

"I don't get it," Key added sotto voce, as if reading my thoughts aloud. "I mean, nothing against your auntie—but this guy is pretty hot stuff, like an Italian film star. The staff and the clientele all stopped talking when he walked in, and the waitress is still drooling on her shirt-front. He's dripping with as many furs as your aunt Lily is, not to mention the designer gold trim and custom-made clothes. This guy could get any babe. So pardon me—can you clarify—exactly what draws him to your aunt?"

"I guess you were right all along," I agreed with a laugh. "He's attracted to her figure." When Key said nothing, I added: "Fifty million."

I hung up to the sound of her groans.

I REALIZED THAT I probably knew Lily Rad better than anyone else *could* know such an eccentric; despite the difference in our ages, we had much in common. For starters, I knew I owed Lily everything. It was Lily, for instance, who had first discovered my chess abilities when I was only three years old. Who had convinced my father and my uncle that these leanings of mine should be developed and exploited—over my mother's irritated, and eventually angry, objections.

It was this bond with Lily that made my phone conversation with Key seem so odd. Though I hadn't seen my aunt in a number of years—and she had also dropped out of the chess world—I found it hard to swallow that a person who'd been an older sister to me, as well as mentor and mother, could suddenly be lobotomized by hormones over some good-looking hunk. No, something was wrong with this picture. Lily just wasn't the type.

Lily Rad had long earned a reputation as the Elizabeth Taylor of chess. With her voluptuous curves, jewels, furs, designer cars, and cash liquidity bordering upon the obscene, Lily had single-handedly brought glamour to professional chess; she'd filled that enormous black hole of Soviet lassitude—all that remained back in the seventies after Bobby Fischer had departed the game.

But Lily wasn't all just panache and pizzazz. People had flocked to her games in droves, and not only to observe her cleavage. Thirty years ago, in her chess-playing prime, my aunt Lily had boasted an ELO rating approaching that of the more recent Hungarian chess whizzes, the Polgar sisters. And for twenty of those years, Lily's best friend and coach—my father, Alexander Solarin—had honed her brilliant defenses and helped keep her star soaring high in the chess empyrean.

After my father's death, Lily had returned to her former chess coach and mentor: the brilliant chess diagnostician and historian of the ancient art of the game, who happened also to be Lily's grandfather and her only living relative, Mordecai Rad.

But then, on the morning of her fiftieth birthday, the lights were suddenly and surprisingly extinguished on Lily's chess marquee.

On the morning of her birthday, so the story goes, Lily was running a bit late for her breakfast appointment with her grandfather. Her chauffeur had pulled the limo from her apartment building out onto Central Park South, and he'd managed to maneuver deftly through the thick morning traffic, down the West Side Highway. They had just passed Canal Street when, up ahead in the sky, they saw the first plane hit the first tower.

Thousands of cars screeched to a halt, the highway in instant gridlock. All drivers were staring up at that long, dark plume of smoke, unfolding like the tail of a big, black bird—a silent omen.

In panic, in the backseat of the limo, Lily tried desperately to tune her TV to the news—any news—but she flipped through the channels in vain. Everything was static. She was going mad.

Her grandfather was at the top of that building. They had an appointment to meet at nine o'clock, at a restaurant called Windows on the World. And Mordecai had a special treat for Lily, something that he wanted to reveal to his only descendant on this special day, her fiftieth birthday: September 11, 2001.

IN A WAY, LILY and I were both orphans. We'd each lost our closest relative, the person who had done the most to train us in our chosen field. I had never questioned for a moment why Lily had closed up her vast apartment on Central Park South that very same week of her grandfather's death, why she'd packed a single bag—as she later wrote me—and headed for England. Though she bore no great love for the British, Lily had been born in England, her late mother was English, so she carried dual citizenship. She just couldn't face New York. I'd barely heard a word from her since. Until today.

But at this moment, I knew that the one individual I desperately needed to see—perhaps the only person who knew all the players in our lives, the only one who might hold the key to my mother's disappearance, perhaps even to those cryptic messages that seemed somehow related to my father's death—was Lily Rad.

I HEARD A PHONE RINGING.

It took me a moment to realize this time it wasn't the desk phone, it was the cell phone in my trouser pocket. I was surprised it even worked in this remote region of

Colorado. In fact, I'd only given out this number to a handful of people.

I yanked the phone from my pocket and read the incoming caller ID: Rodolfo Boujaron, my boss back in Washington, D.C. Rodo would just be arriving for work at his famous restaurant, Sutalde, to learn that the chickadee he believed had been working his night shift had flown the coop.

But in all fairness to myself, if I'd ever had to ask my boss's permission first, I would likely never have gotten any time off at all. Rodo was a workaholic who thought everyone else should be, too. He liked to keep 24/7 surveillance on all his employees, because "the fires must always be *stroked,*" as he'd say in that accent, so thick you could cut it with a meat cleaver.

At this moment, however, I was in no mood to deal with Rodo's rantings, so I waited until I saw the VOICE MESSAGE sign pop on my phone screen, then I listened to what he'd recorded:

"Bonjour, Neskato Geldo!"

That was Rodo's nickname for me in his native Basque—"Little Cinder Girl"—a reference to my job as a firebird: the person who stokes the coals.

"So! You are sneaking away in the dead of the night and leaving me to discover Le Cygne this morning, in your place! I hope she will not produce the . . . aruatza. *How you say? The* œuf? *If she makes the mistake, it's you who cleans it up! You abandon your post with no warning—for some* boum d'anniversaire*—so Le Cygne tells me. Very well. But you MUST return back here at the ovens before Monday, to make the new fire. So ungrateful! You will please recollect why you even have a job: that it was I who rescued you from the CIA!"*

Rodo clicked off—he was clearly lathering himself into one of his typical Basque-Hispano-French snits. But his blathering wasn't quite as bizarre as it sounded, once you learned to read Rodo's multi-*lingo*-isms:

The "*Cygne*"—the swan—whom he'd suggested might lay an egg on the night shift during my absence was my colleague, Leda the Lesbian, who'd happily agreed to pinch-hit for me, if necessary, until my return.

When it came to maintaining those huge wood ovens for which the restaurant Sutalde was known (hence its name in Basque: "The Hearth"), Leda—as glamorous as she appeared when on display (as she often was)—was no slouch back in the kitchens, either. She swung a mean shovel; she knew the difference between hot ashes and embers. And she preferred taking over my Friday night solo hitch on the graveyard shift, to her customary cocktail-hour duties on the floor of the restaurant, where overjazzed and overpaid male "K Street lobbyists" were always hitting on her.

When it came to Rodo's comment about gratitude, however, the "CIA" that he'd "rescued me from" was not the Central Intelligence Agency of the U.S. government, but merely the Culinary Institute of America in rural New York—a training ground for master chefs, and the only school I'd ever flunked out of. I'd spent a fruitless six months there just after high school. When I couldn't think of anything I wanted to study at any college, my uncle Slava felt I should prepare myself to get a job in the only other thing I'd ever known how to do, besides chess—something that Nim had trained me in himself when I was young. That was cooking.

In short order, I'd found the CIA atmosphere a bit like storm trooper boot camp: endless classes in accounting and business management, memorizing vast repertoires—of terminology more than of technique. When I'd dropped out in frustration, feeling I was a failure in everything I'd ever done, Slava urged me into an underpaid apprenticeship—no dropouts, cop-outs, time-outs, or waffling permitted—at the only four-star establishment in the world that specialized exclusively in open-hearth cuisine: that is, cooking with live coals, embers, ash, and fire.

But now, almost four years into my five-year contract, if I took a good hard look in the mirror I had to confess that I'd turned into as much of an isolated loner—even living smack in the midst of Our Nation's Capital—as my mother was, here in hermetic retreat atop her very own Colorado mountain.

In my case, I could explain it away with ease: After all, I was contractually tied to the obsessively slave-driving schedule of Monsieur Rodolfo Boujaron, the restaurateur-entrepreneur who'd become my boss, my mentor, even my landlord. With Rodo standing over me these past four years, cracking the proverbial whip, I'd had no *time* for a social life.

In fact, my all-consuming job at Sutalde, that my uncle had so prudently locked me into, now provided me exactly the same structure—the practice, the tension, the time clocks—that had been woefully lacking in my life ever since my father had died and I'd had to abandon the game of chess. The task of preparing and maintaining the fire for a full week of cooking each week required all the diligence of minding an infant or tending a flock of young animals: You couldn't afford to blink.

But if that mirror told me the unblinking truth about myself, I'd have to admit that my job, these past four years, had provided me a lot more than structure or diligence or discipline. Living with the fire as I did—looking into those flames and embers day after day so I could manage their height and heat and strength—had taught me a new way of *seeing*. And thanks to Rodo's recent vituperous rantings, I'd just seen something new: I'd seen that my mother might have left me another clue—one that I ought to have noticed the very moment I walked in the door.

The fire. Under the circumstances, how could it be here at all?

I hunkered down beside the hearth for a better look at the log in the pit. It was a seasoned white pine of at least thirty caliper inches—a log that would burn faster than a denser hardwood from a broadleaf tree. Though it was clear that my mother, as a mountain girl, knew plenty about building fires, how could she have created *this* fire without prior planning—not to mention without loads of assistance?

In the hour or so I'd been here, no one had applied fresh kindling, or enlivened the embers with a bellows or blowpipe—nothing to speed the intensity of the heat. Yet this fire was a pretty mature one with flames six inches high, which meant that it had been burning for three hours. Given the steady, even nature of the flame, somebody had stayed around tending this fire for well over an hour until it was really established.

I checked my watch. This meant that my mother must have vanished from the lodge even more recently than it had first appeared—perhaps only half an hour before I'd arrived. But if so—vanished to where? And was she alone? And if she—or they—had departed by a door or a window, why were there no tracks, other than mine, in the snow?

My head was aching from this cacophony of clues that all seemed to lead toward nothing more than background noise. But then, yet another sour note leapt out at me: Just how had my boss Rodo known that I'd left to attend a *"boum anniversaire,"* as he called it—a birthday party? Given Mother's lifelong reluctance about even mentioning her birth date, I'd told no one why I was leaving or where I was going—not even Leda the Swan, as Rodo's message said. No matter how contradictory things might appear, I *knew* there must be a theme to my mother's disappearance hidden here somewhere. And there was one more place that I hadn't yet searched.

I plunged my hand into my pocket and grabbed the wooden chess queen I'd rescued from the billiard table. With my thumbnail, I scraped off the bottom circle of felt. Within the hollowed-out queen, I saw that something hard and firm had been inserted. I jimmied it out: a tiny bit of cardboard. I took it over to the window light and pried it open. When I read the three words printed there, I nearly fainted.

опáсно берéчься пожáр

Beside it were the faded traces of the phoenix—just as I remembered from that bleak, awful day at Zagorsk. I remembered that I'd found it in my pocket then, too. The bird seemed to be flying up to heaven, enshrined in an eight-pointed star.

I could scarcely breathe. But before I could come to grips with anything—before I could fathom what in God's name this might mean—I heard the sound of a car horn outside.

I looked out the window and saw Key's Toyota pulling up into the snowy parking space, just behind my car. Key emerged from the driver's side, followed by—from the backseat—a man dressed in furs who helped out my aunt Lily, similarly attired. All three of them were headed straight for the front door.

In panic, I shoved the cardboard back into my pocket, along with the chess piece. I raced to the mudroom; the outer doors were just swinging open. Before I could speak, my eyes flashed past the two women—right to the "gigolo" of my aunt Lily.

As he stepped over the threshhold, he was shaking

loose snow from the high fur collar of his coat. His eyes met mine, and he smiled—a cold smile, a smile filled with danger. It was no more than an instant before I understood why.

Standing there before me, in my mother's isolated mountain retreat, as if we two were completely alone in time and space, was the man who had killed my father.

The boy who had won the Last Game. Vartan Azov.

BLACK AND WHITE

It is here that the symbolism of black and white, already present in the squares of the chess board, takes on its full value: the white army is that of light, the black army is that of darkness . . . each of which is fighting in the name of a principle, or that of the spirit and darkness in man; these are the two forms of the 'holy war': the 'lesser holy war' and the 'greater holy war,' according to a saying of the prophet Mohammed . . .

In a holy war it is possible that each of the combatants may legitimately consider himself as the protagonist of Light fighting the darkness. This again is the consequence of the double meaning of every symbol: what for one is the expression of the Spirit, may be the image of dark 'matter' in the eyes of the other.

—TITUS BURCKHARDT, *The Symbolism of Chess*

Everything looks worse in black and white.

—PAUL SIMON, *Kodachrome*

TIME HAD STOPPED. I WAS LOST.

My eyes were locked with those of Vartan Azov—dark purple, nearly black, and bottomless as a pit. I could see those eyes as they gazed at me across a chessboard. When I was a child of eleven, his eyes hadn't frightened me. Why should they terrify me now?

Yet I could feel myself slipping down—a kind of vertigo, as if I were sliding into a deep, dark hole where there was no way out. Just as I'd experienced so many years ago, in that one awful instant in the game when I'd understood what I had done. I could feel my father then, watching me from across that room as I had slowly plummeted into psychological space, out of control, falling and falling—like that boy with wings who'd flown too near the sun.

Vartan Azov's eyes were unblinking now, as always, as he stood there in my mudroom looking over the heads of Lily and Nokomis, looking directly at me as if we were completely alone, as if there were only the two of us in the world, in an intimate dance. With the black-and-white squares of a chessboard in between. What game had we been playing then? What game were we playing now?

"You know what they say," Nokomis announced, breaking the spell as she tilted her head toward Vartan and Lily. "Politics makes strange bedfellows."

She'd kicked off her boots, tossed off her parka, yanked off her cap—releasing that waterfall of black hair that tumbled to her waist—and she was marching from the mudroom past me in her stocking feet. She plopped down on the hearth wall, shot me a wry smile, and added, "Or perhaps the motto of the United States Marine Corps?"

" 'Many are called but few are chosen'?" I guessed gamely, knowing my friend's compulsive predilection for epigrammatizing. I actually felt relieved, for once, to play her game. But she could tell by my face that something was not as it seemed.

"Nope," she said with raised brow. " 'We're just looking for a few good men.' "

"What on *earth* are you talking about?" asked Lily as she stepped into the room. She had stripped to her skintight ski outfit, which clung to every curve.

"Consorting with the enemy," I suggested, indicating Vartan. I grabbed Lily by the arm, took her aside, and hissed, "Have you blanked out *all* of the past? What were you thinking, bringing *him* along? Besides, he's young enough to be your son!"

"Grandmaster Azov is my protégé," Lily announced indignantly.

"Is that what they're calling them these days?" I cited Key's earlier observation.

Pretty unlikely, since Lily and I both knew that Azov's ELO ranking was two hundred points higher than hers had ever been.

"He's a grandmaster?" said Key. "Grandmaster of what?"

I let that pass, since Mother had eradicated all mention of chess from our family vocabulary. Lily remained undaunted—though she was about to unload some further unexpected information to my already overloaded brain.

"Please don't blame *me* for Vartan's presence here," she informed me calmly. "After all—your mother invited him! All *I* did was to give him a ride!"

Just as I was recovering from that broadside, a small, damp rodent—about four inches tall and sporting soggy, fuchsia hair ribbons—came barreling into the room. The disgusting beast flew into the air and leapt into Aunt Lily's waiting arms. It lapped her face with its equally bright pink tongue.

"My darling Zsa-Zsa," said Aunt Lily, cooing at the beast, "you and Alexandra haven't been introduced! She would love to hold you for a moment, wouldn't she?" And before I could protest, she'd palmed the writhing thing off to me.

"I'm afraid I'm still searching for a line for this one," Key admitted, watching our doggie display with amusement.

"How about 'Familiarity breeds contempt'?" I quipped. But I should never have opened my mouth: The revolting dog tried to stick its tongue beween my teeth. I tossed it back to Lily in disgust.

While we three were playing patty-cake, my archnemesis Vartan Azov had likewise removed his furs and stepped into the room. He was dressed all in black, a turtleneck sweater and slim trousers, with a simple gold neck chain that cost more than any chess tournament winnings I'd ever heard of. He ran his hand through his unruly mop of black curls, as he was gazing around at the totem carvings and sweeping expanse of our family lodge.

I could certainly see why his appearance had stopped traffic at the Mother Lode. Apparently, over the past decade my erstwhile opponent had been working out with something more physically strenuous than a chessboard. But pretty is as pretty does, as Key might say. His good looks didn't make his presence here—most especially under these circumstances—any more palatable to me. Why on earth would my mother invite here the very man whose last appearance in our lives had heralded the end of my chess career and resulted in my father's death?

Vartan Azov was crossing the room directly to where I stood beside the fire—there seemed to be no avenue of escape.

"This is a remarkable house," he said, in that soft Ukrainian accent—a voice that had always seemed so sinister when he was a boy. He was looking up toward the skylights filled with rosy light. "I've not seen anything like it anywhere. The front doors—the stonework, these carved animals looking down upon us. Who built it all?"

Nokomis answered; it was a well-known tale in these parts.

"This place is legendary," she said. "It was the last joint project—maybe the *only* joint project—between the Diné and the Hopi. They've been fighting turf wars over the outside cattle and oil intruders ever since. They built this lodge for Alexandra's ancestor. They say she was the first Anglo medicine woman."

"My mother's great-grandmother," I added, "a real character, by all accounts. She was born in a covered wagon and stayed on to study the local pharmaceuticals industry."

Lily rolled her eyes at me, as if to suggest it must've been mainly hallucinogenic mushrooms, if the decor was any indication.

"I can't believe it," my aunt chimed in. "How could Cat have been holed up here all these years? Charm is one thing, but what about the amenities?" She strolled around the room with Zsa-Zsa wriggling beneath her arm, and with one bloodred-lacquered fingernail she left a trail through the furniture dust. "I mean, the important questions. Where's the nearest beauty salon? Who picks up and delivers the laundry?"

"Not to mention where's the so-called kitchen," I agreed, motioning to the hearth. "Mother is not exactly prepared for entertaining." Which only served to make this birthday *boum* all the stranger still.

"I've never met your mother," Vartan commented, "though naturally, I was a great admirer of your father. I would never have imposed upon you like this, but I was so honored when she offered her invitation to stay here—"

"*Stay* here?" I said, nearly choking on the words.

"Cat insisted that we must stay here at the house," Lily confirmed. "She said there was plenty of room for everyone, and that there were no decent hotels nearby."

Right on both counts—unfortunately for me. But there was another problem, as Lily was quick to point out.

"It seems that Cat still hasn't returned from her outing. That isn't like her," she said. "After all, we've dropped everything to come here. Has she left any inkling that might explain why she invited us all, and then left?"

"Nothing conspicuous," I said evasively. What else *could* I say?

Thank God I'd had the presence of mind to stash that lethal game in the pillow sack before Vartan Azov landed on my doorstep. But Mother's encrypted note atop the piano, along with the hollow black queen and her contents, were still burning a hole in my pocket. Not to mention my brain.

How could a cardboard plaque suddenly surface here when, so far as I knew, it was only seen by my father and me ten years ago and thousands of miles away? In the shock and pandemonium following my father's death at Zagorsk, I'd hardly thought of that strange woman and the message she'd handed me just before the game. Then later, I'd assumed the card had disappeared, just as she had. Until now.

I needed to get Vartan Azov out of the way—and quickly—so I could broach some of these issues with my aunt. But before I could think *how,* I saw that Lily had halted before the British campaign desk and set Zsa-Zsa down on the floor. She was following with her fingertips the trail of wire that led from the telephone to a hole in the side of the desk. She yanked at the drawer, to no avail.

"Those damned drawers always stick," I told her from across the room. But my heart was churning again: How could I not have thought of something so obvious first? Inside that drawer was my mother's rustic answering machine. I went over as Lily pried the drawer open with a letter opener. This certainly wasn't my choice of audience to listen to Mother's private tape, but beggars can't be choosers, as Key would say.

Lily glanced up at me and pushed the Play button. Vartan and Nokomis came over to join us at the desk.

There were the two messages I'd left from D.C., then a few from Aunt Lily—in her case, moaning about having to make a trip into the "Wasteland," as she referred to Mother's remote mountain hideaway. I was in for a few unpleasant surprises, starting with *another* "birthday invitee"—a voice that, unfortunately, I knew only too well:

"*Catherine, dearest,*" came the affected, upper-class accent of our nearest neighbor (which is to say, five thousand acres away), Rosemary Livingston—a voice rendered perhaps even more abrasive than usual by the scratchy tape.

"*How I HATE the idea of missing your WONDERFUL soiree!*" Rosemary oozed. "*Basil and I shall be away. But Sage will be thrilled to come—with bells on! And our new neighbor says to tell you that he can make it, too. Toodle-oo!*"

The only proposition less pleasant than spending time with the boring, officious billionaire Basil Livingston and his status-hunting wife, Rosemary, was the idea of being forced to pass even an instant more time with their pretentious daughter, Sage—the professional prom queen and emerita Pep Club president—who had already tortured me through six years of grammar school and high school. Especially a Sage, as Rosemary had mentioned, "with bells on."

But at least it sounded like we had a brief respite before her descent upon us, if the planned party was to be a soiree and not an afternoon gig.

My big question was why the Livingstons had been invited at all, given my mother's strong distaste for how Basil Livingston had raked in his several fortunes—mostly at civilization's expense.

In brief, as an early venture capitalist, Basil had deployed his control of OPM (Other People's Money) to buy up huge chunks of the Colorado Plateau and turn it over to oil development—including lands that were contested as sacred by the local Indian tribes. These were some of the turf wars that Key had alluded to.

As for inviting this "new neighbor" that Rosemary had mentioned—what on earth was Mother thinking?—she'd never fraternized with the locals. This birthday bash was starting to sound more and more like the makings of an Alice in Wonderland party: Anything might crawl out from under the nearest teacup.

And the next message—the unfamiliar voice of a man with a German accent—only served to confirm my worst fears:

"*Grüssgott, mein Liebchen,*" the caller said. "*Ich bedaure sehr . . . Ja—please excuse—my English is not so good. I hope you will be understanding of all of my meanings. This is your old friend Professor Wittgenstein, from Vienna. I am in great surprise to learn of your party. When did you plan it? I hope you will receive the gift I sent in time for the important day. Please open it at once so that the contents do not spoil. I regret that I cannot come—a true sacrifice. For my absence, my only defense is that I must attend the King's Chess Tourney, in India . . .*"

I felt that old danger signal coming on again, as I pushed the machine's Pause button and glanced up at Lily. Fortunately, she seemed, for the moment, completely at sea. But it was clear to me that there were a few too many dangling key words here—the most obvious, of course, being "chess."

As for the mysterious "Professor Wittgenstein of Vienna," I wasn't sure how long it had taken Mother to catch on, or how quickly Lily would guess. But, accent or no, it had taken *me* exactly twelve seconds to "understand all of his meanings"—including who the caller actually was.

The *real* Ludwig von Wittgenstein—the eminent Viennese philosopher—had by now been dead for more than fifty years. He was famous for his incomprehensible works like the *Tractatus.* But more to the purpose of this message were the two obscure texts that Wittgenstein had privately printed and given to his students at Cambridge University in England. These were in two small notebooks bound with paper covers—one colored brown and the other blue—which were ever thereafter called "The Blue and Brown Books." Their main topic was language games.

Lily and I were acquainted, of course, with someone who was an obsessive devotee of such games, and who'd even published a tractatus or two of his own, including one on the subject of these very Wittgenstein texts. The clincher was that he was also born with the genetic idiosyncrasy of one blue eye and one brown one. This was my uncle Slava: Dr. Ladislaus Nim.

I knew that this tersely worded phone message in disguised voice from an uncle who never used phones must contain some critical kernel of meaning, which likely only my mother would understand. Perhaps something that had caused her to depart the house before any of her eclectic assortment of guests arrived.

But if it was so upsetting or even dangerous, why would she leave the message on the machine instead of erasing it? Furthermore, why would Nim allude to chess, a game that Mother despised? A game she knew nothing whatever about? Given the clues he had left, what else could it all mean? It seemed this message wasn't meant just for my mother—it must also be intended for *me.*

Before I could think further, Lily had hit the Play button on the answering machine again, and I got my answer:

"But as for lighting the candles on your cake," the voice I now knew as Nim's said, in that chilling Viennese accent, *"I suggest it is time to hand the lighted match to*

someone else. When the phoenix rises again from the ashes, take care, or you might get burnt."

"BEEP BEEP! END OF TAPE!" screeched the creaky answering machine.

And thank God, because I really couldn't stand to hear any more.

There could be no mistake—my uncle's passion for "language games," all those cleverly calibrated code words like "sacrifice," "King's Tourney," "India," and "defense" . . . No, this message was inextricably connected with whatever was going on here today. And missing his point might prove just as final, as irrevocable, as making that one fatal move. I knew I had to get rid of this tape right now, before Vartan Azov, standing just beside me—or anyone else—had the chance to figure out the connection.

I yanked the cassette from the answering machine, went over to the fire, and tossed it in. As I watched the Mylar and its plastic casing bubble and melt into the flames, the adrenaline started to pound behind my eyes again, like a hot, pulsing ache, like staring into a fire that was far too bright.

I squeezed my eyes shut—the better to see inside.

That last game I'd played in Russia—the dreaded game that my mother had left for me here, only hours ago, inside our piano—was a variation universally known in chess parlance as the King's Indian Defense. I'd lost that game ten years ago, due to a blunder arising from a risk I'd taken much earlier in the game—a risk I should never have taken, since I couldn't really see all the ramifications of where it might lead.

What was the risk I'd taken in that game? I had sacrificed my Black Queen.

And now I knew, beyond doubt, that whoever or whatever had actually killed my father ten years ago—somehow my Black Queen sacrifice in that game was connected. It was a message that had come back to haunt us. At this moment, something had become as clear to me as the black-and-white squares on a chessboard.

My mother was in truly serious danger right now—perhaps as grave as my father's ten years ago. And she had just passed that lighted match to me.

THE CHARCOAL BURNERS

Like all other associations, the Carbonari, or charcoal-burners, lay claim to a very high antiquity. . . . Similar societies arose in many mountainous countries, and they surrounded themselves with that mysticism of which we have seen so many examples. Their fidelity to each other and to the society was so great that it became in Italy a proverbial expression to say "On the faith of a Carbonaro." . . . In order to avoid all suspicion of criminal association, they employed themselves in cutting wood and making charcoal. . . . They recognized each other by sign, by touch, and by words.

—CHARLES WILLIAM HECKETHORN, *The Secret Societies of All Ages & Countries*

Among the secret societies of Italy none was more comprehensive in its political objectives than that of the Carbonari. In the early 1820s they were more than just a power in the land, and boasted branches and sub-societies as far afield as Poland, France and Germany. The history of these 'Charcoal-burners', according to themselves, started in Scotland.

—ARKON DARAUL, *A History of Secret Societies*

But I am half a Scot by birth, and bred a whole one.

—LORD BYRON, *Don Juan*, Canto X

VIAREGGIO, ITALY
AUGUST 15, 1822

IT WAS THE HEAT OF THE DOG DAYS. HERE UNDER the blazing Tuscan sun, on this isolated stretch of beach along the Ligurian coast, the pebbled sands formed a griddle so intense that already now, at mid-morning, one could bake *pané* upon its surface. In the distance across the waters, the isles of Elba, Capraia, and little Gorgona arose like shimmering apparitions from the sea.

At the center of the crescent of beach, enfolded by its high surrounding mountains, a small group of men had assembled. Their horses could not bear the scalding sands and had been left within a nearby copse of trees.

George Gordon, Lord Byron, waited apart from the others. He'd seated himself upon a large black rock lapped by the waves—ostensibly so that his famous Romantic profile, immortalized in so many paintings, would be silhouetted to best advantage against the backdrop of the glittering sea. But in fact the hidden deformity of his feet since birth had nearly prevented Byron, this morning, from leaving his carriage at all. His pale white skin, which earned him the nickname "Alba," was shaded by a broad straw hat.

From here, unhappily, he had excellent vantage to observe each detail of the dreadful scene unfolding on the beach. Captain Roberts—master of Byron's ship, the *Bolivar,* which lay at anchor in the bay—oversaw the preparations of the men. They were building a large bonfire. Byron's aide-de-camp, Edward John Trelawney—called "the pirate" for his wild, darkly handsome looks and eccentric passions—had now set up the iron cage that served as a furnace.

The half-dozen Luccan soldiers attending them had exhumed the corpse from its temporary grave—hastily dug where the body had first washed up. The cadaver scarcely resembled a human being: The face had been picked clean by fish, and the putrefied flesh was stained a dark and ghastly indigo color. Identification had been made by the familiar short jacket with the small volume of poetry in the pocket.

Now they placed the body into the furnace cage, atop the dry balsam boughs and driftwood they'd gathered from the beach. Such cadres of soldiers were a necessary presence at any such exhumation, Byron had been informed, to ensure that the proper immolation procedures were followed against the yellow fever from the Americas that was now rampaging along the coast.

Byron watched as Trelawney poured the wine and salts and oil on the cadaver. The roaring flame leapt up like a biblical pillar of God into the stark morning sky. A single seagull circled high above the flaming column, and the men tried to chase it away with cries as they flapped their shirts into the air.

The heat of the sands, inflamed by the fire, made the atmosphere around Byron seem unreal—the salts had turned the flames strange, unearthly colors; even the air was tremulous and wavy. He felt truly ill. But for a reason known only to himself, he could not leave.

Byron stared into the flames, disgusted as the corpse burst open from the intensity of the heat and its brains, pressed against the red-hot bars of the iron cage, seethed and bubbled and boiled, as if in a cauldron. It could just as well be the carcass of a sheep, he thought. What a nauseating and degrading sight. His beloved friend's earthly reality was vaporized into white-hot ash before his very eyes.

So this was death.

We are all dead now, in one way or another, Byron thought bitterly. But Percy Shelley had drunk enough of death's dark passions to last a lifetime, hadn't he?

These past six years, throughout all their peregrinations, the lives of the two famous poets were inextricably entangled. Beginning with their self-imposed exiles from England—which had been undertaken in the same month and year, if not for the same reasons—and throughout their residence in Switzerland. Then Venice, which Byron had quit over two years ago; and now his grand palazzo here in nearby Pisa, which Shelley had departed only hours before his death. They'd both been stalked by death—hunted and haunted, nearly sucked down themselves into the long, cruel vortex that had begun to spin in the wake of their individual escapes from Albion.

There was the suicide of Shelley's first wife, Harriet, six years ago, when Shelley ran off to the Continent with the sixteen-year-old Mary Godwin, now his wife. Then the suicide of Mary's half sister, Fanny, who'd been left behind in London with their cruel stepmother when the lovers had escaped. This blow was followed by the death of Percy and Mary's little son, William. And just last February, the death in Rome from consumption of Shelley's friend and poetic idol, "Adonais"—the young John Keats.

Byron himself was still reeling from the death, only months ago, of his five-year-old daughter, Allegra—his "natural" child by Mary Shelley's stepsister, Claire. A few weeks before Shelley's death by drowning, he'd told Byron that he'd witnessed an apparition: Percy had imagined he'd seen Byron's little dead daughter beckoning to him from the sea, beckoning him to join her beneath the waves. And now this ghastly end for poor Shelley himself:

First the death by water; then the death by fire.

Despite the suffocating heat, Byron felt a terrible chill as he replayed in his mind the scene of his friend's last hours.

In the late afternoon of July 8, Shelley had departed Byron's grand Palazzo Lanfranchi at Pisa and had raced to his small boat, the *Ariel,* moored just down the coast. Against all advice or common sense, with no warning to anyone, Shelley had cast off at once and had sailed into the darkening belly of a coming storm. *Why?* thought

Byron. *Unless he was being pursued. But by whom? And to what end?*

Yet in hindsight, this seemed the only plausible explanation—as Byron had now understood for the first time, only this morning. Byron had suddenly seen, in a flash of comprehension, something he should have seen at once: Percy Shelley's mysterious death by drowning was no accident. It had to do with something—or was sought by someone—aboard that ship. Byron now had no doubt that when the *Ariel* was raised from her watery grave, as she soon would be, they'd see that she had been rammed by a felucca or some other large craft, intent upon boarding her. But he also guessed that whatever had been sought had not been found.

For, as Byron had realized only this morning, Percy Shelley—a man who'd never believed in immortality—might have managed to send one last message from beyond the grave.

Byron turned toward the sea so that the others, preoccupied by the fire, would not notice when he surreptitiously fished from his wallet the thin volume that he'd managed to keep hold of: Shelley's copy of John Keats's last poems, published not long before Keats's death in Rome.

This waterlogged book had been found on the body, just as Shelley had left it: shoved within the pocket of his short, ill-fitting schoolboy's jacket. It was still turned open and marked at Shelley's favorite poem by Keats, "The Fall of Hyperion," about the mythological battle between the Titans and those new gods, led by Zeus, who were soon to replace them. After the famous mythological battle, which every schoolboy knew, only Hyperion, the sun god and last of the Titans, still survives.

This was a poem that Byron had never much cared for—and that Keats himself hadn't even liked enough to finish. But it seemed to Byron significant that Percy had taken pains to keep it on his person, even at his death. He had surely marked this one passage for a reason:

Anon rushed by the bright Hyperion;
His flaming robes streamed out behind his heels,
And gave a roar, as if of earthly fire . . .
On he flared . . .

At this premature end to a poem that was destined always to remain unfinished, the sun god seems to set himself aflame and whisk into oblivion in a ball of his own incandescence—rather like a phoenix. Rather like poor Percy, immolated there upon the pyre.

But most critical was something that none of the others seemed to have noticed when the book was found: At just the spot where Keats had laid down his pen, Shelley had taken his own up, and had carefully drawn a small mark at the side of the page—a kind of intaglio, with something printed inside. The ink was badly faded from the long exposure to the salt seawater, but Byron was sure he could still make it out by closer examination. That was why he had brought it here with him this morning.

Ripping the page loose from the book, Byron slipped the volume away again and carefully studied the small drawing his friend had made at the edge. Shelley had drawn a triangle, which enclosed three tiny circles or balls, each in a different colored ink.

Byron knew these colors well, for several reasons. First, they were his own—the colors of his matrilineal Scots family heraldry, which went back to before the time of the Norman Conquest. Though that was merely an accident of birth, it hadn't helped his sojourn in Italy that Lord Byron had always displayed these colors proudly upon his enormous carriage, a vehicle patterned after that of the deposed, deceased emperor of France, Napoleon Bonaparte. For as Byron should know better than anyone, in secret or in esoteric parlance these particular colors signified far more.

The three spheres that Shelley had drawn in the triangle were colored black, blue, and red. The black stood for coal, which signified "Faith." Blue symbolized smoke, meaning "Hope." And red was flame, for "Charity." Together, the three colors represented the life cycle of fire. And further—depicted as they were here, within a triangle, the universal symbol for "Fire"—they stood for the destruction by fire of the old world as prophesied by Saint John in the Book of Revelation, and the coming of a new world order.

This very symbol—these tricolored orbs within an equilateral triangle—had also been chosen as the secret insignia of an underground group that intended to carry out that same revolution, at least here in Italy. They called themselves the Carbonari—the Charcoal Burners.

In the aftermath of twenty-five years of French revolution, terror, and conquest that had nearly shattered all of Europe, there was only one rumor more frightful than rumors of war. And that was the rumor of internal insurrection, of a movement from within—one that might demand independence from *all* external overlords, from all imposed rule of any kind.

During these past two years, George Gordon, Lord Byron, had shared the same roof with his married Venetian mistress, Teresa Guiccioli, a girl half his age who'd been exiled from Venice, along with her brother, her cousin, and her father—but minus the cuckolded husband.

These were the notorious Gambas—the "Gambitti," as they were called in the popular press—highly placed members of the Carbonaria, the very group that had sworn eternal enmity to all forms of tyranny—though it had failed in its attempted coup, during last year's Carnival, to drive the Austrian rulers from Northern Italy. Instead, the Gambas themselves had been exiled from three Italian cities in succession. And Byron had followed them to each new encampment.

This was the reason why Byron's every contact, whether in person or in writing, was now being assiduously tracked by, and reported to, the official overlords of all three parts of Italy: the Austrian Habsburgs in the north, the Spanish Bourbons in the south, and the Vatican itself in the central Papal States.

Lord Byron was the secret capo of the *Cacciatori Mericani*—"The Americans," as the popular, populist branch of the underground society was known. He'd financed from his own private funds the weapons, shot, and powder of the recent abortive Carbonari insurrection—and more.

He'd supplied his friend Ali Pasha the new secret weapon to use in his rebellion against the Turks—the repeating rifle—which Byron had had designed for him in America.

And Byron was now funding the Hetairia ton Philikon, or Friendly Society—a secret group that supported the thrust to drive the Ottoman Turks from Greece.

Lord Byron was surely everything that the imperialist dragons had most cause to fear—an implacable foe of tyrants and their reigns. The powers understood that he was exactly the ferment such an insurrection wanted. And he was rich enough that, if necessary, he could also water it from his own well.

But in the past year all three of these nascent insurrections had been brutally repressed, severed at the jugular—sometimes literally. Indeed, after Ali Pasha's death seven months ago, it was told, he'd been buried at two different locations: his body at Janina, his head at Constantinople. Seven months. Why had it taken him so long to see it? Not until this morning.

It was nearly seven months since Ali Pasha's death, and still no word, no sign . . . At first, Byron had assumed there'd been a change in plan. After all, much had changed in the past two years while Ali was isolated at Janina. But the pasha had always vowed that if he were ever at risk, he would find Byron by any means, via his Secret Service—which was, after all, the vastest and most powerful such organization ever forged in history.

If this were to prove impossible, then in the pasha's final hours on earth, he would destroy himself inside the great fortress of Demir Kule—along with his treasure, his followers, and even the beloved and beautiful Vasiliki—before letting anything fall prey to the Turks.

But now Ali Pasha was dead, and by all reports the fortress of Demir Kule had been seized intact. Despite Byron's repeated attempts to discover any news of the fate of Vasiliki or the others who'd been taken to Constantinople, there was as yet no word. Nor had Byron received the object that was intended to be protected by himself and by the Carbonaria.

Percy's book of poems seemed to hold the only clue. If Byron had read correctly, only half of his message was contained in the triangle he'd drawn. The other part was the poem itself: the passage Percy had marked in Keats's "Fall of Hyperion." Putting those two clues together, the full message would read:

The old Solar God will be destroyed by a far more dangerous flame—an eternal flame.

If this was correct, then Byron had grasped at once that it was he *himself* who had most to fear. He must act, and quickly. For if Ali Pasha was dead without the promised bombast—if there was no word from survivors who'd been closest to him—Vasiliki, his advisers, his Secret Service, the Bektashi sheikhs—if Percy Shelley had been pursued from Byron's Pisan palazzo and driven into that storm, to his death—all this could mean just one thing: Everyone believed that the chess piece had reached its appointed destination, that Byron had received it—everyone, that is, except whoever had escaped from Janina.

And what had become of the missing Black Queen?

Byron needed to get away and think, and to lay a plan before the others arrived aboard his ship with Percy's ashes. It might already be too late.

Byron crumpled in his hand the page containing the message. Adopting his customary expression of detached disdain, he rose from his seat and limped painfully across the hot sands to where Trelawney still tended the fire. The dark, wild features of the "Cockney Corsair" were blackened further by soot from the blaze, and with those flashing white teeth and trailing mustachios, the man appeared more than slightly mad. Byron shuddered as he tossed the crumpled paper indifferently into the flame. He made sure that the paper had caught and burned before turning to speak to the others.

"Don't repeat this farce with me," he said. "Let my carcass rot where it falls. This Pagan Paean to a dead poet, I confess, has quite undone me—I need a bit of a sea change, to cleanse my mental image of this horror."

He went back to the shore—and with a quick nod toward Captain Roberts to confirm their prior agreement to meet afterward on the ship, Byron tossed his wide-brimmed hat aside, stripped off his shirt, and dove into the sea, cutting through the waves with strong and powerful strokes. The water was warm as blood already at mid-morning; the sun scalded "Alba's" fair skin. He knew it would be a short mile swim to the *Bolivar*—nothing to a man who'd already swum the Hellespont, but a long enough one that it would let him clear his mind to think. But though the rhythm of his strokes, the salt water lapping over his shoulders, helped to calm his agitation, his thoughts kept returning to one thing: No matter how he tried—and wildly improbable though it might seem—there was only one person Byron could think of to whom Percy Shelley's message might refer, one individual who might hold the critical clue to the fate of Ali Pasha's missing treasure. Byron himself had never met her, but her reputation preceded her.

She was Italian by birth—a wealthy widow. Beside her vast riches, Lord Byron knew that his own considerable fortune would pale by comparison. She had once been world renowned, though she now was living in semi-isolation here in Rome. But in her youth, it was said that she'd bravely fought on horseback with guns for the liberation of her land from foreign powers—just as Byron and the Charcoal Burners were essaying to do right now.

Despite this woman's personal contributions to the cause of freedom, however, it was she who'd given birth to the world's last Titan-like "solar god"—as Keats had described it: Her son was an imperial tyrant whose short-lived reign had terrorized all of Europe, and then swiftly burned itself out. Like Percy Shelley. In the end, this woman's son had succeeded only in replanting the virulent seed of monarchy back into the world in force. He'd died barely one year ago, in anguish and obscurity.

As Byron felt the sun burning into his naked skin, he strove harder through the teeming waters to reach his ship. If he was right, he knew he had little time to lose in order to set his plan in motion.

And it was no small irony to Byron that, had this son of the Roman widow lived, today, August 15, would have been his birthday—a day commemorated throughout Europe, in his behalf, those past fifteen years until his death.

The woman whom Lord Byron believed might hold

the key to locating the missing Black Queen of Ali Pasha was Napoleon's mother: Letizia Ramolino Bonaparte.

PALAZZO RINUCCINI, ROME
SEPTEMBER 8, 1822

Here [in Italy] there are as yet but the sparks of the volcano, but the ground is hot and the air sultry . . . there is a great commotion in people's minds, which will lead to nobody knows what. . . . The 'king-times' are fast finishing. There will be blood shed like water, and tears like mist; but the peoples will conquer in the end. I shall not live to see it, but I foresee it.

—LORD BYRON

It was a warm and balmy morning, but Madame Mère had arranged to have all the fires flickering in the hearths throughout the palazzo, candles lit in each room. The costly Aubusson carpets had all been brushed, the Canova sculptures of her famous children had all been dusted. Madame's servants were attired in their finest green-and-gold livery and her brother, Cardinal Joseph Fesch, would soon arrive from his nearby Palazzo Falconieri to help greet the guests to whom she always opened her home on this one day each year. For today was an important day in the holy calendar, a day that Madame Mère had vowed she would never ignore and always honor: the Nativity of the Blessed Virgin.

She'd been performing this ritual for more than fifty years—ever since she had taken her vow to the Virgin. After all, hadn't her favorite son been born on the Feast Day of the Assumption of the Blessed Virgin into heaven? That weak little baby whose birth had come so suddenly and unexpectedly early, when she—young Letizia, only age eighteen—had already lost two previous infants. So she'd made a vow on that day to Our

Lady that she would always honor *Her* birth without fail, and that she would consecrate her children to the Blessed Virgin.

Though the child's father had insisted upon naming the new infant Neapolus after an obscure Egyptian martyr instead of Carlo-Maria, as Letizia herself would have preferred, Letizia had made sure to christen all her daughters with the prenom of Maria: Maria Anna, who would later be known as Elisa, the Grand Duchess of Tuscany; Maria Paula, called Pauline, the Princess Borghese; and Maria Annunziata, later called Caroline, Queen of Naples. And they called *her* Madame Mère—Our Lady Mother.

The Queen of Heaven had indeed blessed all the girls with health and beauty, while their brother, later known as Napoleon, had given them wealth and power. But none of it was to last. These gifts had all dissipated, just like those roiling mists she still could recall surrounding her native isle of Corsica.

Now, as Madame Mère moved through the flower-filled, candlelit rooms of her vast Roman palazzo, she knew that this world would not last either. Madame Mère knew, with a palpitating heart, that this tribute to the Virgin today might prove to be her last in a very long time. Here she was, an old woman left nearly alone, her family all dead or scattered, dressed in perpetual mourning attire and living in an environment so alien to her, surrounded only by transitory things: wealth, possessions, memories.

But one of those memories may have suddenly come back to haunt her.

For only this morning Letizia had received a message, a hand-delivered note from someone whom she had neither seen nor heard from in all these many years, throughout the rise and fall of the Bonaparte Empire—not since Letizia and her family had departed the wild mountains of Corsica nearly thirty years ago. It was from someone whom Letizia had come to believe, by now, must be dead.

Letizia slipped the note from the bodice of her black mourning dress and read it again—perhaps for the twentieth time since she'd received it this morning. It was not signed, but there could be no mistaking who had written it. It was written in the ancient Tifinagh script, the Tamasheq tongue of the Tuareg Berbers of the deep Sahara. This language had always been a secret code used by only one person in communiqués with her mother's family.

It was for this reason that Madame Mère had sent urgently for her brother the cardinal to arrive here at once before the other guests. And to bring the Englishwoman along with him—that other Maria who'd just recently returned to Rome. Only these two might be able to help Letizia in her dreadful plight.

For if this man whom they called the Falcon had indeed arisen as if from the dead, Letizia knew precisely what she herself would be called upon to do.

Despite the warmth of the many fires in her chambers, Letizia felt that all too familiar chill from the depths of her own past as she read the fateful lines once more:

The Firebird has arisen. The Eight return.

TASSILI N'AGGER, THE SAHARA
AUTUMN EQUINOX, 1822

> *We are immortal, and do not forget,*
> *We are eternal, and to us the past*
> *Is, as the future, present.*
> —LORD BYRON, *Manfred*

Charlot stood on the high mesa, surveying the vast red desert. His white burnoose flapped about him in the breeze like the wings of a large bird. His long hair floated free, the color of the coppery sands that stretched before him. Nowhere on earth could one find a desert of this precise hue: the color of blood. The color of life.

This inhospitable spot, high on a cliff in the deepest Sahara, a place where only wild goats and eagles chose to live. It had not always been so. Behind him on the fabled cliffs of the Tassili were five thousand years of carvings and paintings—burnt sienna, ocher, raw umber, white—paintings that told the story of this desert and those who had peopled it in the mists of time, a story that was still unfolding.

This was his birthplace—what the Arabs called one's *watar,* or homeland—though he had not been here since he was a babe in arms. Here was where his life had begun, Charlot thought. He was born into the Game. And here, perhaps, was where the Game was destined to end—once he had solved the mystery. That's why he had returned to this ancient wilderness, this tapestry of brilliant light and of dark secrets: to find the truth.

The desert Berbers believed he was destined to be the one to solve it. His birth had been foretold. The oldest Berber legend spoke of a child born before his time, with blue eyes and red hair, who would possess the Second Sight. Charlot closed his eyes and inhaled the scent of this place, sand and salt and cinnabar, evoking his own most primal physical memories.

He'd been thrust into the world early—red and raw and screaming. His mother, Mireille, an orphan of sixteen, had fled her convent in the Basque Pyrenees and journeyed here across two continents, into the deep desert, to protect a dangerous secret. She had been what they called a *thayyib,* a woman who had known a man only once: his father. Charlot's birth, here on the cliffs of the Tassili, was midwifed by an indigo-veiled Berber prince with blue-tinted skin, one of the "blue men" of the Kel Rela Tuareg. This was Shahin, the desert falcon, who was to serve as parent, godparent, and tutor for this chosen child.

Across the vast desert before him now, as far as Charlot could see, the silent red sands shifted as they had for untold centuries, moving restlessly, like a living, breathing thing—sands that seemed a part of him, sands that erased all memory . . .

All but his own, that is. Charlot's terrible gift of remembering was always with him—even the memory of those things that had not yet come to pass. When he was a child, they had called him the Little Prophet. He'd foreseen the rise and fall of empires, the futures of great men, like Napoleon and Alexander of Russia—or like that of his true father, whom he'd only met once: Prince Charles-Maurice de Talleyrand.

Charlot's memory of the future had always been like an unstoppable wellspring. He could foresee it, though he might not be able to change it. But of course the greatest gift could also be a curse.

To him, the world was like a chess game, where each move that one made generated a myriad of potential moves—and at the same time revealed an underlying strategy, as implacable as destiny, that drove one relentlessly onward. Like the game of chess, like the paintings on the rock, like the eternal sands—for him, the past and the future were always present.

For Charlot had been born, as it was foretold, beneath the gaze of the ancient goddess, the White Queen, whose image was painted in the hollow of the great stone wall. She'd been known across all cultures and throughout all times. She hovered above him now like an avenging angel, carved high on the sheer stone cliff. The Tuareg called her Q'ar—"the Charioteer."

It was she, they said, who had spangled the nighttime

sky with glittering stars. And she who had first set the Game upon its adamantine course. Charlot had journeyed here from across the sea to lay his eyes upon her for the first time since his birth. It was she alone, they said, who might reveal—perhaps only to the chosen one—the secret behind the Game.

CHARLOT AWAKENED before dawn and tossed off the woolen djellaba he'd used as a cover against the open night air. Something was terribly wrong, though he couldn't yet sense what it was.

Here in this spot—a difficult four-day hike over treacherous terrain from the valley below—he knew he was well protected. But there was no hiding from the fact that something was amiss.

He rose from his makeshift bed for a better view. Away to the east, toward Mecca, he could make out the thin ribbon of red that ran across the horizon, portending the sun. But he did not yet have enough light to make out his surroundings. As he stood there in the silence atop the mesa, Charlot heard a sound—only meters away. First, a soft footstep on gravel, then the sound of human breathing.

He was terrified to make a false step, or even to move.

"Al-Kalim—it is I," someone whispered—though there was no one within miles to hear.

Only one man would address him as Al-Kalim: the Seer. "Shahin!" cried Charlot. He felt the strong, firm hands press his wrists—the hands of the man who'd always been mother and father, brother and guide.

"But how have you found me?" said Charlot. And why had Shahin risked his life to cross the seas and the desert? To come through this treacherous canyon by night? To arrive here before dawn? Whatever had brought him to this place must be urgent beyond imagining.

But more important: *Why hadn't Charlot foreseen it?*

The sun broke over the horizon, licking the rolling dunes in the distance with a warm pink glow. Shahin's hands still firmly grasped Charlot's in his own, as if he could not bear to let him go. After a long moment, he released Charlot and drew back his indigo veils.

In the rosy light, Charlot could see the craggy, hawklike features of Shahin for the first time. But what he saw in that face actually frightened him. In the twenty-nine years of his life, Charlot had never seen his mentor betray any emotion at all, under any circumstance, much less the emotion that Charlot could see written on Shahin's face right now, which terrified him: pain.

Why could Charlot still not see inside?

But Shahin was struggling to speak: "My son . . ." he began, nearly choking on the words.

Although Charlot had always thought of Shahin as his parent, this was the first time that the elder man had ever addressed him in this fashion.

"Al-Kalim," Shahin continued, "I would never ask you to use that great gift that was bestowed upon you by Allah, your gift of the Vision, if this were not a matter of the gravest importance. A crisis has occurred that has driven me to cross the sea from France. Something of great value may have fallen into evil hands, something I learned of only months ago . . ."

Charlot, with fear gripping his heart, understood that if Shahin had come for him here in the desert with such urgency, the crisis must be grave indeed. But Shahin's next words were more shocking still.

"It has to do with my son," he added.

"Your . . . *son*?" repeated Charlot, fearing that he'd not heard correctly.

"Yes, I have a son. He is greatly beloved," Shahin told

him. "And like you, he was chosen for a life that is not always ours to question. From his earliest years, he has been initiated into a secret order. His training was nearly complete—ahead of its time, for he is only fourteen years old. Six months ago, we received word that a crisis had occurred: My son had been sent upon an important mission by the highest shaikh—the *Pir* of his order—in an attempt to help avert this crisis. But it seems that the boy has never arrived at his destination."

"What was his mission? And what was his intended destination?" Charlot asked—though he realized, in a state of panic, that this was the first time he'd ever had to ask such a question. *Why didn't he already know the answer?*

"My son and a companion in this mission were bound for Venice," Shahin answered, though he was looking at Charlot strangely, as if the same question had just struck him, too: *How could Charlot not know?*

"We have reason to fear that my son, Kauri, and his companion were abducted." Shahin paused, then added, "I have learned that they had in their possession an important piece of the Montglane Service."

THE KING'S INDIAN DEFENSE

[The King's Indian Defense] is generally considered the most complex and most interesting of all the Indian Defenses. . . . Theoretically, White ought to have the advantage because his position is freer. But Black's position is solid and full of resource; a tenacious player can accomplish miracles with this defense.

—FRED REINFELD, *Complete Book of Chess Openings*

Black will . . . allow White to create a strong pawn centre and proceed to attack it. Other common features are Black's attempts to open the black-squared long diagonal and a pawn storm by Black's King-side pawns.

—EDWARD R. BRACE, *An Illustrated History of Chess*

THE SILENCE WAS BROKEN BY THE SOUND OF splintering wood.

I glanced across the room from where I stood by the hearth and saw that Lily had disconnected Mother's answering machine and pulled the spaghetti of wires from the drawer; they were splayed across the campaign desk. With Key and Vartan looking on, she was using the dagger-shaped letter opener to pry the stuck drawer all the way out of the desk. From the sound of it, she was deconstructing the thing.

"What are you doing?" I said in alarm. "That desk is one hundred years old!"

"I hate to destroy an authentic souvenir of British colonial warfare—it must mean so much to you," my aunt said. "However, your mother and I once found some objects of immeasurable value hidden in drawers that were jammed just like this one. She must have known something like this would set off a few bells for me." She went on hacking in frustration.

"That campaign desk is awfully flimsy to keep anything of value," I pointed out. It was just a lightweight box with drawers, on collapsible legs or "horses"—of the sort British officers hauled by pack mules on campaigns through treacherous mountain regions from the Khyber Pass to Kashmir. "Besides, for as long as I can recall, that drawer has always jammed."

"Time to unjam it, then," Lily insisted.

"Amen to that," Key agreed, grabbing up the heavy stone paperweight lying on the desk and handing it to Lily. "You know what they say: 'Better late than never.' "

Lily grasped the rock weight and swung it down onto the drawer with force. I could hear the soft wood splintering further, but she still couldn't yank the drawer all the way out.

Zsa-Zsa, crazed by all the noise and excitement, was squeaking frantically and bouncing around everyone's legs. She sounded something like a colony of rats going down at sea. I picked her up and tucked her under my arm, squishing her into temporary silence.

"Permit me?" Vartan offered Lily politely, taking the tools from her hands.

He stuck the letter opener between the desk and the side of the drawer and hammered it with the paperweight, jimmying it until the soft wood cracked loose from the drawer's base. Lily gave one good tug on the handle and the drawer was released.

Vartan held the damaged drawer in his hands and studied the sides and base, while Key knelt on the floor and stretched her arm back into the open hole as far as she could reach. She felt around inside.

"There's nothing there that I can touch," Key said,

tipping back on her haunches. "But my arm won't reach all the way to the back."

"Permit me," Vartan repeated, and he set down the drawer and squatted beside her, sliding his hand back into the open cavity of the desk. He seemed to take quite a long time feeling around. At last, he withdrew his arm and looked up at the three of us with no expression as we stood there expectantly.

"I can't find anything back there," Vartan said, standing up and brushing the dust from his sleeve.

Maybe it was my natural suspicion or just my jangled nerves, but I didn't believe him. Lily was right. Something *could* be hidden there. After all, these desks might've had to be lightweight for transport—but they also had to be secure. For decades, they'd been used to carry battle plans and strategies, messages with secret codes from headquarters, field units, and spies.

I palmed off Zsa-Zsa to Lily once more and yanked open the other drawer of the campaign desk, rummaging around inside until I found the flashlight we always kept there. Brushing Key and Vartan to one side, I bent forward and swept the flashlight around, exploring inside the desk. But Vartan was correct: There was nothing in there at all. So what had made that drawer stick all these years?

I picked up the damaged drawer from the floor where Vartan had put it, and I looked it over myself. Though I saw nothing amiss, I shoved the answering machine and tools aside and I set the drawer atop the desk, pulling out the other drawer to dump out its contents. Comparing the two side by side, it seemed that the rear panel of the damaged drawer was slightly higher than that of the other drawer.

I glanced at Lily, still holding the wriggling Zsa-Zsa. She nodded to me as if to confirm that she'd known all along. Then I turned to confront Vartan Azov.

"It seems there's a secret compartment here," I said.

"I know," he said softly. "I noticed it earlier. But I thought it best that I should not mention it." His voice was still polite, but his cold smile had returned—a smile like a warning.

"Not *mention* it?" I said, in disbelief.

"As you've said yourself, that drawer has been—do you say, *stuck*?—for a very long time. We've no idea what is hidden there," he said, adding with irony, "maybe something valuable—like battle plans left from the Crimean War."

This wasn't entirely implausible, since my father had actually grown up in the Soviet Crimea—but it was highly unlikely. It wasn't even his desk. And though I was as nervous as anyone about looking inside that secret compartment, I'd had about enough of Mr. Vartan Azov's high-handed logic and steely glances. I turned on my heel and headed for the door.

"Where are you going?" Vartan's voice shot after me like a bullet.

"To get a hacksaw," I tossed over my shoulder, and kept on moving. After all, I reasoned, I could hardly deploy Lily's rock-smashing technique. Even if the contents had nothing to do with Mother, there might be something fragile or valuable tucked away in that panel.

But Vartan had crossed the room, swiftly and silently, and was suddenly there beside me, his hand on my arm, propelling me toward the door right into the mudroom. Inside the cloistering closet he slammed the inner doors shut and leaned against them, blocking any exit.

We were jammed there together in the tiny space between the food locker and the coat hooks that were laden with so many fur and down-stuffed parkas, I could feel the static electricity plastering my hair to the wall. But before I could protest this preemption, Vartan had grasped me by both arms. He spoke quickly, under his breath so no one outside could hear.

"Alexandra, you must listen to me, this is extremely important," he said. "I know things you need to know. Crucial things. We must speak—*right now*—before you go about opening any more cupboards or drawers around here."

"We have nothing to talk about," I snapped, with a bitterness that surprised me. I extracted myself from his grasp. "I don't know what on earth you're doing here—why Mother would even invite you—"

"But *I* know why she asked me," Vartan interrupted. "Though I never spoke with her, she didn't have to say it. She needed information—and so do you. I was the only other person *there* on that day, who may be able to provide it."

I didn't have to ask what he meant by *there*—or what the day in question was. But this hardly prepared me for what came next.

"Xie," he said, "don't you understand? We must speak about your father's murder."

I felt as if I'd been socked in the stomach; for a moment my wind was gone. No one had called me Xie—my father's preferred nickname for me, short for Alexie—in the ten years since my chess-playing youth. Hearing it now, coupled with *Your father's murder,* made me feel completely disarmed.

Here it was again, that thing we never spoke about, the thing I never thought of. But my suppressed past had managed to penetrate the crushing, suffocating space of the mudroom and was staring me in the face with that horrid Ukrainian sangfroid. As customary, I retreated into complete denial.

"His murder?" I said, shaking my head in disbelief—as if that would somehow clear the air. "But the Russian authorities maintained at the time that my father's death was an accident, that the guard on that roof shot him in error, believing that someone was absconding with something valuable from the treasury."

Vartan Azov had suddenly turned his dark eyes upon me with attentiveness. That strange purple gleam was burning from within, like a flame being blown alive.

"Perhaps your father *was* escaping the treasury with something of great value," he said slowly, as if he'd just spotted a hidden move, an oblique opening he'd previously overlooked. "Perhaps your father was leaving with something whose value he himself might have only just grasped at that moment. But whatever did happen on that day, Alexandra, it is certain to me that your mother would never have asked me to come all this distance just now—to this remote spot, along with you and Lily Rad—unless she believed, as I do, that your father's death ten years ago must be directly related to the assassination of Taras Petrossian, just two weeks ago, in London."

"Taras Petrossian!" I cried aloud, though Vartan silenced me with a swift glance toward the inner doors.

Taras Petrossian was the rich entrepreneur and business mogul who, ten years ago, had organized our Russian chess tourney! He'd been there, that day at Zagorsk. I knew very little more than this about the man. But at this moment Vartan Azov—arrogant bastard or no—suddenly had my full attention.

"How was Petrossian killed?" I wanted to know. "And why? And what was he doing in London?"

"He was organizing a big chess exhibition there, with grandmasters from every country," Vartan said, one eyebrow slightly raised, as if he'd assumed I would already know that. "Petrossian fled to England several years ago with plenty of money, when the corrupt capitalist oligarchy he'd created in Russia was seized, along with that of many others, by the Russian state. But he hadn't completely escaped, as he might have imagined. Just two weeks ago, Petrossian was found dead in his bed, in his posh hotel suite in Mayfair. It's believed he was poisoned, a tried-and-true Russian methodology. Petrossian had often spoken out against the *Siloviki*. But the arm of that brotherhood has a very long reach for those whom they wish to silence—"

When I seemed confused by the term, Vartan added, "In Russian, it means something like 'The Power Guys.' The group who replaced the KGB just after the Soviet Union collapsed. Today, they're called the FSB—the Federal Security Bureau. Their members and methods remain the same; only the name has changed. They are far more powerful than the KGB ever was—a State unto themselves, with no outside controls. These Siloviki, I believe, were responsible for your father's murder—after all, the guard who shot him was surely in their employ."

What he was suggesting seemed crazy: KGB gunmen with poison up their sleeves. But I could feel that awful chill of recognition begin to creep into my spine again. It *had* been Taras Petrossian, as I now recalled, who'd relocated that last game of ours outside of Moscow, to Zagorsk. If he'd now been assassinated, it might give more credence to my mother's fears all these years. Not to mention her disappearance, and the clues she'd left that pointed to that last game. Perhaps she had been right in her suspicions all along. As Key might say, "Just because you're paranoid, it doesn't mean that they're not out to get you."

But there was something more that I needed to know, something that didn't make sense.

"What did you mean a moment ago," I asked Vartan, "when you said that my father might have been 'escaping the treasury with something of value'—which only he might understand?" Vartan smiled enigmatically, as if I'd just passed some important esoteric test.

"It didn't occur to me myself," he admitted, "until you mentioned the 'official' explanation of your father's death. I think it likely that your father *was* leaving the building that morning with something of enormous value, something that others could only intuit might be in his possession, but which they could not *see.*" When I looked mystified, he added: "I suspect he was leaving the building that morning with *information.*"

"Information?" I objected. "What sort of information could possibly be so valuable that someone would want to kill him?"

"Whatever it was," he told me, "it must have been something which apparently he could not be permitted to pass along to anyone."

"Even assuming my father *did* get information about something as dangerous as you're suggesting, how could he possibly have discovered it so quickly there at the Zagorsk treasury? As you yourself know, we were only inside that building for a few brief minutes," I pointed out. "And during that entire time, *my father spoke to no one who could have given him such information.*"

"Perhaps *he* spoke to no one," he agreed. "But someone *did* speak to *him.*"

An image of that morning, which I'd so long suppressed, had begun to form in my mind. *My father had left me for a moment, that morning at the treasury. He'd crossed the room to look inside a large glass case. And then someone went over and joined him there—*

"*You* spoke to my father!" I cried.

This time, Vartan didn't try to silence me. He merely nodded in confirmation.

"Yes," he said. "I went and stood beside your father as he was looking into a large display case. Inside that glass case, he and I saw a golden chess piece covered with jewels. I told him it had just been newly rediscovered in the cellars of the Hermitage at Petersburg, along with Schliemann's treasures of Troy. It was said that the piece had once belonged to Charlemagne and perhaps to Catherine the Great. I explained to your father that it had been brought to Zagorsk and put on display for this last game. It was just at that moment when your father suddenly turned away, he took you by the hand, and you both left that place."

We had fled outside onto the steps of the treasury, where my father had met his death.

Vartan was watching me closely now as I struggled to keep from betraying all those dark and long-repressed emotions that were, to my great regret, surfacing. But something still didn't jibe.

"It doesn't make sense," I told Vartan. "Why would someone want to kill my father just to prevent him from passing on dangerous information, when everyone seems to have known all about this rare chess piece and its history—including you?"

But no sooner had these words escaped than I knew the answer.

"Because that chess piece must have meant something completely different to *him* than it did to anyone else," Vartan said with a flush of excitement. "Whatever your father recognized when he saw that piece, his reaction was surely not what those who were observing him had expected, or they would never have brought it to be displayed there at that game. Though they might not have guessed what your father had discovered, he had to be stopped before he could tell anyone else who might understand!"

The pieces and pawns certainly seemed to be massing at center board. Vartan was on to something. But I still couldn't see the forest for the trees.

"Mother always believed that my father's death was

no accident," I admitted, leaving out the small detail that she'd also imagined that the bullet might have been intended for *me*. "And she always believed that chess had something to do with it. But if you're right, and my father's death *is* somehow linked with Taras Petrossian's, what would connect it all to that chess piece at Zagorsk?"

"I don't know—but something *must*," Vartan told me. "I still remember the expression on your father's face that morning as he stared into the glass case at that chess piece—almost as if he didn't hear a word I was saying. And when he turned away to go, he didn't look at all like a man who was thinking about a chess game."

"What did he look like?" I asked with urgency.

But Vartan was looking at me as if he were trying to make sense of it himself. "I'd say he looked frightened," he told me. "*More* than frightened. Terrified, though he quickly hid it from me."

"Terrified?"

What could possibly have frightened my father so much after only a few quick moments inside that treasury at Zagorsk? But with Vartan's next words, I felt as if someone had plunged an icy blade into my heart:

"I can't explain it myself," Vartan admitted, "unless, for some reason, it might have meant something significant to your father that the chess piece in that glass case was the Black Queen."

VARTAN OPENED THE DOORS and we reentered the octagon. I could hardly tell him what the Black Queen meant to *me*. I knew that if everything he'd just told me was true, then my mother's disappearance might well be connected to the deaths of both my father and Petrossian. We might all be in danger. But before I'd gone three paces, I stopped in my tracks. I'd been so riveted by Vartan's private revelations that I'd completely forgotten about Lily and Key.

The two of them were down on the floor in front of the campaign desk with the empty desk drawer between them, as nearby Zsa-Zsa drooled on the Persian rug. Lily had been saying something privately to Key, but they both stood up as we came in; Lily was clutching what looked like a sharp steel nail file. I saw bits of splintered wood scattered here and there.

"Time waits for no man," said Key. "While you two have been cloistered in there—taking each other's confessions or whatever you were up to—look what we've found."

She waved something in the air that looked like a piece of old, creased paper. As we approached, Lily regarded me with gravity. Her clear gray eyes seemed oddly veiled, almost like a warning.

"You may look," she admonished me, "but please don't touch. No more of your extravagant impulses around that fire. If what we've just discovered in that drawer is what I believe it may be, it is extremely rare, as your mother would surely attest if she were here. Indeed, I suspect this document may be the very reason she's *not* here."

Key carefully opened the brittle paper and held it up before us.

Vartan and I leaned forward for a better look. On closer observation, it seemed to be a piece of fabric—so old and soiled that it had stiffened with age like parchment—upon which an illustration had been drawn with a sort of rusty-red solution that had bled across the fabric in places, leaving dark stains, though the figures could still be made out. It was the drawing of a chessboard of sixty-four squares where each square had been filled with a different strange, esoteric-looking symbol. I couldn't make heads or tails of what it was supposed to mean.

But Lily was about to enlighten us all.

"I don't know how or when your mother may have obtained this drawing," she said, "but if my suspicions are correct, this cloth is the third and final piece of the puzzle that we were missing nearly thirty years ago."

"Piece of *what* puzzle?" I asked, in extreme frustration.

"Have you ever heard," said Lily, "of the Montglane Service?"

LILY HAD A STORY to tell us, she said. But in order to tell it before other guests might arrive, she begged me not to ask questions until she had told it all, without distractions or interruptions. And in order to do so, she informed us, she needed to sit upon something other than the floor or a rock wall—all that seemed available in our cluttered but chair-less lodge.

Key and Vartan trooped up and down the spiral stairs, collecting cushions, ottomans, and benches until Lily was now ensconced with Zsa-Zsa in a pile of plumpy pillows beside the fire, with Key perched on the piano bench and Vartan on a high library stool nearby, to listen.

Meanwhile, I'd set myself the task I did best: cooking. It always helped clear my mind and at least we'd have something for everyone to eat if others showed up as announced. Now I watched the copper kettle hanging low over the fire, the handfuls of freeze-dried vittles that I'd foraged from the food locker—shallots, celery, carrots, chanterelles, and beef cubes—as they plumped up in their broth of stock, strong red wine, splashes of Worcestershire, lemon juice, cognac, parsley, bay and thyme: Alexandra's time-tested campfire *Boeuf Bourguignonne*.

Letting it bubble away for a few hours as I stewed in my own juices, I reasoned, might be just the recipe I needed. I confess, I felt I'd had enough shocks in one morning to last me at least until supper. But Lily's confession was about to top that pile.

"Nearly thirty years ago," Lily told me, "we all made a solemn vow to your mother that we would never again speak of the Game. But now, with this drawing, I know that I *must* tell the story. I think that's what your mother intended, too," she added, "or she would never have hidden something so critically important here in that jammed desk drawer. And though I've no idea why she would dream of inviting all those others here today, she would never have invited anyone on such significant a date as her birthday unless it had to do with the Game."

"The game?" Vartan took the words from my mouth.

Although I was surprised to learn that Mother's obsession about her birthday might have something to do with chess, I still figured that if it was thirty years ago, it couldn't be the game that killed my father. Then something occurred to me.

"Whatever this game was that you were sworn to secrecy about," I said to Lily, "is that why Mother always tried to keep me from playing chess?"

It wasn't until this last that I recalled that no one outside of my immediate family had ever *known* that I'd been a serious chess champion, much less about our longtime family altercations over it. Key, despite a raised brow, tried not to look too surprised.

"Alexandra," said Lily, "you've misunderstood your mother's motives all these years. But it isn't your fault. I'm extremely sorry to confess that all of us—Ladislaus Nim and I, even your father—agreed it was best to keep you in the dark. We truly believed that once we'd buried the pieces, once they were hidden where no one could find them, once the other team was destroyed, then the

Game would be over and done with for a very long time, perhaps forever. And by the time you were born, and we'd discovered your early passion and skill, so many years had passed that we all felt sure you would be safe to play chess. It was only your mother who knew differently, it seems."

Lily paused and added softly, almost as if speaking to herself, "It was never the game of chess that Cat feared, but quite another Game: a Game that destroyed my family and may have killed your father—the most dangerous Game imaginable."

"But what Game was it?" I said. "And what kind of pieces did you bury?"

"An ancient Game," Lily told me, "a Game that was based upon a rare and valuable bejeweled Mesopotamian chess set that once belonged to Charlemagne. It was believed to contain dangerous powers and to be possessed of a curse."

Vartan, just beside me, had firmly grasped my elbow. I felt that familiar jolt of recognition, something triggered in the recesses of my mind. But Lily hadn't finished.

"The pieces and board were buried for a thousand years within a fortress in the Pyrenees," she went on, "a fortress that later became Montglane Abbey. Then during the French Revolution the chess set—by then called the Montglane Service—was dug up by the nuns and scattered for safekeeping. It disappeared for nearly two hundred years. Many sought to find it, for it was believed that whenever these pieces were reassembled the Service would unleash an uncontrollable power into the world like a force of nature, a force that could determine the very rise and fall of civilizations.

"But in the end," she said, "much of the Service *was* reassembled: twenty-six pieces and pawns from the initial thirty-two, along with a jewel-embroidered cloth that had originally covered the board. Only six pieces and the board itself were missing."

Lily paused to regard each of us in turn, her gray eyes resting at last upon me.

"The person who finally succeeded, after two hundred years, in this daunting task of reassembling the Montglane Service and defeating the opposing team was also the individual responsible for its reinterment, thirty years ago, when we thought the Game had ended: your mother."

"My mother?" It was all I could muster.

Lily nodded. "Cat's disappearance today can mean only one thing. I suspected it when I first heard her telephone message inviting me here. It now appears that this was only the first step in drawing us all out on center board like this. Now I fear that my suspicions were right: The Game has begun anew."

"But if this Game ever really existed, if it was so dangerous," I protested, "why would she risk setting it in motion again, as you're saying, by inviting us here?"

"She had no choice," said Lily. "As in all chess games, it's White that must have made the first move. Black can only counter. Perhaps her move would be the sudden appearance of the long-sought third part of the puzzle that your mother has left here for us to find. Perhaps we'll discover some different clues to her strategy and tactics—"

"But Mother's never played chess in her life! She hates chess," I pointed out.

"Alexandra," said Lily, "today—Cat's birthday, the fourth day of the fourth month—is a critical date in the history of the Game. Your mother is the Black Queen."

LILY'S TALE BEGAN with a chess tourney she'd attended with my mother thirty years ago, the first time she and my mother had met my father, Alexander Solarin. During a recess in that match, my father's opponent had died under mysterious circumstances, which later proved to be murder. This seemingly isolated event, this death at a chess game, would be the first in an onslaught that would soon sweep Lily and my mother into the vortex of the Game.

For several hours, as we three sat in silence, Lily recounted a long and complex story that I can only summarize here.

THE GRANDMASTER'S TALE

One month after that tourney at the Metropolitan Club, Cat Velis departed New York upon a long-planned consulting assignment in North Africa for her firm. A few months later Mordecai, my grandfather and chess coach, sent me to Algiers to join her.

Cat and I knew nothing of this most dangerous of all games in which we ourselves, as we soon discovered, were mere pawns. But Mordecai had long been a player. He knew that Cat had been chosen for a higher calling and that when it came to close maneuvers, she might need my help.

In the Casbah of Algiers, Cat and I met with a mysterious recluse, the widow of the former Dutch consul to Algeria, and a friend of my grandfather, Minnie Renselaas. The Black Queen. She gave us a diary written by a nun during the French Revolution that recounted the history of the Montglane Service and the role that this nun, Mireille, had played in it. Mireille's diary later proved vital to understanding the nature of the Game.

Minnie Renselaas enlisted Cat and me to penetrate deep into the desert, to the Tassili Mountains, and retrieve eight of the pieces she'd buried there. We braved Saharan sandstorms and pursuit by the secret police, as well as a vicious opponent, the "Old Man of the Mountain," an Arab named El-Marad who, we soon discovered, was the White King. But at last we found Minnie's pieces hidden in a cave in the Tassili protected by bats. We clawed in the rubble to extract the eight pieces.

I shall never forget the moment when I first saw their mysterious glow: a King and a Queen, several pawns, a Knight, and a camel, all of a strange gold or a silvery material, and caked with uncut jewels in a rainbow of colors. There was something otherworldly about them.

After many travails, at last we returned with the pieces. We reached a port not far from Algiers, only to be seized by the same dark forces still pursuing us. El-Marad and his thugs kidnapped me, but your mother brought reinforcements to my rescue; she struck El-Marad on the head with her heavy satchel of chess pieces. We escaped and brought the bag of pieces to Minnie Renselaas in the Casbah. But our adventure was far from over.

With Alexander Solarin, Cat and I escaped from Algeria by sea, pursued by a dreadful storm, the Sirocco, that nearly tore our ship apart. During months of boat repairs on an island, we read the diary of the nun Mireille, which enabled us to solve some of the mystery of the Montglane Service. When our ship was ready, we three crossed the Atlantic by sea and arrived in New York.

There we discovered we had not left all the villains behind in Algeria, as we'd hoped. A group of scoundrels lay in wait—my mother and my uncle among them! And another six pieces had been hidden in those *jammed drawers* in a secretary in my family's apartment. We defeated the last of the White Team and captured these extra six pieces.

At my grandfather's house in Manhattan's Diamond District, we all assembled: Cat Velis, Alexander Solarin, Ladislaus Nim—all of us players on the Black Team.

Only one was missing, Minnie Renselaas herself, the Black Queen.

Minnie had left the Game. But she'd left something behind as a parting gift for Cat: the last pages of the nun Mireille's diary, which revealed the secret of the marvelous chess set. It was a formula that, if solved, could do far more than create or destroy civilizations. It could transform both energy and matter and much, much else.

Indeed, in Mireille's diary she stated that she had worked alongside the famous physicist, Fourier, in Grenoble to solve the formula herself, and she claimed she had succeeded in 1830, after nearly thirty years. She possessed seventeen pieces—more than half of the set—as well as the cloth, embroidered with symbols, that had once covered the board. The bejeweled chessboard itself had been cut into four pieces and buried in Russia by Catherine the Great. But the Abbess of Montglane, herself imprisoned in Russia soon thereafter, had secretly drawn it from memory on the lining of her abbatial gown, in her own blood. This drawing Mireille also now possessed.

But though Mireille had only had seventeen pieces of the Montglane Service back then, we ourselves now had twenty-six, including those of the opposing team and others that had been buried for many years, as well as the cloth that covered the board—perhaps enough to solve the formula, despite its clear dangers. We were only missing six of the pieces and the board itself. But Cat believed that by hiding the pieces for once and all where no one could ever find them, she could stop this dangerous Game.

As of today, I believe we've learned she was mistaken.

WHEN LILY HAD finished her story, she looked drained. She arose, leaving Zsa-Zsa sacked out like a wet sock in the pile of pillows, and she crossed the room to the desk where the soiled piece of fabric lay open to expose its illustrated chessboard, a painting that we now understood had been drawn, nearly two hundred years ago, in abbatial blood. Lily ran her fingers over the strange array of symbols.

The air in the room was filled with the rich scent of bubbling beef and wine; you could hear the log cracking from time to time. For a very long time, nobody spoke.

At last, it was Vartan who broke the silence.

"My God," he said, his voice low, "what this Game has cost you all. It is hard to imagine that such a thing ever existed—or that it might really be happening again. But I don't understand one thing: If what you say is true—if this chess service is so dangerous; if Alexandra's mother already owns so many pieces of the puzzle; if the Game has begun again and White has made its first move, but nobody knows who are the players—what would she gain by inviting so many people here today? And do you know what is this formula she spoke of?"

Key was looking at me with an expression suggesting she might already know.

"I think the answer may be staring us in the face," said Key, speaking for the first time. We all turned to look at her, as she sat there beside the piano.

"Or at least, it's cooking our dinner," she added with a smile. "I may not know much about chess, but I do know a lot about calories."

"Calories?" said Lily in astonishment. "Like the kind you *eat*?"

"There's no such thing as a calorie," I pointed out. I thought I could see where Key might be going with this.

"Well, I'm sorry, but I beg to differ," said Lily, patting her waist. "I've packed on a few of those nonexistent 'things' in my time."

"I'm afraid I do not understand," Vartan chimed in.

"We were talking about a dangerous game of chess where people were killed. Now are we discussing food?"

"A calorie isn't food," I said. "It's a unit of thermal measure. And I think Key here may have just resolved an important problem. My mother knows that Nokomis Key is my only friend here in the valley, and that if I ever had a problem she'd be the first and *only* one I would turn to, to help resolve it. That's Key's job, she's a calorimetrician. She flies into remote regions and studies the thermal properties of everything from geysers to volcanoes. I think Key's right. That's why my mother built this fire: as a big, fat, calorie-laden clue."

"Excuse me," said Lily. Looking more than exhausted, she went over and swept Key aside. "I need to recline for a moment on some of my thermal properties. What on *earth* are you two talking about?"

Vartan looked lost as well.

"I'm saying that my mother is underneath that log—or at least, she *was*," I told them. "She must have had the tree placed here months ago, on removable props, so when she was ready she could exit through the stone air shaft under the floor and light the fire from below. I think the shaft may vent to a cave just downhill."

"Isn't that a rather Faustian exit?" said Lily. "And what does it have to do with the Montglane Service or the game of chess?"

"It has *nothing* to do with it," I said. "This isn't about a chess game—that's the whole point, don't you see?"

"It has to do with the formula," Key pointed out with a smile. This was, after all, her area of expertise. "You know, the formula you told us the nun Mireille worked on in Grenoble, with Jean-Baptiste Joseph Fourier. The same Fourier who was also the author of *The Analytic Theory of Heat*."

When our two brilliant grandmasters sat there like

lumps, staring at us with blank expressions, I figured it was time to clarify.

"Mother didn't invite us all here and then leave us in the lurch because she was trying to make a clever defense in a chess game," I told them. "As Lily said, she's already made *her* move by inviting us here and leaving that piece of cloth right where she hoped Lily might find it."

I paused and looked Key in the eye. How right she was—it was time to get cooking, and all those clues Mother had left now seemed to fall into place.

"Mother invited us here," I said, "because she wants us to collect the pieces and solve the formula of the Montglane Service."

"Did you ever discover what the formula was?" Key repeated Vartan's question.

"Yes, in a way—though I've never believed it myself," said Lily. "Alexandra's parents and her uncle seemed to think it possible that it was true. You may judge for yourselves from what I've already told you. Minnie Renselaas claimed it was true. She claimed she was leaving the Game because of the formula created two hundred years ago. She claimed that she, herself, was the nun Mireille de Remy who'd solved the formula for the elixir of life."

THE VESSEL

Hexagram 50: The Vessel

The Vessel means making and using symbols as fire uses wood. Offer something to the spirits through cooking it. . . . This brightens the understanding of the ear and eye and lets you see invisible things.

—STEPHEN KARCHER, *Total I Ching*

I HID THE DRAWING OF THE CHESSBOARD INSIDE the piano and shut the lid until we could figure out what to do with it. My compadres were unloading their luggage from Key's car, and Lily had just taken Zsa-Zsa outside in the snow. I stayed indoors to finish cooking our dinner. And to think.

I'd raked the ashes and stuffed more kindling beneath the huge log. As I stirred the *Boeuf Bourguignonne,* the liquid bubbled away in the copper kettle hanging from its hook above the fire. I added a splash of burgundy and stock to thin the broth.

My mind was bubbling pretty actively, too. But instead of clarifying something within my mental vessel, the bubbling seemed only to have congealed into a lumpy mass at the bottom of the pot. After hearing Lily's tale and its outcome, I knew I had too many ingredients interacting with one another. And each new idea only seemed to ignite more questions.

For instance, if there really was such a powerful formula as this longevity elixir that some nun had been able to solve nearly two hundred years ago, then why hadn't anyone done it since—namely my parents? While Lily had indicated that she'd never believed the whole story herself, she claimed that the others *had.* But Uncle Slava and my parents were all professional scientists. If their team had put together so many pieces of the puzzle, why would they hide them instead of trying to solve it themselves?

But it seems, as Lily told us, that no one knew where the pieces of the Montglane Service had been buried and who had buried them. As the Black Queen, my mother was the only one who knew to which of the four she'd assigned each piece for hiding. And my father alone, with his prodigious chess memory, was the one she allowed to know where the pieces were actually hidden. Now that my father was dead and my mother was missing, the trail was cold. The pieces could likely never be found again.

Which led to my next question: If Mother really wanted us to solve this formula now, thirty years later—and if she was passing the torch to me, as all indications seemed to suggest—then why had she hidden all the pieces so no one could ever find them? Why had she failed to include some kind of map?

A map.

On the other hand, maybe Mother *had* left a map, I thought, in the form of the drawing of that chessboard and those other messages I'd already retrieved. I touched the chess piece that still lay concealed in my pocket: the Black Queen. Too many clues pointed to this one piece. Especially Lily's story. Somehow *she* must tie it all together. But how? I knew I needed to ask Lily one more critical—

I heard tramping and voices in the mudroom. I hung my soup ladle on an overhead hook and went to help with the bags. I instantly wished I hadn't.

Lily had picked up Zsa-Zsa from the snow, but

couldn't get back inside. Key wasn't exaggerating when she'd mentioned on the phone my aunt's pile of designer luggage: valises were piled everywhere, even blocking the inner door. How had they ever fit all this into one simple Aston Martin?

"How did you bring all this over from London? The *Queen Mary*?" Key was asking Lily.

"Some of these can't go up the spiral stairs," I pointed out. "But we can't leave them here."

Vartan and Key agreed to haul only those that Lily had designated as most critical up the stairs. They'd remove the excess bags to the spot of my choosing: under the billiard table, where no one would trip over them.

The moment they'd departed the mudroom with the first load, I crawled over the piles of bags, pulled Lily and Zsa-Zsa inside, and shut the outer doors.

"Aunt Lily," I said, "you told us that no one but my father knew where each of the pieces was hidden. But we *do* know a few things. You know which pieces you buried or hid yourself, and Uncle Slava does, too, with his own. If you could remember which pieces your team was missing at the end, then we'd only have to figure out my parents' two parts of the puzzle."

"I was only given two of the pieces myself to hide," Lily admitted. "That leaves twenty-four pieces for the others. But only your mother knows if they each got eight. For the six missing pieces, I'm not sure after all these years that my memory is perfect. But I think I recall that we were missing four White pieces: two silver pawns, a Knight, and the White King. And the two Black pieces were a gold pawn and a Bishop."

I paused, not certain that I'd heard correctly.

"Then . . . the pieces that Mother captured and that you all buried or hid included everything else except those six?" I said.

If Vartan's story was true, there was one piece that *must* have been missing from the cache they'd buried thirty years ago. He'd seen it, alongside my father, at Zagorsk. Hadn't he?

Vartan and Key were coming back down the spiral stairs at the end of the room. I couldn't wait—I had to know now.

"Your team possessed the Black Queen?" I asked her.

"Oh yes, that was the most important piece of them all, according to Mireille's diary," said Lily. "The Abbess of Montglane took it to Russia herself, along with the chessboard she'd cut into parts. The Black Queen was in the possession of Catherine the Great, then seized by her son Paul on the empress's death. Finally it was passed to Mireille by Catherine's grandson, Emperor Alexander of Russia. Cat and I found it among Minnie's cache in that Tassili cave."

"Are you sure?" I asked her, my voice weakening along with my grip on the situation.

"How could I forget, with all those bats in that cave?" said Lily. "My memory might not be perfect about the *missing* pieces, but I held the Black Queen in my own hands. It was so important, I feel sure your mother must have buried that piece herself."

My temples were throbbing again, and I felt that same churning in my stomach. But Key and Vartan had just arrived for another haul of bags.

"You look as if you've just seen the proverbial ghost," Key said, regarding me strangely.

She could say that again. But it was a real one: the ghost of my dead father at Zagorsk. My suspicions were back in full gear. How could Vartan's and Lily's versions of the Black Queen both be true? Was this part of my mother's message? One thing was sure: The Black Queen in my pocket wasn't the only one "behind the eight ball."

As I was thinking this over, my ears were assaulted by the deafening clamor of the fire-engine bell ringing just above the front door. Vartan stared up at it in horror. Some visitor, undaunted at the prospect of having his hand bitten off by the bear outside, had reached into its maw and twisted our unique front-door chime.

Zsa-Zsa started yapping hysterically at the noisy bell. Lily retreated with her into the lodge.

I shoved aside a few bags and stood on tiptoe to peer out through the eagle's glass eyeballs. There on our doorstep was a massed gaggle of folks in hooded parkas and furs. Though I couldn't see faces, their identities weren't to be a mystery for long: Across the snowy expanse I glimpsed with sinking heart the BMW parked just beside my car. It was sporting vanity plates that read SAGESSE.

Vartan, from behind, whispered in my ear. "Is it someone you know?"

As if anyone we *didn't* know well would ever make the trek to this place.

"It is someone I'd like to *forget* I know," I told him, sotto voce. "But it does seem to be someone who's been invited."

Sage Livingston wasn't a girl who might graciously accept cooling her heels on the front doorstep, especially if she'd arrived with an entourage. With a sigh of resignation I threw open the doors. I was in for yet another unpleasant surprise.

"Oh no—the Botany Club." Key took the words out of my mouth.

She meant the botanically named Livingstons, *all* of them—Basil, Rosemary, and Sage—a family of whom Key liked to quip: "If they'd had more children, they'd have called them Parsley and Thyme."

But in my youth, they'd never seemed much of a joke.

Now they were one more puzzle on my mother's invitation list.

"Darling! It's been truly *forever*!" gushed Rosemary, as she swept into our constricted mudroom before the rest.

Sporting dark glasses and swathed in her extravagant, hooded lynx cape, Sage's mother looked even more youthful than I'd remembered. She briefly enfolded me in her cloud of endangered animal skins and bussed me with an "air kiss" at either cheek.

She was followed by my old archnemesis, her flawlessly perfect ash-blond daughter, Sage. Sage's dad, Basil, due to the clear constrictions of our broom-closet entry chamber, lagged with another man just outside the door—no doubt our "new neighbor"—a craggy, sun-leathered chap in jeans, sheepskin jacket, western boots, and hand-blocked Stetson. Alongside the haughty Basil with his silvery sideburns and haute couture Livingston women, our new arrival seemed somewhat out of place at this ball.

"Aren't we expected to come inside?" Sage demanded by way of cheery greeting, though it was the first time we'd laid eyes on each other in years.

She glanced past her mother toward the inner doors where Key stood, and raised one perfectly plucked eyebrow as if astonished she should find *her* here. There'd been little love lost over the years between Nokomis Key and Sage Livingston, for a variety of reasons.

No one seemed about to remove wet togs or to introduce me to our external guest. Vartan parted the wall of hanging coats and furs, stepped over some luggage, and addressed Rosemary with a charm I didn't know chess players possessed.

"Please permit me to remove your wrap," he offered in that soft voice I'd always regarded as sinister. Under these close conditions, I realized it might be interpreted slightly differently in a boudoir.

Sage herself, a longtime collector of designer men as well as clothes, shot Vartan a meaningful look that might bring a bull elephant to its knees. He didn't seem to notice, but offered to take her coat as well. I introduced them. Then I squeezed past this intimate threesome, heading outside to greet the two men. I shook hands with Basil.

"I thought you and Rosemary were out of town and couldn't make it," I mentioned.

"We changed our plans," Basil replied with a smile. "We wouldn't have missed your mother's first birthday party for the world."

And just how did he know that it was?

"So sorry, we seem to be here earlier than expected," Basil's companion said as he peered into the luggage-and-coat-jammed entryway.

He had a warm gravelly voice and was much younger than Basil, perhaps in his mid-thirties. Pulling off his leather gloves, he tucked them beneath his arm and took my hand in both of his. His palms were firm and calloused from hard work.

"I'm your new neighbor, Galen March," he introduced himself. "I'm the person your mother convinced to buy Sky Ranch. And you must be Alexandra. I'm so glad Cat invited me today so I could meet you. She's told me a good deal about you."

And nothing at all about you, I thought.

I thanked him briefly and headed back to help clear a path for the new arrivals.

Things just got stranger and stranger. I knew Sky Ranch well. Well enough to wonder why anyone would ever dream of buying it. It was the last and only private parcel in these parts. Over twenty thousand acres, with a price tag of at least fifteen million dollars, it spread across mountaintops between the reservations, national forest, and our family lands. But it was all bleak rock high above timberline, with no water and air so thin you couldn't raise herds or grow crops. The land had sat idle for so many decades that locals called it Ghost Ranch. The only buyers who could afford it today were those who could exploit it in other ways—ski areas or mineral rights. And these wouldn't be the sort that my mother would ever welcome to her neighborhood, let alone to her birthday party.

Mr. Galen March's story deserved investigation, but not right now. Since I couldn't postpone the inevitable forever, I invited Basil and Galen to enter. With the men in my wake, I elbowed my way through the mudroom past Vartan Azov and the doting Livingston ladies, grabbed up a few more valises for Key to stash beneath the billiard table, and went back inside to stir my pot of stew.

No sooner had I set foot inside than I was confronted by Lily.

"How do you know these people? Why are they here?" she hissed.

"They were invited," I told her, mystified by her closed expression. "Our neighbors, the Livingstons. I was only expecting their daughter, Sage—you heard the message. They used to be social muckety-mucks back East, but they've lived out here for years. They own Redlands, their ranch just near here, on the Colorado Plateau."

"They own a good deal more than that," Lily informed me under her breath.

But Basil Livingston had just arrived to join us. I was about to introduce him when Basil surprisingly bowed over Lily's hand. When he stood, his distinguished face seemed also to have taken on a tight mask.

"Hello, Basil," said Lily. "What brings *you* so far from London? As you see, Vartan and I had to leave rather suddenly ourselves. Oh, and tell me, were you able to continue the chess tournament after the dreadful death of your colleague, Taras Petrossian?"

A CLOSED POSITION

A position with extensive interlocked pawn chains and little room for manœuvre by the pieces. Most men will still be on the board and most of the pieces will be behind the pawns creating a cramped position with few opportunities for exchanges.

—EDWARD R. BRACE, *An Illustrated Dictionary of Chess*

THE SUN SETS EARLY IN THE MOUNTAINS. BY THE time we'd gotten the guests and luggage moved inside, a silvery glow was all that still sifted through the skylights above, casting the animal carvings overhead into sinister silhouettes.

Galen March seemed to be quite taken with Key the moment he met her. He offered to help and followed her around, pitching in as she turned on the lamps around the octagon, threw a fresh bedsheet over the billiard table, and drew up the stools and benches all around it.

Lily explained my mother's absence to the newcomers by claiming a family crisis, which, technically, it really was. She lied to the others, saying Cat had phoned with apologies and the wish that we'd enjoy ourselves in her absence.

Since we lacked the necessary number of wineglasses, Vartan filled some teacups with vodka from the tray on the sideboard and some coffee cups with hearty red wine. A few sips seemed to loosen everyone up a bit.

Taking our seats around the table, it was clear we had too many players to sort things out—a party of eight: Key and Lily and Vartan, the three Livingstons, myself and Galen March. With everyone looking a bit uneasy, we raised our cups and glasses in toast to our absent hostess.

The only thing we all appeared to have in common was my mother's invitation. But I knew well from my experiences in chess that appearances can be deceiving.

For instance, Basil Livingston had been unconvincingly vague with Lily about the role he'd so recently played at that chess tournament in London. He was just a silent partner, he said, a financier; he'd hardly even known the late tournament organizer, Taras Petrossian.

But Basil did seem to be on a first-name basis with both Lily and Vartan Azov. How well did he know *them*? How likely was it to have been mere coincidence that all four of them, including Rosemary, had been in Mayfair two weeks ago, on the very day that Taras Petrossian was killed?

"Do *you* enjoy chess?" Vartan was asking Sage Livingston, who'd seated herself as closely as possible beside him.

Sage shook her head and was about to reply when I jumped up and suggested that I start serving dinner. The thing was, no one in this group except Vartan and Lily knew about my life as the little queen of chess. Or why I'd quit.

I went around the makeshift dining table, dishing up boiled potatoes, tiny peas, and the *Boeuf Bourguignonne.* I preferred this vantage point: Moving around the table, I could listen in and read the expressions of the others without focusing attention on myself.

Under the circumstances, this seemed an absolute necessity. After all, it was my mother herself who'd invited them all here today. This might be my only opportunity to observe these seven all together. And if even a part of Vartan's revelations were true, someone here might have played a part in my mother's disappearance, my father's death, or Taras Petrossian's murder.

"So you finance these chess tournaments?" Galen March commented to Basil across the table. "An unusual hobby. You must like the game."

Interesting choice of words, I thought, as I ladled up Basil's stew.

"Not really," he said. "This Petrossian chap arranged that tournament. I knew him through my venture capital firm, based in Washington, D.C. We finance all sorts of business ventures around the world. When the Berlin Wall fell, we helped former Iron Curtain folks—entrepreneurs like Petrossian—get on their feet. During glasnost, perestroika, he owned a chain of restaurants and clubs. Used chess as a publicity stunt, I think. When Putin's troops cracked down on capitalists—oligarchs, they called them—we helped him move his operation farther west. Simple as that."

Basil took a bite of his *Bourguignonne* as I moved on to Sage's plate.

"So you mean," Lily said drily, "that it was really Petrossian's interest in *Das Kapital,* not in the Game, that got him killed?"

"The police said those rumors were quite ungrounded," Basil shot back, ignoring her other implications. "The official report said Petrossian died of heart failure. But you know the British press with their conspiracy theories," he added, sipping his wine. "They'll likely never stop questioning even Princess Diana's death."

At the mention of the "official report," Vartan had slipped a guarded sideways glance at me. I didn't need to guess what he was thinking. I ladled some extra peas onto his plate and moved on to Lily, just as Galen March chimed in again.

"You say you're based in D.C.?" he asked Basil. "Isn't that a pretty long commute to your job? Or from there to London or to Russia?"

Basil smiled with barely suppressed condescension. "Some businesses run themselves. We often pass through D.C. en route from shopping or theater in London, and my wife, Rosemary, visits the capital quite often for her own undertakings—but for myself, I prefer to stay here at Redlands where I can act like a rancher."

The glamorous Rosemary Livingston rolled her eyes toward her husband, then smiled across at Galen March. "You know what they say about the way to make a small fortune in ranching." Galen looked stumped. She said, "You *start* with a *large* one!"

Everyone laughed politely and turned to their meals and their neighbors as I took my place beside Key and helped myself to some chow. But I knew that what Rosemary had just mentioned was no joke. Basil Livingston's fortune—not to mention his business clout—were both legendary in these parts.

I should know plenty about it. Basil was essentially in the same field my parents had worked in, as well as Key: energy. The only difference? What they all studied and supported, Basil exploited.

The Livingstons' ranch at Redlands, for instance—forty thousand acres of the Colorado Plateau—wasn't just a range for grazing cattle and for entertaining CEOs and heads of state. Redlands also sat atop part of the world's largest known cache of industrial-grade uranium.

Then in D.C., not far from where I lived along the river, Basil kept a building jam-packed with his own K Street lobbyists. They'd pushed through the kind of legislation that infuriated my mother—tax benefits for investors in Arctic oil futures and tax breaks for owners of gas-guzzling SUVs.

All the more reason to question not just the audience but the timing of Mother's invitation to us all here today—an invitation, I reminded myself, that was sent out just about the same moment as the death in London of Basil's "colleague," Taras Petrossian, the very man who'd also arranged the tournament, ten years ago in Russia, where my father was killed.

I looked around the table at Mother's invitees: Sage Livingston chatting up Vartan Azov, Galen March attentively listening to Key, Rosemary Livingston whispering an aside to her hubby, and Lily Rad feeding bits of *Bourguignonne* to Zsa-Zsa, who sat in her lap.

If Lily was right and there was a larger Game going on, a dangerous Game, I still couldn't tell the pawns from the pieces. The scenario around this table seemed to me more like a patchwork of blindfold matches against unknown opponents, all of them making covered moves. I knew it was time to start cutting away some of the underbrush for a new line of perspective. And I suddenly thought I knew just where to start.

There was only one individual, of all those who were seated at this table of eight, whom my mother had *not* invited here today. I'd invited her myself—as Mother had surely known I would. She'd been my best and only friend since the age of twelve. Pun inevitable, I realized that she alone might provide the missing *key* to this whole dilemma.

I WAS TWELVE years old. My father was dead.

I'd been yanked out of school in New York by my mother, at Christmas break, and deposited in another school in the Rocky Mountains of Colorado—far away from anyone or anything I'd ever known.

I'd been forbidden to play or even to mention chess.

On my first day at my new school, a perky blonde with a ponytail came up to me in the hallway.

"You're new here," she said. Then, in a manner suggesting that everything depended on my reply, she added, "At the school where you went before, were you *popular*?"

In all my twelve years—at school, in all my world travel for chess competitions—I'd never been asked that question. I wasn't sure how to reply.

"I don't know," I told my interrogator. "What do you mean by *popular*?"

For a moment she looked as stumped by my question as I'd been by hers.

"*Popular* means," she finally said, "that other children want you to like them. They copy what you do or what you wear, and they do what you tell them to because they want to join your group."

"You mean, my team?" I said, confused.

Then I bit my tongue. I wasn't to mention chess.

But I'd been competing since the age of six. I had no group, and the only team I knew were my adult coaches like my father or the "seconds" who helped replay my games. In hindsight, if I'd ever bothered to ask other students at my public school in midtown Manhattan, they'd likely have viewed me as the quintessential nerd.

"Your team? You play sports, then. You look like you're used to winning. So you must have been popular. I'm Sage Livingston. I'm the most popular girl in this school. You can be my new friend."

This hallway encounter with Sage was to prove a high point of our relationship, which would quickly run downhill. The catalyst for that swift decline was my unexpected friendship with Nokomis Key.

While Sage was bouncing around with pom-poms or a tennis racket, Key was teaching me how to ride an Appaloosa bareback and showing me when the fields of névé, summer snow, were ready for us to glissade down—occupations that my mother approved of more than she did my attending Sage's elite Denver "do's" at the Cherry Creek Country Club.

Sage's father, Basil, might be as rich as Croesus. Her mother, Rosemary, might be atop every social register from Denver to D.C. But the one aspiration that had always eluded Sage was her hope of heaven: a card-carrying membership in the DAR—Daughters of the American Revolution—those women who claimed descent from heroes of the American Revolution. Their headquarters in Washington, D.C., including Constitution Hall, took up a city block within spitting distance of the White House. In the century or more since their founding, they'd held more social clout in Washington than Mayflower descendants or any other elitist heritage group.

And that was the real rub, that is, what rubbed Sage Livingston's fur the wrong way when it came to Nokomis Key. While Key worked her way through school at odd jobs in hotels and resorts—from chambermaid to park ranger—whenever Rosemary and Sage went to Washington, as they often did, they were always listed in the society pages as cochairs for benefits and fund-raisers for a number of noted public institutions.

But Key was *herself* a public institution—though one that, arguably, very few knew of in these parts. Key's mother was descended from a long line of Algonquin and Iroquois tribes going back to Powhatan—the *real* "First Americans." But her father was descended from one of Washington's most famous first families: that of the author of our national anthem, "The Star-Spangled Banner"—Mr. Francis Scott Key.

Unlike the Livingston ladies, if Key ever dropped into our nation's capital, the DAR would roll out the proverbial red rug straight across that bridge and right into the tiny park that both bore her famous ancestor's name, a bridge and a park that, coincidentally, would land you right at my own front door.

Washington, D.C.

I don't know how it flashed into my mind just at that moment. It wasn't only the "Key connection," but the whole plethora: Basil's business intrigues "inside the Beltway," Rosemary's social aspirations, Sage's genealogical obsession, and my own lengthy residence there under orders of my uncle Slava—himself, according to Lily, a key player in the Game. It was all too suspicious.

But if Mother wanted to focus my attention on D.C., why did she invite us all to Colorado? Were the two somehow connected? There was only one place I could think of to find out.

I'd naturally assumed, given my mother's impoverished capabilities with puzzles, that each of her encrypted clues would lead to something concrete, like that placard from Russia or the game tucked inside the piano.

But maybe my first assumption had been wrong.

Excusing myself, I got up from the table and went over to the hearth to rotate a few embers. As I stirred the fire with the poker, I slipped a hand in my pocket and touched the Black Queen and the bits of paper still tucked in there.

I already knew from some of our discoveries—the chess piece, the cardboard, the ancient chess map—and from what I'd learned about them, that there were two Black Queens and a larger Game going on: a dangerous Game.

In my mind I went over everything I'd discovered since this morning:

The bogus phone number with two missing digits.
The puzzle that led me to the game in the piano.
The missing Black Queen exchanged for the eight ball in the billiard rack.

The message hidden in the Queen that came from my game in Russia.
The ancient chessboard drawing we'd found stashed in Mother's desk.

This all seemed clear and straightforward, just like my mother herself. But I was positive beyond doubt that they *had* to hold the key to something more—

And then, of course, I got it.

Oh lord, how could I have been so stupid? Hadn't I cut my baby teeth on puzzles like these? I wanted to scream and stomp and tear my hair, which might have been improvident in the circumstance, with that table of diners seated across the room..

But wasn't that the very first puzzle I'd had to solve, before I could even gain access to the house? The missing digits of that "phone number"—64?

Not only was 64 the number of squares on a chessboard, but it was also the last code to the combination of the lockbox where mother had hidden the key to our lodge.

The chessboard provides the key!

Like the Red Sea parting, at last I felt I could see down that long, long file into the very heart of the Game. And if that first message held more than one level of meaning, so would the others, I was sure.

Just as I was sure, despite Mother's seemingly paradoxical choice of invitees, that we were all somehow connected. But connected how? I needed to figure this out, and now, while the players were all still seated around the table.

I slipped to the far side of the hearth where I would be partly concealed by the copper hood, and I extracted from my pocket the only one of the messages that was written in my mother's own hand. It read:

WASHINGTON
LUXURY CAR
VIRGIN ISLES
ELVIS LIVES

AS ABOVE, SO BELOW

Washington, D.C., was definitely at the top of the list. So maybe, just as the chessboard had provided the key to our house, this code would give the key to the rest. I racked my brain and then squeezed a little harder, but with Luxury Cars and Virgin Isles I could come up with nothing. I knew that the first three clues—DC-LX-VI—added up to 666, the Number of the Beast. So I took a fresh look at the bigger picture, starting with the next step. Bingo.

ELVIS LIVES

There were just two other anagrams you could create from Velis, my mother's name: these were *evils* and *veils*. The Book of Revelation or Apocalypse, where the Beast appears, is where Saint John reveals what will happen at the end of the world. And from my word-mongering childhood, I knew that it also derives from something very similar to those two spellings of Mother's name—apocalypse, *apokalyptein,* meaning "extract from the cover." Or revelation, *re-valare,* meaning "remove the veil."

As for the last line—*As Above, So Below*—that was the clincher. And if I was right, it had little to do with that chess game hidden in the piano. That was just a ruse to shock me into paying attention—as it certainly had.

In fact, it was clear that if I hadn't been so quick to jump to conclusions about Mother's ability to form puzzles, I might have seen it at once. Indeed, this would explain why Mother invited us here to Colorado in the first place—to a spot called Four Corners, high in the Rocky Mountains, at the very heart of the four mountains that mark the original Navajo corners of the birthplace of the world. A cosmic chessboard, if ever there was one.

The entire message, all parts taken together, would read:

The chessboard provides the key
Remove the Veil from Evils

As Above, So Below

And if the chessboard provided the key to removing that veil, as Mother's message suggested, then whatever it was that I revealed or discovered, here in the high country—like that ancient map we'd found—must be connected, just as I'd suspected, with that earthly chessboard "below."

For as I knew, there was only one city in all of history that had been specifically created to resemble the perfect square of a chessboard: the city that I called home.

That's where the next move of the Game must take place.

THE VEIL

Shall we write about the things not to be spoken of?
Shall we divulge the things not to be divulged?
Shall we pronounce the things not to be pronounced?
—EMPEROR JULIAN, "Hymn to the Mother of the Gods"

THE ROYAL HAREM
DAR EL-MAKHZEN PALACE
FEZ, MOROCCO
WINTER SOLSTICE, 1822

HAIDÉE PULLED ON HER VEIL AS SHE HASTENED across the vast inner courtyard of the royal harem. She was escorted by two burly eunuchs she had never seen before this morning. Along with the rest of the harem inmates, she'd been awakened at dawn, aroused from slumber by a cadre of palace guards who'd ordered them all to dress and prepare themselves as quickly as possible for evacuation from the premises.

Haidée herself was peremptorily singled out by the chief of the guard, who had notified her that she was summoned at once to the outer court connecting the harem with the palace.

There'd been pandemonium, of course, when the women had understood the reason for this terrifying command. For Sultan Mulay Suliman, descendant of the Prophet and scourge of the faith, had just died of apoplexy. He was succeeded by his nephew, Abdul-Rahman, who would surely possess a harem and courtiers of his own to occupy the palace quarters. As everyone knew, in earlier such changes of succession there had been widespread auctions of human flesh, even mass carnage to eliminate all threat from the outgoing retinue.

Hence, as the concubines, odalisques, and eunuchs had dressed within the warm cocoon of the harem—embraced by familiar scents of rosewater, lavender, honey, and mint, in the only home most of them had ever known—there'd been frightened speculation among them regarding just what this shocking turn of events might mean to any or to each. Whatever it was, they could hold little hope.

Haidée, as a captive with no relationship to the royal family, didn't have to speculate about what fate held in store for her. Why would she be called to the outer court, and she alone among all the harem's occupants? It could mean but one thing. Somehow they'd discovered *who she was*—and worse, what that large lump of black coal was, which, eleven months ago, had been found in her possession and seized by the sultan.

Now as she crossed the open-roofed courtyard with her muscular escorts at each side, they passed the fountains of heated waters that splashed into basins as they did all winter, to protect the pools of fish. The filigreed white fretwork of the Moorish porticoes around the court had retained its lacy resilience for six hundred years, it was said, because the original plaster was mixed with the pulverized bones of Christian slaves. Haidée hoped this was not the fate that lay in store for her at this most critical juncture. She felt her heart pounding between excitement and fear of the unknown.

For nearly a year now, Haidée had been held here as an odalisque or chamber servant, in obscure captivity, surrounded by the sultan's eunuchs and slaves. The royal palace of Dar el-Makhzen was sprawled across two hundred acres replete with magnificent gardens and pools, mosques and military barracks, harems and *hamams*. This wing of the palace, its chambers and bathhouses connected by courtyards and gardens with roofs open to the winter skies, could accommodate one thousand wives and concubines, along with an enormous staff to provide support.

But to Haidée, open as it might seem, it had been stifling beyond imagining. Locked away among hundreds of others here in the harem with its iron grilles, its doors and windows shuttered against the world, she was isolated, yet never alone.

And Kauri—the only protector and friend she'd had on earth, the only person who might find her imprisoned here in this landlocked fortress—had been seized by slave traders, along with all of their crew, the very moment their captured ship had been hauled into port. She could still vividly recall the horror of the event.

Off the Adriatic coast just before Venice, their ship was skirting the seaport of Pirene—"The Fire"—where an ancient stone lighthouse had stood since Roman times warning ships off the rocky point. It was here that the last of the rogue corsairs, the notorious Pirates of Pirene, still plied their evil trade: selling European slaves into Muslim lands, where they were called White Gold.

From the moment when she and Kauri had first realized their plight, that their ship was about to be boarded by the Slovenian corsairs, they had known too well that this unexpected turn could prove a horror beyond all imagining.

The ship's small crew and their two young passengers would certainly be pillaged of their goods, then sold at auction in the slave markets. Girls like Haidée were sold into marriage or prostitution, but the fate of a boy like Kauri could be far worse. The slavers drove such boys into the desert where they castrated each with a knife and buried him in the hot sands to stanch the bleeding.

If the boy lived he would be highly coveted and later could be sold at a premium throughout the Turkish Empire as a eunuch harem guard, or even into the Papal States to be trained as a castrato musician.

Their one hope had been that the Barbary Coast of Africa, after decades of bombardment by the British, the Americans, and the French, was now closed to all such trafficking. Five years ago under treaty eighty thousand European slaves had been released from North African bondage and Mediterranean lanes were again open to normal sea trade.

But there was still one place that accepted such human booty, the only Mediterranean land that had never been controlled by either the Ottoman Empire or Christian Europe: the sultanate of Morocco. A land of complete isolation—its capital tucked away from the coast, between the Rif and the Atlas mountains, at Fez—Morocco had suffered for thirty years under the iron rule of Sultan Mulay Suliman.

After the months she had spent as a captive servant in his harem, Haidée had by now learned much of this sultan's rule, none of which had calmed her constant fears. Though himself descended from the Prophet, Suliman had early embraced the ideals of the Sunni Islamic reformer, Mohammed ibn Abd al-Wahhab of Arabia. Wahhabi zealots had succeeded in helping the ruler of Arabia, ibn-Saud, briefly snatch back large swaths of Arabian lands captured by the Ottoman Turks.

Although this triumph was short-lived, Wahhabi zeal had ignited a fire in the heart of Mulay Suliman of Morocco, who'd ruthessly purged his religious house, without and within. He'd cut off trade with the decadent Turks and the atheistic French with their ill-fated Revolution-cum-Empire; he'd suppressed the cults of saint worship among the Shi'a and dismantled the Sufi brotherhoods.

Indeed, there was only one people that Mulay Suliman had been unable either to control or suppress in these past thirty years of his rule: the Sufi Berbers on the other side of the mountains.

This was what had terrified Haidée most in these many months of her imprisonment. And after this morning's revelation, she feared the worst. For Kauri, wherever he might be—if it had ever been discovered that he was both a Sufi and a Berber—wouldn't have been maimed or sold. He'd have been killed.

And Haidée, who all this time had carefully guarded the secret Ali Pasha had entrusted her with, now would have not even the glimmer of hope that she'd ever again see the outside world as a free person. She would never be able to locate the Black Queen that was seized, recover it, and place it into rightful hands.

But despite her despair at this moment, as she pulled up her veil more tightly and passed with her escorts through the long open gallery that led to the outer court, she could not help clinging to the one thought that had run over and over in her mind these past eleven months:

When she and Kauri had first realized where their ship had been brought—just before they'd touched dock on Moroccan soil, perhaps to be parted forever—Kauri had told her that there was but one man in Morocco who might help them if they could ever reach him, a man highly regarded by the Baba Shemimi himself—a master of the *Tarik'at*, or Secret Path. He was a Sufi recluse known as the Old Man of the Mountain. If either of them managed to escape their captors, they must seek this man.

Haidée prayed now that in the few brief moments she might be permitted to spend outside this cloistered space, she could think and act quickly in her own behalf. Or all would truly be lost.

THE ATLAS MOUNTAINS

Shahin and Charlot reached the final descent of the last mountain range just as the setting sun touched the high peak of snowcapped Mount Zerhūn in the distance. It had taken three months to complete the difficult journey to this spot from the Tassili deep in the Sahara, across the winter desert into Tlemçen. There, they'd traded their camels for horses, more adapted to the wintry climate and mountainous terrain that lay ahead here in Kabylia, home of the Kabyle Berbers in the high Atlas Mountains.

Charlot, like Shahin, wore the indigo *litham* of the Tuareg, whom the Arabs called Muleththemin, the Veiled People, and the Greeks called Glaukoi, the Blue Men, for the pale blue tint of their fair skin. Shahin himself was a Targui, a noble of the Kel Rela Tuareg who had for millennia controlled and maintained the roads that crossed the vast Sahara—they'd dug the wells, maintained pasturage for livestock, and provided armed security. From ancient times, the Tuareg had been the most highly revered among the desert dwellers, by traders and pilgrims alike.

And the veil—here in the mountains as in the desert—had protected both men from far more than just the weather. By wearing it, the two travelers had remained always *dakhil-ak,* under the protection of the Amazigh, or Berbers, as the Arabs called them.

In their thousand-mile journey over often uninhabitable terrain, Charlot and Shahin had acquired far more from the Amazigh along their path than fodder and fresh changes of steeds. They'd also acquired information, enough to cause them to alter their intended path north toward the sea and to divert west toward the mountains.

For there was but one land where Shahin's son and his

comrade might have been taken—to Morocco—and but one man who might help them in their quest—a great Sufi master, if only they could find him. He was called the Old Man of the Mountain.

HERE ON THE BLUFF Charlot drew his horse to a halt beside his companion. Then he unwound his indigo *litham* and folded it into his saddlebag—as Shahin did, too. So close to Fez, it was best to be prudent in case they were sighted. The veil that had served as protection in the desert and the mountains might prove a great danger now that they had crossed the high Atlas into Sunni lands.

The two men gazed across the vast valley, sheltered by the high mountains, where birds circled below. This magical spot lay at the center of a rare confluence of waters: creeks, waterfalls, springs, rivers. There beneath them, surrounded by vegetation, spread a sea of tile roofs, lacquered a brilliant green and glittering in the slanted winter light, a city submerged in time—as in fact it was.

This was Fez, the holy city of the Shurafa—true descendants of the Prophet—and a sacred spot to all three branches of Islam, but most especially to the Shi'a; here on the mountain lay the tomb of Idris, great-grandson of Muhammad's daughter Fatima and the first of the Prophet's family to reach the Maghreb, the western lands, more than one thousand years before—a land of great beauty and dark omens.

"There is a proverb in Tamazight, the Kabyle language," Shahin said. "It is *Aman d'Iman*—Water is Life. Water explains the longevity of Fez, a city that is in itself almost a sacred fountain. There are many ancient caves cut by the waters, concealing ancient mysteries—the perfect place to shelter what we are seeking." He paused, then added quietly, "I feel certain that my son is here."

THE TWO MEN SAT beside the flickering fire within the open cave above Fez in which they'd taken shelter at nightfall. Shahin had set aside his *talac* stick, which marked his noble rank among the Kel Rela drum group, and he'd removed his double-crossed baldric, the fringed goatskin bands the Tuareg wore crisscrossed over each shoulder. They'd dined on a rabbit they'd caught and cooked.

But what was left unspoken now, as it had been throughout their long journey, still lay just beneath the surface, whispering like shifting sands.

Charlot knew he had not completely lost his gift, but he could not command it, either. Crossing the desert he'd often felt the Sight tugging at him like a tattered waif at the hem of one's burnoose. At those moments he'd been able to inform Shahin which men in the marketplace were trustworthy, which were rapacious, which had a wife and children to support, which had an ax to grind. All this was possible to him, as it had been from birth.

But of what real value was such limited foresight, given the daunting task that faced them just ahead? When it came to finding Shahin's son, the Sight had been blocked by something. It wasn't that he couldn't see *anything*—it was more like an optical illusion, a shimmering oasis of palms in the desert, where you know there is no water. When it came to the boy Kauri, Charlot could catch a glimmering vision—but he knew it wasn't real.

Now, in the flickering firelight, as they watched their horses nearby munching at the fodder provided from saddlebags, Shahin spoke.

"Have you wondered why only the Tuareg men wear the indigo *litham,* yet the women go unveiled?" he asked Charlot. "Our veil is a tradition older than Islam; the Arabs themselves were surprised to find this custom when they first arrived in our lands. Some think the veil provides us protection against desert sands; others believe it is against the evil eye. But the veil is quite significant to the history of our drum groups. In ancient times it was spoken of as the evil mouth."

"The evil mouth?"

"It refers to the ancient mysteries: 'those things that must not be spoken of by mouth.' These have existed in every land and culture for all time," Shahin said. "However, among the initiated these mysteries *may* be communicated by drum."

From Shahin, Charlot knew that the Tuareg tribes, known as drum groups, each was descended from a female progenitor. And each drum chief, often also a woman, kept the tribe's sacred drum, believed to be endowed with mystic power.

The Tuareg, like those Sufi Janissaries who controlled most of the Ottoman lands, for hundreds of years had used their secret drum language to send signals across the vast expanses of their dominions. So powerful was this drum tongue that in lands that kept slaves, the drum itself was forbidden.

"And these ancient mysteries of the Tuareg—the evil mouth and the veil—these are connected with your young son?" Charlot asked.

"You still cannot see him?" Shahin said. Though his face bore no expression, Charlot could hear the thought: *Even when he must be so close by?*

Charlot shook his head, then rubbed his hands over his face and ran his fingers through his red hair, seeking to stimulate his addled brain. He looked up at Shahin's face, carved like an ancient bronze. Shahin's golden eyes were trained intently upon him in the firelight. Waiting.

Forcing a small smile, Charlot said, "Tell me about him. Perhaps it will help us to find him, like giving the scent of water to a thirsty camel in the desert. Your son is called Kauri. It's an unusual name."

"My son was born on the Bandiagara Cliffs," he said. "Dogon country. *Kauri* is the Dogon word for *cowrie*, a marine mollusk indigenous to the Indian Ocean, a shell that we Africans have used as our monetary currency for thousands of years. But among the Dogon this small shell, the *kauri*, also bears deep meaning and power. It connects with the hidden meaning of the universe, for the Dogon symbolizing the source of both numbers and words. My wife chose this name for our child."

When he saw Charlot's dark blue eyes observing him in amazement, he added, "My wife—Kauri's mother—was very young when we married but already she held great powers among her people." Shahin continued, "Her name was Bazu—in the Dogon tongue it means 'the female fire'—for she was one of the Masters of Fire."

A blacksmith!

Charlot felt a shock in grasping just what this revelation meant. Blacksmiths everywhere throughout the desert lands and elsewhere were an ostracized profession, though it was true that they bore enormous powers. They were called Masters of Fire, for they created weapons, pottery, tools. They were feared, for they possessed secret skills and spoke a secret language known only to themselves; they commanded both hidden techniques of the initiate and diabolical powers attributed to ancient spirits.

"And this was your wife? Kauri's mother?" said Charlot in amazement. "But how did you come to meet or to marry such a woman?" *And without my knowing it!* Charlot felt weakened with exhaustion by these revelations.

Shahin was silent for a moment, his golden eyes clouded. At last he said, "It had all been foretold, just as it came to pass—both my marriage and the birth of our son, as well as my wife Bazu's early death."

"Foretold?" said Charlot. His creeping terror had returned in force.

"Foretold by *you,* Al-Kalim," said Shahin.

I foretold it. But I cannot remember it.

Charlot stared at him. His mouth was dry with fear.

"This is why, when I found you three months ago in the Tassili, I felt the shock of loss," said Shahin. "Fifteen years ago, when you were but a boy of Kauri's age just at the brink of manhood, you *saw* what I have just told you. You said I would produce a son who must be kept hidden, for he would be descended from a Master of Fire. He would be trained by those who possess great wisdom of the ancient mysteries—those mysteries that lie at the heart of the chess set we know as the Montglane Service, a secret that is believed to hold the power to create or to destroy civilizations. When al-Jabir ibn Hayyan designed the chess set one thousand years ago, he called it the Service of the *Tarik'at*—the Sufi path, the Secret Way."

"From whom did your son learn these mysteries?" asked Charlot.

"At the age of three, when Kauri's mother died, he was raised under the tutelage and protection of the great Bektashi Sufi *Pir,* the Baba Shemimi. I've learned that when the Turks attacked Janina in January, my son was called upon to help rescue an important chess piece held by Ali Pasha. When Janina fell, Kauri was headed with an unknown companion for the coast. This was the last we have heard of him."

"You must tell me what you know of the history of

the service," said Charlot. "Tell me now—before we descend the mountain at dawn to find your son."

Charlot sat staring into the fire, watching the molten heat as he tried to feel his way within himself. And Shahin began his tale.

THE TALE OF THE BLUE MAN

In the year 773, by the Western calendar, al-Jabir ibn Hayyan had been hard at work for eight years. With hundreds of skilled artisans assisting, he was creating the chess Service of the *Tarik'at* for the first caliph of the new city of Baghdad, al-Mansur. No one knew of the mysteries contained within it except Jabir himself. They were based upon his great Sufi alchemical work, *The Books of the Balance,* dedicated to his late shaikh Ja'far al-Sadiq, the true father of Shi'a Islam.

Jabir believed he was nearly finished with his masterpiece. But in the summer of that year, the caliph al-Mansur was surprised by the arrival of an important Indian delegation from the mountains of Kashmir, a deputation that ostensibly had been sent to open avenues of trade with the newly established 'Abbasid dynasty at Baghdad. In fact, these men were on a special mission whose purpose no one might ever have guessed. They had brought with them a secret of ancient wisdom, disguised beneath the veil of two gifts of modern science. As a scientist himself, al-Jabir was invited for the presentation of these treasures. This experience would change everything.

The first gift was a set of Indian astronomical tables that recorded the movements of the planetary bodies over the past ten thousand years—celestial events that were scrupulously recorded in the oldest of Indian sagas, such as the Vedas. The second gift was a puzzlement to everyone but the official court chemist, al-Jabir ibn Hayyan.

These were "new numbers"—new to the West. Among other innovations, these Indian numbers had positional value, that is, instead of two lines or two stones representing the number "two" if placed side by side, they represented one plus ten, or "eleven."

More clever still was a place-holding figure that we now call a cipher—from Arabic *sifr,* meaning "empty"—and which Europeans call a zero. These two numerical innovations—today called "Arabic" numerals—would revolutionize Islamic science. Though they would not reach Europe via North Africa for another five centuries, they had already existed in India for more than one thousand years.

Jabir's excitement knew no bounds. He instantly understood the connection between these astronomical tables and the new numbers, in providing deep and complex calculation. And he understood both with respect to another ancient Indian invention that already had been embraced by al-Islam: the game of chess.

It took al-Jabir two more years, but in the end he was able to build these Kashmiri mathematical and astronomical secrets into the chess Service of the *Tarik'at.* Now the chess set would contain not only Sufi alchemical wisdom and the Secret Path, but also *awa'il*—"in the beginning," or pre-Islamic sciences—the ancient wisdom upon which it all was based from the earliest times. It would be, he hoped, a guidebook for those in coming ages who might seek the Way.

In October of 775, only months after Jabir had displayed the service before the Baghdad court, Caliph al-Mansur died. His successor, Caliph al-Mahdi, hired the powerful family of Barmakids to be his viziers, prime ministers of his reign. Originally a Zoroastrian priestly family of fire worshippers from Balkh, the Barmakids were only lately converted to Islam. Jabir convinced them to revive *awa'il,* the ancient sciences, by bringing experts from India to translate the earliest Sanskrit texts into Arabic.

At the very height of this brief revival, Jabir dedicated his *Hundred and Twelve Books* to the Barmakids. But the ulama, religious scholars, and the chief councils of Baghdad protested. They wished to return to the fundamentals by burning all such books and destroying the chess set that, in its depiction of animal and human forms, seemed close to idolatry.

The Barmakids, though, recognized the importance of the service and all its symbols. They saw it as an *imago mundi,* a world image, a representation of how multiplicity is cosmically generated from Unity—from the One.

The very design of the board replicated some of the earliest structures that had been dedicated to the mystery of transformation of spirit and matter, heaven and earth. Among these was the design of the Vedic and Iranian fire altars—even of the great Ka'ab itself, which existed before Islam, built by Abraham and his first son, Ishmael.

Fearing that such a powerful record of wisdom might be destroyed for secular or political reasons, the Barmakid family arranged with al-Jabir to smuggle it to a safe place: to Barcelona, on the sea close to the Basque Pyrenees. There, they hoped that the Moorish governor Ibn al-Arabi, himself a Sufi Berber, might protect it. It was just in time, for the Barmakids themselves fell from power soon after, along with al-Jabir.

It was Ibn al-Arabi of Barcelona who would send the chess set, only three years after receiving it, over the mountains to the court of Charlemagne.

That is how the greatest tool that ever united the ancient wisdoms of the East came to enter the hands of the first great ruler of the West—from whose control it has never truly been relinquished over these past one thousand years.

SHAHIN PAUSED AND studied Charlot in the waning light of the fire, which had burned down to reddish coals. Though Charlot sat upright and cross-legged on the ground, his eyes remained closed. It was nearly dark within the cave now; even the horses were asleep. Just outside the entrance the full moon cast a silvery blue pallor upon the snow.

Charlot opened his eyes and regarded his mentor with an expression of great attentiveness—familiar to Shahin for it had often presaged one of the young man's prophetic insights—as if he were straining to see something partly hidden behind a veil.

"Sacred wisdom and secular power have always been in conflict, have they not?" Charlot said, as if feeling his way. "But it is the *fire* that seems to me especially haunting. Jabir was the father of Islamic alchemy. Fire must be counted the essential ingredient in that process. And if his own protectors at Baghdad, the Barmakids, were descended from Zoroastrian priests or magi, surely their ancestors had once maintained the fire altars with their eternal flame. The word that exists in nearly every tongue, that designates all of these trades—the blacksmith, the shaman, the cook, the butcher, as well as the priest who performs the sacrifice and burns the offering on the altar—all the works in sacrifice and fire that in ancient times were one. This word is *Mageiros:* the Magus, the Grandmaster, the "Thrice-Great" Master of the Mysteries.

"These fire altars, just like the Indian numbers, the astronomical tables, the *awa'il* sciences you spoke of—like the game of chess itself—all originated in northern

India, in Kashmir. But what connects them all together?"

"I hope your gift can answer that question for us," said Shahin.

Charlot regarded him soberly, this man whom he regarded as his only father. "Perhaps I've lost that gift," he said at last, the first time he'd truly admitted the idea, even within the confines of his own mind.

Shahin shook his head slowly. "Al-Kalim, you know that your coming was foretold among our peoples. It was written that one day a *nabi* or prophet would come from the Bahr al-Azraq—the Azure Sea—one who could talk with spirits and follow the *Tarik'at,* the mystic path to knowledge. Like you, he would be a *za'ar,* one who has fair skin, blue eyes, and red hair; he would be born beneath the eyes of the 'goddess,' the figure painted on the Tassili cliffs that my people call the White Queen. For eight thousand years she has waited—for you are the instrument of her retribution, just as it was foretold. It is written: *I will rise again like a phoenix from the ashes on the day when the rocks and stones begin to sing . . . and the desert sands will weep bloodred tears . . . and this will be a day of retribution for the earth . . .*

"You know what has been foretold of you, and what you have foreseen about others," Shahin added. "But there is one thing no man can ever know—one thing that no prophet, regardless how great, can see for himself. And that is his *own* destiny."

"Then you believe that whatever has affected my vision actually may have to do with my own future?" said Charlot, surprised.

"I think one man can lift that veil," Shahin replied. "We go to seek him tomorrow in the Rif. His name is Mulay ad-Darqawi, a great shaikh. It is he whom they call the Old Man of the Mountain."

All things are hidden in their opposites—gain in loss, gift in refusal, honour in humiliation, wealth in poverty, strength in weakness . . . life in death, victory in defeat, power in powerlessness, and so on. Therefore, if a man wish to find, let him be content to lose . . .

—MULAY AL'ARABI AD-DARQAWI, *Rasa'il*

THE BU-BERIH HERMITAGE
THE RIF VALLEY, MOROCCO

The Old Man of the Mountain—Mulay al'Arabi ad-Darqawi, the great shaikh of the Shadhili Sufi order—was dying. He would soon be far beyond this veil of illusion. He had expected death for many months—indeed, had welcomed it.

That is, until just this morning. Now everything was changed and different.

It was God's irony, as the Mulay himself should understand better than anyone. Here he had been prepared to die in peace, melded into the bosom of Allah just as he longed for. But God had a different idea.

Why should it be a surprise? The Mulay had been a Sufi long enough to know that when it came to Allah's ways, the unexpected must always be expected.

And what the Mulay was expecting right now was a message.

He lay beneath the thin coverlet on the slab of stone that had always served as his bed, his hands folded over his breast as he waited. Beside this plinth sat a large skin drum with a single drumstick attached to the side. He'd asked to have it brought here to him in the event he needed it suddenly, as he was quite sure he would.

Flat on his back, he gazed up at the ceiling toward the sole window, the skylight of his isolated hermitage—the *Zawiya*, the "cell" or "corner"—this tiny, whitewashed stone building high atop the mountain that had served for so long as his remote dwelling place. It would serve as his tomb, he thought wryly, once he himself had been turned into a holy relic.

Outside, his followers were already waiting. Hundreds of the faithful knelt upon the snowy ground in silent prayer. Well, let them wait. It's God who makes the schedules here, not me. Why would God keep an old man lingering like this unless it was important?

And why else would He have brought them here to the mountain? First, the Bektashi initiate, Kauri, who'd found shelter here ever since his escape from the slavers. The boy had insisted all these months that he was one of the protectors of the greatest of secrets, along with a girl who was still missing. According to the boy, she had been captured by the sultan Mulay Suliman's forces, which made it difficult if not impossible to find her. The daughter of Ali Pasha Tebeleni, she'd been entrusted with this relic by the great Bektashi *Pir* himself, the Baba Shemimi, nearly one year ago—a relic that the Mulay had always imagined might be no more than a myth.

But as of this morning, lying here on what would soon be his deathbed, the Mulay ad-Darqawi had understood at last that all of the story must indeed be true.

For now, Sultan Suliman was dead. His retinue would soon be scattered like leaves on the wind. The girl must be found before it was too late.

And what had become of the valuable relic that had been entrusted to her?

The shaikh ad-Darqawi knew it was Allah's will that he, and he alone, answer these questions; that he gather his strength from within to accomplish this final task demanded of him. He must not fail.

But to succeed, he first needed the sign.

Through the open hole in the ceiling the Mulay could glimpse the clouds moving across the sky. They looked like handwriting. *The Mystic Pen of God,* he thought.

"The Pen" had long been among the Mulay's favorite suras from the Holy Qur'an, one that helped explain how the Prophet was chosen to write it. For as all things are known to Allah, the Most Merciful and Compassionate, it had been known to Him that Muhammad—*may peace be upon him*—could neither read nor write.

Despite this fact, or perhaps because of it, it was the illiterate Muhammad whom God had chosen as messenger of His revelations. Among His earliest commands to the Prophet were *"Read!"* and *"Write!"* God always tests us, the Mulay thought, by insisting upon something that may at first appear to us, ourselves, to be quite impossible.

It was many decades ago, when Mulay ad-Darqawi was himself a young disciple on the Sufi Path, that he had first gained the skill to separate truth from vanity, wheat from chaff. That he'd learned how one might sow in pain and penury here on earth, in order to reap that otherworldly harvest of joy and riches. And after many years of honing this patience and intuition, at last he had discovered the secret.

Some called it a paradox—like a veil, an illusion that we created for ourselves: something of great value that we couldn't see, though it lay right before our eyes. The followers of 'Isa of Nazareth called it "the Stone that the Builders Rejected." The alchemists spoke of it as the *Prima Materia*—the Primal Matter, the Source.

Each master who'd found the Way had said the same: a discovery of great simplicity, and, like many simple things, breathtaking in its magnitude. Yet it was also wrapped in mystery, for did not the Prophet say, *"Inna lillahi la-sab'ina alfa hijabin min nurin wa zulmatin"*? God has seventy thousand veils of light and darkness?

The Veil! Yes, that's what those scudding clouds resembled—those clouds just over his head! He squinted his eyes, the better to study the clouds. But at that moment, just as the wispy clouds above were moving beyond the Mulay's window of vision, they parted. And there in the sky he thought he saw a large equilateral triangle comprised of clouds, feathery, like an enormous pyramidal tree with many branches.

In a flash of insight, the Mulay ad-Darqawi saw the meaning. Behind the Veil lay the Tree of Illumination.

Behind *this* veil, as the Mulay now understood, lay the illumination of the *Tariq'at,* the Secret Way that was hidden in the chess set created by al-Jabir ibn Hayyan more than one thousand years ago, and that piece now sought by his fellow Sufis—the piece the Baba Shemimi had protected.

The boy himself, though he'd held it in his hands, had never seen it, for it was veiled by a dark material. In confidence, he revealed to the shaikh Darqawi that he'd been told it was a most important piece that might be the key to all: the Black Queen.

Thanks to his vision, the Mulay now believed he knew precisely where this piece must have been hidden by the sultan Suliman or his forces. Just like the *Prima Materia,* like the secret Stone, it would be hidden in plain view, but it would be veiled. If he died now, before sharing this vision, the thousand-year-old secret might die with him.

The old man marshaled what power he could to put aside his coverlet, arise from his plinth, and stand without aid on bare feet upon the cold stone floor. With frail and trembling hands he grasped the drumstick as firmly as he could and took a deep breath. He needed all his strength to beat the familiar tattoo of the Shadhili Sufis.

The Mulay commended his soul into the hands of Allah.

And he began to beat the drum.

KAURI HEARD A sound that he had not heard since he'd left the White Land: the sound of the Sufi tattoo! This could only mean that something of great importance was happening. The crowds of mourners heard it, too; one by one, they looked up from their kneeling prayers.

As Kauri knelt in the snow alongside these hundreds of others who had drawn together here awaiting the shaikh Darqawi's death, he strained to make out the weak sound of the drum, trying to divine the meaning of its message. But he was frustrated, for it was unlike any other cadence he'd ever heard. Just as each drum had a voice of its own, he knew that each rhythm held a different import, one that could be completely grasped only by the ear initiated into its specific significance.

But more shocking than the sound of this incomprehensible drumbeat was the location from which it derived: the *Zawiya,* the stone cell of shaikh Darqawi where the saint lay dying. The crowds murmured in amazement. It could only be Darqawi himself who beat the tattoo. Kauri prayed that this also meant there existed hope of some kind.

For ten months, ever since his escape from those slave merchants who'd clapped him in chains at dockside, Kauri had sought in vain to learn the fate of Haidée and the chess piece called the Black Queen. No effort on his part, nor on that of the Shadhili Sufis, even of the shaikh himself, had turned up a trace of either. It was as if the girl and that critical key to al-Jabir's sacred legacy had both been swallowed by the earth.

As Kauri listened, it seemed the drumbeats from within became steadily firmer and stronger. Then he noticed a stirring at the fringe of the crowd outside. One by one, men were rising to their feet to clear a path for something moving in their direction. Though Kauri could not yet make out just what it was, there was whispering.

"Two horsemen," said his neighbor in a choked voice that mingled awe and fear. "They say perhaps they are angels. The saint is drumming the sacred beat of the *Pen*!"

Kauri looked at the man in amazement, but the man was looking past him. Kauri glanced back over his own shoulder to where the crowd was parting for whatever came their way.

A tall man astride a pale horse moved through the crowd, with another man behind him. When Kauri caught a glimpse of the white desert robes, the coppery hair swinging loose about his shoulders, it recalled those forbidden icons of "Esus the Nasrani" that the priests had kept in their fortress monastery of St. Pantaleon, on the Isle of Pines, the place where the Black Queen had been hidden.

But the horseman who followed was more of a revelation. He wore the indigo *litham*!

Kauri sprang to his feet and rushed forward along with the others.

It was his father, Shahin!

THE AL-QARAWIYYAN MOSQUE
FEZ, MOROCCO

The glow of sunset was gone from the skies; darkness had set in. The lacquered tile roofs of the al-Qarawiyyan Mosque glittered in the torchlight of the courtyard. The keyhole arches around the court's periphery were already deep in shadow as Charlot, alone, crossed the vast open expanse of the black-and-white-tiled floor, en route to *Isha*, the last evening prayer.

He'd arrived as late as possible, but still with enough

time to enter the mosque with the last group of worshippers for the day. By now Shahin and Kauri, already within, would have secured their hiding place as planned. Shahin had deemed it best for Charlot to arrive separately, after nightfall. For though his red hair was now completely concealed beneath a turban and his heavy djellaba, by day the cornflower blue of his eyes would be conspicuous.

When Charlot reached the fountain court the last stragglers were performing their ablutions before entering the sanctum. Beside them at the basin he quickly removed his shoes, careful to keep his eyes always downcast. When he'd finished washing his hands, face, and feet, he surreptitiously tucked his shoes into the pouch beneath his robe so they wouldn't be found here once everyone had departed the mosque for the night.

Lagging until the others had entered, he pushed open the great carved doors of the mosque and stepped into the dim, hushed interior—a forest of white pillars stretching in all directions, hundreds of them as far as the eye could see. Between these, worshippers already lay prostrate on their prayer rugs, facing east.

Charlot paused near the door to gauge the terrain from the drawing of the mosque the shaikh had provided them.

Despite the warmth of Charlot's garments and the warm dull glow provided by oil lamps throughout the great hall, he could not help but feel a terrible chill. He trembled, for what he was doing was not only highly dangerous; it was forbidden.

The al-Qarawiyyan was one of the oldest and most sacred of mosques, founded nearly a thousand years ago by Fatima, a wealthy woman from its namesake city, Kairuan in Tunisia—the fourth sacred city of Islam after Mecca, Medina, and Jerusalem.

So sacred was al-Qarawiyyan that mere entry by a *gi-*

aour, an infidel like himself, might be punishable by death. Though he'd been raised by Shahin and knew much of Shahin's faith, one could scarcely overlook that Charlot's mother had been a novitiate nun and his natural father a bishop of the Catholic Church in France.

Indeed, in every regard, to spend the night here within this sacred precinct, as the shaikh had recommended, was completely unthinkable. They would be trapped here like birds in a sack, with no recourse to their natural element.

But the shaikh ad-Darqawi had assured them—in a lofty tone suggesting he was already well conversant in the tongues of angels—that he had it on highest authority that the chess piece would be found within the great mosque of al-Qarawiyyan and that he knew where it was hidden:

"Behind the veil, within a tree. Follow the parable in 'The Verse of Light,' and you will surely find it."

> *God doth guide whom He will to His Light:*
> *God doth set forth parables for men:*
> *and God doth know all things.*
>
> —QUR'AN, SURA XXIV: 35, *"The Verse of Light"*

" 'The Verse of Light' is part of a famous sura in the Qur'an," Kauri explained to Charlot in a whisper.

They were hiding behind a heavy tapestry in the funereal annex of the mosque, where the two had been seated on the floor, concealed with Shahin these many hours, ever since the *Isha* prayer ended and the mosque was locked up for the night.

According to the shaikh ad-Darqawi, the only occupant of the vast mosque from now until dawn would be the *Muwaqqit,* the Keeper of Time. But he remained all night in his private chamber high in the minaret, relying upon sophisticated instruments—an astrolabe and a pendulum clock, gifts to the famous mosque from Louis XIV of France—to make his important calculation: the precise moment for *Fajr,* the next of the five canonical prayers prescribed by the Prophet, which took place between first light and sunrise. They should be safe in this alcove until then, when the gates were unlocked. Then they could mingle with the morning worshippers and depart.

Kauri went on speaking in a whisper, though there was no one nearby to hear. " 'The Verse of Light' begins by affirming that it's meant to be taken as a parable—a kind of encrypted code concerning 'God's Light.' It gives five keys: a niche, a lamp, a glass, a tree, and some oil. According to my teacher, the Baba Shemimi, these are the five secret steps to illumination if we can decipher the meaning, although scholars have debated its meaning for hundreds of years without any real resolution. I'm not sure how Shaikh Darqawi thought this would lead here to the mosque or help us find the Black Queen—"

Kauri stopped when he noticed Charlot's sudden change of expression, as if the latter had been overcome by some unbidden emotion. His face had gone white; he seemed to have trouble breathing in the cloistered space. Without warning, he'd precipitously jumped to his feet and pushed aside the heavy curtain. Kauri glanced quickly to his father for guidance, but Shahin was on his feet as well and had grasped Charlot by the arm. He seemed quite as upset as Charlot.

"What is it?" Kauri said, stepping out to draw the men back behind the tapestry before they were found.

Charlot shook his head, his blue eyes clouded over as he gazed at Shahin.

"My *destiny,* you said, did you not?" he asked Shahin with a bitter little smile. "Perhaps it was never anything about *Kauri* that blocked my vision. My God. How can this be? Yet I still cannot see it."

"Father, what is it?" Kauri repeated, still in a whisper.

Shahin told his son, "What you've just told us must be impossible. A total paradox. For the piece we've come here to find in the mosque tonight—the chess piece that you brought out of Albania eleven months ago—*cannot* be the Black Queen of al-Jabir ibn Hayyan. For *we* possess the Black Queen. It once belonged to Catherine the Great. It was retrieved from her grandson Alexander more than fifteen years ago—secured for us by Charlot's own father, Prince Talleyrand. How could Ali Pasha also have possessed it?"

"But," said Kauri, "the Baba Shemimi claimed that the Albanian Bektashis and Ali Pasha have possessed this piece for more than thirty years! Haidée was chosen by the Baba because her natural father, Lord Byron, had a hand in its history. We were to take it to him for protection."

Charlot said to Kauri, "We must find this girl at once. Her role may be critical to everything ahead. But first, is there any way that you can decipher that parable?"

"I believe I may have done so already," said Kauri. "We must begin at the place of prayer."

IT WAS NEARLY MIDNIGHT—once they felt sure that the *Muwaqqit* was well asleep—when Shahin, Charlot, and Kauri crept down the steps from their alcove in the loft of the Funereal Mosque.

The Great Mosque was deserted. The expanse beneath its five vaulted domes was hushed as an open sea beneath a starlit sky.

Kauri had said that the only spot in the mosque that "wore a veil," as the shaikh had stressed, was the alcove where the prayer niche was located—the niche itself being the first step in the parable of "The Verse of Light."

Within this same niche lay the *lamp* that was always kept burning, which in turn was contained in the *glass* surrounding it "like a brilliant star, lit from a Blessed *tree*." The tree in the "Verse" was an olive tree, which produced a luminous light from ever-burning *oil*—a magic oil, in this case, for "fire scarcely touched it."

The three men silently slipped by the marble pillars and headed to the prayer niche at the far end of the mosque. Once they'd reached it and passed through the curtain, they stood together before the niche and gazed into the lamp within its sparkling glass container.

At last, it was Charlot who spoke. "You said that the next step in the Qur'anic verse would be a tree, but I see nothing like that here."

"We must pull aside the veil," said Shahin, pointing to the screening curtain they'd just passed through. "The tree must be on the other side, inside the mosque."

When they pulled back the drapery to reenter the mosque, they saw what they had not recognized before as the final key: There before them, suspended by its heavy golden chain from the central dome of the great al-Qarawiyyan Mosque, was the enormous chandelier, glittering with light from the thousands of oil lamps, many with luminous cutout stars and suns. From this vantage point, seeing it hanging there from the central dome, it resembled an ancient drawing of the World Tree.

"The tree and the oil both here together—the sign," said Shahin. "Not the illumination that the Baba Shemimi seeks for my son, perhaps. But at least we may be enlightened enough to discover whether there is another Black Queen up there."

They were fortunate that the gearing mechanism for the chandelier had been well oiled; they moved it in silence. Still it took extraordinary effort by all three to lower it by the chain—only to discover that the lowest it would reach was just enough to enable the stewards of the mosque to replenish or relight the lamps with long-handled tapers or spouts. When all was done, it hovered ten feet off the ground.

As the sun moved toward its inevitable rise, the three were in serious panic at their plight. How to get up there into the "tree"? At last, a decision was reached.

Kauri, as the lightest in weight of the three, removed his outer garments, stripped down to his shiftlike kaftan, and, with Charlot's help, was hoisted onto his father's shoulders. The boy climbed onto the heavy branches of the chandelier, taking care not to disturb the many flickering bowls of luminous oil.

Shahin and Charlot watched from beneath as—soundlessly and with great dexterity—Kauri ascended the tree, branch by branch. Whenever he shifted his position too far, the enormous chandelier swayed slightly, threatening to spill some oil. Charlot found himself holding his breath. It took a conscious effort to calm his racing pulse.

Kauri reached the top tier of the lowered chandelier—perhaps sixty feet in the air, more than halfway to the dome. He looked down to where Charlot and Shahin waited so far below. Then he shook his head to indicate that there was no Black Queen.

But it has to be here! thought Charlot in a frenzy of anguish and doubt. *How could it not be here?* They'd all been through so much. Their journey across the great desert and the mountains. Kauri's capture and narrow escape from bondage; the plight of the girl, wherever she might be. And then this paradox.

Was Mulay ad-Darqawi's vision as poor as his own had become? Had there been some mistake; had the shaikh misinterpreted the message?

And then he saw it.

Gazing at the gigantic chandelier from beneath, Charlot thought he saw something that wasn't quite aligned. He moved to the exact center of the structure and looked up again. There at the core he saw a dark shadow.

Charlot raised his hand and motioned to Kauri, high above. The boy began his precarious descent—more difficult by far than the trip upward—lowering himself, step by step, and skirting the thousands of dishes of burning oil.

Shahin stood beside Charlot beneath the tree and watched the descent. When Kauri had reached the lowest tier of the chandelier, he swung two-handed from the bottom rung and Shahin wrapped his arms around the boy's legs to catch him. Except for a quick intake of breath by Shahin, all had been accomplished in complete silence.

All three sat on the ground and looked up at the hollow core of the chandelier, where the lump of coal had been inserted. They had to get it out—and as quickly as possible, so they could raise the chandelier again well before the muezzin's call to morning prayer.

Charlot made a sign to Shahin, who stood with legs planted widely apart and held his hands like a stirrup for Charlot to step onto. Charlot climbed to Shahin's shoulders and stood precariously, extending his arm and reaching into the chandelier's core. His fingers brushed the piece but he couldn't quite grasp it. He motioned for Kauri and extended his hand. Kauri clambered up the two men's bodies and swung himself up to the first rung once more, until he was above the chess piece. Reaching inside the chandelier's core, he pressed down on the piece of coal. It was dislodged and moved downward, sliding through the core toward Charlot's extended hand.

At that same moment, a loud chiming like that of a gong shattered the silence in the vast hall. It seemed to come from somewhere high up, toward the entrance. Charlot flinched, momentarily withdrawing his raised hand to correct his balance—when everything suddenly went topsy-turvy. Kauri had snatched at the coal from above, trying to halt its downward progress, but had failed. Shahin staggered under the unbalanced weight, and Charlot toppled from his shoulders to the ground, rolling to one side just as the weighty chunk of coal crashed like a meteor, from ten feet above, onto the carpeted marble floor between them.

Charlot leapt to his feet and snatched up the piece in a panic as the loud chiming continued echoing off marble pillars, magnified on high from the hollowed domes. Kauri swung from the bottom rung of the swaying chandelier and dropped to the floor amid a shower of hot oil. Together the three braced for flight—

And then it stopped.

The chamber was again swallowed in silence.

Charlot glanced back at his two astonished companions. Then he understood, and he laughed despite the danger that still hung in the air around them.

"Twelve chimes, wasn't it?" he said in a whisper. "That would be midnight. I'd forgotten about the *Muwaqqit* and his ruddy French pendulum clock!"

AFTER THE PREDAWN prayer Charlot and his companions, mingling among the other worshippers, moved through the gates of the courtyard into the streets of Fez.

The day was already beginning. The sun shimmered like a filigreed platter through the silvery veil of fog that was just melting away. To reach the nearest gate of the walled city they must pass through the medina, already bustling with merchants of legumes and viands, the air thick with the exotic aromas of rosewater and almonds, sandalwood and saffron and amber. The largest and most complex market district in Morocco, the Fez medina was a confusing labyrinth where, they all knew, it was easy to become hopelessly lost.

But Charlot would not begin to feel secure with this chess piece hidden within the pouch beneath his garments until he could set foot outside of the city's imprisoning walls, which loomed around them everywhere, like those of a medieval fortress. He had to get out—if only long enough to draw his breath.

Furthermore, he knew they must find a suitable place to hide the chess piece in the short term, at least until they could trace the path of the girl who might hold the key to the mystery.

Within the medina, not far from the mosque, lay the famous five-hundred-year-old Attarine Medrassa, one of the most beautiful religious centers in the world with its carved cedar doors and grilles, its walls replete with richly colored tilework and golden calligraphy. The Mulay Darqawi had informed them that the medrassa roof, which was open to the public, provided a bird's-eye view of the entire medina. It would allow them to map out their exit route.

And more important, Charlot was drawn to this spot. Something was awaiting him there—though he couldn't see what it was.

Once on the parapet with his companions, Charlot looked out over the medina, trying to get his bearings. Below lay the maze of narrow streets dotted with shops and souks, fawn-colored houses with small gardens, fountains, and trees.

But immediately beneath them—right here in the al-Attarine souk just below the medrassa's walls—Charlot beheld a remarkable sight. *The* sight. The vision he'd been awaiting. The vision that blocked all the others.

When he realized what it was, his blood froze.

It was a slave market.

He had never seen one in his life, yet how could he be mistaken? There below him were hundreds of women held in enormous fenced-in pens like animals in a barnyard, chained to one another by ankle bracelets. They stood without moving, with bowed heads, all looking at the ground as if ashamed to see the platform toward which they were headed: the platform where the merchants displayed their wares.

But there was one who looked up. She looked directly at him, as it seemed, with those silvery eyes, as if expecting to find him there.

She was only a wisp of a girl, but her beauty was breathtaking. And there was something more. For Charlot now understood exactly *why* he had lost his memory. He knew that even if it cost his life, even if it cost the Game itself, he must save her, he must rescue her from that pit of iniquity. At last he understood everything. He knew who she was and what he must do.

Kauri had grasped Charlot by the arm with urgency.

"My God! It is *she*!" he told Charlot, his voice trembling with emotion. "It's Haidée!"

"I know," Charlot said.

"We must save her!" Kauri said, clinging to Charlot's arm.

"I know," Charlot repeated.

But as he stared down into her eyes, unable to avert his gaze, Charlot knew something else that he could not speak of to anyone until he could understand, himself, just what it all might mean.

He knew that it was Haidée herself who had blocked his vision.

AFTER THEIR BRIEF consultation with Shahin on the parapet, they had arranged their plan, the simplest they could devise on such short notice, though even so it would be fraught with difficulty and danger.

They knew there was no way they could effect an abduction or escape for the girl from so large a crowd. Shahin, they agreed, would depart at once to retrieve their horses for their departure, while Charlot and Kauri, posing as a wealthy French colonial slave trader and his servant, would purchase Haidée at whatever the cost and meet him at the medina's western edge, an isolated area not far from the northwest gate, a place where their exit from the city might be less remarked upon.

As Charlot and Kauri descended into the crowd of purchasers awaiting the first block of humans being prepared for auction, Charlot felt a tension and rising fear that he could barely contain. Slipping among the dense crowd of men, his vision of the pens was blocked for a time. But he did not need to see the faces of those who were held there like livestock awaiting slaughter. He could already smell their fear.

His own fear was scarcely less affecting. They'd begun by auctioning the children. As each lot of young ones was herded from the pens and up onto the auction stand, fifty souls to a parcel, where they could be seen, their clothes were stripped, their hair, ears, eyes, noses, and teeth were examined by the auctioneers, and a starting price for each was put upon their heads. The smaller children were sold in lots of ten or twenty, and the "sucklings" were sold with their mothers—to be sold once again, no doubt, the moment they'd been weaned.

Charlot's mounting revulsion and horror were nearly overwhelming. But he knew he must bring these emotions under control until he could learn precisely where Haidée was. He glanced at Kauri, then nodded toward a man in a striped kaftan, standing just beside them in the throng.

"Sire," Kauri addressed the man in Arabic, "my master is a trader for a prominent sugar plantation in the New World. Women are needed in our colonies, both for slave breeding and for childless planters. My master is sent hither to acquire good breeding stock. But we are unfamiliar with custom at auctions in these parts. Perhaps you would be so kind as to enlighten us as to your procedures. For we've overheard that this auction today might contain a high quality of both black and white gold."

"You have overheard quite correctly," said the other, seemingly pleased to know something that these strangers were ignorant of. "These lots today are directly come from the recently deceased Sultan Mulay Suliman's personal household at the palace, the choicest of flesh. And yes, both procedure and prices often go very differently here than in other slave markets—even than at Marrakech, the largest slave market in Morocco, where five or six thousand humans are sold per year."

"Different? How so?" asked Charlot, his anger at this fellow's callousness beginning to restore a bit of his strength.

"In the Western trade, like at Marrakech," the man said, "you'll find that strong healthy males are in greatest demand to ship to plantations like yours in the European colonies—while for export to the East, eunuch youths bring the highest prices, for they're favored as concubines by wealthy Ottoman Turks. But here in Fez boys between five and ten years may bring no more than two or three hundred dinars each, although young *girls* of that age bring more than double that amount. And a girl that's reached the age to breed—if she's attractive, pubescent, and yet still a virgin—might command something like the value of fifteen hundred dinars, more than one thousand French livres. As these girls are the choicest and most highly sought after here, if you have the money you won't have long to wait. They will always be sold first, just after the children."

They thanked the man for his information. Charlot, in despair at these words, had taken Kauri by the shoulder and now began to propel him to the edge of the crowd so they might quickly gain a better view of the auction platform.

"How can we possibly do it?" Kauri whispered to Charlot. For it was clear that it was now too late ever to procure such an enormous sum, even if they knew how.

Just as they cleared the crowd, Charlot said beneath his breath, "There is one way."

Kauri looked at him with open, questioning eyes. Yes, there was one way, as they both knew, that they could acquire so large a sum quickly, regardless of what such a decision might cost them in the end. But did they really have a choice?

There was no time to think further. Almost as if the hand of fate had grasped him, Charlot felt the terror grasp his spine. He looked back toward the platform with a jolt to see the slender form that he knew was Haidée, her nakedness now covered only by her long, loose abundance of hair, as—with a string of other young girls, chained to one another by a silver cuff attached to the left wrist and ankle of each—she was herded up onto the platform.

As Kauri stood guard, blocking the view of the others, Charlot huddled beneath his own robe as if merely pulling off his outer djellaba. But with one hand he reached beneath his underlying kaftan and removed the Black Queen from her leather pouch so he could see her. Unsheathing his sharp *bousaadi,* he scraped away a bit of the charcoal. Then from the soft, pure gold, he prized out a single, costly stone. It fell into his hand—an emerald the size of a robin's egg. He put the Black Queen back in her pouch, untied the bag from his waist, tossed back his djellaba, and handed the pouch to Kauri.

With the smooth stone still clutched in his palm Charlot, all alone, walked to the front of the crowd to stand directly beneath the platform of those naked and terrified women. But when he looked up he saw only Haidée. She was looking down at him with no fear, with enormous trust.

They both knew what he must do.

Charlot might have lost his vision, but he knew beyond a doubt that this was right.

For he knew that Haidée was the new White Queen.

THE HEARTH

Every Greek state had its prytaneum. . . . On this hearth there burned a perpetual fire. The prytaneum was sacred to Hestia, the personified goddess of the hearth. . . . The question still remains, why was so much importance attached to the maintenance of a perpetual fire? . . . Its history goes back to the embryo state of human civilization.

JAMES GEORGE FRAZER, *The Prytaneum*

WASHINGTON, D.C.
APRIL 6, 2003

MY TAXI DROPPED ME ON M STREET IN THE HEART of Georgetown just as the Jesuit church bells at the end of the block were calling out the end of Sunday night.

But Rodo had left so many unanswered messages on my cell phone to start up the fires that, exhausted as I was, and although I knew Leda would cover for me, I'd already decided not to go home. Instead I would go to the kitchens only a block from where I lived to prepare the new fire for the week, as usual.

To say I was exhausted was the understatement of the millennium. Getting out of Colorado had not gone exactly as planned.

By the time the Livingstons had departed our dinner Friday night, the rest of us were already completely wiped out. Lily and Vartan were still on London time. Key said she'd been up before dawn and needed to get home and get some shut-eye, too. And what with the emotional traumas and psychic bruising I'd been subjected to from the very moment of my arrival on that Colorado mountaintop, my mind was by now so cluttered with potential moves and countermoves that I couldn't see the board for the pieces.

Lily, glancing around at our haggard faces, suggested that it was time to call it a night. We'd readjourn first thing in the morning, she said, when we'd be in a better state to construct a strategy.

According to her idea, this would consist of activity on multiple fronts: She herself would sleuth to learn more about Basil Livingston's activities within the chess world, and Vartan would milk his Russian contacts to discover what he could about the suspicious death of Taras Petrossian. Nokomis would ferret out what possible escape routes my mother might have taken after departing the lodge in Four Corners, to see if she could pick up her trail, while I was assigned the thankless task of contacting my elusive uncle to learn what he might know about her disappearance and what "gift" he had sent her, as he'd said in his mysterious message. We all agreed that finding my mother was top priority—that I'd phone Key on Monday to find out what she'd learned.

Key was on the phone with her crew, checking the status of Lily's car that they'd sent off to Denver on a trailer. That was when the news broke that there would be a change in our plans.

"Oh no," she said, regarding me with a grim expression as she held the phone to her ear. "The Aston Martin got to Denver just fine, but there's a blizzard headed our way from the north. It's already in southern Wyoming. It should hit here before noon tomorrow. Cortez airport has shut down for the weekend, along with everything else."

I'd been in this boat before, so I knew the drill. Although this was only Friday and my return flight to D.C.

wasn't scheduled until Sunday, if a blizzard dumped enough snow here tomorrow I could still miss my connection at Denver. Worse yet, and beyond contemplation, we might all be stranded here in the mountains for days with one bed among us, living on a diet of flash-dried food. So we'd have to depart the mountaintop first thing in the morning—the three of us with Zsa-Zsa and the luggage—well before the snows hit, and make the five-hundred-mile trek through the Rockies in my rental car, which could be dropped at the Denver airport.

Upstairs, I assigned Aunt Lily and her companion Zsa-Zsa the only real bed—my mother's brass bed, tucked into one of the semiprivate alcoves on the octagonal balcony. They were both fast asleep before they even hit the mattress. Vartan helped me pull out futons and sleeping bags, and he offered to help me clean up the after-dinner mess.

My houseguests must have observed that our accommodations here at Mother's octagon were primitive. But I'd neglected to mention that the lodge only sported one small bathroom—on the ground floor under the stairway—with no shower, only a claw-footed tub and a big, old-fashioned iron sink. As I knew from long experience, that was where we'd have to do the dinner dishes, too.

On Key's way out, she glanced in the open bathroom door where Vartan—his cashmere sleeves shoved above his elbows—was swirling dishes around in the sink and rinsing them off in the tub. He passed a wet plate out the door for me to dry.

"Sorry we can't recruit you—no room," I said, motioning to the cramped space.

"There's nothing sexier than seeing a strong man slaving over a sink of hot, sudsy dishes," Key informed us with a wide grin.

I laughed, as Vartan pulled a grimace.

"Now, no matter how much fun this is, you two," she said, "please don't stay up all night playing in the bubbles. You've got a rough road ahead of you tomorrow."

Then she vanished into the night.

"This actually *is* fun," Vartan told me as soon as she'd gone. He was now passing cups and glasses out the door. "I used to help my mother like this in Ukraine when I was little," he went on. "I loved to be in the kitchen and smell the bread baking. I helped with everything—grinding coffee and shelling peas—you couldn't ever get me to leave. The other children said I was fastened to my mother's—how do you say it?—her apron ties? I even learned to play chess on the kitchen table, while she cooked."

I admit I had trouble visualizing the arrogant, ruthless boy chess wizard of my last acquaintance as this self-described mama's boy. Stranger yet was the disparity in our cultures that instantly leapt to mind.

My mother could build a fire. But when it came to cooking, she could barely dip a tea bag in hot water. The only kitchens I'd known as a child were far from cozy: a two-burner hot plate in our apartment in Manhattan, versus my uncle Slava's huge old wood-burning ovens and walk-in fireplace at his mansion on Long Island, where you could cook for a cattle drive—though being such a recluse, he never did. And my chess upbringing itself could hardly be described as idyllic.

"Your kitchen life sounds wonderful to somebody like me, a chef," I told Vartan. "But who taught you chess?"

"That was my mother, too. She got me a little chess set and taught me to play—I was very tiny," he told me, passing the last of the silverware through the door. "It was just after my father was killed."

When Vartan saw my shocked reaction, he reached out and wrapped his wet hands over mine as I still held the silverware in the dishcloth.

"I'm sorry—I thought everyone knew," he explained hastily. Taking the silverware from my hands, he set it down. "It's been in all the chess columns ever since I made grandmaster. But my father's death was nothing like yours."

"What *was* it like?" I said. I felt like weeping. I was ready to drop to the floor from exhaustion. I couldn't think straight. My father was dead, my mother was missing. And now this.

"My father was killed in Afghanistan when I was three," Vartan was explaining. "He was conscripted there as a soldier at the height of the war. But he hadn't served for long, so my mother could receive no pension. We were very poor. That's why eventually she did it."

Vartan's eyes were trained upon me. He'd taken my hands in his again, and now he pressed them tightly. "Xie, are you listening to me?" he said in a tone I hadn't heard before—so urgent it was almost a command to pay attention.

"Let's see," I said. "You were poor, your father was shot in the line of duty. So far am I tracking?" But then I *did* snap to. "That's why who did *what*?" I said.

"My mother," said Vartan. "It was several years before she understood how good I was at chess—how good I *could* be. She wanted to help me in any way she could. I found it hard to forgive her, but I knew that she did what she thought was right by marrying him."

"Marrying who?" I said, though I had grasped it before he said it.

Of course. The man who'd managed the chess tourney where my father was killed, the man who was Basil Livingston's partner in crime, the man who was snuffed out himself by the Siloviki two weeks ago in London. It was none other than Vartan Azov's own stepfather . . .

"Taras Petrossian."

NEEDLESS TO SAY, Vartan and I didn't get much sleep before dawn. His checkered Soviet childhood made my father's—at least, what little I knew of it myself—seem cheery by comparison.

The crux of it was, Vartan had resented and disliked the new stepfather he'd acquired at the age of nine, but was reliant upon him for the sake of his mother's comfort and Vartan's own chess education and training. After Vartan attained his GM ranking—after his mother died, and Petrossian was in self-imposed exile outside Russia—Vartan had little to do with the man. That is, not until this past chess tournament two weeks ago in London.

Still—why had he mentioned nothing about this relationship to us when we were discussing strategies earlier? If it was in "all the chess columns," did Lily already know?

Now, as we sat side by side deep in the pillows beside the waning light of the fire, I found myself too exhausted to protest or even to speak, but still too distraught to adjourn upstairs and try to get some sleep. Vartan had poured us some brandy from the sideboard. As we sipped it, he reached over and rubbed my neck with one hand.

"I'm sorry. I thought you must know all this," he told me as gently as possible, kneading my tense neck tendons. "But if we are indeed involved in that larger Game, as Lily Rad said, I believe that you and I have too many coincidences in our lives *not* to join forces."

Starting with a few suspicious family murders, I thought. But I said nothing.

"I would like to begin this spirit of cooperation," Vartan told me with a smile, "by offering you my skill at something I do even better than I play chess."

He slipped his hand from my neck to beneath my chin and tilted my face up to his. I was about to protest when he added, "This skill is something else that my mother taught me when I was quite small. Something I believe you will need before we leave here tomorrow morning."

He got up and went into the mudroom, returning with my big down-filled parka, which he tossed in my lap. Then he headed to the piano. I sat up in the cushions in alarm as he opened the lid and reached inside. He extracted the drawing of the chessboard, which in my stupor I had somehow completely forgotten.

"You *had* planned to take this with you, hadn't you?" Vartan inquired. When I nodded, he added, "Then you should be grateful your parka is thick enough to conceal it in all that down. And thank heaven that my mother taught me how to sew!"

I'D MADE THIS grueling ten-hour drive often, but even so, all day Saturday I was wrangling with the steering wheel, barely outpacing the snapping winds of the incoming storm. Though I did have the comfort of some extra thermal padding from the drawing of a two-hundred-year-old chessboard hidden inside the down filling of my parka. And the added comfort of my last-minute decision to grab the pillow bag stuffed with that chess set and place it in my rucksack. Just in case there was some further message I'd overlooked.

Just as the blizzard hit Denver, I dropped Lily's entourage and luggage at the front door of the Brown Palace and let the doorman take the car. We got our first meal of the day at the Ship's Tavern just before the restaurant closed. We agreed that we would all touch base later in the week. And I grabbed a few hours of sleep myself, crashing on the sofa in Lily's suite. As it turned out, that would be the last food and sleep I would have for twenty-four hours.

Now at midnight in Georgetown, as I descended the steep flight of stone steps and crossed the wooden foot-bridge over the glassy, shimmering canal, I could see Rodo's world-famous restaurant—Sutalde, The Hearth—there on the low bluff below me, overlooking the river.

Sutalde was unique even for a place steeped in history like Georgetown. Its weathered stone buildings dating from the 1700s were among the earliest still standing in Washington, D.C., and they were seeping with charisma.

I unlocked the front door to the restaurant and switched off the burglar alarm. Though the interior lights were on automatic dousers, I never bothered to turn them on when I came into Sutalde, even so late at night. Across the vast room, where the original barn doors had once been, was a wall of many-paned windows overlooking the canal and the river. As I moved among the damask-draped tables, ghostly in the gloom, I had a panoramic view of the pale celadon green sweep of Key Bridge, illuminated by its tall, slender lanterns all the way across the river. On the far shore, the lights of the high-rise buildings of Rosslyn were reflected in the glittering midnight waters of the wide Potomac.

From those windows to the maître d's desk, extending the length of the room's left wall, ran a rack that stood nearly as tall as I and displayed handmade jugs of Basque cider from every province. It provided a corridor of sorts so that waiters and my boss's favorite diners could get to their destinations without being forced to navigate the forest of tables. Rodo was quite proud of it all—the cider, the display, and the touches of privacy and class it provided. I ducked around the rack and descended the curving flight of stone steps to the kitchens. Here was the magical stone dungeon created by Rodolfo

Boujaron, where most evenings privileged diners, if they had nothing but time on their hands and *beaucoup d'argent,* could watch through an enormous glass wall as their prix fixe eight-course meal was prepared over flames and hot embers by scurrying staff and award-winning master chefs.

Beside the great stone ovens I found Leda the Lesbian sitting on the high chair we used for monitoring the fires. She seemed calm and relaxed, reading a book while smoking her traditional hand-rolled Turkish cigarette in its black lacquered holder and sipping a Pernod pastis, her favorite drink.

The ovens, I noticed with appreciation, had already cooled down and she had mucked them out in preparation for my task for the week ahead, which would save me time tonight.

Rodo was right about one thing. Leda was a swan, a *soignée* creature of both detachment and strength. But she preferred to be called Leda the Lesbian, both as a vocational badge of pride, I think, and a way to keep certain clients at arm's length. I could understand her concerns. I'd be worried about the length of unsolicited arms, too, if I looked as rakish and come-hither as she did.

The sweep of her swanlike neck was exaggerated by a short-cropped silver-blond shock of hair—like a flattop crew cut. Her translucent white skin, artificially arched eyebrows, lips perfectly outlined in bloodred paint, and lacquered cigarette holder all contrived to give her the look of a stylized art nouveau illustration. Not to mention that her costume of preference, weather permitting, was what she was wearing, even now, at midnight beside the cold hearth: nothing but sparkly Rollerblades, a rhinestone-studded T-shirt, and men's satin boxer shorts. Leda was, as the French say, "such a one."

Leda turned in relief when she heard me on the stairs.

I dropped my backpack on the floor, stripped off my down jacket, and carefully folded it and placed it on top.

"The prodigal returns, thank heavens," she said. "Not a moment too soon. 'Massa Rodolpho Legree' has been driving us all in circles ever since you left."

Leda's concept of Rodo as a slave master was shared by anyone who'd ever manned the kilns on his behalf. As in a military drill, obedience became second nature.

By way of demonstration, tired and hungry as I was, I was already on the move to the woodpile. Leda set down her cigarette and drink, slid off her chair, and followed, swishing behind me on her silent Rollerblades to the back wall, where we each pulled a stack of hardwood so I could start building the new fire in all four of the large stone hearths.

"Rodo said if you got here tonight, I should stay and help you," she said. "He said the fire must be done right tonight—it's important."

As if that familiar admonition would help either my bleary eyes or my travel-addled brain get focused, I thought. Not to mention my growling stomach.

"What else is new?" I said as she helped me plop the two large "andiron logs" into place in the first hearth, which would serve to support the others. "But Leda, I haven't really slept in days. I'll get things going here in all the hearths—they'll take a few hours to establish before we can cook. Then if you'll watch the fires, I can go home and get a little shut-eye. I'll be back before sunrise, I promise, to start making the bread."

I'd finished stacking the triangle of upper logs atop the andirons and shoved some crumpled paper beneath. Then I added, "Besides, it's not so urgent everything tonight be done on our drillmaster's schedule. You know the restaurant's always closed Mondays—"

"You don't know what's been happening around here," Leda interrupted, looking uncustomarily concerned as she handed me another pile of paper. "Rodo is holding a big *boum* tomorrow night for a bunch of dignitaries, here in the cellar. It's very private. None of us has been invited even to work the tables. Rodo said he wants only you to help him cook and serve."

I had those first glimmers that something might be terribly wrong. I tried to relax as I shoved some more crumpled paper under the nascent fires. But the timing of this unannounced soiree of Rodo's bothered me—just a weekend away from my mother's in Colorado, a party that Rodo himself had actually *known* about, as I recalled from his voice mail.

"What exactly do you know about this party?" I asked Leda. "Do you have any idea who these 'dignitaries' might be?"

"I heard it might be some high-level muckety-mucks from the government. Nobody knows for sure," she said. She was hunkering down over her blades as she passed me a few more sheets of crumpled paper. "They made all the arrangements with Rodo himself, not the catering manager. They're throwing it on a night when the restaurant isn't even open. It's all very hush-hush."

"Then how did you learn so much?" I asked.

"When he heard you'd left for the weekend, Rodo threw a real hissy fit—that's the first I learned that he wanted you and you alone for tomorrow night," Leda explained. "But as for the *boum*, we all knew there was some private function cooking. The cellar's been reserved for two weeks—"

"Two weeks?" I interrupted.

I might be jumping to conclusions, but this seemed more than synchronicity. I couldn't help hearing Vartan's comment: *You and I have too many coincidences in our lives.* I was growing horribly certain that there was no such thing as a coincidence when it came to the way my life was running these past few days.

"But why would Rodo single me out for this shindig?" I asked Leda, who was kneeling beside me wadding newsprint. "I mean, I'm hardly a seasoned caterer, just an apprentice chef. Has anything happened lately that might prompt this sudden interest in my career?"

Leda glanced up. Her next words confirmed my worst fears.

"Well, actually, there was a man who came by the restaurant a few times this weekend, looking for you," she said. "Maybe he has something to do with the gig tomorrow night."

"What man?" I said, trying to quell that familiar adrenaline rush.

"He didn't give his name or leave a note," Leda told me, getting to her feet and brushing off her hands on her shorts. "He was pretty distinguished—tall and elegant, with an expensive trenchcoat. But mysterious, too. He wore blue-tinted sunglasses so you couldn't quite see his eyes."

Terrific. This was the very last thing I needed—a man of mystery. I tried to focus on Leda, but my eyes went all crooked. I was nearly reeling from four days' deprivation of food, of liquid, of sleep. Synchronicity, serendipity, and strangers be damned, I needed to get home. I needed to lie down in a bed.

"Where are you going?" Leda said as I stumbled toward the steps in a blur.

"We'll discuss it in the morning," I managed to say, as I grabbed my jacket and backpack from the floor on my way out. "The fires will be fine. Rodo will survive. The enigmatic stranger may return. And we who are about to die salute you."

"Okay, I'll be here," Leda said. "And you take care."

I headed up the steps on wobbly legs and staggered into the deserted alley. I glanced at my watch: it was almost two A.M. and not a creature was stirring; the narrow, brick-paved lane was dead as a tomb. It was so silent that you could hear the waters of the Potomac in the distance, lapping the trestles of Key Bridge.

At the end of the alley I turned the corner to my small slate terrace bordering the canal. I fumbled in my pack for the key to my front door, illuminated by the golden pink light of the single streetlamp marking the entrance to the shadowy path that descended into Francis Scott Key Park. The low iron bicycle railing surrounding the terrace was all that kept one from toppling over the side of the sheer rock retaining wall that dropped sixty feet to the motionless surface of the C & O Canal.

My cliffside dwelling provided an astonishing overlook across the vast expanse of the Potomac. People would kill for a view like this, and probably had in the past. But over the years, Rodo had refused to sell this weathered structure, due to its proximity to the Hearth. In exhaustion, I took a deep breath of the river and pulled out my key.

There were two doors, actually, separate entrances. The one at the left led to the main floor with its iron bars and shuttered windows, where Rodo kept important documents and files for his flickering fireside empire. I unlocked the other—the upstairs, where the slave laborer slept, always within handy availability to the fires.

As I was about to step inside, I bumped my toe on something I hadn't noticed, lying there on the step. It was a clear plastic bag with the *Washington Post* inside. I'd never subscribed to the *Post* in my life, and there were no other residents in the alley it might belong to. I was about to dump the bag, paper and all, into the nearby city trash can, when under the limpid pink light of the streetlamp I noticed the yellow stickie that someone had attached with a handwritten note: "*See page A1.*"

I switched on my house lights and stepped inside. Dropping my rucksack on the floor of the foyer, I yanked the newspaper from its plastic bag and pulled it open.

The headlines seemed to be screaming at me from across time and space. I could hear the blood beating in my ears. I could hardly breathe.

April 7, 2003:
TROOPS, TANKS ATTACK CENTRAL BAGHDAD . . .

We'd taken the city at six A.M., Iraqi time—only hours ago, barely long enough to get the news into this paper. In my dazed stupor, I could hardly absorb the rest.

All I could hear was Lily Rad's voice haunting the recesses of my mind:

It was never the game of chess that your mother feared, but another Game . . . the most dangerous Game imaginable . . . based on a rare and valuable chess set from Mesopotamia . . .

Why hadn't I seen it at once? Was I blind?

What event had happened two weeks ago? Two weeks ago when Taras Petrossian mysteriously died in London? Two weeks ago when my mother sent all those invitations to her birthday party?

Two weeks ago—on the morning of March 20—U.S. troops had invaded Iraq. Birthplace of the Montglane Service. Two weeks ago was when the first move had been made. The Game had begun again.

PART TWO

Nigredo

You . . . must search into the causes of things, and endeavour to understand how the process of generation and resuscitation is accomplished by means of decomposition, and how all life is produced out of decay . . . it must perish and be putrefied; again, by the influence of the stars, which works through the elements, it is restored to life, and becomes once more a heavenly thing that has its habitation in the highest region of the firmament.

—BASILIUS VALENTINUS, *The Eighth Key*

THE RETURN

Suddenly I realized that I was no longer a prisoner, neither in body nor in soul; that I was not condemned to death. . . . As I was falling asleep, two Latin words were running through my brain, for no apparent reason: magna mater. *The next morning when I woke I realized what they meant. . . . In ancient Rome candidates to the secret cult of magna mater had to pass through a bath of blood. If they survived, they would be born again.*

—JACQUES BERGIER, *Le Matin des Magiciens*

It is only this initiatory death and resurrection that consecrates a shaman.

—MIRCEA ELIADE, *Shamanism*

DOLENA GEIZEROV, DUHLYIKOH VAHSTOHK (VALLEY OF GEYSERS, THE FAR EAST)

He felt as if he were rising from a great depth, floating toward the surface of a dark sea. A bottomless sea. His eyes were closed but he could sense the darkness beneath him. As he rose toward the light, the pressure on him seemed to increase, a pressure that made it difficult to breathe. With effort, he slid his hand to his chest. Against his skin was a soft piece of cloth, some sort of thin garment or cover with no weight at all.

Why couldn't he breathe?

If he focused on his breath, he found it came more easily, rhythmically. The sound of his own breathing was something strange and new, as if he hadn't ever heard it clearly before. He listened as the sound rose and fell in a soft, gentle cadence.

With his eyes still shut, in his mind's eye he could almost make out an image hovering near him: an image that seemed so important, if only he could grasp it. But he couldn't quite see it. It was all rather vague and blurry around the edges. He tried harder to see it: Perhaps it was a figurine of sorts. Yes, it was the carved figure of a woman, shimmering in a golden light. She was seated within a partially curtained pavilion. Was he the sculptor? Had he been the one to carve it? It seemed so important. If he could just pull the draperies aside with his mind, then he could see within. He could see the figure. But each time he tried to imagine this task, his head was flooded with a brilliant, blinding glare.

With extra effort he finally managed to open his eyelids and tried to focus upon his surroundings. He found himself in some kind of undifferentiated space filled with a strange light, an incandescent glow flickering around him. Beyond, there were impenetrable deep brown shadows, and in the distance a sound that he couldn't identify, like rushing water.

Now he could see his own hand, which still rested upon his chest, faded like a fallen flower petal. It seemed unreal, as if it had moved here of its own accord, as if it were someone else's hand.

Where was he?

He tried to sit up, but found he was too weak even to attempt the effort. His throat was dry and scratchy; he couldn't swallow.

He heard voices whispering nearby, the voices of women.

"Water," he tried to say. The word barely passed his parched lips.

"Yah nyihpuhnyee mahyoo," *said one of the voices: I don't understand you.*

But he had understood her.

"Kah Tohri Eechahs?" *he asked the voice in the same tongue in which she'd addressed him, though he couldn't yet place what it was. What time is it?*

And though he still couldn't make out forms or faces in the flickering half-light, he could see the slender female hand that descended to gently rest over his own hand, where it still lay upon his chest. Then her voice, a different voice from the first—a familiar voice—spoke just beside his ear. It was low and liquid and soothing as a lullaby.

"My son," she said. "At last you have returned."

THE CHEF

But men, whether savage or civilized, must eat.
—Alexandre Dumas, *Grand Dictionnaire de Cuisine*

To know how to eat is to know enough.
—Basque saying

Washington, D.C.
April 7, 2003

At 10:30 on Monday morning I was maneuvering Rodo's Volkswagen Touareg through the misty drizzle of rain, up River Road, headed for Kenwood just north of the District and my boss's palatial villa, Euskal Herria—"the Basque Land."

I was the designated driver to make sure the raw vittles arrived intact. Per Rodo's commands left on my house phone, I'd already picked up the iced crustaceans from Cannon Seafood in Georgetown and the fresh veggies from Eastern Market on Capitol Hill. They'd be washed, scraped, chopped, diced, minced, shredded, mandolined, or *mouli*'d under Rodo's private supervision by his own resident staff of culinary sous-slaves, in preparation for tonight's "hush-hush" dinner at Sutalde.

But though I'd managed to get some sleep and Leda had delivered some fresh hearth-brewed coffee to my doorstep this morning, my nerves were still so raw it took every effort just to be sure that *I* arrived intact.

As I drove up the slick, winding road with windshield wipers slapping against the blur of water, beside me on the passenger seat I grabbed a handful of gooseberries from the small wooden box I'd filched, intended for tonight's fixings, and I popped them into my mouth, washed down by some of Leda's syrupy java. My first fresh food in days. I realized it was also the first time in four days I'd been left alone to think, and I had plenty of food for thought.

The one thought I couldn't stop going over and over in my mind was, as Key might say: Too many cooks spoil the broth. I knew that this bouillabaisse of unlikely coincidences and conflicting clues contained too many potentially lethal ingredients to allow easy digestion. And there were too many folks dishing up more by sleight of hand.

For instance, if the Livingstons and Aunt Lily were all acquainted with Taras Petrossian, the organizer of that last chess tourney where my father was killed, why had no one at dinner—including Vartan Azov—deigned to mention the detail they all surely must have known: that this same chap they'd left recently deceased in London was Vartan's stepfather?

And if everyone who'd been involved in the past had been endangered or even killed—including Lily's family and my own—why would she spill the beans about this Game in front of Vartan and Nokomis Key? Did Lily think they were players, too? And what about the Livingston family and Galen March, who'd all been invited to my mother's, as well? Just how dangerous were they?

But regardless of who the players were or what the Game was, I now realized that there were a few captured pieces of the puzzle I was holding in *my* hand only. In chess we refer to this as "material advantage."

First, as far as I knew, I was the only person—except my late father—who'd discovered that there might be not just one, but two Black Queens of the Montglane Service. And second, other than the mystery person who'd left that *Washington Post* on my doorstep, I might also be the only one who'd connected that jeweled chess set created in Baghdad twelve hundred years ago with events unfolding there right now—or any of it with that other dangerous Game.

But when it came to the Game, I now knew one thing beyond doubt: Lily was mistaken back in Colorado when she'd said we needed a master plan. By my lights it was too early in the Game for strategy. Not when we were still in the opening moves—"the Defense"—as Lily herself had said.

In any chess game, though you need a wide-angle view of the board—the big picture, a long-range strategy—as the game progresses, the landscape will quickly change. To keep your balance, to be able to land on your feet, you must never let the long view distract your attention from those immediate threats always lurking nearby, those close encounters in an ever-shifting sea, with dangerous actions and defensive or aggressive counteractions lapping about you at every side. These require tactics.

This was the part of the game I knew best. This was the part of the game I loved: the part where everything was still potential, where elements like surprise and risk would pay off.

As I swung the Touareg through the big stone gates of Kenwood, I knew exactly where that kind of danger might lie closest at this very moment, where those tactical maneuvers might soon come in handy: less than three hundred yards away up the hill at villa Euskal Herria.

I'D FORGOTTEN UNTIL I entered Kenwood that this week was the Cherry Blossom Festival in D.C., where each year hundreds of thousands of tourists packed the

National Mall to snap photos of the reflecting pool with its mirror images of Japanese cherry trees.

But the little-known cherry trees in Kenwood had apparently been discovered only by the Japanese. Hundreds of Japanese tourists were already here, moving like wraiths through the rain beneath dark umbrellas along the grassy, winding creek. I drove uphill beside them through the astonishing cathedral of black-branched cherry trees, so old and gnarled that they seemed to have been planted a hundred years ago.

At the top of the hill, when I rolled down the window at Rodo's private gates to punch in my intercom code, mist swirled into the car like damp smoke. It was permeated with a heady aroma of cherry blossoms that made me a little dizzy.

Through the fog beyond the high iron gates I could see acres of Rodo's beloved *xapata,* the Basque trees that yield abundant black cherries for Saint John's Day each June. And beyond in the mist, floating above the sea of cherry trees in frothy magenta bloom, lay the sprawling villa Euskal Herria with its Mediterranean tiled roof and vast terraces. Its shutters painted a brilliant *rouge Basque,* the color of cow's blood, and the flamingo-pink stucco walls dripping with vermillion bougainvillea, it was all like something from a Fauve painting. Indeed, everything about Euskal Herria had always seemed illusory and strange—especially here so close to Washington, D.C. It seemed to have been dropped from the skies of Biarritz instead.

When the gates swung open, I drove around the circle drive to the back side of the house where the kitchens, with their wall of French windows, were located. On a clear day, from the enormous tiled terrace, you could see the entire valley beyond. Rodo's silver-haired concierge, Eremon, was already awaiting me there with his crew to unload the car—half a dozen muscular lads all clad in black, with bandannas and *txapelas,* dark berets: the Basque brigade. While Eremon helped me down from the Touareg, they wordlessly set to their task of unloading boxes of fresh produce, eggs, and iced seafood.

I always found it interesting that Rodo—who'd grown up like a wild goat on the Pyrenees passes; whose family crest included a tree, a sheep, and some pigs; who still raked fires for a living and composted his own crops—today maintained a lifestyle involving multiple villas, a permanent staff of servants, and a full-time concierge.

The answer was simple: They were all Basques so they weren't really employees, they were brothers.

According to Rodo, Basques were brothers regardless of what language they spoke—French, Spanish, or Euskera, the Basque tongue. And regardless of where they came from—one of the four Basque provinces belonging to Spain or one of the three that are part of France—they think of the Basque regions as a single country.

As if to reinforce this important point, just above the French windows a favorite, if private, Basque maxim had been set in hand-painted tiles into the stucco wall:

EUSKERA MATHEMATICS
4 + 3 = 1

Eremon and I entered the enormous kitchen through the wall of French windows and the brigade started efficiently unloading the crates across the room.

We found Rodo, his back to us, his compact, muscular body bent with intensity over the stove, stirring something with a big wooden spoon. Rodo's long dark hair, normally brushed up from his neck like a horse's mane to tumble over his collar, was today pulled back into a ponytail—with his customary red beret instead of a chef's toque, to keep it from the food. He was dressed in his usual whites—slacks, open-throat shirt, and espadrilles tied with long ribbons about the ankles—a costume usually worn on festive occasions with the bright red neck kerchief and waist sash. This morning it was covered with a big white butcher's apron.

Rodo did not turn when we entered. He was breaking a large bar of bitter Bayonnais chocolate into pieces and dropping them into the double boiler as he stirred. I assumed this meant that tonight we'd taste his specialty, a version of *Txapel Euskadi: Beret Basque*, a cake he filled with dark liquid chocolate and cherries preserved in liquor. My mouth was watering already.

Without looking up from his task, Rodo muttered, "So! The *neskato geldo* returns from dancing *Jota* all night with the prince!" His favorite little cinder girl, he was calling me. "*Quelle surprise!* Back to the kitchen to rake the ashes! Ha!"

"It wasn't exactly a *Jota* I was dancing out there," I assured him, *Jota* being one of those ebullient Basque dances Rodo loved so much, with high kicks, everyone arms akimbo, leaping off the floor. "I almost got snowed in, in the middle of nowhere. I had to drive through a blizzard to get here in time to help with this unannounced *boum* of yours tonight. I might have been killed! *You're* the one who ought to be grateful!"

I was fuming, but there was method in my fulminations. When it came to dealing with Rodo, I knew from experience that one had to fight fire with fire. And whoever tossed the first match into the fat usually came out on top.

But maybe not this time.

Rodo had dropped his spoon in the chocolate pot and turned to Eremon and me. His stormy black brows were drawn together like a brewing thundercloud as he waved his hand frenetically in the air.

"So! The *hauspo* believes that it is the *su*!" he cried: The bellows thinks it's the fire. I couldn't believe I always put up with this. "Please do not forget who gave you a job! Do not forget who rescued you from—"

"The CIA," I finished for him. "But maybe you deserve a job at that *other* CIA—the Central Intelligence Agency? Or how could you possibly have guessed that I'd left to attend a party? Perhaps you can explain why I had to race back so fast?"

This put Rodo off balance for only an instant. He quickly recovered and, with a snort, he snatched off his red beret and threw it dramatically onto the floor—a favorite technique whenever he was at a loss for words, which wasn't often.

This was followed by a torrent in Euskera of which I could pick up just a few words. It was directed with urgency toward the dignified, silver-haired concierge Eremon, just beside me, who'd said nothing at all since we'd entered.

Eremon nodded in silence, then walked over to the stove, turned off the gas, and removed the wooden spoon that Rodo had forgotten there in the chocolate pot. It looked a mess. After carefully placing it on the spoon holder, the concierge crossed back to the French windows that led outside. There he turned, as if expecting me to follow.

"I must take you back right now for the *geldo*," he said, referring to the embers, apparently to prepare them for tonight's cooking. "Then, after the men have finished cleaning the food, Monsieur Boujaron says he himself will return with the car and bring everything so you can help for tonight's private dinner."

"But why me?" I said, turning to my boss for an explanation. "Who on earth *are* these 'dignitaries' tonight, that there's all this subterfuge? Why's no one allowed even to see them except you and me?"

"No mystery," Rodo said, evading my question. "But you are late for the work. Eremon will explain anything you may need to know en route." He vanished from the kitchen in a huff, shutting the inner door behind him.

My audience with the master now seemed to be at an end. So I followed the stately concierge out onto the terrace and got into the car on the passenger side, while he drove.

Perhaps it was my imagination, or only my limited knowledge of the Basque tongue, but I was fairly sure that I'd picked up two words that had run together in Rodo's recent diatribe. And if I was right, these specific words wouldn't make my mind rest any easier. Not at all.

The first was *arisku*, a word Rodo used all the time around the ovens: It meant "danger." I couldn't fail to recall that same word printed in Russian on a cardboard plaque that still lay, even now, in my pocket. But the second Basque word that had followed on its heels, *zortzi*, was even worse—though it didn't mean "beware the fire."

In Euskera, *zortzi* means "eight."

AS EREMON MANEUVERED the Touareg down River Road back into Georgetown, he never removed his eyes from the road nor his hands from the wheel, deploying the noncity dexterity of a driver who'd been negotiating hairpin mountain turns all his life—as likely he had. But that fixated attentiveness wasn't going to stop me from what I knew I had to do right now: pump him for information—as Rodo had evasively promised—for "anything I needed to know en route."

I'd been acquainted with Eremon, of course, for as many years as I'd been apprenticed to Monsieur

Rodolfo Boujaron. And though I knew much less of the consigliere than I knew of the don, there was one thing I did know: Eremon might play the silver-haired dignitary and chief factotum around Rodo's baronial estate. But away from his official job, Eremon was a dyed-in-the-wool Basque with all the implied traits. That is, he had an off-the-wall sense of humor, an appreciative eye for the ladies (especially Leda), and an inexplicable taste for *Sagardoa*—that god-awful Basque apple cider that even the Spaniards can't drink.

Leda always said that *Sagardoa* reminded her of goats' piss, though I was never sure how she'd come to make that culinary judgment call. Nevertheless, she and I had ourselves both cultivated a taste for the cider, for an obvious reason: Drinking tumblers of bitter, sparkling fermented apple juice in Eremon's company, from time to time, was the only way we could think of to get the scoop on our mutual boss, the guy Leda liked to refer to as "the Maestro of Menus."

And trapped in a car for at least half an hour—as I was now with Eremon—I felt there was, as Key might say, no time like the present.

So imagine my surprise when it was he who broke the ice first, and in a most unexpected fashion.

"I want you to know that E.B. is not angry with you," Eremon assured me.

Eremon always called Rodo "E.B.," short for "Eredolf Boujaron," a Basque "in" joke that he'd shared with Leda and me on one of our very late ciderfest nights. Apparently there are no names or words in Basque that begin with R: hence Eremon's name—Ramon in Spanish, Raymond in French. And Rodolfo seemed almost Italian. This linguistic flaw would seem to make Rodo something of a Basque Basqtard.

But the very fact that he could make quips about a

tyrannical volcano like Rodo showed their relationship was closer than master and servant. Eremon was the only one I could think of who might have a clue as to what Rodo was up to tonight.

"So if he's not *angry* with me," I pointed out, "then why all the burnt chocolate, the beret on the floor, the snit in the Euskeran tongue, the slammed door, the instant ejector button for *moi*?"

Eremon shrugged and smiled enigmatically. All the while, his eyes still clung to the road like Velcro.

"E.B. never knows what to do with you." He warmed to his theme. "You are different. He isn't used to dealing with women. At least, not professionally."

"Leda's different, too," I said, counterpointing with his favorite girl violincello. "She runs the entire cocktail operation. She works like a dog. She makes Sutalde a fortune. Surely Rodo wouldn't slight her that."

"Ah, the swan. She is magnificent," said Eremon, his eyes wavering just a bit. Then he laughed. "But he always tells me, with her, I am barking on the wrong horse."

"I think the expression is 'Barking up the wrong tree.' "

Eremon hit the brakes. We'd come to the stoplight at River Road and Wisconsin. He looked over at me.

"How can one 'bark up a tree'?" he asked, quite sensibly. Unlike my friend Key, I'd never actually given such sayings any thought. So much for folk wisdom.

"So maybe we'd say you're barking at the wrong swan," I agreed.

"One does not bark at swans, either," said Eremon. "Especially not a swan that you are in love with. And I *am* in love with that one, I really think."

Oh no. This chat wasn't exactly the one I'd been hoping to have.

"I'm afraid that, when it comes to observing human

nature, Rodo may be right just this once," I told Eremon. "The swan prefers female companions, I believe."

"Foolishness. That is just some—how do you say it?—phase of a moment. Like those wheels she likes to wear on her feet. This will change—this need for the success, this power over the men. She doesn't need to prove things to everyone," he insisted.

Ah, I thought, that popular chestnut: "She's never known a man like me."

But at least I had Eremon talking, no matter what got him hooked. As the traffic light changed, he started paying a bit more attention to me than to the road. I knew this might be my last opportunity, in the few miles before we reached our destination, to learn what was really going on behind the scenes.

"Speaking of proving things," I said as casually as possible, "I wonder why Monsieur Boujaron didn't ask Leda or anyone else to work tonight's *boum*. After all, if these guests are so important, wouldn't he want to prove *himself*? To make sure things run like clockwork? We all know what a perfectionist he is. But he and I can hardly cover all the bases by ourselves, replace a full restaurant staff. If the amount of food I just hauled up to Kenwood is any indication, we must be expecting a pretty good-sized crowd."

I'd been probing as casually as possible—until I noticed that we'd just passed the Georgetown Library to our left. We'd be arriving at Sutalde at any moment. I decided to turn up the heat. But luckily, it wasn't to be necessary.

Eremon had forked down a side street, avoiding Wisconsin traffic. He stopped at the first four-way stop sign and turned to me.

"No, at most a dozen will be there, I believe," he told me. "I am told that this is a command performance, that many demands were made of E.B.—that the very highest level in haute cuisine was instructed, with many special dishes commanded in advance. This is why we have had to make all these preparations up at Euskal Herria under E.B.'s supervision. This is why he was so anxious to be sure you were here in time, that the fires were properly established last night—so we could start the *Meschoui*."

"The *Meschoui*?" I said, amazed.

It took at least twelve hours to roast a *Meschoui*—a spit-basted, herb-stuffed goat or lamb turned on a rotisserie, a highly coveted dish in Arab lands. They could only cook something like that in the big central hearth at Sutalde. Rodo must have had a crew down there before the crack of dawn to get it going in time for tonight's dinner.

"But who *are* these mystery dignitaries?" I demanded once more.

"Based on the menu, I believe they must be some kind of high-level officials from the Middle East," he told me. "And I have heard many preparations for security. As for why you are the only staff in attendance tonight, I cannot say. But E.B. assured us that everything tonight is only what has been commanded."

"Commanded?" I said, uneasy at the repeat of that word. "Commanded by whom? What kind of security?"

Though I was trying to act unruffled, my heart was pounding like a steel-head drum. It was all too much. Dangerous chess games with mysterious moves, Russian assassinations and familial disappearances, mysterious Middle East dignitaries and invasions of Baghdad. And me with less than eight hours' sleep in the past forty-eight.

"I don't know for certain," Eremon was saying. "All the arrangements were made through E.B. alone. But with so much security above the normal, one could guess. It is my suspicion that this dinner was arranged by the Oval Office."

A WHITE HOUSE command performance? Not bloody likely. That really was the last straw. What further difficulties was my already difficult boss "commanding" me into? If the idea hadn't been so absurd I might've been genuinely angry.

But as Key would say, "If you can't take the heat, get out of the kitchen."

I thought I was about to step into the very kitchen that I'd heated up myself, fewer than ten hours earlier. But in the foggy drizzle, as I descended the steep stone steps to the canal bridge, I couldn't help noticing that some things had changed since my visit here earlier this morning.

A low concrete barrier was now blocking the entrance to the footbridge that crossed the canal, and a small wooden kiosk, no larger than a portable latrine, had been placed just beside it. As I approached, two men suddenly emerged from the booth. They were wearing dark suits and coats and (oddly, given the glowering weather) even darker sunglasses.

"Please state your business," said the first man in a flat, official voice.

"I beg your pardon?" I said, alarmed.

Security, Eremon had said. But this surprise barricade popping up like a mushroom on the deserted bridge seemed beyond the bizarre. I was becoming more nervous by the minute.

"And we need your name, birthdate, and a photo ID," the second man requested in a duplicate monotone, holding out his hand palm-up toward me.

"I'm on my way to work; I'm a chef at Sutalde," I explained, motioning to the stone buildings across the bridge.

I tried to look obliging as I rummaged in my crammed shoulder bag for my driver's license. But I suddenly realized how remote and inaccessible this brushy section of the towpath really was. Women had been murdered along here, one even during a morning jog. And had anyone ever reported having heard them scream?

"How do I know who *you* are?" I asked them. I raised my voice a bit, more to quell my fears than to solicit assistance when none seemed to exist.

Number one had reached into his breast pocket and, like lightning, he flashed his ID beneath my nose. Oh lord, the Secret Service! This did tend to suggest that Eremon's hunch about tonight might be right. Whoever was "commanding" this *boum* had to be pretty high up themselves, or they could hardly commandeer the highest echelons of government security, to provide a private blockade, just to screen folks for a dinner party.

But by now, I was fuming; I was surprised they couldn't detect the smoke of indignation pouring from my ears. I was going to kill Rodo, whenever he deigned to show up, for never alerting me about this showdown at "Checkpoint Charlie"—after what I'd already been through these past forty-eight hours just to get here.

I finally dug out my buried driver's license and I flashed the two thugs back. Show me yours and I'll show you mine. Number one returned to the kiosk to check my name against his instructions. He nodded out the door to number two, who handed me over the concrete hurdle, vaulted after me, escorted me across the canal, and deposited me on my own at the far side of the bridge.

When I entered Sutalde, I was in for yet another jolt. More security guys prowled the upstairs dining room—

maybe half a dozen, all whispering on mouthpieces into their individual walkie-talkies. A few searched beneath the linen-draped tables, while their boss searched behind the long wall rack displaying Rodo's colorful collection of homemade *Sagardoa*.

The Kiosk Twins must have buzzed ahead to announce my arrival, since nobody in the vast dining room seemed to give me a second glance. Finally one of the plainclothesmen came over to speak to me.

"My team will be clearing out of here shortly, once we've finished sweeping the place," he informed me curtly. "Now that you've been processed for admission, you're not to leave these premises until you've been clearance-processed for exit at the end of the night. And we need to search your bag."

Terrific. They went through my stuff, removed my cell phone, and told me they'd give it back later.

I knew it was senseless to argue with these guys. After all, given what I'd just learned these past four days about my own family and circle of friends, who knew when a little unexpected offer of security might come in handy? Besides, even if I wanted out now, upon whom could I call for help against the Secret Service of the United States government?

Once the boys in black had departed, I ducked behind the cider rack, made a quick trip down the spiral stone steps into the dungeon where I found myself, refreshingly, completely alone. Except, that is, for the enormous cadaver of a lamb that was silently revolving on the spit in the central hearth. I raked the hot embers into place beneath the slowly revolving *Meschoui,* to keep the heat steady. Then I checked the flames in all the hearths and ovens, and I brought extra wood and kindling to touch up what needed improvement. But as I placed the new logs, I realized I had a bigger problem.

The rich herbal aroma of the roasting meat wafted

over me, almost reducing me to tears. How long had it been since I'd ingested anything substantial? I knew this carcass couldn't be done yet—and it would be ruined if I started picking at it too soon. Yet for all I knew, Rodo might not show up here for hours with the rest of the dinner fixings or anything I could nibble on. And no other potential sustenance-provider that I knew of had security clearance to get across that bridge. I cursed myself for not making Eremon stop off even at a fast-food place somewhere en route so I could get a snack.

I considered foraging in the food lockers at the back of the dungeon where we kept all our supplies, but I knew it would be pointless. Sutalde was famous for fresh homegrown produce, daily-procured seafood, and healthily raised, recently butchered viands. We mostly kept things on-site that were hard to come by in a pinch—like preserved lemons, vanilla beans, and saffron stamens—nothing resembling actual food that could be popped quickly from a freezer and nuked. Indeed, Rodo had banned freezers and microwaves from the premises.

By now, I could hear those tart gooseberries I'd been foolish enough to eat, already fighting for supremacy with the acids in my stomach. I knew I wouldn't last until dinnertime. I had to be fed. I had in my mind the stark, ugly image of the prisoner of Zenda, starving to death here in her very own dungeon—the last vision before her eyes of delicious, savory meat rotating slowly on a spit.

I was looking at the logs I'd just placed under the *Meschoui,* when I caught a glimpse of something silvery and metallic back there in the ashes. I bent over and peered beneath the rotating spit. For sure, there was a tinfoil lump back behind the coals that you could barely see, half covered with ash. I got the rake and pulled it out: a large oval object I instantly recognized. I fell on my knees and started to grab it with my hands, until I realized what I was doing. I yanked on the asbestos gloves, pulled the object out, and peeled the heavy tinfoil away. I'd never been so happy to see anything—or so grateful to anyone—in my life.

It was a gift from Leda. I recognized not only her style but her taste.

Comfort food: a twice-baked potato stuffed with meat, spinach, and cheese.

IT'S HARD TO imagine how perfectly exquisite a stuffed potato can taste, until you're starving. I ate every bit except the tinfoil.

I thought of phoning Leda, until I recalled that she'd worked the graveyard shift for me and was probably sleeping it off right now. But I resolved to buy her a magnum of Perrier-Jouët, just as soon as I broke out of prison.

Now that I had an infusion of fodder that I could burn off, it ignited a few thoughts that had not occurred before.

For starters, Leda and Eremon each knew more than they were letting on about this dinner party, as evidence revealed. After all, one was my driver and the other my potato-provider, which meant they knew when I'd be arriving here and that I wouldn't have had time to eat. But there was more.

Last night when I was building the fires, I was too exhausted to follow up on Leda's comments about Rodo: How he'd thrown a fit when he learned I'd left town without notice. How he'd been driving the staff like a slavemaster "ever since I'd left." How he was throwing a secret party for "government muckety-mucks" and only I was to help out at the dinner. How he'd insisted that

Leda was to stay on-site until I returned that night, to "help me with the fires."

Then this morning, practically the instant I'd arrived up there at the Kenwood estate with the food, Eremon had raced me back here to the restaurant.

What had Rodo said just after his tantrum this morning—just before he slammed the door behind him? He'd said there was no mystery to worry about. That I was late for work. And that *Eremon will explain anything you need to know en route.*

But what had Eremon actually told me on the way? That Rodo wasn't in charge of this dinner at all—lack of control being something my boss had always hated. That it might involve guests from the Middle East. That security was involved. That from square one, this *boum* had been arranged by the highest echelons of D.C. clout.

Oh, yes—and that he himself, Eremon, was in love with Leda the swan.

Such things seemed like diversionary tactics, drawing my vision away from a sneaking lateral attack. This was not the time to miss the big picture, not the moment to succumb to chess blindness—not here, locked in a dungeon, waiting for the ax to fall.

And then it struck me.

When exactly was it this morning that Rodo went into that tantrum? Exactly *when* did he toss his beret on the floor, lapse into Basque, eject me from his presence? Wasn't this connected with everything Leda and Eremon had hinted at, but hadn't come right out and told me?

It was not my questions about *this* party that had lit Rodo's fire. It was when I'd demanded to know how he'd found out about that *other* party. After I told him I'd driven through a blizzard to get here. After I'd demanded to know how he could possibly have known where I was.

Though I'd had the first glimmer, back in Colorado, of what might be headed my way—I'd missed the main point until it reached out and bit me:

Whatever might happen tonight here in this cellar, it was going to be the next move in the Game.

TACTICS AND STRATEGY

Whereas strategy is abstract and based on long-term goals, tactics are concrete and based on finding the right move now.
—GARRY KASPAROV, *How Life Imitates Chess*

Tactics is knowing what to do when there is something to do. Strategy is knowing what to do when there is nothing to do.
—SAVIELLY TARTAKOWER, POLISH GRANDMASTER

PRACTICE MAKES PERFECT, AS KEY WOULD SAY.

I'd spent half a lifetime practicing cooking in my uncle's big wood-burning ovens and his open hearth out at Montauk Point on Long Island. And now I'd had another nearly four years of apprenticeship here at Sutalde, under the rigorous, if often overbearing, surveillance of the Basque Bonaparte—Monsieur Boujaron.

So one would think that by now, at least when it came to cooking, I'd be able to distinguish a flame from a flimflam.

Yet until this moment it hadn't really hit me that there was something wrong with this scenario. Of course, I'd been a bit preoccupied by things like food and sleep deprivation, by tempestuous tantrums and Secret Service spies. But my first clue that something was wrong should have been the *Meschoui* itself.

It was obvious to the trained eye. After all, the clockwork spit was running just like clockwork; the fire I'd created was producing an even, steady heat; and the lamb itself, rotating at perfect elevation above the hearth, was trussed correctly, so as it turned all sides would be evenly exposed to heat from the firebox. But the dripping pan was missing. The liquid fat, instead of dropping into a water-filled catch-all beneath, to be recycled for basting the meat, had been splashing onto the flagstones below and baking into a black mess for hours. It would be hell to scrub all that off.

None of the master chefs would ever have set up the rotisserie that way—much less Rodo. He'd be infuriated. And Leda, even if she were strong enough to set it up, was no cook. Yet someone must have, since none of this was here when I'd left the cellar at two o'clock this morning.

I privately vowed to get to the bottom of it all just as soon as Rodo arrived. Meanwhile, I hauled down the longest ceramic dripping pan I could find and placed it under the sheep, then poured in some water and got out the basting siphon.

The mystery of this fireplace setup made me recall that other one I'd just left behind in Colorado—what seemed like aeons ago: which also triggered my memory of my arrangement with Key, that I'd phone her on Monday to find out what she'd managed to learn about my mother's disappearance.

I never knew exactly where Key might be found but, given the remote spots where she did her work, she kept her satellite phone beside her at all times. Before I could pull out my cell phone, though, I remembered that the Secret Service had temporarily commandeered it.

There was a phone with an outside line near the restaurant entrance, behind the maître d's desk, so I trotted upstairs to use it; I could put the charges on my card. I wasn't concerned about being overheard or taped by the SS guys, though it was a cinch they'd bugged the place. Key and I had been masters of our own private espionage lingo ever since our youth. When we got going we sometimes had trouble understanding each other or even ourselves.

"Key to the Kingdom," she answered her phone. "Can you read me? Speak now or forever hold your peace." That was "Key" code that she knew it was I phoning and asking whether the coast was clear.

"I read you," I said. "But it's sort of in one ear and out the other." Establishing that others were likely listening in to whatever we said. "So what's new, Pussycat?"

"Oh, you know me," said Key. "A rolling stone gathers no moss, as they say. But time sure flies when you're having a good time."

This meant that she'd rolled on out of Colorado in her vintage bush plane, Ophelia Otter, and was already back up in Wyoming doing her job in Yellowstone National Park, where she'd commuted throughout high school and college. She had been studying geothermal features—geysers, mud holes, the steam vents called fumaroles—all powered by magma from the Yellowstone Caldera, or cauldron, created by the ancient supervolcano that now slept miles beneath the earth's crust.

When Key wasn't screwing around in that crazy plane of hers—running around to events where bush pilots took joy in coasting in onto melting icebergs—she was one of the top experts in the thermal field. And in great demand lately, given the escalating numbers of "hot spots" on our planet.

"What's up with you?" she was saying.

"Oh, you know me, too." I followed our usual patter. "Out of the frying pan, into the fire. That's the problem with chefs, we love those flames. But it's my job to follow orders. As they say, 'Theirs not to make reply, theirs not to reason why, theirs but to do or die—' "

Key and I had been doing our Navajo-Code-Talker routine so long that I was pretty sure she'd know the next line of "The Charge of the Light Brigade"—"Into the valley of Death / Rode the six hundred"—and would grasp it meant I was headed into the proverbial box canyon at this very moment. And it was clear she got the hint with respect to my job and my boss, but Key had a surprise of her own in store.

"That job of yours," she said, in a *tsk-tsk* tone. "It's such a shame you had to rush away like that. You should have stayed: They also serve who only stand and wait, you know. If you'd waited just a bit longer you wouldn't have missed that meeting of the Botany Club, Sunday night. But it's okay—I sat in for you."

"*You?*" I said, in shock.

Nokomis Key was hobnobbing with the Livingstons after I'd left Colorado?

"In a backroom kind of way," Key said offhandedly. "I wasn't actually invited. You know I've never gotten on well with their chairwoman, that Miss Brightstone. She was never the brightest bulb in the chandelier, as they say, but she *can* be illuminating. Sunday night would have interested *you*. The subjects were right up your alley—Exotic Lilies and Russian Herbal Remedies."

Good Lord! Sage met with Lily and Vartan? It sure sounded like it—but how? They were both down in Denver.

"The club must have changed its venue," I suggested. "Was everyone able to get there?"

"It was moved to Molly's place," Key affirmed. "Attendance was slim—but Mr. Skywalker managed to make it."

"Molly's Place" was our standard code for that flamboyant millionairess of the Colorado Gold Rush era, the Unsinkable Molly Brown, and her former stomping ground: Denver. So Sage *was* there! Nor was "Mr. Skywalker" much of a stretch. That would be Galen March, the mysterious recent purchaser of Sky Ranch.

What in God's name were he and Sage Livingston doing hoity-toitying down in Denver (apparently just after my departure) with Vartan and Lily Rad? And how did Key learn of this mysterious coven? It all sounded pretty suspicious.

But the subtext was getting too complex for my limited supply of aphorisms, and Rodo might show up any moment to crash the party. I urgently needed to know how all this might relate to the topic I'd phoned Key about—my mother. So I jettisoned our repertory of quips from *Familiar Quotations* and cut straight to the chase.

"I'm here at work, expecting my boss soon," I told Key. "I'm using the house phone; I really shouldn't tie it up longer. But before we hang up, tell me about your job progress: anything new with the . . . Minerva hot spring lately?"

Key was at Yellowstone and this was all I could think of in a pinch, to connect. Minerva was a famous "stair-step" or terraced hot spring at Yellowstone, a spot that boasted more than ten thousand such dramatic geothermal features, the largest group in the world. Minerva herself, a magnificent steaming waterfall of breathtaking rainbow colors, had been a premiere Yellowstone attraction. I say "had been," since over the past ten years Minerva had inexplicably and mysteriously dried up—the entire enormous hot spring and waterfall had simply vanished, just like my mother.

"Interesting you should ask," said Key, not missing a beat. "I was working on that problem only yesterday. Sunday. Looks like the Yellowstone Caldera's getting warmer. Might cause a new eruption where we're least expecting it. As for Minerva, our defunct hot spring, I think she may make a comeback sooner than we thought."

Did that mean what it sounded like? My heart was pounding.

I was about to ask more. But just at that instant, the front door of the restaurant was flung open and Rodo came barreling in with a large chicken tucked under each arm and one of the sunglassed Secret Service guys in tow, bearing a stack of containers.

"Bonjour encore une fois, Neskato Geldo," Rodo boomed at me while gesturing to the SS chap, like a minion, to set down his stack of foodstuffs on a nearby table.

While the guy's back was turned, Rodo passed by me at the desk and hissed beneath his breath, "I pray you will not be very sorry for using that telephone." Then in a louder voice, he added, "Well, Cinder Girl, let's go downstairs and have a look at our *gros mouton*!"

"Sounds like you gotta go see a man about a sheep," said Key, sotto voce in my ear. She added, "I'll e-mail you my notes about the Botany Club and the results of our geothermal study. You'll find it all fascinating." We signed off.

Of course, Key and I never used e-mail. This just meant she'd get back to me off-line as quickly as she could. It couldn't be quick enough.

As I followed Rodo down the steps to the dungeon, I couldn't keep two nagging questions from my mind.

What had taken place at that clandestine meeting in Denver?

Had Nokomis Key somehow picked up the trail of my mother?

RODO HEFTED THE large chickens one at a time, suspending them by their strings over the hearth. With these birds, unlike the *Meschoui,* no basting would be required due to his dry-roasting method. The birds would have been carefully dried inside and out, sprinkled with rock salt, then trussed using his own unique design—bound by a crisscross lattice cage and attached by a string to a long skewer run horizontally through each bird. This permitted the bird to swing freely above the hearth from heavy hooks embedded in the stone mantel. The heat from the embers first rotated the bird counterclockwise, then clockwise in an endless motion like Foucault's pendulum.

When I finished basting the lamb and returned upstairs for the foodstuffs, per Rodo's command, I found that our dour bridge guards seemed to have been pressed into a bit more than Secret Service. A vast array of containers of food sat just inside the door, with an official-looking seal on each box. Rodo had never been one to let a pair of spare hands go to waste, but this was absurd.

I counted the boxes—there were thirty, just as he'd said—then I dead-bolted the outer doors as he'd instructed, and I started carrying the stacks downstairs to the Dictator of the Dungeon.

For more than an hour we worked together without speaking, but that was par for the course. Rodo's kitchen was always managed in complete silence. Everything functioned with cleanliness, detail, and precision: the kind of skilled precision I knew I needed—like a game of chess. For instance, on an ordinary night at the Hearth, with dozens of workers in the kitchens, the only sound heard might be the soft tap-tapping of a knife slicing vegetables, or, from time to time, the hushed voice of the chief steward or sommelier over the intercom, placing an order from the main dining room upstairs.

Luckily, today all the preprep here had already been handled by others, or we'd never have made it by dinner.

Before I'd even finished hauling the final load of containers downstairs, Rodo already had the baby artichokes, tiny purple and white eggplants, little green and yellow zucchini, and grape tomatoes, like a gorgeous harvest cornucopia, basting in the dripping pans.

But I couldn't help wondering how the meal-serving was going to fare with just the two of us. Mondays like this, when the restaurant was usually closed, were training days for the waiters. They learned to place silver and glassware properly and what to do if a diner (they were never called customers) spilled a drink or a bit of sauce on the tablecloth. If this occurred—even when diners were in mid-meal—half a dozen waiters and busboys would swiftly descend upon the table, whisk everything away without disturbing the diners, quickly remove and replace the cloth, and put everything back as it had been, including the correct drinks and meals before each diner, like a conjuring act. Rodo timed it with a stopwatch: The whole process had to take under forty seconds.

Watching Rodo now as he moved silently back and forth among the hearths, wordlessly handing me subordinate tasks, was an education in itself that could never be taught in any school. You had to see it in action. And only a true perfectionist with plenty of practice could demonstrate Key's favorite motto.

Difficult as Rodo might be, I'd never regretted coming to apprentice here.

Until tonight, that is.

"*Neskato!*" Rodo announced, as I was down on my knees turning the vegetables with the tongs. "I want you to go upstairs now, unplug the intercom and telephone, and bring them here to me."

When I glanced up at him strangely, he slapped his open hand flat against the stone cellar wall and bestowed a rare smile on me.

"See these stones?" he said.

For the first time I took a close look at the hand-hewn rocks of the wall, likely cut and set in place more than two hundred years ago. They were milky-white and shot through with an unusual apricot-colored vein.

"Quartz crystal, it's native here in the soil," Rodo said. "It has excellent properties for transmission of sound waves but will interfere with communications unless they are—how do you say it?—hardwired."

Hence, decommissioning the phone and the intercom. And bolting the doors. Rodo was nobody's fool. He clearly had something to tell me, but although I was dying to hear it, I couldn't help my stomach butterflies knowing that the highest echelons of government security were flitting about just outside that upstairs door.

When I came back with the gear, he took it and put it into the giant refrigerator. Then he turned to me and took my two hands in his.

"I want you to sit on this stool while I tell you a small story," he said.

"I hope it's going to answer some of those questions I asked you this morning," I told him, "that is, if you're really sure that no one can hear us speaking."

"They cannot, which is why we arranged for tonight's dinner to be held down here as well. However, that phone you were speaking on, and my house, Euskal Herria, are perhaps a different matter. More of that later," he said. "There is something first, more important—the reason why we are here. Do you know the story of Olentzero?"

When I shook my head in the negative, taking my seat on the high stool, he added, "With a name like Olentzero, of course he was Basque. It's a legend that we reenact each year at Epiphany. I myself often dance the part of the famous Olentzero, which requires very many high kicks in the air. I will show you sometime."

"Okay," I said, thinking, *Where on earth is this going?*

"You know," said Rodo, "that the Roman Church tells us that the baby Jesus was discovered by three Magi—those Zoroastrian fire worshippers who traveled from Persia. But we think this story isn't quite true. It was Olentzero, a Basque, who first saw the Christ child. Olentzero was a—how you say—a *Charbonnier*, a Charcoal Burner—you know, one of those who traveled through the lands, cutting and burning wood to sell as charcoal for cooking and heat. He was our ancestor. Which is why we Basques are famous for being great cooks—"

"Whoa," I said. "You dragged me back from Colorado through a raging blizzard—and down to this cellar with no food or sleep—just to get me alone and tell a story about some mythical two-thousand-year-old Basque kick-dancer who sold coal?"

I was in a complete fury, but trying to keep it under my breath since I still wasn't sure we couldn't be overheard.

"Not entirely," Rodo said, unperturbed. "You are here because it was the only way I could arrange for us to speak alone before tonight's dinner. And it is critical that we must do so. You do understand that you are in great danger?"

Danger.

That did it. That word again. I felt as if the wind had been knocked out of me. All I could do was stare at him.

"That's better," he said. "For once, a little payment of the attention."

He went over to the hearth and stirred the bouillabaisse for a moment, then returned to me with a grave expression.

"Go ahead now, ask your questions again," he said. "I will answer them."

I decided I had to pull myself together; it seemed it was now or never. I gritted my teeth.

"Okay. Exactly how did you ever learn that I'd gone to Colorado in the first place?" I asked him. "What is this *boum* that's happening tonight? And why do you think I'm in some kind of danger about it? *What does this all have to do with me?*"

"Perhaps you don't know exactly who these Charcoal Burners are?" Rodo changed the topic, though I had noted that he'd said who they *are*, not *were*.

"Whoever they are," I said, "how would that answer any of my questions?"

"It may answer *all* of your questions. And some that you do not even know of just yet," Rodo informed me quite seriously. "The *Charbonniers*—in Italy they were called the *Carbonari*—it's a secret society that has existed for more than two hundred years, though they themselves say they are far more ancient. And they claim they still have tremendous power. Like the Rosicrucians, Freemasons, the Illuminati, these Charcoal Burners also say they possess a secret wisdom only known by the initiated such as themselves. But it is not true. This secret was known in Greece, Egypt, Persia, and even earlier in India—"

"*What* secret?" I said, though I was afraid I already knew what was coming.

"A secret knowledge that was finally written down more than twelve hundred years ago," he said. "Then it was in danger of no longer being kept a secret. Though no one could decipher its meaning, it was hidden in plain view within a chess set created in Baghdad. Then for a thousand years it was buried in the Pyrenees—the Fire Mountains, Euskal Herria—home of the Basques who helped to protect it. But now it has surfaced once more, only weeks ago, which may place you in great danger—unless you can understand *who you are* and what role you shall play tonight—"

Rodo looked at me as if that should answer all my questions. Not a chance.

"What role?" I said. "And who *am* I?"

I felt truly ill. I wanted to crawl under my high stool and weep.

"As I've always told you," said Rodo with a strange smile. "You are *Cendrillon*—or *Neskato Geldo,* the Little Cinder Girl, the one who sleeps in the ashes behind the stove. Then she rises from the ashes to become the queen—as you may find out, only hours from now. But I shall be with you. For it's *they* who are dining here with all this secrecy tonight. It's they who requested that you be present, and they who knew that you'd gone to Colorado. I only learned of your departure too late."

"Why me? I'm afraid I still don't get it," I said, though I was a great deal more than afraid that I actually *did.*

"The one who organized this meal knows you quite well—or so I understand," said Rodo. "The name is Livingston."

BASIL LIVINGSTON.

Of *course* he was a player. Why would I be surprised? But might he not be *more* than that, given his suspicious long-term connections with the recently murdered Taras Petrossian?

I was, however, astonished that I found myself here, buried in this dungeon-cellar with my crazy Basque boss, who seemed to know more than *I* did about the dangers posed by this even crazier Game.

I resolved to hear more. And exceptional though it was, for once Rodo seemed more than ready to open up.

"You perhaps know of the *Chanson de Roland,*" he began, as he started setting a dozen or so clay pots on the hearth, "that medieval story about Charlemagne's famous retreat through the Roncesvalles Pass in the Pyrenees—it contains the key to everything. You are familiar with the *Chanson*?"

"I'm afraid I haven't read it," I admitted, "but I know what it's about. Charlemagne's defeat by the 'Saracen,' as they called them—the Moors. They wiped out his rear flank as his army retreated from Spain back into France. His nephew Roland, hero of the song, was killed there on the pass, wasn't he?"

"Yes, that's the story they've told," Rodo assured me. "But hidden underneath is the real mystery—the true secret of Montglane." He'd dipped his fingertips in olive oil and was oiling the insides of the pots.

"So what do Charlemagne's retreat and this 'secret of Montglane' have to do with tonight's mysterious coven? Or with that chess set you mentioned?" I asked him.

"You understand, Cinder Girl, it was never the Islamic Moors who destroyed Charlemagne's rear flank or who killed his nephew Roland," Rodo told me. "It was the Basques."

"The Basques?"

Now he unwrapped the *boulles* of shepherd's dough from their damp cloths and carefully set one *boulle* in each pot. I handed him the long-handled shovel to push the pots back into the firebox.

Once Rodo had shoveled the ash up around the pots, he turned to me and added, "The Basques had always controlled the Pyrenees. But the *Chanson de Roland* was written hundreds of years *after* the events it tells us about. When the retreat through Roncesvalles Pass actually happened, in AD 778, Charlemagne was not yet powerful or famous. He was still merely Karl, king of the Franks—uneducated northern peasants. It was more than twenty years before he would be anointed Holy Roman Emperor—'Carolus Magnus' or *Karl der*

Grosse, as the Franks call him, Defender of the Faith—by the pope. Karl the Frank *became* Charlemagne because by then he was already the possessor and defender of the chess set that was known as the Montglane Service."

I knew we were definitely on to something. This supported my aunt Lily's story of the legendary chess set and its fabled powers. But Rodo's additions still hadn't answered all my questions.

"I thought that the pope made Charlemagne Holy Roman Emperor in order to get his help defending Christian Europe against incursions by the Muslims," I said, racking my brain for all the medieval trivia I could recall. "In the mere quarter century before Charlemagne's arrival, hadn't the Islamic faith conquered most of the world, including Western Europe?"

"Exactly," Rodo agreed. "And now, only four years after Charlemagne's roust at Roncesvalles, the most powerful possession of Islam had fallen into the hands of Islam's worst enemy."

"But how had Charlemagne been able to get his hands on this chess set so fast?" I asked.

In my interest, I'd temporarily forgotten that I had a job to do and that we were soon to be descended upon by a bevy of undesirable "diners." But Rodo hadn't. He passed me the crate of eggs and a stack of nested copper bowls as he went on.

"It's told that the Service was sent to him by the Moorish governor of Barcelona, though for reasons that are still quite unclear," Rodo told me. "It certainly wasn't for Charlemagne's 'aid' against the Basques, whom he'd never defeated and who were nowhere operating in the vicinity of Barcelona, anyhow.

"It's more likely that the governor himself, Ibn al'Arabi, had some important reason for wanting to hide the set as far from al-Islam as possible—and the

Frankish court at Aix-la-Chapelle, or Aachen, was more than one thousand kilometers north, as the bird would fly."

Rodo paused to review my egg-separation technique. He always insisted it be performed single-handed, with the yolk and whites dropped into separate bowls and the shells flipped into the third. (For the compost heap: Waste not, want not, as Key would say.)

"But why would a Spanish Muslim official want to send something to a Christian monarch more than six hundred miles away, just to keep it from Islamic hands?" I asked.

"Do you know why they called this chess set 'the Montglane Service'?" he replied. "It's a revealing name, for there never was such a place in the Basque Pyrenees back then named Montglane."

"I thought it was a fortress and later an abbey," I said. But then I bit my tongue, for I recalled that it was Lily who'd told me that, not Rodo.

I'd caught myself just in the nick of time. In my distraction, I'd nearly gotten a fleck of egg yolk into the bowl of whites and ruined the whole batch. I tossed the shell—yolk and all—into the compost bowl and wiped my sweaty hands on my butcher's apron before resuming my task. When I glanced over to see if Rodo had noticed my faux pas, I was relieved to see that he was beaming with approval.

"They say that women cannot concentrate on two things at one time," he told me. "And yet here you have done it! I am happy on behalf of the future existence of my famous meringue."

Rodo was the only person I'd ever heard of or even imagined who would attempt a soufflé or meringue over an open hearth. But his pièce de résistance—the *Béret Basque,* that rich *gâteau au chocolat*—called for both.

Rodo remained forever undaunted, even delighted, by such "small challenges."

Now I had a challenge of my own: how to get back to the topic. But Rodo beat me there.

"So you do know something of the story," he said. "Yes, Charlemagne named the place Montglane, and he also created the fortress and a title of nobility to go with it. But all were located extremely far from Barcelona and the Mediterranean in the south, and also very far from his capital in the north at Aachen.

"Instead, he chose the impossible-to-penetrate terrain of the Basque Pyrenees, atop a high mountain. And strangely, this location was not so very far from that exact place of his own disastrous retreat. And he named this spot where he put his fortress: *Montglane*—it means *Le Mont des Glaneurs,* the Mountain of, how you say, the Gleaners. Like the famous painting by Millet."

Rodo demonstrated the gesture with his hands, as if he were swinging a scythe.

"You mean the Reapers?" I said. "The Mountain of Reapers? Why would he call it that?"

I'd set down my copper bowl of yolks in preparation for whipping the whites. But Rodo took the bowl of whites, stuck his finger in it, and shook his head—not ready yet. It had to be the right temperature. He set the bowl down again.

"To each thing its time," he told me. "It's from the Bible. This includes all things, as well as the egg whites. And so is the other, the one about the Reapers. It says, 'Whatever seeds you sow on the earth, that also you shall, ah—*recolte*—collect.' But I can say it much better how it is written in Latin: *Quod Severis Metes.*"

"As ye sow, so shall ye reap?" I guessed.

Rodo nodded. Something about that rang a strange bell in the back of my mind. But I had to let it go.

"Clarify for me," I asked him. "What do sowing and reaping have to do with Charlemagne and that chess set? Why does anyone even want it if it's so dangerous? What does any of it have to do with the Basques, with tonight, or with why *I'm* supposed to be here? I just don't get it."

"Yes, you certainly *do* 'get it,' " Rodo assured me. "You are not *complètement folle*!"

Then briefly testing the egg whites with a finger once more, he nodded, tossed in a handful of tartar, and passed the copper bowl with its whisk to me.

"Think of it!" he added. "More than one thousand years ago this chess set was sent to a remote place; it was guarded so carefully by those who owned it—those who understood and feared its power. It was buried in the ground just like seeds, for they knew it was something that one day would surely bear fruit of a good or an evil kind."

He held up an eggshell in front of my face.

"And now the egg has hatched. But like that harvest gleaned from the mountain of Montglane, it has now risen like a phoenix from the ashes," he finished.

I let the mixed metaphor go by the wayside. "But why me?" I repeated, though it took as much effort as I could muster to remain calm. This was too close to home.

"Because, my dear firebird," said Rodo, "whether you want it or not, you yourself have risen—from that moment two weeks ago—along with that chess set. I know what is the date of your birthday, you see, and so do these others—October 4, exactly opposite your mother's birthday *boum*, announcing her own.

"That is what has placed you into this danger. That is what has convinced them they must examine you tonight, that they believe they know who you really are."

That expression again. But this time, it drove the fear of God into me, like a stake through my heart.

"Who am I?" I repeated.

"I do not know," said my boss, looking far from crazy. "All I know is what others believe. And they believe that *you* are the new White Queen."

THE PYRAMID

Shelley's ashes were later conveyed to Rome and buried where they now lie on the slope of the Protestant cemetery under the shadow of the great grey pyramid of Caius Cestius—that place of pilgrimage for English-speaking people from all over the world for more than a hundred years.

—ISABEL C. CLARKE, *Shelley and Byron*

Pyramid of Caius Cestius: A massive sepulchral monument of brick and stone, at Rome, 114 feet high, incrusted with white marble. Each side of the base measures 90 feet. . . . The pyramid is of the time of Augustus.

— *The Century Dictionary*

The mausoleum of Caius Cestius . . . inspired eighteenth-century garden pyramids including those at the Désert de Retz and Parc Monçeau, as well as the Masonic pyramid that appears on the American dollar bill.

—DIANA KETCHAM, *Le Désert de Retz*

CIMETERO ACATTOLICO DEGLI INGLESI, ROMA
(PROTESTANT CEMETERY OF THE ENGLISH, ROME)
JANUARY 21, 1823

THE "ENGLISH MARIA" STOOD IN THE BITTER FOG beside the stone wall, in the shadow of the enormous, two-thousand-year-old Egyptian pyramid tomb of the Roman senator Caius Cestius. Attired in her plain gray traveling dress and cape, she watched—a little apart from the other mourners, whom she scarcely knew—as the small urn was placed into its shallow grave.

How appropriate, she thought, that Percy Shelley's ashes should be laid here in this ancient, sacred spot, on this special day. The author of *Prometheus Unbound* had been the quintessential Poet of Fire, had he not? And today, January 21, was Maria's favorite holy day, the feast of Saint Agnes, the saint who could not be killed by fire. Even now, Maria's eyes were watering, not from the cold but from the many brushfires that had been lit here on the Aventine Hill to honor the ancient martyr, their smoke mingling with the dank fog from the Tiber below. In England last night, on Saint Agnes's Eve, young girls would have gone to bed hungry, fasting in hopes of a dreamed glimpse of their future husbands, as in the popular romantic poem by John Keats.

But, though Maria herself had long lived in England and knew their customs, she was not English, even if she'd been known as *pittrice Inglese,* an "English paintress," from age seventeen when she was inducted into the Accademia del Disegno at Florence. She was, in fact, a native Italian—born in Livorno more than sixty years ago—who felt more at home here in Italy than she ever would in England, the land of her parents' birth.

And though she had not been back to this sacred spot in more than thirty years, Maria knew, perhaps better than anyone, the mystery that lay beneath the "English" topsoil here on this southernmost hill just outside the gate of ancient Rome. For here in Rome, where Saint Agnes had been martyred, where her feast day would soon be celebrated, lay a mystery far older than either the bones of the saint or the pyramid tomb of Caius Cestius—a mystery perhaps more ancient than Rome itself.

This spot on the Aventine Hill, where Caius Cestius had built his ostentatious pyramid in the time of Jesus and the emperor Augustus, had been a sacred place from the earliest times. It lay just at the edge of the Pomerium, the "apple line," an ancient though invisible boundary just outside the city walls, beyond which the *auspicia urbana,* the official divination to protect the city, could not take place. The *auspicia—avis specio,* "watching the birds"—could only be conducted by the established collegium of priests skilled in studying omens from the sky, whether thunder and lightning, the movements of clouds, or the patterns and cries of birds. But beyond the Pomerium, a different power had held sway.

Beyond this line lay the Horrea, the granaries that fed all of Rome. And here on the Aventine, too, was the most famous temple to the cult of the goddess of grain, Ceres. Her name, Ker, meant growth, and she shared her temple here with Liber and Libera, god and goddess of freedom, virility, the juice of life. They were equal to the more ancient Janus and Janna, god of the two faces, for which the town of Janina in Albania, site of one of her earliest shrines, had been named. But here, Ceres' two great festivals lay outside the boundaries of establishment control: the *feriae sementiuae,* the sowing festivals, which commenced with burning the old fields' stubble with enormous fires in the month named for Janus; and the harvesting or reaping festival, Cerialia, which took place in the month named for the emperor Augustus, whose birth name, Octavian, meant "the Eighth."

The fires lit to Ceres in the first month, the ancients believed, would portend what they reaped in the eighth. QUOD SEVERIS METES, it was written above her temple: *As ye sow, so shall ye reap.*

The mystery behind this was so deep and ancient that it ran in the blood itself: There was no need of auspices performed under the law by church and state or official prognostications; it was performed outside the gate, outside the city.

It was an Eternal Order.

Maria knew that on this day the memory of the past and the divination of the future were somehow linked, as they had been for thousands of years. For today—Saint Agnes's Day, January 21—was the day of Divination by Fire. And here in Rome, the Eternal City, it might also prove to be the day when the secret that Percy Shelley took to his watery grave six months ago—the secret of that order—would rise from his ashes.

At least that is what Maria's friend and patron, Cardinal Joseph Fesch, intended to find out. That is why he and his sister, Letizia Bonaparte, had summoned her here today. After more than thirty years, the Anglo-Italian artist Maria Hadfield Cosway had come home for good.

PALAZZO FALCONIERI
ROMA

> *Through me mankind ceased to foresee death . . .*
> *Blind hopes I made to dwell in them . . .*
> *And more than all I gave them fire.*
>
> —AESCHYLUS, *Prometheus Bound*

George Gordon, Lord Byron, painfully paced the drawing room of Cardinal Joseph Fesch's Palazzo Falconieri. Despite his private wealth, Byron felt out of place here in this lavish mausoleum to a dead emperor. For though the cardinal's nephew, Napoleon Bonaparte, was gone these past two years, the wealth he'd lavished on his relations had remained scarcely hidden here. The damascened walls of this room were no exception, plastered from end to end with the paintings of the finest masters of Europe, and more were stacked upon the floors, including works of the cardinal's longtime protégée, the painter Madame Cosway, at whose request they'd all been peremptorily called here today. Overtly, at least.

The note had taken some time to reach him, for it had been directed at first to Pisa. On the morning he'd received it at his new villa at Genoa—Casa Saluzzo, overlooking Portofino and the sea—Byron had hastily departed before he'd even had time to settle in. He'd abandoned his ménage of lover, family, and unwanted guests, and his menagerie of animals—monkeys, peacocks, dogs, and exotic birds—all scarcely unloaded from his flotilla of boats from Pisa.

For it was clear something important had happened. Or was about to.

Ignoring his fevers and the pains that endlessly pierced his intestines, like those that plagued Prometheus, Byron rode so hard this past week in order to arrive here at Rome that he'd had little time even to bathe or to shave at those dreadful inns where he and his valet, Fletcher, had put up. He realized that he must look a sight by now, but in the circumstance it scarcely mattered.

Now, having been ushered into the palazzo and proffered a crystal cup of the cardinal's excellent claret to settle his stomach, Byron for the first time looked about at the gorgeously appointed drawing room, and in the same instant realized that he not only *felt* out of place, he *smelled* out of place! He was still attired in his riding habit and covered with dust from the road: a close-cropped blue military jacket, mud-splashed boots, and the long, full nankeen cotton pantaloons that covered his deformed foot. With a sigh, he set down the glass of ruby-colored claret and unwound the turbaned scarf he habitually wore outdoors to protect his fair skin from the sun. Much as he longed to leave right now, to send round for Fletcher, to find a place to bathe and change, he knew it was impossible.

Because time was of the essence. And how much of it did he really have?

When Byron was quite young, a soothsayer had predicted that he would not survive his thirty-sixth year, a date that had seemed an eternity away. Yet tomorrow, January 22, Byron would turn thirty-five. In just a few months, he would leave Italy for Greece to fight in and to finance that very War of Independence that his friend, Ali Pasha, had sacrificed his life to launch.

But of course, Ali had also sacrificed something else.

Which could be the only meaning of the message.

For although the note sent to Byron by Letizia Bonaparte was patently written in response to his earlier veiled query about Shelley, the import of the message she expressed in her mélange of languages could not have been plainer:

À Signor Gordon, Lord Byron
Palazzo Lanfranchi, Lung'Arno, Pisa
Chèr Monsieur,

Je vous invite à un vernissage de la pittrice Inglese, Mme Maria Hadfield Cosway, date: le 21 Janvier, 1823, lieu: Palazzo Falconieri, Roma. Nous attendons votre réponse.

Les sujets des peintures suivi:

Siste Viator
Ecce Signum
Urbi et Orbi
Ut Supra, Ut Infra

By this, he was invited to a showing of the paintings of Madame Cosway, a woman whose reputation he knew quite well, given the fame her late husband had enjoyed as royal painter to the Prince of Wales. And she herself was protégée not only of Cardinal Fesch but also, for years in Paris, of the famous French painter, Jacques-Louis David.

It was not this invitation itself, however, but the meaning of the message that had riveted Byron's attention and hastened his departure from Genoa. First, the "subjects" of Madame's "paintings" as they were listed were hardly topics normally chosen by artists. But they were all highly meaningful when one read between the lines.

Siste Viator, "Stop, Traveler": a phrase used on every roadside tomb in ancient Rome.

Ecce Signum, "Behold the sign": this was followed by a small triangle.

Urbi et Orbi, "To the City and the World": a motto of Rome, Eternal City.

Ut Supra, Ut Infra, "As Above, So Below": a motto of alchemy.

Nor could it be coincidence that this invitation was scheduled for the same date and location as poor Percy Shelley's burial, which, thanks to merciful God, had taken place hours before Byron reached Rome. He did not regret having missed it. Try as he might, he could not forget what he'd had to bear on the day of Shelley's cremation, those many months past, nor the fears for his own life he'd harbored ever since.

This message was clear: "Stop seeking and behold what we have found: the sign, the triangle, of the famous Egyptian pyramid tomb at Rome that was adopted by the Carbonari, the Freemasons, and other such groups as a sign among brothers. It represented a new order connecting spirit and matter, the worlds of above and below."

This was the message that Percy Shelley had tried to send him just before he'd been killed. Now Byron understood what it meant, though it chilled him to the core. For even if Letizia Bonaparte and her cohorts knew something of the mystery, or of the missing Black

Queen—as this invitation certainly suggested they did—how could they have guessed that single word? The only word that would definitely bring Byron here to Rome, if nothing else would. The word that Letizia Bonaparte had used to close her letter.

Byron's favorite name, which he'd shared as a password with only one person on earth—Ali Pasha, who was now dead.

But just as he thought that name, he heard the door open and a soft voice spoke it to him from across the room:

"Father, I am your daughter. Haidée."

He had an only daughter, called Haidée,
The greatest heiress of the Eastern Isles;
Besides, so very beautiful was she,
Her dowry was as nothing to her smiles
—LORD BYRON, *Don Juan,* Canto II, CXXVIII

Byron could not contain himself. He could not yet even think of the chess piece she must surely be carrying, for he was beside himself with joy. He was weeping, at first pressing the child to his breast, then holding her away to stare, shaking his head in disbelief, as he felt the hot tears making tracks in the dust that still coated his face.

Good Lord! She was the very image of Vasiliki, who perhaps had been only a few years older than this when Byron had fallen in love with her at Janina. She had those same silvery eyes of Vasia's, which seemed like luminous mirrors, though Haidée also had traits of her father—the cleft chin and that pale, translucent skin that had won him the nickname "Alba," which meant "white."

What a blessing, he thought. For his other daughters had been lost to him in one way or another—through death, separation, scandal, exile. Little Ada, his legitimate child by his wife Annabella, who would now be just seven years old. He'd not seen her since her birth, due to the scandal Lady Byron had put about that had driven Byron into exile these many years—the rumor that his sister Augusta's daughter, Medora, now eight years old, was Byron's child as well.

Then his daughter by Claire Clairmont, Mary Shelley's stepsister, who'd been so besotted with Byron that she'd followed him from London the length and breadth of Europe till she'd accomplished her goal, a child by the famous poet. That was dear little Allegra, who'd died last year at the age of five.

But now this precious jewel-like gift, this incredible beauty—Haidée—a daughter from Vasiliki, perhaps the one woman he'd ever truly loved. A woman who'd placed no claims upon him, who'd sought nothing and had given him everything in return.

And Byron understood that this slip of a girl before him was no ordinary child. Ali Pasha might be her father in name only, but Haidée seemed to possess that inner strength that Byron had rarely glimpsed and had long forgotten. Like one of the pasha's brave, gray-eyed Palikhari troops from the mountains of Albania. Like Arslan the lion, Ali Pasha himself.

How strong the pasha and Vasia must have been to have had the presence of mind, in those final moments, to send to Byron his own daughter for safekeeping, and to place the valuable Queen into her hands. Byron hoped that he would have such strength himself to carry through with what he now understood he must do. But he also knew better than anyone the risk that this involved—not just to himself, but certainly to Haidée as well.

Now that he'd found this daughter, was he prepared to lose her so soon, as he'd lost the others?

But Byron saw something more—that the pasha must long have planned this moment, even as long ago as Haidée's birth. For hadn't he named the girl after their own secret code, Byron's private name for her mother, Vasiliki? And yet he'd never known of his daughter's existence, nor the role for which she may have been chosen—perhaps even trained—from the very beginning.

But what precisely *was* that role? Why was Haidée *here,* of all places, in this Roman palazzo in the very heart of Rome—and today, on the Day of Fire? Who were these others? What role did they play? Why had they lured Byron here with secret codes, rather than bringing Haidée and the chess piece to *him*?

Was this a trap?

And just as urgently, in Byron's role as "Alba," he needed to discover—and quickly—the part he himself now played within this larger Game.

For if he failed now, all hope might indeed be lost for the White Team.

PORTO OSTIA, ROMA
JANUARY 22, 1823

Haidée could scarcely quell those dozens of warring emotions raging within her. She'd tried to come to grips with it all ever since that morning, weeks ago, when she'd first seen Kauri's face beside the others, looking down from that parapet in Fez, that morning when she'd known, against all hope or expectation, that he'd at last found her and she would be saved. She was free finally, delivered to an exotic foreign land that she'd never even dreamed existed—Rome—and to a father whose very existence seemed to her just as exotic and strange.

However, last night due to the strain of Byron's

lengthy and difficult journey, and its impact upon the fragile state of his health—not to mention the proximity of the extensive entourage in residence at the palazzo—he'd slept in the privacy of rooms that his valet Fletcher had acquired. They'd arranged that this morning in darkness hours, before they were to meet the others at their appointed rendezvous at the pyramid, Haidée, with Kauri as her protector, should slip away from the palazzo to meet him.

Now, with Lord Byron clutching his daughter's hand, these three threaded their way through the deserted streets in the silvery predawn fog. Haidée knew, given all she'd learned during their retreat from Morocco, given all that Charlot and Shahin had told them aboard the ship, that Lord Byron himself might be the one person still living who held the key to the mystery of Ali Pasha's Black Queen. And she knew that this morning's private meeting with her newfound father might be her one chance to learn what she so desperately needed to know.

As the three moved away from the center of town past the ancient public baths, toward the outskirts of Rome where the pyramid lay, the young people, at Lord Byron's request, told him of how the Black Queen had been retrieved from its hiding place in Albania, of the ancient Baba Shemimi's arrival over the mountain passes, of the old man's important tale regarding the true history of al-Jabir's creation of the Service of the Tarik'at, and finally, Ali Pasha's last words and brave deeds in the Monastery of St. Pantaleon, just before the arrival of the Turks.

Byron listened attentively until they'd finished. Then, still holding his daughter's hand in his, he pressed the boy's shoulder in thanks as well. "Your mother was very brave," he told Haidée, "to send you off at the very moment when she and the pasha might be facing their own death."

"The last thing my mother said to me was that she loved you very much," Haidée told him, "and the Pasha said he felt the same. At whatever the cost to themselves, Father, they both trusted you entirely to keep the chess piece from the wrong hands. And so, too, did the great Baba who sent Kauri to protect both me and the chess piece.

"But despite all these careful plans," she went on, "things did not happen at all as anyone had expected. Kauri and I set sail by sea, planning to find you at Venice. We thought we did not have far to travel, but we were mistaken. Off the point of Pirene, our ship was captured by corsairs and was diverted to Morocco, where Kauri was seized at the docks by slave merchants. He vanished from my life—I feared, forever. The Black Queen was taken from me by the sultan's men, and I was placed in the royal harem at Fez. I was alone and terrified, surrounded by strangers with no one I could trust. I was saved from a worse fate, I think, only because they did not know who I was. They suspected that I, or that black lump of ore, might have some value that wasn't apparent on the surface."

"And how right they would have been," said Byron grimly, putting his arm about his daughter's shoulder. "You've been very strong in the face of such dangers, my child. Others have died for the secret you were protecting," he said, thinking of Shelley.

"Haidée was very brave," agreed Kauri. "Even though I managed to escape and seek protection in the mountains, I quickly understood that despite my relative freedom, she was as lost to me as I was to her. We couldn't find a trace. Then, when the sultan died, only weeks ago, and she was threatened with slavery along with the rest of the harem, Haidée still maintained silence; she refused to reveal anything about herself or the mission she'd been bound for. She was already at the auction block when we found her."

Haidée could not control the shudder that ran through her at this memory. Byron felt it through her slender shoulder. "It seems a miracle that either of you survived, much less that you managed to rescue the chess piece," he said gravely, pressing her to him as they walked.

"But Kauri never would have found me," said Haidée, "we should never have arrived here at all, never have completed the mission with which the pasha and the Baba entrusted us—if it hadn't been for Kauri's father, Shahin. And his companion, the red-haired man whom they call Charlot—"

Haidée looked past Byron to Kauri with a questioning expression. The boy nodded and said, "It is Charlot whom Haidée wished to speak to you of this morning, before you meet him with the others at the pyramid. That's why we wished to arrange a more private meeting—to discuss with you this man's intimate involvement with the Black Queen."

"But who is this Charlot you speak of?" asked Byron. "And what has he to do with the chess piece?"

"Kauri and I aren't referring to the chess piece," said Haidée. "The true Black Queen, the living one, is Charlot's mother, Mireille."

BYRON FELT ILL, and not only from his stomach difficulties. He had stopped, for he saw that just as the sun rose, they'd reached the gates of the Protestant cemetery and were close to the place of their intended rendezvous, just moments from now. He took a seat on the low stone wall and regarded both Kauri and Haidée gravely.

"Please explain yourselves," he asked them.

"According to Charlot, as he told us on the ship," said

Haidée, "his mother, Mireille, was one of the original nuns at Montglane when the service was first brought to light after a thousand years. She was sent to Kauri's father, Shahin, in the desert. There, her child Charlot was born beneath the eyes of the White Queen, just as it was foretold in the ancient legend."

"My father raised him," Kauri explained. "He told us Charlot possessed the second sight, also predicted one who would help to assemble the pieces and solve the mystery."

"But Charlot claims that his mother possesses something else of tremendous power," Haidée added, "something that makes our entire mission seem . . . impossible."

"If a nun from Montglane is his mother," Byron said, "it does not require any 'second sight' to guess what you have to tell me. This Charlot of whom you speak believes he and his mother are in possession of something he's just learned that *we* own instead. Something the two of you have risked your lives to bring across mountains and seas. Is that not it?"

"But how can it be?" said Haidée. "If his mother helped dig the pieces from the earth at Montglane Abbey with her own bare hands; if she's collected the pieces from the ends of the earth ever since; if she's even received the Black Queen from the tsar of all the Russias, grandson of Catherine the Great, then how can there be a second queen? And if there were, how could the one that was owned by the Bektashi Sufis be the real one?"

"Before trying to answer that question," said Byron, "I suggest we pay cautious and careful attention to what we've been brought to this place to hear. And by whom: Letizia Ramolino Bonaparte, Cardinal Fesch, and even Madame Cosway—all scions of the Church, which, after all, had retained these pieces in Christian hands since the time of Charlemagne."

"But Father," said Haidée, glancing at Kauri for his support, "this must surely be the explanation, the very reason why we all are here! According to Charlot, his mother, the nun Mireille, was sent thirty years ago to Kauri's father, Shahin, in the Sahara by someone who must be the missing connection: Angela-Maria di Pietra Santa. A close friend of the Abbess of Montglane, and also the mother of our two hosts here today, Letizia Ramolino Bonaparte and, by a different father, also of Cardinal Joseph Fesch. Angela-Maria was Napoleon's grandmother! Don't you see, Father? They are on the opposing team!"

"My child," protested Byron, drawing his daughter to him and wrapping his arms around her, "it doesn't matter, this business of teams. It's the chess service itself that is important—the powers it holds, not this foolish Game. That's why the Sufis have sought for so long to retrieve the pieces, to return them to the hands of those who will protect them and never exploit them for individual power—only for the good of all."

"Charlot thinks differently," insisted Haidée. "We are the White Team and they are the Black! And I believe that he and Shahin are on *our* side."

THE PYRAMID, ROMA
JANUARY 22, 1823

Only one dim oil lamp burned in the crypt where they'd gathered, at Letizia Bonaparte's proposal, on the morning after Shelley's funeral. All else within the enormous pyramid was swallowed in darkness, which provided Charlot the first space he'd had to think in since departing Fez.

Letizia had asked them here, she explained, because the artist Madame Cosway had important information to impart to them all. And what better spot than this very pyramid, which contained the crux of the secret Maria had agreed, after so many years, to reveal.

Madame Mère now lit the sconces she'd brought and set them beside the tomb of Caius Cestius. Their flickering light cast shadows upon the high vaulted stone ceiling of the crypt.

Charlot looked at the faces encircled about him. The eight whom Letizia Bonaparte and her brother had brought together in Rome, at Shahin's behest, were all present. And each played a critical role, as Charlot now understood: Letizia and her brother, Cardinal Fesch; Shahin and his son, Kauri; Lord Byron and the painter, Madame Cosway; Charlot himself and Haidée.

Charlot knew that he no longer required such external light to identify the dangers all around him. Only days ago, at that marketplace in Fez, his vision had returned full-force—a situation wholly unexpected, at once as exciting and as frightening as if he'd suddenly found himself amid a meteor shower. The past and the future were again his traveling companions, the contents of his mind lit like a pinwheel of ten thousand glittering sparks in a midnight sky.

Only one thing remained dark to him: Haidée.

"There is one thing no prophet, regardless how great, can see for himself," Shahin had told him that night in the cave above Fez. "And that is his own destiny."

But in that moment when Charlot had first gazed down from that parapet in the medina and seen the girl in the slave market below—though he'd spoken of this to no one since, not even to Shahin—he'd glimpsed for a single dreadful instant just where that destiny might lead.

Though he still could not see precisely *how* his destiny was entwined with hers, Charlot knew that his premonition about Haidée had been a true one, just as he'd first been drawn three months ago to leave France, to journey a thousand miles into the canyons of the Tassili, to find the White Queen, that ancient goddess whose image was painted high on the cliffs, in the hollow of the great stone wall.

And now that he'd found her in flesh and blood, embodied in this young girl, he understood something more: Whatever Madame Cosway had to reveal about it, whatever role these others played, it was Haidée herself who stood at center board, holding the Black Queen, and Charlot must stand with her.

CARDINAL JOSEPH FESCH looked around the candlelit crypt at the others who, he thought, sat huddled like mourners at a funeral.

"Madame Maria Hadfield Cosway is known to many of you by reputation, if not in person until today," he began. "Her parents, Charles and Isabella Hadfield, ran the famous English group of inns in Florence, Carlo's, which catered to British travelers on the Grand Tour, like the historian Edward Gibbon and the biographer James Boswell. Maria grew up surrounded by the aristocracy of the arts and became a great artist herself. When Charles died, Isabella closed up the inns and took Maria and her siblings to England, where Maria was married to the famous painter, Richard Cosway.

"Although my sister, Letizia, and I did not make the acquaintance of Maria Cosway until Napoleon came to power, from then we have remained the closest of friends. I am myself today a sponsor of the girls' school she founded just north of here, at Lodi. We have asked Maria to tell a story involving this very pyramid in which we are seated today, and its connection with her late husband, Richard Cosway, who has recently died in London. The tale she will tell she has never revealed in full to anyone—not even to us ourselves. It took place more than thirty years ago, in 1786, when she went with her husband to Paris. And something happened there that may be of deep concern to everyone here in this chamber."

The cardinal took his seat and deferred to Maria.

As if uncertain how to proceed, she removed her moleskin gloves and set them aside. With her fingertip she took a bit of the soft candle wax from the nearby sconce and rolled it into a ball between her thumb and forefinger.

"*Ma chère madame,*" said Cardinal Fesch, placing his hand over hers to prompt her to continue.

Maria smiled and nodded.

"It was in September of 1786," she began in her soft, lightly inflected Italian, "and my husband Richard Cosway and I had recently crossed *la Manche,* the English Channel, from London. Our reputations had preceded us. We were both award-winning painters, and our salon in London was known to be the most sought-after. Richard had an important commission in France to paint the children of the duc d'Orléans, cousin to Louis XVI, and a great friend of my husband's English patron, the Prince of Wales, now King George IV. At Paris, we were feted by artists and nobility alike. Our friend and colleague, the painter Jacques-Louis David, arranged our presentation at the French court to the king and Marie Antoinette.

"A word must be said here of my husband, Richard. Many envious people in London had long thought ill of him, for he'd come from poverty and had risen very far. Richard did little to assuage these enemies, but bore himself with extravagance and ostentation at all times. He favored a coat of mulberry satin embroidered with strawberries, a large sword that dragged upon the ground, hats heavily laden with ostrich plumes, and shoes with red heels. In the press he was called a 'macaroni'—a fop—and his appearance was likened to his own pet monkey, who some maliciously called his natural child.

"But only privately known was that Richard was also one of the great virtuosi, or arbiters of taste, a connoisseur and collector of rare and valuable antiquities. Not only the famous Gobelin tapestries, but he also possessed twenty-six rooms of rareties: an Egyptian mummy, the relics of saints, Chinese ivories, rare esoteric works from Arabia and India, and even what he believed to be a tail feather of the phoenix.

"Richard himself was of mystical bent, a follower of earlier visionaries like Emanuel Swedenborg. In London, along with my brother, George, an architectural student, we'd attended the private lectures of Thomas Taylor, 'the Platonist,' who'd recently translated secret doctrines of the earliest Greek esoteric writers for avid subscribers to such mysteries, like Ralph Waldo Emerson and William Blake.

"This background is important. For it appears that my husband, unknown to me, had discovered through the duc d'Orléans something involving a great mystery that had been buried for nearly a thousand years in France, a mystery that was about to resurface into the light, not long after that morning, thirty years ago, when we first arrived in France.

"I remember the day. It was Sunday, September 3, 1786, a golden morning that brought Richard and me on an outing to the Halle au Blé, the famous Paris grain market, an enormous rotunda where wheat, peas, rye, lentils, oats, and barley were all sold. It has since burned down, but was then known as one of the most beautifully designed buildings in Paris, with curving stairways, a lofty dome with skylights that flooded everything with daylight like a fairy palace floating through the sky.

"It was there, in that magical, silvery light, that we encountered the person who would soon change everything. But at that moment, so long ago, I could hardly have foreseen how my life and the lives of my family would be so completely altered by events that had just been set in motion.

"The American painter John Trumbull had arrived in the company of his friend, a tall, pale man with copper-blond hair, at whose residence on the Champs-Élysées Trumbull himself was staying. Trumbull's host, we soon learned, was the delegate from the new American Republic to the French court, a statesman whose own fame was shortly to eclipse all our own. His name was Thomas Jefferson.

"By all appearances, Mr. Jefferson was completely captivated by the Halle au Blé; he spoke in rhapsodies about the beauties of its design, and was thrilled with a rush of excitement when John Trumbull mentioned the architectural works of my brother, George, a fellow at the Royal Academy in London.

"Mr. Jefferson insisted upon accompanying us throughout the day. From our meeting at Paris, we four spent the afternoon in the countryside at St. Cloud, where we dined. Then we canceled all evening plans and went instead to Montmartre, to the outdoor garden at the Ruggieris', the family of pyrotechnicians who'd created a lavish display of fireworks; the play 'The Triumph of Vulcan' was performed, about the mysteries of that great underworld figure whom the Greeks called Hephaistos, god of the forge.

"It was this extravagant dramatic display of the underworld mysteries, it seems, that prompted my husband, Richard, to speak so openly to Mr. Jefferson about the great pyramids and fire temples, resembling those of Egypt, that were built in the wilderness pleasure gardens just outside Paris—like those of Parc Monceau, the famous estate of our French patron, the duc d'Orléans. My husband shared with the duc a deep interest in the knowledge of hidden things.

"And just as Jefferson had succeeded Benjamin Franklin as emissary to France, the duc d'Orléans himself had succeeded Franklin as Grand Master of the Paris Freemasons. Their secret initiations often took place among the grottoes and classical ruins of his gardens.

"But more intriguing to Thomas Jefferson was Richard's allusion to another mysterious spot, farther from Paris, en route to Versailles, which was created by the duc's close friend, Nicolas Racine de Monville. According to the duc, so my husband revealed to us that night, this ninety-acre park, filled with strange mystical symbols, concealed a secret as old as the pyramids—indeed, it boasted a pyramid that was an exact replica of this one. Mozart's *Magic Flute* had been performed there.

"There was something more intriguing still about the place—so much so that Mr. Jefferson lost no time in abandoning his ministerial work and arranging a jaunt, only a few days later, into the countryside—with me alone—to view this hidden garden.

"Ever since the tale of that first biblical lost garden, we humans always seem to value things more once they've been lost. In the case of Monsieur Racine de Monville, with the dawn of the French Revolution not far away, he would soon lose his fortune as well as his gardens. The duc d'Orléans would fare far worse: dubbing himself Philippe Égalité, he would side with the Revolution, would vote to condemn his cousin, the king, but be guillotined by the revolutionaries, nonetheless.

"As for Thomas Jefferson and me—we *found* something that day in de Monville's garden, something neither of us had expected: the key to an ancient lost wisdom. The garden itself provided the key.

"It was called le Désert de Retz. In the ancient French parlance, this meant 'the Wilderness of the King'—the Lost Domaine."

THE TALE OF THE ARTIST AND THE ARCHITECT

But gardens also exist in our collective subconscious. The garden was man's first domain, and in the course of centuries he gave it numerous names meaning the Earthly Paradise, Eden. The hanging gardens of Babylon were one of the seven wonders of the world. . . . Our efforts to recreate it always remain works of the imagination.

—OLIVIER CHOPPIN DE JANVRY, *Le Désert de Retz*

I cannot think but that he meant to imitate the Tower of Babel.

—THOMAS BLAIKIE, ROYAL GARDENER,
speaking of the Desert of Retz

We set out from Paris that Friday, September 8, with Mr. Jefferson's elegant carriage and grays, and we crossed the river into the glorious countryside. But nothing would prove more glorious than our destination, the Désert de Retz.

One abandoned the carriage and entered the park on foot through a grotto opening into an enchanted landscape, resembling a Watteau painting of late summer colors, hazy purples and mauves and rust. The rolling hills and meandering paths throughout the park were dotted by copses of copper beeches, pomegranates, mimosas, along with two-hundred-year-old sycamores, maples, lindens, and hornbeams: all trees with meaning for the initiated eye.

At each turn throughout the vista, interesting structures had been created that seemed to appear through sleight of hand, peeking from within a hidden grove or rising magically from a lake.

The stone pyramid was the one Jefferson noted with that same excitement he'd manifested when first viewing the Halle au Blé.

"A model of the tomb of Caius Cestius," he said. "I recognize it from its prototype, that famous Roman structure shaped like an Egyptian pyramid, a 'mountain of fire,' of which your countryman, Piranesi, made so many popular engravings."

He added, "The original of it at Rome possesses unusual properties. The square base measures ninety by ninety—a number of great significance, for it sums up to three hundred and sixty, the number of degrees in a circle. 'Squaring the Circle'! That was the most challenging and important puzzle for the ancients, concealing several meanings. They weren't just trying to discover some dry mathematical formula that would enable them to convert the area of a circle into that of a square, but much, much more. For them, squaring the circle meant a deep kind of *transformation:* transforming the circle that represents the celestial realm into the square, that is, the material world. Bringing heaven to earth, as one might say."

"The 'Alchemical Marriage'—the marriage of Spirit and Matter," I agreed. "Or one might also say, the wedding of the head and the heart. My husband, Richard, and I have been students of ancient mysteries like this one over a great, great many years."

Jefferson laughed, seeming slightly embarrassed by his own unsolicited diatribe.

"As long ago as that?" he said with a winning smile. "Yet you look to be no more than twenty, an unlikely age for an attractive young woman to be impressed with the overweening pontifications of an elder statesman like myself."

"Twenty-six," I told him, returning his smile. "But Mr. Cosway is just *your* age. So I've grown accustomed on a daily basis to the benefits of such thought-provoking wisdom! I hope you'll share even more."

Jefferson seemed quite pleased to hear it, and he tucked my arm beneath his as we strolled on deeper into the park.

"A wedding of the head and the heart, you say?" He repeated my remark, still smiling down at me, rather wryly, from his lofty height. "Ancient wisdom, perhaps, my dear lady. But I find my own head and heart more often bickering with each other, rather than preparing themselves for a trip down the aisle to the altar of marital bliss!"

"What concern could these organs of yours possibly have, that they should be so at odds about it with each other?" I asked him with great amusement.

"Can you not imagine?" he asked me, quite unexpectedly. I shook my head and hoped that the shadow of my bonnet concealed the flush I felt rushing to my face.

Luckily, his next words relieved me considerably. "Then I promise, I shall write you all my thoughts on the topic one day quite soon." Then he added, "But for the moment at least—as the head is in charge of all mathematical and architectural problems such as the bearing weight of an arch or the squaring of a circle, it informs me that this nine-by-nine square of our pyramid has another, more important meaning. When we consult Herodotus, we discover that this very same proportion appeared in the layout of the ancient city of Babylon, a city of nine by nine miles. This evokes a fascinating mathematical puzzle you may not have heard of—a 'magic square'—where each box of this nine-by-nine matrix must be filled with a number, in such fashion that each row, each column, and each diagonal will sum to the same total.

"My predecessor as American delegate to France, Benjamin Franklin, was an expert in magic squares. They were common to the cultures of China, Egypt, and India, he believed. He amused himself completing them whilst sitting in Congress. He could create one, he said, as quickly as he could jot down the numbers in their boxes, and he discovered many ingenious solutions to the formulas."

"Did Dr. Franklin discover a formula for the square of Babylon?" I asked, relieved to be set upon a safer path of inquiry than the direction in which our last had appeared to be headed.

I confess, though, I was reticent to mention the true reason for my interest. I'd done copies myself, for Richard's collection of rare esoteric works, of Albrecht Dürer's famous 1506 copper engraving of a magic square, which showed its relationship to the golden mean of Pythagoras and *The Elements* of Euclid.

"Franklin did even better!" Jefferson seemed delighted that I should ask. "Dr. Franklin believed that in re-creating the ancient formulas for *all* of these squares he could demonstrate that any city built upon such a grid had been created to invoke the specific powers of that formula, along with its specific number, planet, or god.

"Franklin was, of course, a Freemason like our General Washington, and a bit of a mystic. But in truth, there is little that is mystical in such an idea. All great civilizations in ancient times, from China to the Americas, built a new city whenever they first established their new rule. That's what 'civilization' means, after all—*civitas,* of the city, from Sanskrit *çi,* 'to settle, to lie down, to put in roots,' as opposed to the savage or nomad who builds structures he can collapse and carry with him that are often round. By creating cities in the form of a square with such magical properties, the civilized ancients were hoping to invoke a new world order, an order that can only be created by sedentary peoples—architects of order, if you will."

"But what of those cities designed on the plan of a circle, like Vienna, Karlsruhe, or Baghdad?" I asked.

My question was to be answered in an unexpected way, for just at that moment, as we came through the copse of ancient lindens, the underbrush parted and we beheld the tower. Jefferson and I both halted, breathless in astonishment.

The Colonne Détruite—or ruined column, as it was called—was often written of by those who'd seen it, and many drawings and engravings had been made. But none of these did justice to the sheer impact of coming upon it in the woods like this.

It was a house built in the guise of a column—an enormous, crenellated, cream-colored pillar, nearly eighty feet high, with a jagged top that made it appear it had been struck by lightning and broken in two. All around the sides were square and rectangular and oval windows. When we entered, we saw that the center of the vast space was dominated by a spiral stairway, flooded with natural light, which seemed to soar toward the sky. Overhanging the railings were baskets of exotic hothouse flowers mixed with wild vines.

As I preceded Jefferson up the stairs, we marveled at the cleverness of the interior spaces. Each circular floor was divided into oval-shaped rooms with fan-shaped salons fitted in between. There were two floors that lay underground in darkness and four above, all surrounded by windows. Above these, on the uppermost floor, was an attic surrounding the conical skylight, which washed everything on the floors beneath in silvery light. As we passed through the floors, we saw views from the oval windows across the landscape including the pyramid, gothic ruins, temples to gods, a Chinese pavilion, and a Tatar tent. Through all this, we never spoke a word.

"Astonishing," said Jefferson at last, when we'd finished our tour and descended to the ground floor—back to earth again, as it seemed. "Just like the circular cities you asked of, but more like a citadel, a fortress—*the* fortress, for it's a ruined tower of seven stories like the biblical one that once was built as an altar, a ladder to God."

"This entire journey today seems symbolic," I agreed. "From an artist's eye, it's like a story that's been painted upon the land: the tale of Babylon throughout the Bible. First, its legendary history as a succession of wondrous gardens—Eden on the Tigris and Euphrates, or the Hanging Gardens of Babylon, one of the Seven Wonders of the World. Then its conjunction with the four elements. Earth—the magic square you described in the pyramid. Then those twin biblical catastrophes—the destruction of the Tower of Babel, symbolizing air, the sky, the language, the voice—and the great Flood of Mesopotamia, signifying water. And last, of course, in the Apocalypse—the final destruction of the once-great city. Its end by fire."

"Indeed," said Jefferson. "When the Eden of the East, Babylon, is destroyed, though, it is replaced, according to John in the Book of Revelation, by another magic square, a twelve-by-twelve matrix that descends from the sky: the New Jerusalem."

WHEN MARIA COSWAY completed this story, she looked around the room at the others, then bowed her head in contemplation. No one spoke for a very long time.

But there was something strange in this tale, as Haidée knew. She glanced at Kauri beside her, and he nodded once in confirmation. At last Haidée, who'd sat quietly between Kauri and Byron, got to her feet and came around the room to Maria's side, placing her hand on the older woman's shoulder.

"Madame Cosway," said Haidée, "you have told us a story very different from what any of us had been led to believe. We all understand that your tale is meant to allude to that other matrix, of eight by eight. The chessboard. Yet even before Mr. Jefferson could have known of the Montglane Service, even before it was ever removed from the ground, he had the idea that it was really the board itself—the matrix, as he called it—rather than the pieces, that might be the most important part. Did he say where he got this idea?"

"Everyone knows," said Maria, "that after Thomas Jefferson's European sojourn, he went on to become American secretary of state, then vice president, then third president of the United States. Some believe he was also a Freemason, but I know that was not the case. He didn't care for joining orders invented by others; he had always preferred creating a new order of his own.

"It is also widely known that Jefferson was a great scholar and a student of architecture, especially of the designs of that fifteenth-century Venetian, Andrea della Gondola, nicknamed 'Palladio' after Pallas Athene, patroness of Athena. The man who, during the Renaissance, had revived architecture *all'antica*—reconstructions of the ancient Roman forms. What is less known, but more significant, is that Jefferson was also a student of the works of Palladio's great master, Vitruvius Pollio, the first-century architect whose works, the *Ten Books on Architecture,* had just been rediscovered in Palladio's day. These books are critical to any understanding of the roots of ancient architecture and its meaning, whether by Palladio or by Jefferson, and the influence of these books is revealed in everything either of them ever built.

"Vitruvius explains the importance of symmetry and proportion in building a temple with respect to the human body. Of siting a city and planning the directions of the streets with respect to the eight directions of the winds. The effects of the zodiac, the sun, the moon, and the planets upon the construction of a new religious or civil site."

"I don't follow how this answers my daughter's question," said Byron. "What do the works of Palladio, much less Vitruvius, two thousand years ago, have to do with the importance of the chessboard we've come here to discuss? Have you an answer?"

"The chessboard doesn't provide the answer," said Maria cryptically. "It provides the key."

"Ah," said Haidée, glancing toward Byron. "The architect Vitruvius *also* lived at Rome in the time of Jesus and Augustus—and of Caius Cestius, too. You mean, madame, that it was *Vitruvius* who designed this very pyramid with its cosmic proportions. 'Squaring the Circle'—bringing heaven to earth here in Rome!"

"Indeed," said Maria Cosway with a smile. "And Jefferson, great student of architecture that he was, understood the meaning of it all the very moment he went to the Désert. As soon as possible, Jefferson traveled to each city he could in Europe, studied the layout, and bought expensive, accurate engravings of the plans of each. At the dawn of the French Revolution he returned home from Europe and I never saw him again, though we continued an intermittent correspondence.

"But someone else shared his intimate confidence," she explained. "A prizewinning Italian architect, a member of the Royal Academy who'd studied in both London and Rome, a student of the works of both Palladio and Vitruvius, an expert in *disegno all' antica.* And a classmate and intimate friend of our colleague John Trumbull, who'd introduced us to Jefferson at the Halle au Blé that day. Jefferson and Trumbull lured this man to America with an important architectural commission. He stayed there until his death. It is through *him* that I know much of what I have told you here today."

"Who was this architect with whom Jefferson was so intimate, in whom he placed such confidence?" asked Byron.

"My brother, George Hadfield," Maria said.

Haidée's heart was now thumping so loudly she thought it might be heard by the others. She knew she was close to the truth. Though still standing beside Maria, she saw Kauri cast her a warning glance. "What was the commission your brother received?" Haidée asked the older woman.

"In 1790," said Maria, "as soon as Jefferson returned from Europe, and the very moment that George Washington was elected first president, Jefferson persuaded the president to have Congress purchase a piece of land in the form of a Pythagorean square, that is, one based on the number ten.

"Through the heart of this square ran three rivers, meeting at the center to form the letter Y—a Pythagorean symbol. As soon as a designer was chosen—Pierre l'Enfant—Jefferson presented him with all the maps he'd collected of the European cities. But in Jefferson's letter to L'Enfant, there was a caveat: '*They are none of them however comparable to the old Babylon.*' My brother, George Hadfield, was hired by Jefferson and Trumbull to complete the map—as well as the design and construction of the Capitol building—for this great new city."

"Astounding!" said Byron. "The chessboard, the biblical city of Babylon, and the new city created by Jefferson and Washington are all based upon the same plan! You've explained the significance of their design as 'magic squares,' and the deeper meaning that might entail. But what of their differences? These may be important, too."

They certainly were, as Haidée had grasped in a flash.

And now she understood the importance of the Baba Shemimi's story. She understood the meaning of Kauri's warning glance, for this was what the Sufis surely had most feared all along. The chessboard was the key.

Al-Jabir's chessboard square of eight by eight—as even the Baba had pointed out from square one—had twenty-eight squares around its perimeter, the number of letters in the Arabic alphabet.

The nine-by-nine square of the Egyptian pyramid, of the ancient city of Babylon, had a perimeter of thirty-two squares: the letters of the Persian alphabet.

But a ten-by-ten square would contain thirty-six squares around its perimeter, representing not letters of an alphabet, but rather the 360 degrees of a circle.

The new city that Jefferson had built on three rivers, the city that he had even been first to occupy as a sitting president of the United States, had *itself* been designed to bring heaven to earth, to unite the head and the heart—to square the circle.

That city was Washington, D.C.

THE QUEEN ADVANCES

It had taken longer for a woman [the queen] to appear beside the king on the Russian chessboard than in any other non-Muslim country, including China.

—MARILYN YALOM, *Birth of the Chess Queen*

WHITE QUEEN? HOW COULD I BE THE WHITE queen in this Game when my mother—if one believed Aunt Lily's version—was the Black Queen? Though we hadn't always been on the best of terms, Mother and I could hardly be on opposite sides—especially in a Game as dangerous as this one was purported to be. And what on earth did our birthdays have to do with it?

I knew I needed to talk to Lily, and fast, to untie this unanticipated knot. But before I could begin unraveling anything, another queen had arrived on the scene—the very last person on earth I hoped to see just at this moment, though I surely might have known. It was none other than that Queen Mother and Queen Bee all rolled into one: Rosemary Livingston.

Though it was only a few days since I'd last seen Sage's mother enveloped in her clouds of fur, back in Colorado, I was as nonplussed as always by her appearance here tonight. And I don't mean just her arrival.

Rosemary made her usual impression as she descended the sweep of stone steps into the cellar, surrounded by men. Some of her exotic escorts were dressed in white desert robes and others, like Basil, were clad in elegant business suits. Rosemary herself wore a trailing gown of shimmering bronze-colored silk the exact color of her eyes and hair, her tresses partly covered with a shawl of sari silk so fine and opalescent that it seemed to be made of pure spun gold.

Rosemary's appearance had always stopped traffic, but never more so than here and now, in her natural element, surrounded by a gaggle of goggling males. But I quickly realized these were no ordinary oglers—many of these men I recognized from the Fortune 500. If a bomb were dropped in Rosemary's wake just now, I thought, the news of it might drop the New York Stock Exchange twelve hundred points by tomorrow morning.

Rosemary's powerful sense of presence, like a heady perfume, wasn't anything you could really put your finger on, much less aspire to imitate. But I'd often attempted, in my own mind, to define it.

There were women like my aunt Lily who could carry off the kind of flamboyant glamour that was always part and parcel of their own celebrity. There were others, like Sage, who had polished their chiseled looks into the flawless perfection of the born-again beauty queen. My mother herself had always seemed innately to possess a different kind of aura: the healthy beauty and grace of a wild creature, naturally adapted for survival in the forest or jungle—perhaps the reason she'd been nicknamed Cat. Rosemary Livingston, on the other hand, had managed almost alchemically to combine bits of each of these traits into a powerful presence all her own: a kind of regal elegance that at first glimpse fairly took your breath away, leaving you grateful to be touched by the glimmer of her golden presence.

That is, until you actually got to know her.

Now, as Basil removed her wrap just on the other side of the curved glass partition that separated the private dining room from the hearth, Rosemary was blowing a *moue* at me, something between a pout and a kiss.

Though Rodo had told me plenty, at least enough to raise the hair on my neck, I wished like mad that I'd had time to pump him for more information on whatever he knew about this dinner. I couldn't help wondering exactly what the Livingstons were doing, apparently hosting this strange entourage of multinational millionaires. But given those connections that I myself had only recently made involving the chess set, the Game, and Baghdad, it did not seem to me to bode well that many of these diners seemed themselves to be noted figures from the Middle East.

And though as a serving girl myself at this gig I hadn't exactly been introduced to them, I knew these were not just high-level muckety-mucks, as Leda and Eremon had guessed, but there were a few whom I thought I'd even recognized as sheikhs or princes of royal families. No wonder security was at an all-time high over on the canal footbridge!

And beneath everything, of course—with a deep-seated unease after Rodo's recent edification about my own projected role—I was desperate to know what it all had to do with the Game. Or more specifically, with *me.*

But these thoughts were cut short, for Rodo had taken me firmly by the arm and was ushering me out to greet the group.

"Mademoiselle Alexandra and I have a special meal prepared for you tonight," Rodo assured Basil. "Your guests and madame's have, I hope, prepared yourselves for something unique. You will each find your *menu du soir* at your table."

He squeezed my arm tightly from beneath his own: a far-from-subtle hint that I should keep our prior conversation under my chef's cloche and follow his commands until otherwise notified.

Having made certain that everyone was seated within

viewing distance of our performance back at the hearth, Rodo dragged me off to beyond the glass wall and hissed in my ear, "*Faites attention.* Tonight when you serve the food you must be the . . . *entzula.* Not the *jongleur des mots, comme d'habitude*!"

That is, I should be a "listener" and should avoid my usual "word juggler" behavior, whatever that was supposed to mean.

"If these guys are who I think they are, they all speak French, too," I hissed back at him under my breath. "So why don't you stick with talking in Euzkera? Then nobody will understand you—including, if I'm lucky, me!"

With that, Rodo made like a clam and shut up.

The bouillabaisse was followed by the *bacalao*—an enormous cod poached in a Basque lemon sauce with olives, accompanied by heaps of the steamy *boulles* of ash-baked shepherd's bread.

My mouth was watering—that stuffed potato at lunch seemed to have worn off—but I held my ground and pushed my serving cart back and forth, planting dishes on the table for each course, removing them to the larder where I slipped them into the dishwashing machine to await the morning staff.

It did occur to me that this was almost the mirror image of my mother's birthday *boum,* where I'd made a point to glean as much information as I could about this deadly Game in the midst of which I'd found myself.

But though Rodo had told me to be the listener here as well, I couldn't follow the dinner conversation, due to my duties. Everyone seemed quite chatty until I came into the room to serve each course. And though there were many compliments for Rodo's brilliant cuisine, the talk then seemed to drift away as I swept the dishes off and lay the fresh food before the diners.

Perhaps it was my imagination—or Rodo's sinister

suggestion just before their arrival—but they didn't seem to be worried that I might overhear their dinner conversation. They seemed to be *watching* me.

It wasn't until the *Meschoui* course—his pièce de résistance—that Rodo left the hearth and accompanied me to the dining room. Traditionally, the lamb must be served still on its spit, with everyone gathered around, all standing up, so they can pull pieces of the succulent, herb-infused meat from the carcass with their fingers.

I couldn't wait to see Rosemary Livingston attempting this feat in her costly gown of Parisian silk. But one of the desert princes had moved swiftly to rectify matters.

"Permit me," he said. "Women should never be required to stand beside the men at a *Meschoui*!" Motioning for Rosemary to remain seated, he personally pulled a small plate of lamb just for her, which gentlemanly Basil delivered to her place at table.

This seemed just the opportunity the Queen Bee had been awaiting. Once she was left alone at the table, with Rodo rotating the spit for the men gathered around the lamb, she motioned for me to bring the water pitcher to replenish her glass.

Though I suspected, given Rodo's cautionary glance in my direction, that it was a ruse, I bent over the table and poured the water. Rosemary, regardless of her snobbery, was not to be put off by convention when she wanted something. Deftly circumventing the table to come around and buss me at either cheek with her trademark "air kiss," she held me away and breathed, "Darling! After hearing of that dreadful storm due to arrive, Basil and I never hoped to see you back here so quickly from Colorado. We're delighted! And we do hope your mother got over her crisis—or whatever took her away. We ourselves, of course, took the Lear back to the East Coast that very same night!"

Hardly surprising. I knew that the Livingstons kept a stable of pilots and designer planes at the ready at all times, on their private tarmac in Redlands, in the event that Rosemary might get a craving to go off somewhere and shop till she dropped—though of course, they might have offered *us* a lift, too, instead of leaving us stranded in the path of that incoming storm.

As if she'd read my mind, Rosemary added, "You know, if we'd realized you were going down to Denver we might have dropped you and the others, along with Sage and our neighbor, Mr. March."

"Oh, I wish I'd known," I told her in the same lofty tone. "But don't let me keep you from your meal; the *Meschoui* is a Sutalde specialty. Rodo almost never prepares it; he'll be upset if my gabbing with the guests lets yours grow cold before you've even tasted it."

"Then sit beside me for a moment," Rosemary said, in the most ingratiating tone I'd ever heard from her. She slipped back to her place and patted the empty seat just beside her with a smile.

I was in shock at this lapse of protocol—here before all these dignitaries—especially on the part of the biggest snob I'd ever met. But her next words were even more flabbergasting.

"I'm sure that your employer, Monsieur Boujaron, won't mind if you and I chat for just a moment," she assured me. "I've already told him you were a family friend."

Friend! What a concept!

I made my way around to her side of the table, replenished a few water glasses, and glanced once, quickly, in Rodo's direction. He'd raised one eyebrow slightly as if to ask if I was okay.

When I reached Rosemary's side, I said, "Well, Mr. Boujaron is looking our way. I'd better get back to the kitchen. As you see from your menu, there are three more courses following this one. And as wonderful as the cuisine is, we don't want it spoiled by ruining the timing. Nor would you want to be here all night."

Rosemary grasped me by the arm in a deathlike vise and pulled me down to the chair beside her. I was so surprised, I nearly spilled the water pitcher in her lap.

"I said I'd like to talk," she announced—under her breath yet in a tone that qualified as one of imperial command.

My heart was racing. What in God's name did she think she was up to? Could someone be killed at a private dinner party in a famous restaurant when Secret Service were crawling all around outside? But I couldn't help recall, with sinking spirits, Rodo's comment about the blocked communications down here in the cellar. So I set the pitcher down on the table and nodded.

"Sure. I guess a few moments won't matter," I said with as much calm as I could muster, peeling her fingers carefully away. "What took Sage and Galen to Denver?"

Rosemary's face shut down. "You know perfectly well what they were doing there," she said. "Your little half-breed friend Nokomis Key has already passed you the word, hasn't she?"

There were spies everywhere.

Then with steely eyes, she unleashed the persona with which I was more familiar. "Exactly whom do you believe you are dealing with, my girl? Do you have any possible conception of *who I am*?"

I thought of saying that I was having trouble just figuring out who *I* was. But, given Rosemary's most recent reaction, not to mention the composition of this mysterious group, I thought we all might be best served if I'd checked my levity, along with that cell phone, at the door.

"Who you *are*?" I finally said. "You mean—other than Rosemary Livingston? My former neighbor?"

Rosemary sighed with enormous impatience and tapped her nail on the plate of *Meschoui* before her, which she still hadn't touched.

"I told Basil this was all foolishness—a *dinner,* for heaven's sake—but he simply wouldn't listen," she said, almost as if to herself. Then she looked back at me with narrowed eyes.

"You *do* know who Vartan Azov actually is, of course?" she said. "I mean, apart from his *avocation* as a world-class chess master."

When I shook my head, confused, she added, "Naturally we've known Vartan since he was just a boy. He was then the stepson of Taras Petrossian, Basil's business associate who's just passed away in London. Vartan never likes to speak of their relationship. Nor the fact that he himself is sole heir to the Petrossian estate, which is quite extensive."

Much as I hoped to avoid showing what I felt at this revelation, I couldn't help staring and quickly averted my gaze. Of course Petrossian was rich. He'd been an "oligarch" during the brief heyday of Russian capitalism, hadn't he? And, too, Basil Livingston would hardly have had truck with anyone who wasn't.

But Rosemary hadn't quite finished. Indeed, she seemed to be waxing on her poisonous theme with unprecedented gusto.

"I wonder if you could explain for me," she said, her voice still low, "exactly how Vartan Azov, a Ukrainian subject, managed to obtain a visa for the United States with such short notice, just to attend a party? Or why he and Lily Rad—if they were really in such a hurry to reach Colorado—decided to *drive together* cross-country in a private car?"

I kicked myself for being a mental midget. If Rosemary was trying to throw suspicion upon my friends, she was doing a really great job. Why had it never occurred to *me* to ask such questions?

But the very instant that I did ask those same questions of myself, that was all it took to strike the final, lethal chord of terror up my spine. I was relieved I was still sitting down. My limbic system was wreaking havoc with my visceral reponses; I was drenched in cold sweat.

But I couldn't help hearing that one particular phrase, like a clash of symbols in my mind—the phrase that pulled everything together in a way that I really couldn't bear to understand:

Naturally we've known Vartan since he was just a boy . . .

If the Livingstons had known Vartan Azov since he was a boy—if they'd known him ever since the time when he was Taras Petrossian's stepson and they'd been involved all that time with Petrossian himself—then this meant that they'd *all* been intimately connected. Even from the very first moment that my father and I had set foot in Russia.

Which meant that *they all* must have been involved in that very Last Game, the one that took my father's life.

THE GAME HAD certainly advanced. In those few words of aside, I'd quickly realized, Rosemary Livingston had not only shown her true colors, but perhaps provided a good deal more than food for thought.

As I served the next three courses—the daube of wild mushrooms, the poultry with vegetables and spicy greens braised in pan drippings, and the *gâteau au chocolat* thick with brandy-soaked Basque cherries—I hung out like the proverbial fly on the wall and tried to get a better glance at the board I was playing on. I learned a lot, if only through innuendo.

Though Rodo had soon rescued me from the clutches of our hostess and got me back to my more comfortable habitat, raking ashes and serving vittles, I still couldn't stop the refrain running through my head: that most of those who'd been my mother's guests only days ago in the Colorado Rockies, had turned out to be somehow intimately connected with one another as well—in a way that suggested they were therefore also suspiciously connected with my father's death.

This meant that they certainly were all players in the Game.

Now all I needed to grasp was how they were connected with *me*. What role did *I* play? The Sixty-Four-Square Question, as Key might say—and as Rodo, in his own way, had earlier tried to point out. I couldn't wait to get him alone after closing time, to pump him about the real inception of this gala meal. Whose idea had it been? How was it initially arranged? How had it been set up—replete with all the high-level dignitaries and the *haut* security force?

But despite all those unanswered questions floating in the forefront of my consciousness, there was one thing I was sure that I *had* deciphered, one thing that lay lurking within the deep recesses of my mind.

Something else had happened ten years ago. Something besides my father's death and besides my mother's decision to yank me out of school in New York and relocate us both to the Octagon in the wilds of the Rocky Mountains—something that almost seemed like an inexplicable chess move within a larger Game.

For ten years ago, as I now recalled, the Livingston family had pulled up roots in Denver and become our full-time neighbors. They'd moved to their ranch in Redlands, on the Colorado Plateau.

IT WAS AFTER MIDNIGHT when the Livingstons departed with the last of their guests. Rodo and I were both too exhausted for a lengthy chat. He said he'd like to meet me tomorrow morning and take me somewhere private where we could do a postmortem on what had been going on tonight.

That sounded good to me. A field trip with Rodo would also spare me the ire of the master chefs and Leda—not to mention the dishwashing crew—when they discovered what we'd left them to clean up after tonight.

I was moving the kettles and pans to the larder, where they could be left soaking in water for the next few hours, when I moved the dripping pan and saw those awful burned drippings glommed onto the slate floor underneath. I pointed it out to Rodo.

"Who set up that spit with the *mouton*?" I asked him. "Whoever it was, they really left a mess. You should have had me do it, or you should have done it yourself. Who'd you send down here as helpers this morning—the Basque Brigade?"

Rodo shook his head sadly at the baked-in black goo. He trickled some water onto it from the pitcher, then sprinkled it with a bit of baking soda.

"Just a friend," he said. "I shall correct it tomorrow. Right now I shall retrieve our cell phones. You had best go to bed yourself and get you some sleep."

This was so unlike my boss—whom the chefs called the Euzkaldun Exterminator—that it fairly took my breath. The real Rodo would have leveled his contempt like an AK-47 assault rifle at anyone for a transgression even half this bad. He must be slipping after the exertion of tonight, I reasoned.

I myself was nearly slipping into a coma from exhaustion by the time Rodo had returned from the bridge patrol with our cell phones. Once he'd locked the door behind us it was once again the wee hours. Becoming a tradition for me. The footbridge was open, the gumshoes gone, and their carrel and concrete barriers conveniently removed.

We parted at the end of the bridge where Rodo wished me a good night's sleep and said he'd phone tomorrow and arrange to pick me up. It was after one A.M. when I headed down the alley to my pied à terre overlooking the canal.

When I reached the terrace at the usually shadowy entrance to Key Park, everything was as black as the inside of a wool sock. The streetlamp had burned out, which happened more often than I liked to think. It was too dark to see, so I fumbled for my keys and finally located the right one by touch. But when I opened the door to my hallway there was something wrong. I noticed a dim light that seemed to be glowing at the top of the stairs.

Could I have left a lamp on this morning by mistake?

After all I'd been through these past four days, I had the right to be worried. I pulled out my cell phone and dialed Rodo's number. He couldn't be more than a block or two away—likely hadn't even reached his car yet—but there was no answer, so I hung up. I could easily punch Redial if I found something up there that was really wrong.

I crept soundlessly up the stairs until I reached the door to my apartment. It didn't have a lock of its own, but I always shut it when I left the house. Now it was slightly ajar. And there was no doubt: a lamp was lit inside. I was about to hit Redial when I heard a familiar voice from within.

"Where have you been, my dear? I've been waiting here for you half the night."

I pushed the door and it swung open. There, seated in

my comfy leather chair as if he owned the place, lamplight falling on his coppery curls, a glass of my best sherry in one hand and an open book upon his lap, sat my uncle Slava.

Dr. Ladislaus Nim.

THE MIDDLE GAME

Middlegame: The part of the game that follows the opening phase. It is the most difficult and the most beautiful part, where a lively imagination has great opportunity to create wonderful combinations.

—NATHAN DIVINSKY, *The Batsford Chess Encyclopedia*

NIM REGARDED ME WITH HIS WRY SMILE, BUT for only a moment. I must have looked like a complete wreck. As if he'd grasped everything that had happened, he set down his glass and book and came over to me; without a word he enfolded me in his arms.

I had no idea of the real state of my frazzled nerves. But the instant he hugged me the floodgates opened and I found myself sobbing uncontrollably into his sleeve. Frightened as I'd been only seconds ago, I felt it turn to relief. For the first time in as long as I could recall, I found myself under the protection of someone I could trust completely. He stroked my hair with one hand, as if I were his pet, and I began to relax.

My father had nicknamed my uncle "Slava," a kind of Russian double entendre—short for Ladislav, the pronunciation of his name, but also the Russian word for a "Glory," the eight-pointed star that forms a halo in Russian icons for figures like God, the Virgin, or angels. *My* Slava was definitely ensconced in his own aura, replete with a coppery halo of hair. And although now that I was grown, like everyone else I called him Nim, I still thought of him as my guardian angel.

He was the most fascinating person I'd ever known—

I think because he'd kept a trait that most of us possess as children, but few of us manage to retain as we grow older. Nim remained fascinating because he was always *fascinated*—by anything and everything. His favorite admonition summed up this philosophy: Whenever I'd wheedled to be amused or entertained as a child, he'd say, "Only the boring are bored."

Whether fascinating or mysterious to others, Nim had been the most stable ingredient in my young life. After my father's death and the estrangement from Mother that followed my removal from the world of chess, my uncle had given me two important gifts that helped me survive—gifts that were also the means we'd employed all these years to communicate with each other so we didn't have to speak about the deeper things that clearly we both found so painful: the arts of cooking and of puzzles.

And my intriguing uncle was here just now, tonight, to bestow a third gift—something I'd never expected or sought or even wanted.

But now—cradled in his arms, my sobs subsiding—I felt myself sinking into exhausted oblivion, too weary to ask my many questions, too heavy with fatigue to understand the answer my uncle was here to give me, that "gift" that was about to change everything: the knowledge of my own past.

"DOESN'T HE EVER *feed* you, this employer of yours? When was the last time you ate?" Nim was asking me, irritably.

Despite the caustic tone he was regarding me with grave concern with those strange bicolored eyes—one blue, one brown—that seemed always to look at you and through you at once. His brow furrowed, his elbows propped on my kitchen table, he watched every swallow I took as I tucked into my second helping of the delicious soup he'd prepared from things he'd foraged in my barren kitchen. He'd whipped up this soup to revive me, after I'd apparently blacked out in his arms and he'd laid me out cold on the living room sofa.

"I guess Rodo and I both overlooked that I haven't had time to eat much lately," I admitted. "Things have been so confused these past few days. I think the last real meal I had was what I prepared myself, back in Colorado."

"Colorado!" Nim exclaimed under his breath as he glanced once, quickly, toward the window. Then he lowered his voice further. "So that's where you've been. I've been hunting you here for days. I've been by that restaurant of yours more than once."

So he was the trench-coated mystery man who'd been lurking around Sutalde.

But suddenly, without warning, Nim had slapped his hand flat on my nearby kitchen counter with a loud *smack*. "Cockroach," he said, holding up his empty palm with one brow slightly raised as in warning. "I noticed one, but there may be others. When you've finished your soup, let's go toss this outside."

I understood: That empty palm suggested my place was "bugged" in a different fashion, so we couldn't talk here. My eyes were scratchy from my weeping jag, my head ached from lack of sleep. But hungry or exhausted or not, I understood as well as he did the urgency of our situation. We really needed to speak.

"I'm pretty tired already," I told my uncle with a yawn that I didn't need to fake. "Let's go right now and get it done. Then I can get back and catch some sleep."

Pulling my big coffee mug down from its hook over the stove, I ladled it full of the soup. I made a mental note to jot down later the magical meld of flavors Nim had managed to concoct from the dusty tins and paper packets he'd tossed together: a rich, creamy corn chowder laced with curry and lemon juice, sprinkled with toasted coconut, crabmeat, and chopped jalapeño peppers. Astonishing. Once again my uncle had demonstrated what he'd always prided himself on: creating a magical meal just by rummaging through the refuse of an ordinary kitchen cupboard. He'd do Rodo proud.

We slipped on our outdoors coats. I stuck the spoon in my cup and followed him down the darkened steps and into the wet black night. Both the canal towpath below us and the meandering footpath leading into Key Park were black and deserted, so we walked uphill to M Street where the streetlamps always shimmered golden pools of light throughout the night. By unspoken consensus we turned left toward the lighted span of Key Bridge.

"I'm glad you brought the soup along. You will finish that, please." Nim nodded toward the big cup as he tossed his arm across my shoulders. "My dear, I'm seriously concerned about your health. You look a wreck. But I'm not nearly as worried about what's already happened to you—you can explain all that to me later—as I fear what may be *about* to happen. What on earth suddenly possessed you to up and take off for Colorado?"

"Mother's birthday party," I said between slurps of the fabulous soup. "You were invited yourself. Or at least, so you said in your voice message—"

"My message!" he said, taking his arm from my shoulder.

"*Jawohl,* Herr Professor Doktor Wittgenstein," I said. "You declined to attend, you were running off to India for a chess tournament. I heard the message on Mother's machine. We all did."

"All!" cried Nim. He'd stopped cold in his tracks just as we reached the upper corner of Key Park and the entrance to the bridge. "Perhaps first, after all, you'd best tell me exactly what did happen in Colorado. Who else was there?"

So there under the streetlamp at the park's edge, as we heard the clock chime two A.M., I quickly filled in my uncle on the arrival, one by one, of Mother's mysterious motley crew of birthday invitees and what I'd learned about each. He winced at a few names—principally Basil and Vartan. But he was paying close attention when I told him Lily's story of the Game, as if he were trying to reconstruct the moves of an important chess match they'd all played years ago. As he likely was.

I'd almost reached the critical parts about our finding the chessboard in the drawer, and what Vartan had revealed to me about the Russian Black Queen and my father's death, when suddenly my uncle cut in with barely concealed impatience.

"And what of your *mother* all this while, when all these 'guests' were arriving?" he said. "Did she tell you nothing that might have explained her actions? Did she say why she took such a foolish risk to throw this party on her own birth date, despite the obvious dangers? Who else was invited? Who didn't attend? Good lord—after all those names you've just told me, I pray she had the presence not to mention the gift I sent."

I was still so obliterated due to my deep-sleep deprivation that I wasn't sure if I'd heard him correctly. Was it possible that he really didn't know?

"But Mother was never there at the party at all," I told him. "It seems she left the house only shortly before I arrived. She never returned. She simply vanished. We hoped, Aunt Lily and I, that *you* might have some idea where she was."

I'd never seen this expression on my uncle's face: He seemed thunderstruck, as if I were speaking some exotic tongue that he simply couldn't comprehend. At last those bicolored eyes of his focused upon me in the lamplight.

"Gone," he said. "This is far worse than I'd conceived. You must come with me. There's something you really must learn about."

So he *hadn't* known Mother was missing. *"This is far worse than I'd conceived,"* he'd said. But how could it be? Nim always knew everything. If *he* didn't know, then where *was* my mother?

At this moment, alone with my uncle in Georgetown somewhere between midnight and dawn, I suddenly realized that I felt too deeply depressed even to plumb the depths of my own depression.

Together Nim and I crossed the road to the opposite side of Key Bridge. Then we hiked along the bridge sidewalk till we reached the midpoint, high above the water. Nim motioned for me to sit beside him on the concrete base that supported the celadon bridge railing.

We were sitting in a puddle of milky pink light cast by the lanterns high above us. The eerie glow turned my uncle's coppery curls to gold. From time to time a car came across the bridge, but the drivers never noticed us seated there, only feet away from them, just behind our protective barrier.

Then Nim glanced down at the cup in my hand. "But I see you haven't finished your soup, though you surely need it. It must be cold by now."

Obediently I took another spoonful—it still tasted great, so I tilted the cup to my lips and swilled it down.

Then I looked at my uncle, awaiting his revelation.

"I must begin," he informed me, "by saying that your mother has always had a mind of her own. A stubborn streak."

As if that were news to *me*!

"Only a few weeks ago," he went on, "shortly before I knew she was planning this mad confrontation that she had the effrontery to call a 'birthday party,' I'd sent her an important parcel." He paused, then added, "A very important parcel."

I was pretty sure I knew what the contents of that parcel might be. It was likely what was hidden in the lining of my parka right at this very moment. But if Nim was ready to talk, I wasn't about to interrupt his informative train of thought with such trivia as Vartan Azov's sewing skills. My uncle might well be the only person who possessed the missing pieces of the puzzle I needed in this most dangerous of all games.

But there was one thing I needed to know.

"*When* exactly did you send this parcel to my mother?" I asked.

"It means nothing to ask *when* I sent it," said Nim. "Only *why*. It's an object of enormous importance, though not mine to give. It belonged to someone else—I was surprised to receive it. I sent it on to your mother."

"Okay, then *why*?" I asked.

"Because *Cat* was the Black Queen—the one in charge," he said, glancing at me with impatience. "I don't know how much Lily Rad has spilled to all of you, as you told me she did. But her imprudence might well have placed all of us—especially *you*—in terrible danger."

Nim removed my soup cup and set it on the pavement. Then he took my hands in his as he went on speaking. "It was the drawing of a chessboard," he told me. "Thirty years ago, when your mother first became custodian of the other pieces, that part of the puzzle was missing, though we knew from a diary that it originally had been captured by the nun who was known as Mireille."

"Lily told us about her. Lily said she'd read that diary," I told him. "She said she claimed she was still alive—that her name was Minnie, and that my mother had somehow replaced her as the Black Queen."

It took more than an hour for me to fill him in on all that had happened. Knowing Nim's obsession with detail, I tried to leave out nothing. The puzzles Mother had left me, the phone message with the key, the eight ball, the game in the piano, the card tucked inside the Black Queen, the drawing of the chessboard hidden in the desk, and lastly, Vartan's revelation of what transpired just before my father's death and our mutual conviction that his death was no accident.

I realized that my uncle was the only one with whom I'd yet shared what I had deduced from this: the possible existence of a second Black Queen, which might have led to my father's death.

During this entire time, as he followed each word intently, Nim said nothing and showed no reaction, though I was sure he was taking copious mental notes. When I'd finished everything, he shook his head.

"Your story only serves to confirm my worst fears, and my conviction that we must find out what has become of your mother. I hold myself responsible for Cat's disappearance," he said. "There's something I've never told you, my dear. I believe I must always have been deeply in love with your mother. And it was I myself—long before she ever met your father—who foolishly lured Cat into this most dangerous Game."

When Nim saw my reaction, he placed his hand on my shoulder.

"Perhaps I shouldn't have revealed to you how I felt, Alexandra," he said. "I assure you that I've never shared these feelings with your mother. But from what you've said, she's surely in danger. If you and I hope to help her,

I've no choice than to be as honest and direct with you as possible—much as it might go against my cryptographic nature." He regarded me with that familiar ironic smile.

I didn't smile back. Openness was one thing, but I'd just about had it with these post-meridian surprises from every quarter.

"Then it's time to decrypt a few things, starting now," I told him sharply, making every effort to draw myself out of oblivion. "What would these long-suppressed feelings of yours about my mother have to do with her disappearance, much less with the chess set or the Game?"

"After that unsolicited confession of mine, you've the right to ask me anything. And I hope you will," my uncle told me. "The moment Cat received my packet with that drawing of the chessboard—the final piece of the puzzle, once we could decode it—she must immediately have understood that the Game was once more afoot. However, rather than her consulting with an expert code-breaker like myself, as I'd hoped and expected, she announced she was throwing that mad tea party, and then she disappeared!"

This would explain the "why" of my uncle's previous comment—why he'd sent my mother that packet with so little fanfare. Clearly he still hoped, ten years after my father's death, that he could be her cryptographer, her confidant—or perhaps something more.

Could there be some reason why she *hadn't* turned to him?

"After Sascha's death," Nim said, reading my mind, "Cat never trusted me—never trusted any of us. She felt we'd all betrayed her, betrayed your father, and most of all, betrayed *you*. That's why she took you away."

"How did you all betray me?"

But then I knew the answer. Because of chess.

"I remember the day it happened, the day she first drew away from us all. It was the day we all realized what a strange little animal we were harboring in our midst," Nim said with a smile. "But come, let's walk as I tell you, it will warm us."

He stood, took me by the hand, and pulled me to my feet, stuffing my empty coffee mug and spoon into his trench-coat pocket.

"You were only three years old," he said. "We were at my place on the tip of Long Island, Montauk Point—all of us, as we often were on weekends during the summers. That was the day we discovered, my dear girl, who and what you really were. That was the day that began our estrangement from your mother."

So we crossed the bridge to Virginia as foggy midnight crept toward rosy dawn. And Ladislaus Nim began his tale . . .

THE CRYPTOGRAPHER'S TALE

The sky was blue, the grass was green. The fountain splashed into the pool at the edge of the lawn, and in the distance beyond the crescent of beach, as far as the eye could see, spread the expanse of little whitecapped waves of the Atlantic Ocean. Your mother was swimming laps, cutting through the waves, as lithe as a dolphin.

On the grassy lawn, Lily Rad and your father sat in lacy white wicker lawn chairs, with a pitcher of iced limeade and two frosty glasses. They were playing chess.

Your father, Sascha—the great grandmaster Aleksandr Solarin—had given up tournament play shortly after he came to America. But he'd still needed a job. There was a special provision that I knew of, a fast track to citizenship for someone gifted in physics, as your father was.

As soon as was practicable, both your parents took well-paying but unobtrusive jobs with the U.S. government. Then you were born. Cat thought tournament chess too dangerous, especially once they'd had a child; Sascha agreed, though he still coached Lily on weekends.

You'd always seemed fascinated by the board, those little black-and-white pieces on black-and-white squares. Sometimes you even stuck them in your mouth and looked quite proud to have done so.

On this particular day you'd been toddling about the lawn as they two began their play. I'd pulled up my chair so I could observe the game and your mother's swimming at once. Aleksandr and Lily were so intent that none of us paid much attention when you were suddenly there, clinging to a table leg to hold yourself upright, those large green eyes peering across the board as you watched their play.

I distinctly recall that it was just at move 32 of the Nimzo-Indian Defense. Lily, playing White, had somehow got herself caught between a fork and a pin. Though I'm sure your father could have extricated himself from a similar trap, it was clear that, to her at least, there seemed to be no way forward and no way back.

She'd turned to me for a moment to jest that if I refreshed her limeade glass it might refresh her point of view when, all at once, still clinging to the table, you reached forward with one chubby child's fist and plucked her Knight from the board. To my complete astonishment, you set it down in position to check your father's king!

Everyone was silent for a very long moment—dumbstruck was more like it—as we understood what had occurred. But as it slowly sank in, just what the long-range ramifications of such an event might be, the tension around the chessboard built up like that within the interior of a pressure cooker.

"Cat will be furious," Sascha was the first to remark, softly and in a voice completely devoid of all intonation.

"But it's incredible," said Lily between thin lips. "What if it's not an accident? What if she's truly a prodigy?"

"*Not* a broccoli," little Alexandra announced firmly to the group.

Everyone laughed. Your father plucked you up and set you on his lap.

But once Sascha and Lily had reconstructed that game hours later, as they always did after each such coaching session, they saw that the move made by a three-year-old toddler had been the only viable one that might enable Lily to draw that game.

The lid of the problem had been opened. And there would never be any chance of putting it back shut.

NIM PAUSED AND LOOKED down at me in the dim light. I saw we'd reached Rosslyn on the Virginia side of the bridge. It was dark and isolated, with the high-rise office buildings all shut down for the night. Wired as I was, I knew I needed to go home and crawl into bed. But my uncle hadn't quite finished.

"Cat came up the lawn after her dip in the sea that day," he told me. "She was brushing sand from her feet and drying her hair with the edge of her toweling robe. Then she saw us all seated on the lawn around that chessboard, with you—her innocent little daughter in your father's lap—holding a chess piece in your hand.

"No one had to say it—Cat knew. She turned on her

heel and left us without a word. She would never forgive us for putting you into the Game."

At last Nim fell silent. I thought it was time to intervene, or at least turn back, so we wouldn't be out here all night.

"Now that I know about that larger Game from you and Aunt Lily," I said, "it certainly explains why Mother didn't trust the lot of you. And why she was so afraid for me. But it doesn't explain the party or her disappearance."

"That wasn't all," Nim said.

What wasn't all?

"That wasn't all that was in the parcel I sent to Cat," he said, again reading my mind. "That card you found—the placard with the picture of a phoenix on one side, a firebird on the other, and some words in Russian. Almost like a calling card someone thought I would recognize. But though it was quite beyond me, there was something else I must show you—" He eyed me suspiciously. "What on *earth* is it now?"

I'm sure I looked like I might black out again, though this time not for lack of food or sleep. I couldn't believe this was happening. I reached into my pants pocket, pulled out the card, and handed it to my uncle.

" 'Danger—Beware the Fire,' " I told him. "Maybe it meant nothing to you but I can tell you what it means to *me*. That card was given to me just before my father died. How did you get it?"

He bowed his head over it for a long moment there on the darkened pavement. Then he looked up at me with a strange expression and handed the card back to me.

"I've something to show you," he said.

He reached into his trench coat and extracted a small leather folder the size of a wallet. He held it carefully in his hand like a relic, looking down at it. Then he opened my hands and placed the leather wallet in them. He kept his hands around mine for a moment, then finally released them.

When I opened the folder, even here in the dim light of Rosslyn, I could make out details of a worn black-and-white photo that was tinted with aquarelles to resemble a color image: It seemed to be a family of four.

Two little boys—perhaps four and eight years old—were seated on a garden bench. They both wore loose tunics belted at the waist, with knickers; their pale hair fell in loose ringlets. They looked into the camera with uncertain smiles as if they'd never had their picture taken before. Just behind them stood a muscular man with unruly hair and intense dark eyes, looking fiercely protective. But it was the woman who stood beside him that had caused my blood to turn to ice.

"It's myself and your father, little Sascha," Nim was saying in a choked voice I'd never heard. "We're sitting on the stone seat of our garden in Krym, the Crimea. And those are our parents. It's the only photo that exists of our family. We were still happy. It was taken not so long before we learned we would have to flee."

I couldn't tear my eyes from that image. Fear clutched at my heart. Those chiseled features I could never forget, her white-blond hair even paler than my father's had been.

Nim's voice seemed to come through a tunnel thousands of miles long. "God knows how it could be," he was saying, "but I know that only one person could have possessed this photo after all this time, one person who would understand its importance, who could have sent it to me along with that card and the chessboard drawing. Only one."

He paused and looked at me gravely. "What it means, my dear, is that regardless of what I've believed all these years—and as impossible as it might seem to me even now—that woman in the photo, my mother, is still alive."

She certainly *was* alive. I myself could testify.

She was the woman at Zagorsk.

TWO WOMEN

Deux femmes nous ont donné les premieres exemples de la gourmandise:
Ève, en mangeant une pomme dans le Paradis;
Proserpine, en mangeant une grenade en enfer.

(*Two women have given us the first examples of greed:*
Eve, in eating an apple in Paradise;
Persephone, in eating a pomegranate in Hell.)
—Alexandre Dumas, *Le Grand Dictionnaire de Cuisine*

I was awakened by the loud warblings of a male wren just outside my bedroom window. I was familiar with the drill. This same guy showed up each spring, always singing the same old tune. He was hopping around excitedly, trying to convince his spouse to check out a potential nest location just under my eaves where he'd shoved some twigs and grasses into a cubbyhole and was coaxing her to come rearrange the furniture herself, so he could nail down the mortgage before somebody else spotted this prime piece of real estate—one of the few locales on the canal that roving cats couldn't get at.

But suddenly, it dawned on me that if this wren was awake, singing his head off, it must already be well past dawn. I sat up in bed to check the time, but my alarm clock was nowhere to be seen. Someone had removed it.

My head was throbbing. How long had I slept? How had I gotten here, into my own pajamas and my own bed? All recollection seemed to have been wiped.

But then yesterday's events started to trickle back into my addled brain.

Rodo's strange behavior yesterday, from Euskal Herria to Sutalde. That dinner, ushered in by SS officials and hosted by my least favorite personae on the planet, the Livingstons. Finally, Nim's unexpected appearance inside my apartment, and our post-midnight stroll across the bridge. When he'd shown me that photo—

The whole thing returned and hit me like the proverbial ton of bricks.

That mysterious blond woman at Zagorsk, the woman who'd tried to warn me—she was my grandmother!

That was the last thing I remembered telling my uncle last night before all went blank. The woman in his weathered family photo was the woman who'd given me that card ten years ago, only moments before my father's death.

At this particular moment, however, that warbling wren outside jarred me into dealing with more pressing issues. I suddenly recalled that my boss, Rodo, was supposed to phone me this morning to make arrangements to meet him for breakfast, so he could give me whatever urgent information he had left unsaid last night. I'd better phone *him*—

But when I glanced around, I saw that my bedroom phone had disappeared, too!

I was about to jump from bed when the bedroom door swung open. There was Nim with a tray in his hands and a smile on his face.

"A Russian-Greek bearing gifts," he said. "I hope you slept well. I took every precaution that you should. Oh, and—my apologies—I laced your soup last night with half a bottle of grappa. Enough fermented grape pulp to ensure that an ox would get a good night's sleep. You certainly needed it. I barely managed to get you home and upstairs on your own steam *and* make myself a bed on that lumpy sofa. You need to eat this now, though. A good breakfast will help what lies ahead."

So at least I'd still been conscious last night, despite how unconscious I was right now of what else we may have discussed.

Much as I needed to speak with Rodo—under my nose just now was that steaming pot of coffee and another of hot milk, a tumbler of fresh juice, and a stack of my uncle's famous buttermilk pancakes along with a crock of sweet butter, a bowl of fresh blueberries, and a beaker of warm maple syrup. It smelled even better than it looked.

Where had Nim found all these ingredients in my barren larder? But I didn't need to ask.

"I've had a word with Mr. Boujaron, your employer," Nim told me. "He phoned here earlier, but I'd removed the phone from your room. I refreshed his memory of who I was—the principal reference on your contract with him. And I explained that after your taxing week you needed some rest. He came to see the wisdom of giving you the day off work. And he sent over a minion with a few ingredients I'd requested."

"It looks like you made him an offer he couldn't refuse," I said with a grin, tucking the big napkin into the neck of my pajama top. It was one of the good damask ones from Sutalde. God bless Nim.

Then I tucked into the wonderful food, as well. My urgent need to hear the rest of Rodo's story from last night began to wane. My uncle's prized flapjacks, as always, had that thin, delicate crust that kept the syrup on the outside, so they never got soggy, and the insides stayed lighter than froth. He'd never disclosed his secret of making them that way.

As I relished this fare, Nim sat on the edge of my bed in silence, gazing out the window until I'd finished my meal and wiped the last bit of maple syrup from my chin. Only then did he speak.

"I've been doing a lot of thinking, my dear," he told me. "After our conversation last night on the bridge—once you'd told me you'd actually *seen* the woman in the photo, and she'd given you that card, I could scarcely sleep. By dawn, however, I believe I'd resolved a great deal. Not only what may have motivated your mother to do as she's done with that party, but more important, I think I've discovered the secret behind the appearance of that chessboard, as well as the puzzle of the second Black Queen."

When Nim saw my alarmed expression, he smiled and shook his head.

"I swept your place for bugs first thing this morning," he assured me. "I've removed them all. They were amateurs, whoever placed those detection devices—some in the telephones and one in your alarm clock—the first places one would think to look." He stood, picked up the breakfast tray, and headed for the door. "Happily, we're now free to speak without further resort to alfresco meals at midnight on Key Bridge."

"Maybe these guys *here* were amateurs," I said, "but the guys last night on the footbridge guarding the restaurant both had Secret Service badges. They were certainly pros. My boss seemed pretty chummy with them, too, though he made sure they couldn't overhear us when he told me, just before that private dinner, what he knew about the Basque version of the story of the Montglane Service."

"And what, precisely, was that?" Nim had halted at the door.

"He said he'd tell me the rest this morning," I said, "but thanks to you and your grappa, I overslept. Last night Rodo gave me the Basque scoop on the *Chanson de Roland;* that in fact it was Basques and not the

Moors who'd defeated Charlemagne's rear guard at the Roncesvalles Pass; that the Moors gave Charlemagne the chess set in thanks; and that he then buried it a million miles from his palace in Aachen, right back in the Pyrenees at Montglane. Rodo told me what Montglane really means: 'Mountain of Gleaners.' Then, just before the others arrived, he was explaining about sowing and reaping, and how it related to my birthday being the opposite of my mother's—"

But I stopped, for Nim's bicolored eyes had grown cold and faraway. He still stood in the doorway holding my breakfast tray, but suddenly he looked like a different person altogether.

"Why did Boujaron mention your birth date?" he demanded. "Did he explain?"

"Rodo said it was important," I said, unnerved by his intensity. "He said I might be in danger because of it, that I should keep my eyes and ears peeled for clues during last night's dinner."

"But there must have been something more," he insisted. "Did he say what it might signify for these people?"

"He told me that the people coming last night *knew* that my birth date was October 4, opposite my mother's birthday and the party she threw this past weekend. Oh, and then he said something even stranger, that they thought they knew who I really was."

"And who was that?" asked Nim, his expression so grim it almost made me tremble.

"You're sure no one can hear us?" I whispered.

He nodded.

I said, "I'm not sure I understood it myself. But Rodo said, for some reason, they imagined that *I* was the new White Queen."

"GOOD LORD, I MUST be going completely mad," Nim said. "Or perhaps I'm just growing inattentive as I grow older. But one thing is clear to me now: If Rodolfo Boujaron told you that much, then *someone* knows more than I'd imagined. Indeed, they've managed to gather a great deal more insight than I myself had understood until this very moment.

"But combining what you yourself have told me with what I came to grasp just last night," my uncle added, "I think I now understand everything. Though it will take some explanation and examination."

Quel relief, I thought, at last somebody understands. But it no longer sounded like news I longed to hear.

Nim had insisted that I get dressed and put down another cup or two of his java before he began to fill me in on the epiphanies he'd had since just last night. Now, in my living room, we both sat on the sofa where he'd bedded down last night. The wallet with its weathered photo was propped open between us. Nim touched the image carefully with one fingertip.

"Our father, Iosif Pavlos Solarin, a Greek sailor, fell in love with a Russian girl and married her—our mother, Tatiana," he told me. "He built a small fishing fleet on the Black Sea and never wanted to leave. As boys, my brother, Sascha, and I thought our mother to be the most beautiful woman we'd ever seen. Of course, on the isolated tip of the Crimean peninsula where we lived, we hadn't seen many women. But it wasn't just her beauty. There was something magical about our mother. It's hard to explain."

"You don't have to. I made her acquaintance at Zagorsk," I reminded him.

Tatiana Solarin. Privately, I could hardly bear to look at this color-tinted photo. Her image alone brought back all the pain of these past ten years. But now that that first question—*Who was she?*—had been answered, it only gave rise to an unstoppable onslaught of further questions.

What had her warning that day really meant? *Danger, Beware the Fire?* Did she know about the Black Queen that we would soon find inside the treasury? Did she know the risk to my father the moment he saw it?

Had my father recognized her on that bleak wintry day at Zagorsk? He must have—after all, she was his mother. But how could she still look the same then, just ten years ago, as she did in this faded photo before me that had been taken when my father and uncle were little boys? Furthermore, if everyone had been assuming she was dead all these years, as Nim assured me, then where had she been hiding? And what—or who—had prompted her to resurface only now?

I was about to find out.

"When Sascha was six years old and I was ten," Nim began, "one night at our isolated house on the coast of Krym, there was a terrible storm. We boys were asleep in our room downstairs, when we heard a tapping at the windows and we saw a woman in a long dark cape standing outside in the storm. When we let her in through the window, she introduced herself as our grandmother Minerva, who'd come from a distant land on an urgent mission to find our mother. This woman was Minnie Renselaas. And from the moment she stepped through that window, all our lives were instantly to change."

"Minnie—she's the one that Aunt Lily told us had claimed to be Mireille," I said, "the French nun who lived forever."

But I swiftly cursed myself for interrupting, for Nim had something more important to reveal.

"Minnie told us we must all flee at once," he went on. "She'd brought with her three chess pieces—a golden pawn, a silver elephant, and a horse. My father was sent ahead through the storm with these pieces, so he could prepare the boat for the rest of our family's escape. But soldiers arrived at the house before we made our exit, and they captured our mother, while Minnie fled through the upper windows with us children. We hid on the cliffs in the rain until the soldiers were gone, then tried to reach Father's ship at Sevastopol. But little Sascha couldn't climb quickly enough. I was sent ahead, alone, to my father at the ship."

Nim looked at me gravely. "I'd reached my father's ship at Sevastopol. We waited for hours for Minnie and Sascha to arrive. But at last when they didn't appear, per my father's promise to Mother, we were forced to depart for America. Many days later, Minnie had to place Sascha in an orphanage so she could return to try to find our mother and rescue her. But all seemed lost."

It's true I had known that my father was raised in a Russian orphanage, but he'd always refused to discuss it any further. Now I understood *why*. Mother wasn't the only one of my parents trying to protect me from the Game.

"Cat is the only other one who ever knew the rest of our story," Nim told me. "Sascha and I—who were parted at that moment in Krym—did not know it ourselves until many years later when, thanks to your mother, we met at last and we told it to each other and to her. Father had died shortly after he and I reached America. I'd lost my mother, my brother, and Minnie all in one night, with no way to trace them. As far as I knew until many years later, none of them had survived."

"But now we both *know* that your mother is alive," I said. "I can understand, if she'd been captured and put in prison as you thought, why she might have been incommunicado all those years. But she was *there* at Zagorsk ten years ago: She gave me this card. And now you think she sent you the chessboard, too. How did she get her hands on it? And why wait so long?"

"I haven't all the answers yet," Nim admitted. "But I do have one answer, I believe. To understand it, you would have to know the famous fable of The Firebird that appears on your card, and what it means to us Russians."

"What does the Firebird mean?" I said, though I thought I had my first inkling.

"It might explain why my mother still lives, how she survived," Nim told me. When I looked surprised, he added, "What if Minnie *did* manage to locate our mother after leaving Sascha in that orphanage? What if Minnie found her in prison just as we'd all supposed—about to be sacrificed by the Soviet authorities as another casualty of the Game? What would Minnie have exchanged to secure our mother's release?"

I didn't have to ask. There was only one item I knew of that was definitely in the hands of the Russians.

"The Black Queen!" I cried.

"My thinking exactly," said Nim with a pleased smile. "And this would especially make sense if Minnie had managed to create a copy of the queen and had retained the original herself! It would explain the double-queen gambit you've discovered."

"But then, where did your mother disappear after her release? And how did she get that drawing of the chessboard you said she'd sent you?" I asked. "You said you thought you'd solved that puzzle, too."

"That drawing of the chessboard by the Abbess of Montglane was a piece of the puzzle that we *know*, according to the nun Mireille's journal, she had in her possession," Nim explained. "But it was never passed on to Cat with the other pieces. Therefore, Minnie must have given it to someone else for safekeeping."

"To *your* mother!" I said.

"Wherever our mother has been all these years," said Nim, "there's one thing that's clear. That card she gave you and your father contained both a phoenix and a firebird. But it said *Beware the Fire.* The Firebird is nothing like the Phoenix, which bursts into flame each five hundred years and rises from its own ashes. The tale of the Phoenix is one of self-sacrifice and rebirth."

"Then what *does* the Firebird mean?" I said, breathless enough with anticipation that I was at risk of passing out yet again.

"It gives up its golden feather—something of enormous value, just like Minnie's Black Queen—in order to bring Prince Ivan, who's been killed by his ruthless brothers, back to life. When the Firebird appears, the message to be understood is: *Recalled to Life.*"

RECALLED TO LIFE

This is a secret service altogether. My credentials, entries and memoranda, are all comprehended in the one line, "Recalled to Life" . . .

—CHARLES DICKENS, *A Tale of Two Cities*

Remembering is for those who have forgotten.

—PLOTINUS

BRUMICH EEL, KYRIIN ELKONOMU (FIRE MOUNTAIN, DWELLING PLACE OF THE DEAD)

The sounds of rushing water seemed to have been with him always, night and day. Dolena Geizerov, the Valley of Geysers, the woman had told him. Healing waters created by fires beneath the earth. Waters that had brought him back to life.

Here in the meadow, high atop the cliffs, lay those steaming, silent pools that he'd been bathed in by the elders. Their milky, opaque waters from deep in the earth, variously colored by the layers of dissolved clay, shone in rich tones, vermillion, flamingo, ocher, lemon, peach, each with its own medicinal properties.

Far beneath him on the sheer rock cliff water bubbled within the sinkhole, growing more and more agitated—until suddenly, Velikan the Giant erupted in a steam explosion, shocking him as it always did, spewing its powerful rainbow of steaming water thirty feet into the air. Then on down the canyon as far as the eye could see, one by one they went off as if synchronized by clockwork and gushed over the sides, their boiling waterfalls tumbling into the torrential river far below that rushed onward to the sea. This constant throbbing, deafening roar of the explosive surge of waters was nonetheless somehow strangely soothing, he thought—rhythmic like life, like the breath of the earth itself.

But now as he moved diagonally up the uneven slope to higher ground, he took care to follow in the woman's tracks so he wouldn't fall. One couldn't maintain footing across this slippery slope of mud and wet rock. Though his high-laced moccasins were made of bearskin for a better grip, and the oiled fur tops kept them warm, snow was sifting through the limpid sunlight. The tumultuous clouds of steam from below melted the flakes even before they touched the ground, turning the wet mosses and lichens to a gummy paste.

He'd walked these ravines every day for months until he was strong enough for this trip. But he knew he was still weak for so long a trek as today's would be—they'd already come seven versts through the canyon of geysers, and higher still lay the tundra, meadowlands, and the taiga, a tangle of slender birch, scrub spruce, and pine. They were now moving into terra incognita.

As they left the roaring waters behind, climbing higher into the mountains, into the silence of a new and snowy world, he felt the fear begin to grip him—the fear that comes with emptiness, uncertainty about the unknown.

It was foolish of him to feel that way, he knew, when after all, to him everything was part of the void, that greater unknown. He'd long ago stopped asking where he was, or how long he had been here. He'd even ceased asking who he was. She'd told him that no one could provide that answer for him—that it was important he should discover it on his own.

But as they reached the end of the steep ravine, the

woman stopped and side by side they gazed out across the valley. He saw it there in the distance across the valley floor—their destination: that enormous cone far across the valley, all dressed in snow, which seemed to arise from nowhere like a mystical pyramid viewed across an ancient plain. The volcano had deep runnels in the sides and the top was crushed in, with smoke pouring out as if it had recently been struck by lightning.

He felt a kind of fascinated awe at the sight, a mixture of terror and love, as if a forceful hand had just gripped his heart. And the blinding light had suddenly, unexpectedly returned.

"In the Kamchal tongue, it is called Brumich Eel—Mountain of Fire," the woman beside him was saying. "It is one of more than two hundred volcanoes here on this peninsula, called apagachuch, the excitable ones, for many of these are always active. A single explosion of one has lasted for twenty-four hours, pouring lava, destroying trees, and followed by earthquake and tidal wave.

"This one, Mount Kamchatka, Klyutchevskaya in Russian, erupted just ten years ago, raining ash and embers more than one vershok deep over everything. The Chukchi shamans to the north of here believe it is the sacred mountain of the dead. The dead live inside the cone and they hurl rocks down at anyone who should try to approach them. They plunge beneath the mountain, under the sea. The summit is covered with bones of the whales they have devoured."

He could barely see across the valley, the fire in his head had grown so bright—nearly obliterating everything else.

"Why did the elders believe that you must bring me to that place?" he asked her, squeezing his eyes shut.

But the light was still there. And then he began to see.

"I am not taking you there," she said. "We are going

together. Each of us owes our own tribute to the dead. For we have each been recalled to life."

ON THE SUMMIT, *at the very lip of the collapsed cone, they could look down within to the molten lake of hot lava that bubbled and seethed inside. Sulfurous fumes floated skyward. Some said they were poisonous.*

It had taken two days to reach this spot, fifteen thousand feet above the sea. It was now after twilight, and as the moon rose above the waters of the ocean in the far distance, a dark shadow slowly began to creep across its milky white surface.

"This eclipse of the moon is why we have come here tonight," the woman spoke beside him. "This is our gift to the dead—the eclipse of the past for those in this pit, that they may sleep in peace. For they shall never again have a present or a future, as we ourselves shall."

"But how will I have a future—or even a present," he asked in fear, "when I can remember nothing at all of my past?"

"Can you not?" the woman said softly. She'd reached inside her fur-lined vest and extracted something small. "Can you remember this?" she asked, holding it out to him in the palm of her hand.

Just at that moment, the last of the moon was eaten by shadow and they were cast temporarily into darkness. There was only that awful red glow from the pit beneath.

But he'd seen that flash of fire again in his head—and he'd suddenly seen something else. His glimpse had been long enough that he knew exactly what that object had been in her palm.

It was the black queen from a chessboard.

"You were there," he said. "There at the monastery. There was going to be a game—and then just before—"

The rest he couldn't remember. But in that flash, as he'd looked at the black queen, he had caught just a glimpse of his own past as well. And now he knew one thing beyond doubt.

"My name is Sascha," he said. "And you are my mother, Tatiana."

THE KEY

There are seven keys to the great gate,
Being eight in one and one in eight.
—Aleister Crowley, *AHA*

I STILL COULDN'T FIND THE KEY, THOUGH NIM'S story last night had resolved a few paradoxes for me.

If Minnie had a duplicate Black Queen that she'd used to secure Tatiana's release forty years ago, that would account for the second queen that had appeared before my father's eyes at Zagorsk.

If Minnie had given Tatiana the abbess's drawing of the chessboard to protect, that would explain why that important ingredient had been missing from my mother's final cache of pieces.

I couldn't forget that this same key piece of the puzzle was currently sewn up inside my feathery jacket. Nor could I forget that first encrypted clue I'd received from my mother in Colorado, the clue I'd had to unravel before I could even unlock our house—those square numbers that resolved themselves into that final message: *The chessboard provides the key.*

But despite all my uncle's solutions and resolutions last night, there were still too many questions on one side and too few answers on the other.

So while Nim did the breakfast dishes, I whipped out my paper and pen to jot down what I still needed to know.

For starters, it wasn't only answers that were missing. My mother *herself* was missing, and apparently my newly discovered grandmother had vanished, too. Where were they? What role did each of them play? And what role did everyone else play in this Game?

But when I looked at my notes, I realized I was still missing the larger point: whom to trust?

For instance, my aunt Lily. When I'd last seen her, she'd offered as part of her "strategy" to try to sleuth out the chess and, possibly, the underworld connections of Basil Livingston—a man with whom, she'd failed to mention, she might have far more than a nodding acquaintance. After all, Basil was a chess organizer, wasn't he? And these past two years since her grandfather's death, when Lily had left New York, she'd been living in London—Basil's second home. Now, several days after I'd departed Colorado, Lily still hadn't reported in on that mysterious late-night meeting of hers I'd learned about, in Denver, with Basil's daughter, Sage.

Then there was Vartan Azov, who'd graciously agreed to check out the Taras Petrossian connection, mentioning only later that the very person he was to "investigate" was actually his late stepfather. If Petrossian had indeed been poisoned in London, as Vartan seemed to believe, it was odd he'd never mentioned what Rosemary Livingston subsequently told me: that Vartan was sole heir to Petrossian's estate.

Then Rosemary herself, who had given away more than she'd gotten from me last night. For instance, that she seemed to spend as much time not just in D.C., but in London, as her hubby, Basil, did. That they could be whisked inconspicuously from one part of the globe to another without even changing clothes, much less filing a flight plan. That they could command their own private, State-level dinner replete with the requisite security, for guests who operated at the highest echelons of international wealth and power. And of infinitely more interest: that they'd been on a first-name basis with the late Taras Petrossian and his stepson, Vartan Azov, ever since Vartan was "just a boy."

Last but not least was that feisty Basque, my boss, Rodolfo Boujaron, who seemed to know more than he was letting on about everything and maybe every*one*. There was his unique Basque pedigree for the Game itself and the background of Montglane, which no one else had mentioned. But there was also his foreknowledge of my mother's birthday *boum,* and his mention of the meaning of our birth dates—a strange idea that no one else had suggested, that she and I might be imagined, by some, to be on opposing teams.

In reviewing what I'd written while Nim was still splashing in the kitchen, I jotted down some ancillary characters like Nokomis and Sage or Leda and Eremon—people I knew well, but who were likely only pawns in the Game, bit players if they were players at all.

However, an unknown quantity emerged from this picture, one that stuck out on the page like the proverbial sore thumb: the only person of all those my mother had invited to her birthday *boum* whom I'd never heard of prior to the party.

Galen March.

But then, as I tried to go over in my mind the events of that day, and his role in them, something struck me for the first time: No one else had really seemed to know him all that well, either!

It's true that the Livingstons had arrived with Galen and introduced him as a "new neighbor," and that he'd later hopped a ride on their plane to Denver along with Sage. But I now recalled that at dinner last Friday he'd actually spent his time asking *other* people questions, as if it were the first time he'd ever met any of them. Indeed, it seemed I had it only on *his* word that he'd ever met my mother either! What was his connection, if any, to the recent death of Taras Petrossian? Yes, further research was definitely called for on the highly improbable owner of Sky Ranch.

Of course, when it came to Nim, I knew that in these past hours together, my normally enigmatic uncle had opened his bosom and his wounds to me, probably more than to anyone else in his life. I needn't ask how he broke into my place last night, for I was sure he'd done it the same way he'd entertained me through my childhood: He could crack almost any safe or pick any lock. But I would have to probe a bit further into other topics. There were still a few open questions to which perhaps only Nim could provide the answers.

Even though my inquiries might just lead to a long trail of red herrings, it was worth at least checking to see if any of them might prove to be real bait. For instance:

When had Nim first lured my mother into the Game, as he'd told me he had? And why?

What did Mother's birth date—or mine—have to do with our roles?

What were those jobs with the U.S. government that my uncle told me he'd helped to arrange for my parents, even before I was born? Why had they never discussed their work in front of me?

And more to the recent point, back in Colorado: How had my mother come up with all those clues and puzzles she'd left for me, if Nim hadn't helped provide them?

I was about to jot a few more thoughts on my list when Nim arrived in the living room, drying his hands on the towel he'd tucked into his waistband.

"Now down to business," he said. "I agreed to the demands of that employer of yours that I release you into his custody before nightfall," adding with his wry smile, "Do you work the swing shift, or is there some vampirism involved?"

"Rodo's a bloodsucker, all right," I agreed. "Which

reminds me, you've never met anyone from Sutalde, right?"

"Except for that meals-on-wheels wench this morning—the platinum blonde on Rollerblades who delivered your breakfast makings," he told me. "But we never met. She left them in the downstairs hall and departed before I could proffer any gratuity."

"That's Leda, she's the cocktail manager. But no one else?" I said. "You've never set foot inside Sutalde or seen the stone ovens?"

Nim shook his head. "There's some mystery about the place, I take it?"

"A few dangling plot elements I need to pull together," I told him. "Yesterday morning in my absence, someone set up the rotisserie spit there incorrectly, so that burnt lard got baked onto the hearth. That's never happened before—the place is like boot camp—yet Rodo didn't seem at all fazed. And the night before, when I got home here after midnight, someone had left the April seventh edition of the *Washington Post,* with a note, at my door downstairs. That wasn't you?"

Nim raised a brow and removed his kitchen towel. "Do you still have that note and the paper? I'd like to have a look."

I rummaged around in one of my baskets of books and extracted the *Post* for him, with its yellow stickie still attached.

"See?" I pointed out. "The note says *See page A1*. I think the headline is the key: *Troops, Tanks Attack Central Baghdad.* It's all about U.S. troops' entry into Baghdad—the very place where the chess service was first created. Then it mentions that the invasion itself began a little over two weeks earlier, the very day when my mother phoned in all those birthday invitations and the Game was launched once more. I think whoever left that newspaper for me was trying to point out that these two things—Baghdad and the Game—have somehow been reconnected, perhaps very much as they were twelve hundred years ago."

"That's not all," Nim interjected. He'd folded back the paper while I spoke and skimmed the rest of the article. Now he glanced up at me and added, "I believe that the saying is, 'The Devil is in the details.' "

He and Key would have made a fine pair, I thought.

But aloud I said, "Do embellish."

"This article goes on to describe what the invading troops had done to secure the area. There is, however, an interesting remark further along about a 'convoy of Russian diplomats' departing the city. The convoy was accidentally strafed by American forces, and several were injured. Yet U.S. Central Command claimed no U.S. or British forces were operating in the area at the time, the obvious question being—" He raised his brow again, this time to urge my response.

"Um—was someone actually after the Russians?" I hazarded a guess.

Without a direct reply, Nim handed me the *Post*, folded back to page 1 again. "That's *still* not all. Read further," he suggested, pointing to another article I hadn't noticed before:

At Airport, Probe Leads Army to Secret Room

I scanned it quickly. In a "VIP terminal" at Baghdad airport, apparently U.S. soldiers had found what they "suspect was a hideaway for president Saddam Hussein. Elaborately appointed, it has a carved mahogany door, gold-plated bathroom fixtures and a verandah opening onto a rose garden. But its most intriguing feature is a wood-paneled office with a false door that leads to a basement room." The troops found weapons there.

"But," the article went on, "they believe there is something more: a secret exit."

"A secret departure terminal, a secret room, a secret exit, and a convoy of Russians the source of whose injuries is unaccounted for. What does this tell us?" said Nim, when he saw that I'd finished reading.

I remembered my uncle's enjoinder to me when I was young, never to overlook the obvious point that whatever was done could also be undone, in chess as in life: the "Vice Versa Factor," as he liked to call it. It seemed he wished to invoke the factor here.

"What goes out can also come in?" I suggested.

"Precisely," he said, with a look that somehow managed to mix satisfaction at finding something important with concern about what he'd inadvertently uncovered. "And what or whom do you suppose might have come *into* Baghdad through that secret terminal, that secret room, that secret exit—and might also have left by the same route only shortly before the invasion? Only shortly before your mother sent her party invitations?"

"You mean something arrived there from Russia?" I asked.

Nim nodded and went over to get his trench coat. He pulled from his pocket the same wallet as before, but this time he opened the wallet and extracted a piece of folded paper. He unfolded it and handed it over to me.

"I rarely search on the Web, as you know," my uncle told me. "But thanks to your mother's foolishness with that gathering of hers, this time I felt it might be important to do so."

Nim's Vice Versa Factor, supported by his thirty years as a computer technocrat, had convinced him never to surf anything. "If you're investigating *them*," he'd told me often enough, "they're likely also investigating *you*."

The bit of paper he'd handed me was the smeared printout of a press release, dated March 19, from a

Russian news agency I'd never heard of. It began by announcing the "Christian-Islamic peacemaking mission" that had just returned to Russia from Baghdad. The rest was a real eye-opener.

Among the luminaries—which included Russian Orthodox bishops, a Supreme Mufti, and head of the Russian Muslim council—was a name I might have known, had I still been a player in the world of chess. It was a cinch, however, that everyone *else* at Mother's dinner must have known it: Kirsan Ilyumzhinov, president of the Russian republic of Kalmykia, and a self-made billionaire at the age of forty.

Of more immediate import, however, was the interesting fact that his excellency, the president of the little-known republic of Kalmykia, was also the current president of FIDE, the World Chess Federation, not to mention the highest bankroller in the history of the game. He'd sponsored tourneys in Las Vegas, and even built a chess city, with checkerboard streets and buildings shaped like pieces, in his own hometown!

I stared at my uncle, rendered totally speechless. This guy made Taras Petrossian and Basil Livingston look like a pair of patzers. Could he be for real?

"Whoever strafed that convoy of diplomats yesterday made their move a bit too late," Nim told me grimly. "Whatever might once have been hidden in Baghdad certainly has been removed by now. Your mother must have known that; it would even explain why she threw her party with the odd guest list you've described. Whoever has left this newspaper on your doorstep Monday before dawn must have known it, too. I think we had best review your mother's list of invitees a bit more closely."

I handed my notes to him, and he scrutinized everything. Then he sat beside me on the sofa and flipped to a fresh page on my yellow pad.

"Let's begin with this chap, March," he said. "You've spelled his first name G-A-L-E-N, but if you use the Gaelic spelling, it works perfectly." He printed the name. Then beneath it he wrote each letter in alphabetical order, like so:

Gaelen March
aa c ee g h l m n r

This was a game we'd played when I was small—name anagrams. But practiced though I might be, I was no match for my uncle. The moment he'd unscrambled the anagram in writing for me, I looked up at him in horror.

It read: *Charlemagne.*

"Not very tactful, is it?" Nim said with a grimace. "Giving away your hand and your likely agenda, along with your calling card."

I couldn't believe it! Galen March had not only moved up my list of suspicious figures in this Game—he'd just landed smack on top!

But Nim hadn't quite finished. "Naturally, given the medieval saga that your Basque employer spun for you yesterday, this would suggest to us some connection between him and your new neighbor," he said, studying my sheet of notes in more detail. "And speaking of Monsieur Boujaron, the sooner you learn what he has to tell you, the better. From these observations you've written here, I suspect that whatever he knows may prove quite important. Since I failed to inquire, will he be coming by here for his postponed meeting with you tonight?"

"I forgot to tell you," I said, "now that our morning appointment was deferred, I don't know if I'll even see him today. Rodo normally cooks on the dinner shift and I work the fires on the graveyard shift after he's left for the night. That's why he wanted to be sure I was available tonight. I should phone and find out when we can reschedule our talk."

But when I glanced around, I noticed that the living room phone seemed to have vanished from its place, as well. I went over and grabbed my shoulder bag from the table where I'd left it, and I rummaged around until I found my cell phone to call Rodo. But before I'd even flipped the cover open to power it on, Nim crossed the room and snatched it from my hand.

"Where did you get this?" he snapped. "How long have you had it?"

I stared at him. "A few years, I guess," I said, confused. "Rodo insists on having us all at his beck and call."

But Nim had put his finger to my lips. Now he went to retrieve the yellow pad and scribbled something. He handed both the pad and pencil to me with a sharp look. Then he studied my phone that he still held in his palm.

"Write your answers," his scrawl read. *"Has anyone recently handled this phone but yourself?"*

I started to shake my head, when in horror I recalled exactly who *had,* and I cursed myself. *"The Secret Service,"* I wrote. *"Last night."*

And they'd held on to it for hours—enough time to plant a bomb or anything else, I thought.

"Have I taught you nothing, all these years?" Nim muttered beneath his breath when he saw my message. Then he scribbled again, *"Did you use it at all, after it was returned?"*

I was once again about to reply in the negative, when I realized that I had.

"Only once, to phone Rodo," I wrote, and handed back the pad.

Nim put his hand briefly over his eyes and shook his head. Then he wrote on the pad again. This time it took so long that I was on tenterhooks. But when I actually read it, my breakfast did a swift toss in my stomach and threatened to land in my throat.

"*Then you've activated it, too,*" Nim had written. "*When they seized it, they got every phone number, message, or code. All now in their possession. If you've turned it on even once since then, they've overheard all that we've said in this room, too.*"

Good God, how could this be happening?

I was about to write more, but Nim grabbed my arm and ushered me to the kitchen sink, where he tore all our notes into shreds, including my earlier observations, lit a match, and burned them. He washed the ashes down through the garbage disposal.

"You can phone Boujaron in a moment," he said aloud. Without a word, we left the phone on the table and went downstairs and outside.

"It's too late now," my uncle told me. "I'm not sure what they've heard, but we can't let on that *we* know they've learned anything. At this moment, we must take everything of value out of your place with us, and get to someplace where we can't be overheard. Only then can we try to reassess the situation sanely."

Why hadn't I thought of that phone first thing this morning, the moment he'd told me why he'd removed the others? Whatever we'd said on the bridge last night might be safe, maybe even our breakfast chat, which was in another room. But what had we said this morning, in the vicinity of the cell phone? I felt my hysteria rising.

"Oh," I said with tears in my eyes, "I'm so sorry, Uncle Slava. It's all my fault."

Nim put one arm around me, drew me to him, and kissed my hair as he had when I was tiny. "Don't worry," he said softly. "But I'm afraid this does alter our timetable a bit."

"Our timetable?" I said, looking up at him, his face blurry.

"It means," he said, "that no matter what amount of time we *thought* we had to find your mother, we now haven't any."

TOO MANY QUEENS

Dark conspiracies, secret societies, midnight meetings of desperate men, impossible plots—these were the order of the day . . .

—DUFF COOPER, *Talleyrand*

VALENÇAY, THE LOIRE VALLEY
JUNE 8, 1823

Only in France can one know the full horror of provincial life.

—TALLEYRAND

CHARLES-MAURICE DE TALLEYRAND-PÉRIGORD, Prince de Bénévent, sat in the small pony cart wedged between the two little children who were dressed in their linen gardening tunics and big straw hats. They were following the servants and Talleyrand's recently returned chef, Carême, who went before them through the herb and vegetable gardens with baskets and cutting shears, letting the children help select the fresh produce and flowers for this evening's dinner and table decorations as they did each morning. For Talleyrand it was customary never to dine with fewer than sixteen at the table.

As Carême pointed his scissors at various bushes and vines, nasturtiums and purple rhubarb and small artichokes and bunches of fragrant bay leaves and small colorful squashes toppled into the servants' baskets. Talleyrand smiled as the children clapped their small hands.

Maurice's gratitude knew no bounds for the fact that

Carême had agreed to come to Valençay, and for a number of reasons. It was only coincidence, however, that today was Carême's birthday. He'd told the children that he was preparing a special surprise for dessert tonight, for himself as well as for them—a pièce montée, one of those architecturally designed constructions of moulded and spun sugar for which he'd first become internationally famous.

Antonin Carême was today the most celebrated chef in Europe, made even more famous with the publication, last autumn, of his book *Maître d'Hôtel Français,* more than a cookbook in its scholarly erudition, for in it he compared both ancient and modern cuisines and explained the importance of foods in various cultures as connected with each of the four seasons. He drew many of his examples from the twelve years of early experience he'd garnered as chef in Talleyrand's kitchens, both in Paris and especially here at Valençay, where he'd prepared, with Talleyrand's intimate involvement, a separate menu for each day of each and every year.

Having served in the intervening years as master chef to other luminaries—including the Prince of Wales at Brighton; Lord Charles Stewart, the British ambassador at Vienna; and Alexander I, tsar of Russia—Carême had now returned, at Talleyrand's insistent request, to spend these few summer months recuperating at Valençay while his new employers finished renovating their palace in Paris. Then, despite the serious lung ailment from which all chefs of his era suffered, he would assume his tasks as master chef to the only people who could afford his full-time employment—James and Betty de Rothschild.

This morning's jaunt through the twenty-five acres of kitchen gardens with Carême and the children was just a pretext, of course, though morning outings like this had long been a favorite custom here at Valençay.

But this morning was special in many ways, for one,

because Maurice Talleyrand, at nearly seventy, dearly loved spending time like this with his nephews' children, two-year-old Charles-Angélique, Charlotte's child by his nephew Alexandre, and Edmond and Dorothée's daughter Pauline—little "Minette"—who was nearly three and whom he called his guardian angel.

Maurice had no legitimate children of his own. Charlotte herself, mother of little Charles-Angélique, was the beloved adopted daughter of "unknown parentage" whom Maurice had mysteriously brought back, nearly twenty years ago, from his annual trip to the spa at Bourbon-l'Archambault, and whom he and Madame Talleyrand had subsequently raised, treating her as their own and spoiling her as best they could. They dressed Charlotte in fancy costumes, Spanish, Polish, Neapolitan, gypsy attire, and threw fancy *bals d'enfants* that were all the talk of Paris, where the children learned to dance boleros, mazurkas, and tarantellas.

But in these twenty years, how everything had changed—Maurice himself most of all. In those years of royalty, revolution, negotiation, diplomacy, and flight, he'd served so many governments: the French parliament under Louis XVI, the Directory, the Consulate and the Empire under Napoleon. He'd even served as Regent of France himself, until the restoration of Louis XVIII.

Meanwhile, the Game itself had had as many fluctuations of fortune. Maurice's erstwhile wife, the Princesse de Talleyrand, the former Catherine Noel Worlée Grand—the White Queen—was by now long gone. Nearly eight years ago, at a time when Talleyrand himself had been taken by surprise, stranded at the Congress of Vienna with other heads of state, all believing they were dividing up Europe, Napoleon had escaped from Elba and returned in triumph to Paris to rule for his infamous Hundred Days. Catherine herself had fled from Paris to London with her Spanish lover. Maurice now paid her a stipend never to return closer than twenty kilometers to Paris.

The Game was over, and with Maurice's help the Black Team had captured the preponderance of pieces. Napoleon was deposed and dead. And the Bourbons—a family, as Maurice said, that had learned nothing and forgotten nothing—was now restored to power under Louis XVIII, a king who was himself seduced and ruled by the Ultras, that party of sinister men who wished to turn back the clock and revoke the constitution of France and all that the Revolution had stood for.

And now Maurice himself was put out to pasture, too—paid off with the meaningless title "High Chancellor" and a stipend, but removed from politics, living here a two days' journey from Paris, at his palatial forty-thousand-acre estate in the Loire Valley, a gift, so many years ago, of the emperor Napoleon.

Put to pasture, perhaps—but not alone. Dorothée de Courland, the former Duchess of Dino and one of the richest women in Europe, whom he'd married to his nephew Edmond when she was just sixteen, had remained Maurice's life companion ever since Vienna. Except, of course, for her brief public reconciliation with Edmond only months before Pauline was born.

But Maurice had come here to the kitchen gardens with the children this morning for another, more important, reason: desperation. He sat in the pony cart between the two children—his natural daughter Pauline, "Minette," by his beloved "Petite Marmousin," Dorothée, the Duchess of Dino. And little Charles-Angélique, the child of his other natural daughter, Charlotte. And he experienced an emotion that he felt hard-pressed to describe, even within the confines of his own mind.

He'd felt it for days now, as if something frightening were about to happen, something life-altering, something strange: a feeling that was neither joy nor bitterness, a feeling more like a sense of loss.

And yet, it might prove to be exactly the opposite.

Maurice had felt passion in the arms of many women, including his wife. And he felt a caring, almost avuncular love for Pauline's mother, Dorothée, now thirty, who'd shared his life and his bed these past eight years. But the sense of loss Maurice felt, as he knew very well, was for the one woman he'd ever deeply loved: Charlotte's mother.

Mireille.

He'd had to conceal from his darling Charlotte her mother's very existence, due to the dangers ever present—even now that this round of the Game was over. He had only the vaguest sense of what it might have meant if Mireille had stayed, if she'd abandoned that mission that had so consumed her. If she'd forgotten all about the Montglane Service, and that bloody, horrible, life-destroying Game. What might his life have been like, if only she'd remained beside him? If they'd married? If they'd raised their two children together?

Their *two* children. There. It was out at last.

That was why Maurice had insisted, this morning, upon taking little Charles-Angélique and Minette for a drive in their pony cart to look at the plants and flowers. An ordinary outing with one's family—something Maurice had never experienced, even when he himself had been a child. He wondered what it would feel like if these children were *their* children—his and Mireille's.

He'd only felt an inkling of it once—that single night, twenty years ago now, when Mireille had met him in the steamy baths at Bourbon-l'Archambault. That night of radiant joy for Maurice, when he'd seen their two children together for the very first time.

That night, twenty years ago, when Mireille had

agreed at last to give over little Charlotte to Maurice, so the child might be raised by her natural father.

That night, twenty years ago, when Mireille had departed with their ten-year-old son, a boy whom Maurice had come to believe he would never see again on this earth.

But that belief had now been irrevocably dispelled, just two nights ago, when he'd received that letter by midnight post.

Maurice reached into his blouse and extracted the paper—a letter dated three days ago, from Paris.

Sire:

I must see you on a matter of extreme importance to us both.

I have just learned that you are not in residence at Paris.

I shall come to you at Valençay in three days' time.

Yours obediently,
Charlot

HERE AT VALENÇAY, the lavish house with its many domes was built into the back of the hill so that the kitchens, instead of being dungeons, were flooded with light and looked out upon the rose gardens, the billowing branches laden with pastel petals.

Maurice Talleyrand sat there in a garden chair, just out-of-doors, where he could enjoy the scent of the roses and still observe the process under way inside. Though he'd seen Carême perform this magic so often in the past, he could almost describe it blindfolded. It had always been his favorite.

Maurice himself had spent many hours with many chefs in many kitchens. One of his greatest pleasures had always rested upon the planning and enjoyment of a meal, especially in his profession. For Maurice considered a well-planned meal the greatest lubricant to successful and well-oiled diplomacy. At the Congress of Vienna, his only message to his new master, Louis XVIII, back in Paris, had been, "Here, we have more need of casseroles than of instructions." And Carême had provided them all.

But tonight's meal, as Maurice well understood, might prove the most difficult and delicately balanced of his own long and distinguished career. Tonight—for the first time in nearly twenty years—he would see his son. He and Charlot, no longer a boy, would have many critical questions to ask, many things to reveal to each other.

But the only one who might have *all* the answers to even the most vital of their questions, as Maurice knew, was the man he himself had insisted upon bringing here to Valençay, the very moment he'd received that letter: A man who'd been close to Maurice's heart, had earned his trust, and knew many of those secrets. A man who, as a child, had been rejected by his own family yet gone on to stellar success—just as Maurice had, on both counts. A man who'd carried out Maurice's missions behind the scenes these many years throughout the courts of Europe. A man who'd been closest to being Maurice's son—in spirit, if not in flesh.

This was the man who was now entertaining the kitchen staff in the cuisine just beyond these windows, while preparing what they'd planned for the children's dinner.

He was the only one living, except Maurice himself, who knew the entire story.

It was the famous chef, Marie-Antoine, "Antonin," Carême.

THE COPPER POT of melted sugar bubbled on the stove. Carême swirled it gently before the attentive eyes of the children and the kitchen staff of more than thirty, all riveted by the aura of the great maître d'hôtel, the master chef. With the aid of only young Kimberly, his apprentice from Brighton, Carême proceeded. He sprinkled a bit of tartar into the boiling molten sugar, and the bubbles grew large and porous, as if made of glass.

It was nearly ready.

Then the maître did something that always astonished those who were unfamiliar with the art of the pâtissier. He plunged his bare hand into a nearby bowl of ice water that had been prepared for the occasion, then quickly plunged the hand into the volcanic sugar, then back once more into the ice water. The children squealed in horror, and many among the crowd of scullions gasped.

Then he took his sharp knife as well, plunged it into the molten sugar, then into the ice water, and it cracked from the knife. "*Bien!*" Carême announced to his astonished audience. "We are ready to spin!"

For more than an hour, the group watched in silence as the maître, with young Kimberly quickly handing him his implements, performed the work of a skilled surgeon, a master stonemason, and an architect all in one.

Scalding sugar flew from the copper spout to the waiting mould. It swirled around the inside of the mould, which had been precoated with fragrant nut-oil so that it would later release its cooled form. Then, when all the various moulds had been filled and the requisite shapes created, the master—using the spinning forks he'd designed himself—threw sparkling ribbons of sugar into the air like a Venetian glassblower, twisted them into the plaited ropes called *cheveux d'anges*, angels' hair, and cut them into long, columnar pieces.

Talleyrand watched through the windows from the

rose garden. When Carême had finished the most difficult and dangerous part of the process, from which he must not be distracted, and the pieces were all hardened like rock crystal, Maurice entered the kitchen and took a seat near the children.

He knew so well, after Carême's years in his service, that the garrulous chef would not be able to resist this large audience for much longer, pontificating upon his skills and knowledge, despite the strain this exercise had already taken upon his clearly fragile health. And Maurice wanted to hear what he would say.

Maurice watched with the others as Carême began his assembly by melting the tips of each section against hot coals from the brazier, so it would stick to the other parts with its own sugary glue. But each time he bent over the coals and breathed the smoke, he could hardly suppress his coughing, the curse of his profession: black lung from constant enclosure with charcoal fumes. Kimberly poured some champagne, which Carême sipped as he worked. And as he assembled his myriad pieces, and little by little a complex and fascinating structure began to emerge, the chef at last cleared his throat to speak to the prince and his staff.

"You have all heard the tale of my life," Carême began, "how, like the story of Cendrillon, my journey went from the ashes of obscurity to the palaces of Europe. How, as a ragged child who'd been abandoned by my father at the gates of Paris, I was first discovered and put into the service of the noted pâtissier, Bailly. And how I eventually came to serve beneath Prince Talleyrand's chef, the great Boucher, formerly of the house of Condé."

The very mention of the name Boucher had always struck awe throughout the kitchens of Europe. For all knew that Boucher was once the renowned maître d'hôtel to the Prince de Condé, scion of one of the most powerful families in France.

Following in a long line of Condé chefs—beginning with the almost legendary Vâtel, who'd committed suicide by falling on his sword when the seafood failed to arrive in time for a banquet—Boucher himself had for years trained apprenticed scullions and sous-chefs in the Condé kitchens at both Paris and Chantilly. These men later went on to become master chefs in the great houses of Europe and America—including Thomas Jefferson's enslaved chef, James Hemings, who'd studied under Boucher's tutelage during the American diplomat's five-year tenure in France.

Then, when Louis-Joseph, the reigning Prince de Condé, had fled the country to lead an Austrian army against revolutionary France, it was Talleyrand who'd rescued his chef, Boucher, from the depredations of the mob and given him employment.

And then it was Boucher who'd discovered the young *tourtier*, the tart-maker, in Bailly's pastry shop and brought him to the attention of Monseigneur Talleyrand.

"Cinderella, yes indeed," added the master chef. "And with a name like mine, Carême—short for *quarantième*, the forty days of Lent that begin with *dies cinerum*, Ash Wednesday—one would imagine that I'd have been more interested in ashes and sackcloth, that is, in the ancient tradition of fasting, rather than the art of feasting!

"But from each of my great tutors and my patrons, I've discovered something most mysterious about the connection between these two things—feasting and fasting—and of their connection with fire. However, I get ahead of myself. First, it is of this creation that I am building now, for the prince and his guests and family tonight, that I wish to speak."

Carême glanced toward Talleyrand, who nodded for

him to continue. The chef rolled out a parchment with strange designs drawn upon it of arcs and lines, and he unmolded one of the sugar forms upon it, in the shape of an octagon perhaps one meter in diameter. Then one by one, he unmolded progressively smaller octagons and placed each atop the last, like stair steps. Lastly, with his tongs, he plucked up one of his twisted columns and touched it briefly to the coals, before resuming both his assembly process and his story.

"It was from Bailly, the master pâtissier, that I first learned the wonderful art of the *architecture* of cuisine," he said, "for he let me study by night and copy those designs of ancient buildings he'd borrowed from the print rooms of the Louvre. I came to understand that the fine arts are five in number, to wit: painting, sculpture, poetry, music, and architecture, whose highest expression is confectionary. I learned to draw, with the steady and skilled hand of a seasoned architect and geometrician, those structures of the ancients—Greece, Rome, Egypt, India, China—that one day I would create as architectural masterpieces in spun sugar, like this one.

"This is the greatest of the early structures, seminal to all that inspired Vitruvius. It is called the Tower of Winds, a famous tower of eight sides in Athens, containing a planetarium and an elaborate water clock, which Andronicus of Cyrrhus built one hundred years before Christ, and which is still standing today. Vitruvius tells us, 'Some have held that there are only four winds. . . . But more careful investigators tell us that there are eight.' Eight: a sacred number, for it lies at the root of the most ancient temple designs of Persia and India in deep antiquity."

Everyone watched closely, as the maître's fingers flew back and forth across the board with those architectural components he'd miraculously crafted himself. When he had finished the structure, it stood two meters high from the table and towered over all, an octagonal tower with astonishing detail, including grillework at the windows and the designs of frescoes around the top, representing the personae of the eight winds. Everyone in the room applauded, including the prince himself.

WHEN THE STAFF had returned to their duties, Talleyrand escorted the master chef into the gardens. "Yours is truly a remarkable achievement, as always," Talleyrand said. "But I have missed something, I fear, my dear Antonin. For just before you began your magical architectural reconstruction of what must surely be one of the most remarkable structures of early Greece, you'd mentioned some mystery that prompted you to build the Tour des Vents. It was something, I recall, to do with feast and famine—with Lenten sackcloth and ash? Though I confess, I still do not make the connection."

"Yes, your highness," said Carême, pausing only for a moment to look his patron and mentor in the eye. For they both knew what Talleyrand was secretly asking. "Vitruvius himself shows us how—by erecting a gnomon to track the sun and by using a compass to construct a simple circle—we can give birth to the octagon, the most sacred structure, as the ancients knew, for it is the divine intermediary between circle and square.

"In China, the octagon is the *Ba'gua,* the oldest form of divination. In India, the square of eight is called the *Ashtapada*—"the spider"—the oldest board game that we know of. It is also the base of the mandala upon which they construct the Hindu and Persian fire temples. Less known, but surely known to Vitruvius, is that these represent the earliest forms of the *altar* where the sacrifice was made, where things could be "altered"—where heaven was brought down to earth in ancient times, like lightning from the sky. During the eight fire festivals that took place each year, the fire sacrifice to God and the feast of the people were both one."

He added, "That is why the center of the house, the center of the temple, and the center of the city itself were called the *focus*—that is, the hearth. We chefs are all blessed. For to be a chef or magus, a master of fire, of the feast and sacrifice, was once the holiest profession."

But Carême could not go on. Despite the fresh air in the garden, or perhaps because of it, his chronic cough had returned to grasp him by the throat once more.

"You sacrifice *yourself* to that holy profession and those coals of yours, my friend," observed Talleyrand, raising a hand to call for a steward, who ran from the house with another coupe of champagne and gave it to the chef. When the servant had left, Talleyrand added, "You know why I have brought you here, of course?"

Carême nodded, still sipping the champagne as he tried to recover his breath.

"That's why I hastened to come, sire—though perhaps I ought not to have, for as you see, I am ill," he managed to choke out at last. "It's the woman, is it not? She has come back, somehow—the woman who came to Paris late that night, so many years ago, when I was first sous-chef under Boucher at your palace, the Hôtel Galliffet on the rue de Bac. That woman who later appeared at Bourbon-l'Archambault, with Charlotte. It's the woman for whom you've had me collect all those pieces. Mireille—"

"We must not speak of it openly, my trusted friend," Talleyrand interrupted. "You and I are the only people on earth who know the story. And though we must share it with someone quite soon—tonight, in fact—I wish you to save your strength for that encounter. You are the only one who may be in a position to help us, for as you are aware, you're the only one I have trusted to know the entire truth."

Carême nodded to indicate that he was once more prepared to serve the man he had always referred to as his greatest patron. And much more.

"Is the woman herself expected at Valençay tonight?" asked Carême.

"No. It is her son who arrives," said Talleyrand, placing his hand upon the chef's shoulder with unaccustomed familiarity. Then, after a long breath, he added softly, "That is—her son and mine."

MAURICE WANTED TO WEEP as he regarded his son for only the second time in his life. In a rush, it brought back the memory of all the bitterness that had followed their parting, so many years ago, at Bourbon-l'Archambault.

Now that the household had been fed and the children put to bed, Maurice sat and watched until the sunset had seeped into lavender twilight—his favorite time of the day. Yet his mind was filled with a thousand warring emotions.

Carême had left them alone to speak, but agreed he would soon rejoin them, along with a small cask of the aged Madeira and some of the answers they both were seeking.

Now Maurice gazed across the small garden table that the chef had provisioned for them beneath the boughs of an enormous linden tree within the park. He studied the romantic-looking young man that his own passion had produced more than thirty years ago. It was an astonishingly painful experience.

Charlot, just come from Paris and still in his riding

clothes, had only taken time to brush off the dust from the road and to put on a clean shirt and cravat. His coppery hair was pulled back onto his nape in a tidy queue, from which only a few unruly wisps had managed to escape. Even this small thing was so evocative of his mother's sweet-smelling mass of strawberry locks, in which Maurice could still remember burying his face whenever they had made love.

Before she'd left him.

But in all other details, as Maurice forced his thoughts back, he saw that Charlot more closely resembled his natural father: Those cold blue eyes that seemed to assure one that they would reveal none of their owner's innermost thoughts. That high brow, the strong cleft chin and retroussé nose were all marks of the long, noble line of the Talleyrands of Périgord. And those surprisingly sensual lips—it was a mouth that bespoke the born connoisseur of fine wines, beautiful women, all the voluptuary arts.

But his son, as Maurice had quickly discerned, could be none of those things.

When it came to bloodlines, that was why Maurice had followed Charlot's earlier request—when as a mere boy Charlot had suggested that his father arrange to marry Charlotte into Talleyrand's own family that she might not share her brother's fate. Thanks largely to the folly of his parents in not marrying, as an illegitimate child Charlot would never hold rights of primogeniture, even to inherit his father's own estates. Indeed—for there was little Maurice could do about it under French law—Charlot's physical features would likely be his chief inheritance through the noble line of Talleyrand-Périgord.

But even Charlot's features themselves, Maurice realized, seemed to rebel against their inborn disposition.

His mouth might suggest overt sensuality, but the set of it showed that inner determination that had manifested itself in bringing him here, from whatever distant land, for some critical purpose, a purpose that, from Charlot's expression, was clearly not his mother's, but his own.

And those eyes that at first glance had seemed so icy and self-contained. At their indigo depths Maurice discerned some secret, a mystery that, it was also clear, he'd traveled this distance prepared to share with his father, and no one else.

It was this alone that gave Maurice his first glimmer of hope that this visit, this reunion, perhaps after all would not prove to be what he'd been imagining and fearing, these past twenty years. And Maurice knew it was time for him to disclose something, too.

"My son," he began, "Antonin Carême will soon return to join us, as he must. For during those years when I had to perform certain critical tasks for your mother, Antonin was the man I trusted with my very life—with all our lives.

"Before he returns, though, while we are alone, let us speak frankly. It is long overdue. In my capacity as your natural father, I seek and beg your forgiveness. If I were not of the age I am, nor the disposition, I would go down upon one knee, at this very moment, and kiss your hand to implore you—"

But he stopped, for Charlot had leapt up and come around the table. He drew his father to his feet and kissed his two hands instead. Then he embraced him.

"I see what you are feeling, Father," he told him. "But you may rest in assurance, I am not here for what you believe."

Talleyrand looked at him, at first in shock, then with a guarded smile. "I'd quite forgotten that skill of yours," he admitted, "your ability to read thoughts or to prophesy."

"I'd nearly forgotten it *myself,*" Charlot said, returning his smile. "But I've not come hither to seek my sister Charlotte, as you seem to be fearing at this moment. No, as far as I am concerned—for I can see that you love Charlotte dearly and want to protect her—she needn't know anything about us at all. Nor need she, in future, ever have anything to do with the Montglane Service, or the Game."

"But I thought that the Game had ended!" cried Talleyrand. "It *cannot* begin again. To prevent it, Mireille permitted little Charlotte to be raised by me, where she'd be safe. Away from the service, away from the pieces—away from the Game! And away from the Black Queen—her mother—for that was the prophecy."

"The prophecy was wrong," said Charlot. He was no longer smiling, though he still held his father's hands in his own. "It appears that the Game has begun again."

"Again!" cried Talleyrand in horror. Then he lowered his voice, though there was no one about to hear. "But it was *you,* Charlot, who first told the prophecy. 'The Game will only begin again,' you said it had been foretold, 'when the opposite is born from the ashes.' How can you still claim your sister is safe if it's begun anew? You know that Charlotte's birthday, October 4, is just opposite that of your mother's—the Black Queen. Does that not mean, if a new Game should begin, that Charlotte would become the White Queen—just as we've all believed these many years?"

"I was mistaken," said Charlot softly. "The Game has begun again. White has made the first move and an important Black piece has surfaced."

"But . . ." muttered Talleyrand. "I don't understand."

As he saw Carême head back across the lawn, Talleyrand sank to his seat once more, looked up at Charlot, and added, "With the assistance of Antonin Carême inside those households and palaces, we'd collected nearly all of the pieces from Russia and Britain! My wife, Madame Grand, the White Queen, is decommissioned, her forces disbanded or dead! Mireille's been in hiding for years, where no one can find her or the pieces. Yet you say it's begun again? How could White make a move, and yet Charlotte still be safe? What important Black piece could the other team possibly possess that we haven't captured?"

"That is precisely what I've come here to discover from you and Carême," said Charlot, kneeling beside his father on the grass. "But I know it's true, for I have seen it myself. I've seen the new White Queen, just a slip of a girl, but with great power behind her. I've held in my hands the valuable chess piece the White Team has captured, and which she now possesses. That piece is the Black Queen of the Montglane Service."

"Impossible!" cried Talleyrand. "That's the piece that Antonin brought back with his own hands from Alexander of Russia! It belonged to the Abbess of Montglane herself. Alexander had promised to secure it for your mother, Mireille, long before he ever became tsar. And he kept that promise!"

"I know," said Charlot. "I helped my mother hide it when it was first retrieved from Russia. But the one the White Team has seems to have been hidden longer. That's what I've come hither to discover—in hopes that Carême might help us find a clue as to how there could possibly be *two* Black Queens."

"But if the Game has begun anew, as you say," said Talleyrand, "if the White Team has suddenly surfaced with this powerful piece and made their first move, why did they take you into their confidence? Why did they show it to *you*?"

"Don't you see, Father?" said Charlot. "That's what was wrong with my interpretation of the prophecy. The

White Team *has* arisen from the ashes of its opposite. But not in the way I'd imagined. I couldn't see it, for it involved me, myself."

When Talleyrand still looked mystified, Charlot added, "Father, I am the new White King."

THE FOUR SEASONS

Seminate aurum vestrum in terram albam foliatum. *'Sow your gold in the white foliated earth.' Alchemy (often called 'Celestial Agriculture') borrows numerous analogies from farming . . . the epigram . . . stresses the need to observe 'as in a mirror' the lesson of the grain of wheat . . . the excellent treatise (Secretum) published in Leyden in 1599 . . . compared the operations of wheat farming in detail to the operations of the alchemical Work.*

—Stanislas Klossowski de Rola, *The Golden Game*

We were out of time, according to Nim. The enemy—whoever he might be—now had the inside track. I'd placed my missing mother and the rest of us in danger. And all because I'd been a complete nitwit and ignored the warning signals, though they'd been flashing as brightly as semiphores on the tarmac, as Key would say.

And what about me? Here I was, for heaven's sake, bursting into weeping jags—three of them, just in the past twelve hours—wiping away tears, letting my uncle kiss my head and make it all well, and generally behaving as if I were twelve years old again.

When I'd actually *been* twelve, if memory served, I'd been better than this: a world-class child chess champion who'd seen her father murdered before her eyes and who'd managed to survive it and go on. What was wrong with me now? I couldn't think my way out of the proverbial paper bag.

My current behavior could only be explained by one thing: that these past ten years of mixing Sage Livingston's Miss Personality recipe in the Molotov-cocktail-shaker of Rodo Boujaron's open-hearth bombast must have resulted in softening whatever I'd once regarded as brains into pulp-stuffed banana fritters.

I had to snap out of it.

Metaphor, simile, and hyperbole be damned—along with the torpedoes, as Key also might say, "Full speed ahead."

Nim and I kept up a steady stream of idle chitchat, background noise to deflect our snoopers, while he meticulously searched everything in my place. Including me. He had a little scanning wand, the size of a tiny wire whisk, and with it he gave the once-over to my clothes, china, linens, books, furnishings, and the chess set he'd pulled from my backpack, which he then set up on the living room table. I handed him the missing black queen I'd been carrying around in my pocket. After examining it, he set it in its place on the board as well.

He picked up my backpack and shoved some fresh clothes from the cupboard into it, and stuffed in that front section of the newspaper, too. Then he turned to me.

"I think we've tidied your flat as much as we can for the moment," he said aloud. "Will that be all, before we head outdoors for our walk?"

I shook my head to indicate there was still something more. I handed him my ski parka, and with a significant look, I said aloud, "I should phone Rodo about tonight's schedule before you and I get too far afield. I do work for the guy, you know."

Nim was feeling the back of the down-filled jacket, where the chess map was concealed. It was just slightly stiffer than the rest. He raised his brow.

I started to nod, then I got an idea. "In fact, it might be best if I phone Rodo from along our walk," I said. "He had a few errands. I can check with him from where we stop, to make sure that I'm getting everything he needs."

"Well, we're off then," said Nim, as he held out the jacket for me to slip into. "Your carriage awaits, madame."

Just before leaving, he plucked my dangerous cell phone from where we'd left it on the table, and he slipped it between the sofa cushions as if it had been accidentally dropped. Then he offered me his arm.

When I glanced down, I saw the Swiss Army knife in his palm. He handed it to me with a smile. "To more penetrating insights," he said, squeezing my coat meaningfully, as we went out the door.

When we reached M Street, the heart of Georgetown, the place was glutted with tourists, spilled over here from the Cherry Blossom Festival on the National Mall. Outside every restaurant there were lines of them queued up on the pavement, hungrily awaiting a table or a space at an oyster bar. We had to slalom out into the streets to get past them. The sidewalks of Georgetown provide enough of an obstacle course on their own, what with doggy droppings, slippery and smelly fruits from the famous ginkgo trees, inch-deep holes from missing sidewalk bricks, bicyclists dodging up onto the pavement to avoid the swerving taxis, and truckers double-parked just outside open metal basement doors, unloading their crates of vegetables and beer into the cellars.

But the tourists were the worst, always behaving as if they owned the city of Washington, D.C. Of course, whenever I took the time to think about it, I realized that they actually *did*.

"This place makes Manhattan itself seem quite calming," commented Nim, still protectively holding my backpack in one hand and my arm in the other as he eyed the profusion of chaos all around him. "But I'm taking you somewhere a bit more civilized right now, where we can continue our conversation and lay a plan."

"I was serious. I do have an errand to run," I told him. "It's really urgent—and only a block or so from here."

But Nim had his own observations about errands in need of running.

"First things first," he said. "I do know when you've last eaten. But just when did you last *bathe*?"

Bathe? Was it that obvious? I tried not to sniff at myself right here on a public thoroughfare to try to find out. The truth was, I couldn't remember, but surely not since before I'd left for Colorado, as I now realized.

Even so, I had a first of my own, something more urgent to attend to immediately, for it very well might not wait.

"Why didn't you mention this fastidiousness of yours when we were still at my apartment?" I demanded. "I could have jumped in the shower there."

"Your flat?" he snorted. "A campground has more amenities. Besides, it's too dangerous to return. We can do your errand if it's really important—but only if it's en route to my hotel."

"Hotel?" I said, staring up at him in astonishment.

"Naturally," he said, amused. "I've been here days, as I said, hunting for you. Where did you expect me to stay—in your unprovisioned dwelling place? Or in some local park?"

In truth, I don't know *what* I'd expected. But it was just as hard to imagine someone as secretive as Nim actually staying beneath the roof of a public house.

"What hotel?" I said.

"You'll like it," he assured me. "Quite a welcome change from that barren, eavesdropper-riddled flat of yours. And at least you'll be clean. It boasts, among its other amenities, a competition-length lap pool and the finest Roman bath in the city, not to mention enough privacy that we may plan the next part of our campaign. It's just at the end of this street, not far at all. The Four Seasons."

PERHAPS BECAUSE I was descended from a line of self-proclaimed *philosophes*—masters of complexity theory like my uncle Slava, who'd always preferred the roundabout route to Truth—I myself had never bought into the idea that the first or the fastest answer to a problem was necessarily the right one; no Occam's Razor girl, *moi.* But in my immediate case, speed seemed to be of the essence, just as in lightning chess, and the simplest solution seemed best. As we walked, I succinctly shared my plan with Nim, and he approved.

The Koppie Shoppe, with its phonetically spelled name that dated back to the 1960s, was located halfway down the next block of M Street. It was lodged between a dim sum diner and a tapas dive whose chief promotional technique was a giant fan that blew food fumes out into the street. Nim and I had to work our way through the queues of ravenously anticipatory tourists to reach our destination and get in the door.

The Shoppe sold office supplies in the front of the store and had a copy shop with printers in the back. It was the only place around town I knew of that had a machine large enough to scan a full front page of the *Washington Post,* not to mention an eighteenth-century chessboard drawing written in blood.

It was also, fortuitously, the only place I knew of whose copy department manager, Stuart, was a fan of leftovers from a four-star Basque restaurant, and of the sous-chef who could smuggle them to him upon occasion—as well as of said sous-chef's long-legged sidekick, who could out-Rollerblade him over the cobblestones of Prospect Street.

In Georgetown, as within any other insulated tribal community, outsiders were mistrusted and milked for whatever they were worth or left in the streets to starve, as with these ravenous tourists just outside. But among locals, who were understood to be men of honor, there was an unspoken system of barter and exchange called tit for tat. In Russia, my father had called it *blat*. Either way, it works out to reciprocity.

In my case, Stuart respected my confidentiality. He let me do my own private copying, usually stuff for Rodo, on the big machine when no one else was around. He also let me use the unisex employee bathroom, a big plus, given my improvised agenda for today.

I left Nim in the front of the store among the office supplies, to pick out the de rigueur cardboard mailing cylinders, tape, labels, and small stapler required for my plan, while I took the backpack, went back to the copy department, waved to Stuart who was running a big noisy print job, and then went into the powder room, where I locked the door.

I extracted the *Washington Post* from my backpack, spread the front pages on the floor, removed my parka, and—holding it upside-down, so as not to spill its feathery contents—used the miniature scissors from Nim's Swiss Army knife to carefully pick loose the threads that Vartan Azov had stitched in.

It was nearly impossible to extract the chessboard without filling the place with down, but at last I managed to get the chessboard drawing cleaned off enough to slip, unfolded, between the first few pages of the *Post*. Rolling them up together, I stuck them in the satchel. Then I swept the down feathers off the floor with damp toilet paper, as best I could, tossed the paper into the toilet, and flushed.

Step Number One completed.

The soft tap at the bathroom door, as prearranged, told me that Nim was prepared to take over his part: Step Number Two.

I opened the door. He stood outside with his bag of just-purchased office supplies. I exchanged my down jacket for the plastic bag, then exchanged places with him in the bathroom.

While he locked himself inside so he could staple the lining back into my jacket, I went back to the copy room with my stash. The racket of the job that was running there was deafening. I appreciated the noise, so I could concentrate on what I had to do and not have to chat.

Stuart, with gestures, set up the big machine and turned it over to me. I set the first page of the *Post* facedown on the platen and ran off four clean copies. Then I flipped to the page where I'd inserted the drawing of the chessboard. It stuck out a bit, a little wider than the newspaper page that was supposed to be concealing it, but my pal across the room seemed occupied with his print run.

I set the chess drawing facedown with the newsprint covering the top, and ran four copies of that, as well. Then, for good measure, I made four copies of the other page of the *Post* where the front-page articles had spilled over. When I was done, I sorted the large copied pages into four piles, with the chessboard tucked into the middle of each one. I yanked the cardboard cylinders from Nim's plastic bag, quickly rolled each pile of papers tightly, and started fitting them, one at a time, into their cardboard mailing tubes.

Just then, the racket came to a sudden halt.

"Drat! Paper jam," said Stuart. "Alex, come over here a sec and hold this tray up for me, will you? This thing's been jamming all day, and the repairman never showed up. I'll have to stay myself tonight to clean it and find out what's wrong."

My heart was pounding. I didn't want to stop with the job half done, but what could I do? I quickly rolled up all the papers, including the originals, and put them in the plastic bag. Then I went to help him unjam the other copying machine.

"By the way," said Stuart, as I held up the heavy tray so he could pull loose the paper jam, "I'm not sure you need to do what you're doing over there."

"What I'm doing?" I said, as calmly as I could manage to force out.

How did *he* know what I was doing?

"I mean," he said, struggling to extract the culprit, a shredded, ink-stained paper, from where it was trapped, then yanking it out, "if you're copying that for your boss, Mr. Boujaron, he's already been in here earlier this morning with another fella. They had me run some copies of the same darned thing—yesterday's front page, right? I don't get it. I mean, the whole paper costs less than just a few of these full-size copies. What's the attraction?"

Good God! My pulse shot up like a meteor as I struggled not to panic.

Not to mention—what exactly *was* the attraction? Was Rodo the one who'd had my house and my cell phone bugged? Had he heard our conversation about the *Post*? Who was his sidekick this morning? And why was he making copies of that front page?

I knew I had to say *something* to deflect Stuart's curiosity. But I also needed to get out of here fast. Nim was waiting out front and he'd be wondering, in a sweat, what had happened to that "instant errand."

"I'm not sure myself what the attraction is. You know my boss," I told him as I helped slide the tray back in place. "For all I know, maybe Boujaron's wallpapering a new room with yesterday's headlines. But he sent me to make a few extra copies. Thanks so much for saving my neck!"

I slapped a ten-dollar bill on the counter on account, grabbed the plastic bag and my backpack, and blew Stuart a kiss on my way out the door.

Outside on the street, Nim took the backpack with a concerned expression.

"What kept you?" he asked as we plowed back through the throngs.

"Cripes," I told him. "Let's just do this. I'll fill you in later."

Without a further word, we hoofed it to the Georgetown post office two blocks away and just around the corner, and scrambled up the stone steps. Nim provided a defensive blockade as I slipped behind a counter, where I rolled the rest of my stash into the cylinders, sealed them with the tape he'd bought, and made out the labels—one to Aunt Lily, one to Nokomis Key, one each to the post office boxes of Nim and my mother. The one with the original drawing of the chessboard I sent to myself, right here at the Georgetown post office. Then for extra safety, I filled out one of those big yellow cards and signed it, so the post office would hold my mail for me until further notice.

At least this way, I thought, as my uncle and I walked back down the stone steps of the Georgetown post office, no matter what happened to me or to the others, the sacrifice that was made by a dying abbess, two hundred years ago in a Russian prison, would not have been in vain.

I TOOK A HOT, soapy shower and washed the three-day-old Colorado dust from my hair in the most elegant marble bathroom I'd ever seen in my life. Then, sporting nothing but the thick toweling robe that I'd found in the room and the designer swimsuit graciously provided me by the Four Seasons concièrge, I went down to where my uncle said he'd meet me, in the athletic club on the lower floor of the hotel.

First, I did thirty laps in the lane—by reservation only—that Nim had arranged for me in their private lap pool. Then I joined him in the enormous marble Roman Jacuzzi bath, which, if drained, would have comfortably slept fifty full-grown sumo wrestlers.

I had to concede it to my uncle: Wealth and comfort had their appealing points.

But I knew that if this Game I'd been thrown into was really as dangerous as everyone kept saying, I wouldn't have much longer to enjoy *anything*, especally if I kept sitting around doing pattycakes here in the steamy water.

As if my uncle had read my mind, he moved across the hot pool to sit on the marble shelf beside me. "Given that we don't know whatever may lie ahead of you just now," he said, "I thought you could only be assisted in it by being given a hot bath and a decent meal."

"Last wish?" I asked him with a smile. "I'll never forget it. My mind's working better already, I can tell. And I learned something really important today."

"About your boss Boujaron at the copy shop. You told me," he said. "That does raise some questions, of which we already have many. But there's something—"

"No, I discovered something I think is more important than that," I said. "I learned whom I could trust."

When he focused his bicolored eyes on me with curiosity, I added, "At the post office, and even before, I didn't have to think for one second before filling out those mailing labels. I knew who could be trusted with copies of the board. Not just you and my mother, who already had it, but Aunt Lily and my friend Nokomis Key, as well."

"Ah," said Nim. "Your friend Key's first name is Nokomis? So that must explain it."

"Explain what?" I said.

And that quickly, I was getting the uncomfortable feeling again that there was something headed in my direction I really didn't want to meet up with.

"While you were bathing, I picked up my messages from last night," said Nim. "Almost no one knows I'm here—just my caretaker. Yet there was a fax waiting for me here from last night—from one 'Selene Luna, Hank Tallchap's grandmother.' "

I was puzzled for just a moment, then I saw that Nim was smiling, and I got it too. "Selene" and "Luna" both meant "moon."

" 'By the shores of Gitchee Gumee, By the shining Big Sea Waters . . . ' " I quoted.

" 'Stood the wigwam of Nokomis, *Daughter of the Moon,* Nokomis,' " Nim finished for me. "So this friend of yours, does she really resemble Hiawatha's grandmother from the famous poem by Henry Wadsworth Longfellow?"

"Only in how she *thinks,*" I told him. "She could raise a warrior brave single-handed. And you'd be surprised that she knows more about cooking up secret codes than anyone I've ever known except *you.* Indian smoke signals, she calls them. So apart from puzzling out how she managed to find me, what was her message?"

"I confess, for once I was at a loss there, too," Nim said. "But now that I know who she is, clearly it was encoded for your eyes only."

He reached over for his toweling robe beside the pool, pulled out the fax, and handed it to me.

It did take a minute. But when I got it, I turned slightly

green. How could it be? Nobody had seen that coded message but me!

"What is it?" said Nim in alarm, his hand on my shoulder.

I could only shake my head. I couldn't speak.

Kitty's had a reversal of fortunes, it read. *She's coming back from the Virgin Isles, she leased a luxury car, she'll be in DC tomorrow. She says you have her number and the rest of her contact info. She's still in apartment A1.*

The message was still the same: *A1* meant it had to do with Russians and a secret room in Baghdad. But the reversal of fortune was definitely the key. I reversed the message in my mind. Instead of DC-LX-VI in Roman numerals, which added to 6-6-6, it would now read: IV-XL-CD, which added to 4-4-4. Three numbers, I noticed, that when multiplied added to 64, the number of squares on a chessboard!

The chessboard provides the key.

And if Kitty-Cat was taking an alternate route to the one she'd left atop that piano in Colorado, it meant that my mother was, possibly even at this very moment, right here in Washington, D.C.!

I'd dawdled here too long. I'd just turned to my uncle to tell him we had to go, and I started to step out of the Roman bath. But just at that moment I was confronted by absolutely the worst thing I could imagine in my wildest dreams. Around the corner came three figures I could hardly visualize together—certainly not in my current state of deshabille, with nowhere to run or hide:

Sage Livingston, Galen March, and my boss, Rodolfo Boujaron.

PART THREE

Rubedo

The Arabic saying 'Blood has flowed, the danger is past,' expresses succinctly the central idea of all sacrifice: that the offering appeases the power. . . . The driving-force behind the mechanism of sacrifice, the most characteristic of the symbolic inferences of blood, the zodiacal symbol of Libra representing divine legality, the inner conscience of man . . . for example in alchemy, when matter passes from the white stage (albedo) *to the red* (rubedo) *. . .*

—J. E. CIRLOT, *A Dictionary of Symbols:* "Blood"

The Prometheus myth . . . is an illustration of sublimation . . . which confirms the alchemic relation between the volatile and fixed principles. . . . At the same time suffering (like that of Prometheus) corresponds to sublimation because of its association wth the colour red—the third colour in the alchemical Magnum Opus, *coming after black and white.*

—J. E. CIRLOT, *A Dictionary of Symbols:* "Prometheus"

FIRE IN THE HEAD

I went out to the hazel wood,
Because a fire was in my head . . .
—W. B. YEATS, "The Song of the Wandering Aengus"

Yeats's Aengus . . . had the fire in his head that shamans everywhere believe is their source of enlightenment, illuminating visions of other realities. The shamanic journey begins and ends in the mind . . .
—TOM COWAN, *Fire in the Head*

KORYAKSKOE RAYIRIN YAYAI
(HOUSE OF THE DRUM, LAND OF THE KORYAK)

Within the yurt, the shaman was drumming softly as the others sat in a circle around the fire and chanted in the beautiful rhythms that Aleksandr had come to love. He sat outside the tent flap and listened. He loved the sounds of the shamans for they tranquilized his thoughts, creating a kind of harmonic that seemed to flow through his body and helped to heal his frayed and damaged nerves.

But often, when these rhythms stopped, the fire would return: the fire that filled his head with that burning light, that searing pain—not physical, more like something that emanated from within his psyche.

He had no real sense of time yet, either. He was unsure of how long he'd been here—a few days, maybe a week or more—or of how long they'd traveled to reach this place, all that distance across miles of seemingly impenetrable taiga. Toward the end of the journey, when his newly seasoned legs had failed him in the snows, when he'd become too weak to keep up the pace, they'd sent the sled with dogs to bring him the rest of the way.

The dogs were wonderful. He remembered what they were called: Samoyeds. He'd watched them with interest as they'd bounded through the snowy fields before the sled. When they were unleashed from the harness at night, he'd embraced them, and they'd licked his hands and face. Had he had a dog like this when he was young?

But he was no longer that boy, young Sascha, the self he knew best, the only self he really knew at all. He was now a grown man who remembered so little, his past seemed a foreign land, even unto himself. She'd told him his name.

Aleksandr Solarin.

And the woman who'd brought him here—the lovely blond woman who sat beside him now, waiting outside the tent for the others to call them when they were ready for the healing—she was his mother, Tatiana.

Before they'd first set out on this mission, she'd told him what she could about his state. "At the beginning," she said, "you were in a coma, you did not move, you could hardly breathe. The chief shaman, the Etugen, came down from the north to assist in your healing in the mineral waters. She is the one whom the Chukchi call qacikechca*—"similar to a man"—a female shaman from the aboriginal line, the* enenilit*, those with the spirit, those with great power. But despite all the strong herbs and skilled techniques the elders had employed to heal your flesh, the Etugen said you would only recover your spirit if you could begin the crossing—the journey from the people of the dead, the Peninelau, to* *the place of the living—through the effort of your own will.*

"After a very long time, you came to that state that we would call a stupor, although sometimes, for a month or longer, you still moved in and out of consciousness. At last, you've become as you are now, aware and conscious, able to eat, walk, read, even speak in several languages—but these are all skills that you possessed in your early youth. We must expect the rest to return more slowly, for you have had a great shock.

"The Etugen says that yours is not only a wound of the flesh, but of the spirit. It is dangerous to probe this psychic wound while it is still healing—already it comes to you in flashes. You are sometimes attacked by sleeplessness, a kind of seizure of distress or hysteria caused by what may seem irrational fears. But the Etugen believes these fears are real—that we must permit the true cause of your trauma to surface naturally, despite how long it may require and as difficult as it may seem.

"Then, when your flesh is well enough for you to make the physical part of the journey," she added, "we will head toward the north, to begin that other journey of healing your soul. For you have lived among the dead, you have the fire in your head—you have passed the tests to become a hetolatigiu*—'one-looking-into'—a prophet shaman."*

But Solarin knew in despair that all he wanted was his life back. As more of his memories returned, bit by bit, the more hopeless he felt at how much he'd really lost of all those intervening blank years. He could not even remember how many of them there were, that he was unble to remember. Bitterest of all to him now, he couldn't access the contents of his memory—couldn't recall those whom he'd loved or hated, cursed or cherished.

Yet there was one thing he could *remember.*

The game of chess.

Whenever he thought of it—especially of one game in particular—the fire began to rise in his head again. He knew that something about that game must be the key to it all: all his lost memory, all the traumas and nightmares, the hopes and fears.

But he knew, too, that just as his mother and the shaman had advised, it was best to watch and wait. For by pressing too hard and fast to grasp those cherished memories, he might be in the greater danger of killing the golden goose and losing it all.

Along their journey to the north, whenever they'd reached a stopping place where they could speak, he would tell his mother whatever he'd been able to remember, some small vapor, something rising like a mist from his past.

For instance, that night when he was a child, when Tatiana had given him a glass of warm milk and put him to bed. He could see his bedroom with the fig tree just outside. It was somewhere near the cliffs and the sea. It was raining. They'd had to flee. This much he'd remembered all on his own. The first memory—a great sense of accomplishment and release.

And now as they went, Tatiana—like a painter filling color into a drawing that was as yet only half-sketched on the canvas—would share more details of whatever she could retrieve for him from this part of his life.

"That night you recalled is important," she told him. "It was in late December of 1953—the night when all our lives changed. That night in the rain, our grandmother Minnie arrived at our house, which lay along a wild, sparsely occupied stretch of coast on the Black Sea. Though part of the Soviet Union, this spot was a sheltered oasis far from the terrors and purges elsewhere—or so we believed. Minnie brought with her

something that our family, across many generations, had always vowed to protect."

"I do not recall her," said Solarin, though with stirring excitement, for he'd just had another glimmer. "But I remember more of that night. Men broke into our house; I ran out and hid on the cliff. I somehow escaped. But you were captured by those men—" He looked at his mother in shock. "I never saw you again until that day at the monastery!"

Tatiana nodded and said, "Minnie had chosen that moment to arrive with a treasure she'd spent eight months scouring Russia to locate. For just eight months earlier, Yusuf Stalin—who'd ruled Russia for twenty-five years with a fist of steel—had died. In those ensuing months after his death, the entire world had changed for better or worse: Iraq, Jordan, and England had all gained new young rulers. Russia had developed the hydrogen bomb. And only shortly before that night of Minnie's arrival at our house, the longtime head of the Soviet secret police—Lavrentii Beria, the most feared and hated man in Russia—was executed before a firing squad. Indeed, Stalin's death and the vacuum it left was what had prompted Minnie's frantic eight-month search to excavate as much as she could of the hidden treasure—three valuable gold and silver, bejeweled chess pieces, which she begged us to hide. She believed we were safe to do so, with a boat nearby at your father's disposal."

At the mention of the chess pieces, Solarin had felt the fire returning. He struggled to hold it back. There was something else he had to know. "Who were those men who captured you?" he asked, his voice shaking. "And how did you manage to disappear for so long?"

Tatiana did not answer directly. "It has always been easy to disappear in Russia," she said calmly. "Millions did so, if rarely by choice."

"But if the old regime was dismantled," said Solarin,

"who were those men who were after the treasure? Who captured you? And where did they take you?"

"The usual place," said Tatiana. "The Glavny Upravlenie Lagerey, the Main Administration for Camps—'Gulag' for short—those forced labor camps that have existed since the time of the tsars. The 'Administration' it refers to is always the secret police, whether called Okhrana under Tsar Nikolas, or under the Soviets the Chekha, the NKVD, the KGB."

"You were put into a prison camp?" Solarin said, astonished. "But how in God's name did you manage to survive all that time? I was only a small boy when they took you!"

"I should not have survived," Tatiana told him. "But after little more than a year, Minnie at last discovered where I'd been taken, to a camp in Siberia. A place of desolation. And she bartered for my escape."

"She secured your release, you mean?" said Solarin. "But how?"

"No, my escape," said his mother. "For if the politburo had ever learned of my release, all of our lives would have remained in danger all these many years. Minnie bought my freedom in another way, and for quite another reason. I have remained here, hidden among the Koryak and Chukchi ever since. Thanks to this, I was not only able to rescue your broken body, but to save you, too, for I hold many powers myself that I've acquired over many years from these great masters of the fire."

"But how did you rescue me," Solarin asked his mother, "and what did Minnie give the Soviets—or the Gulag guards—to effect your escape?"

But before the last question was out of his mouth, Solarin knew the answer. In horror he suddenly saw, with the force of brilliant illumination, the glimmering shape that had hovered at the periphery of his vision all these many months.

"Minnie gave them the Black Queen!" he cried.

"No," said Tatiana. "Minnie gave them the chessboard. It was I myself who gave them the Black Queen."

JIHAD

The conquest of Spain and Africa by Islam had made the king of the Franks the master of the Christian Occident. It is therefore strictly correct to say that without Mohammed Charlemagne would have been inconceivable.

—HENRI PIRENNE, *Mohammed and Charlemagne*

SAGE LIVINGSTON, RODO BOUJARON, AND MONsieur "Charlemagne d'Anagram" himself, my suspicious new Colorado neighbor, Galen March. These were the very last folks on the planet I wanted to see at this precise moment, especially en masse like this, with me half-naked. I felt like gagging. But I managed to pull on my plush velour robe and knot the sash, the only thing I could think to do when confronted by this unexpected trio of mismatched coconspirators.

Nim had stepped from the steamy Roman bath and tugged his arms into his own robe. With one deft sweep, he plucked Key's fax from my hand, shoved it back into his pocket, and handed me a towel for my dripping hair.

He muttered from the side of his mouth, "You're acquainted with these people, I take it?" When I merely nodded, he added, "Then timely introductions might prove to be in order."

But our Charm School Queen beat me to it.

"Alexandra!" Sage exclaimed, crossing the space to me with the two men in tow. "How astonishing to find you here at the same hotel where Galen himself is staying. He and I were searching all of Georgetown for you until your employer here was kind enough to point us in the right direction; it was he who suggested you might be visiting your uncle at the Four Seasons."

Before I could respond or react to this startling remark, Sage had turned her charms upon Nim, extending one flawlessly manicured hand and bestowing an even more polished smile. "And you must be Dr. Ladislaus Nim, the noted scientist of whom we've all heard so much. I'm Sage Livingston, Alexandra's neighbor from Colorado. Delighted to meet you."

Heard so much of *Nim*? The Man of Mystery himself? Hardly from Mother or *me*. And just how could Rodo pin down our whereabouts so fast, without the use of those bugging devices I thought we'd just ditched?

Nim was shaking hands all around, as dignified as one could be in such attire. At this moment, however, I was cold and dripping—not to mention more than desperate to figure out the rest of Key's fax about Mother still stashed in my uncle's pocket. I decided to excuse myself and head for the locker room to dry off, in hopes I might escape by a back door and follow up with Nim on these and other questions.

But our "Hostess with the Mostest," it would appear, had yet another surprise up her sleeve.

"Dr. Nim," Sage was saying, in a sultry sotto voce, "surely you, of all people, must know just who we all are, and why we're all here. So you must understand, as well, why we must speak and why time is of the essence."

Who we all *are*?

I tried not to glance at my uncle. But really—what gave here?

Sage was sounding less like the pretentious bit of fluff of my longtime acquaintance and a bit more like Mata Hari. Was it actually possible that the Sage standing before me right now, the one mindlessly toying with her diamond tennis bracelet and pouting, could be heiress to more than just the Livingston oil fields and uranium mines? Might she be heiress to all those intriguing Livingston intrigues as well?

But just as that unbidden thought about Sage had done its best to bite me from behind, the shade of her mother reared its unattractive head. *Exactly whom do you believe you are dealing with?* Rosemary had asked me that night at the restaurant. *Do you have any possible conception of who I am?*

I decided—at least under these cold, wet circumstances—that it was time to blow the whistle. I'd definitely had enough.

"What exactly do you *mean,*" I asked Sage in irritation, "that Nim must know 'Who We Are'? Let's see. . . . reading from left to right, you all look a lot like my uncle, my boss, and a couple of my mother's neighbors—"

I paused, for Sage, completely ignoring me, had sighed with understated elegance, lips pressed together and nostrils slightly flared. Glancing meaningfully toward the reception desk, she whispered directly to Nim, "Isn't there someplace we can go and speak privately, the five of us? Just as soon, of course, as you and Alexandra have had time to dry off and change. You must know very well what we need to discuss."

I was about to object, but Nim took me by surprise. "My room. Ten minutes," he told her, nodding to the gang of three. Then he tore a bit of paper from the piece in his pocket and scribbled his room number down.

What on earth was he thinking? He knew better than anyone that my mother was in danger—maybe right here in D.C.—and that I had to get out of here now. And yet we were fraternizing once more with the enemy, about to throw another extended tea party. I was really fuming.

When Nim hit the lockers, I doubled back quickly and grabbed Sage by the arm.

Galen and Rodo were already well ahead, halfway up the stairs to the athletic club's private entrance and hopefully out of earshot of my questions. But the moment I began, I found I'd been corked up so long that when uncorked, I just couldn't seem to stop.

"Who called this meeting?" I demanded of Sage. "Was it you or Tom and Jerry up there? Why were you and March looking 'all over Georgetown' for me today? What are you both doing in Washington, anyway? Why did you both race down to Denver last Sunday just after I'd left? What did you have to talk about with Vartan Azov and Lily Rad?"

It was clearly no secret that I knew all this—Rosemary had already let the cat out of the bag that she knew I'd had a report from Nokomis Key.

Now Sage coolly regarded me with that lofty, condescending expression that had always filled me with the desire to wipe it off her face with a Brillo pad. Then she smiled, and the familiar Miss Popularity returned, double-barreled dimples and all.

"You really ought to ask your uncle those questions—not me," she told me sweetly. "After all, he's agreed we would all meet. It's only ten minutes from now, as he's just said."

Sage started up the stairs once more, but again I grabbed her by the arm. She looked at me in shocked surprise. Bloody hell! I was surprising even myself. I must have been nearly snarling in her face in my frustration.

Maybe I'd never shown my true colors toward Sage before, but from my perspective this had been a pretty rough week, even before it received any help from her and her awful family. Besides, I was in no mood to get the brush-off from a girl whose entire prior accomplishment in life, so far as I knew, was to be a card-carrying Teen Goddess. People were in danger. I needed information. Now.

"You're here. We're alone. I'm asking *you,*" I told her. "What would be the advantage in waiting ten more minutes to ask my uncle something you could tell me right away?"

"I was only trying to help, after all," said Sage. "It's your uncle we've come to meet with, as you must realize. Galen insisted we had to find him. He said it was urgent. That's why we went to Denver to question the others after your mother came up missing at that party. And when even *you* didn't seem to have a clue where she had gone—"

She cut off when I'd glanced around quickly to see if anyone could overhear us. This was more than I'd expected. Galen March was hunting for Nim? But why? I was almost in shock.

Then I looked up the long flight of stairs and saw that Galen himself was headed back down them, coming right toward us. I panicked and dragged Sage into the ladies' locker room where he could hardly follow. Still holding her by the arm, I checked under the stall doors to be certain we were completely alone.

When I turned back to Sage, I was nearly panting with anticipation. I knew I had to ask the question—though I confess I was genuinely terrified to hear what her answer might be. Sage was staring at me as if I might start frothing at the mouth. I would have laughed if the situation hadn't been quite so grave.

As Key would say, I bit the bullet.

"Why would Galen March be chasing after my uncle?" I asked. "After all, they'd never met each other, until just moments ago, in this club."

Right?

"I never really inquired," said Sage with her customary sangfroid.

She was treading carefully, no doubt, so as not to excite me more than necessary, though I noticed that she was eyeing the nearby fire alarm box, as if contemplating how hard it might be to break the glass and pull the handle to summon help.

I was about to press further, but Sage hadn't finished. With her next words, I nearly blacked out.

"I just assumed they must know each other. After all, it was your uncle who put up the money to purchase Sky Ranch."

I HAD NEVER BEFORE studied my uncle through the bottom of a brandy snifter, but I'd accepted this stiff belt he'd proffered the moment I'd arrived, wet and bedraggled, from the club.

Now, dried off and dressed in the fresh change of clothes he'd earlier stuffed into my backpack, I was peering through the glass as I sipped the last of my cognac, curled barefoot in a comfy chair behind one of those exotic flower arrangements the Four Seasons is famous for. I tried to remember their names: the orange and purple were birds of paradise, the green and white were yucca plants, the fuschia were wild ginger, the plum were cymbidiums . . . or was it cymbidia? I'd never been much at Latin.

Nim came around the table and removed the glass from my hand. "That's quite enough for one morning," he informed me. "I want you relaxed, not comatose. Why don't you pull up your chair and join the group?"

The group.

He was referring to the motley trio seated on rich brocade chairs that were scattered about the lavish suite.

Nim padded back and forth over the luxurious carpeting, fixing them drinks of their own.

I really couldn't believe all this was happening.

I felt truly ill, and that cognac had hardly helped relieve my confusion or pain.

I knew I somehow had to get to the bottom of things. But for the first time I felt completely and utterly alone.

Thank God I'd done those thirty laps in the pool today, before reality set in.

Thank God I'd pinched Key's fax from Nim's robe in the bathroom just now.

Because my beloved uncle Slava—the one person I'd always trusted with my confidences and my life, more even than my own parents—now appeared to have a ton of explaining to do. At this point, I wasn't sure how much he *could* just explain away. After all, as my mother used to say when I was a child, "A lie by omission is still a lie."

As he'd requested, I pulled my chair from behind the table of flowers to "join the group," and I seized this opportunity for a quick mental recap.

How much fact or speculation had I myself shared with Nim since last night?

How much of his input was a "lie by omission"—versus actual commission?

I couldn't state that he'd outright lied, but he'd certainly misled me. For starters, his every remark in the past twenty-four hours had seemed to imply that he'd never met Rodo or Galen—even as far as this morning, when he'd deciphered the latter's code name and had pointed out how the two might be linked through Charlemagne and the chess set.

This picture of blissful ignorance certainly shifted, once you squinted a bit closer at a few unobtrusive facts. Like the fact that Rodo had known right where Nim was staying in D.C., when no one else had, including me. Or the fact that Nim had footed the multimillion-dollar bill for a worthless Colorado ranch purportedly owned by Galen March.

Once you read a bit of that fine print, it might well appear that my uncle had been well acquainted—and well before today—with everybody here in the room, with the possible exception of Sage Livingston.

Of course, that's only if you assumed that Sage *herself* was telling the truth.

"Clearly, we seem to have been protecting the wrong person all along," said Nim to the room in general, when everyone had been refreshed with refreshments. "Cat outwitted everyone with that disappearing act of hers, though I've no conception of *why*. Any ideas?"

"Just as clearly," Rodo volunteered, "she didn't trust any of us to protect either her *or* Alexandra. Why else would she have taken such critical matters into her own hands, as she has done?"

But even as he talked, I knew I couldn't take this for even one teensy second longer. I was all but sure I'd explode.

"Um, I *thought* none of you had ever met before?" I said sweetly, my eyes all the while shooting daggers at Nim across the room.

"We haven't," he said, in disgust. "We were kept apart for a purpose. This was all your mother's idea from the very beginning. I should say, it really began from the moment of your father's death. This is what comes of dealing with a woman who's let her maternal instincts seize control of her mental faculties. She'd had a fine brain before *you* were born. What a mess."

Great. Now *I* was responsible for whatever wild scheme these folks had been up to, while I myself had been kept completely in the dark.

"Perhaps you can explain," I said to Nim, as I motioned to Galen. "Are you the owner of Sky Ranch, as Sage says you are? Or is *he*?"

"Cat asked me to purchase the place," Nim said. "A kind of buffer zone from the land speculators, as she explained it. She had someone act as a 'front' to deceive the local residents as to our involvement. Though I never knew who, I now assume that would be Mr. March. Apparently, it was Miss Livingston here who helped instrument the sale in privacy."

Sage? Why would Mother involve *her*? She hated all the Livingston clan. Though it might explain how Sage had learned who the real owner was, this scenario was making less sense by the moment, even less than inviting them all to her bloody birthday party. I felt like screaming.

And there were still a few large chunks missing. But I didn't need to ask: The Potemkin of the Pyrenees was about to volunteer.

"Your mother and I have been friends for years," Rodo told me. "I don't believe that she would like me to discuss the precise nature of our relationship here, since she has taken such pains to keep us all apart for so many years. Nonetheless, I shall say that she did request me to employ you, once you'd abandoned that awful CIA place, and she told me she would provide excellent references. In answer to your earlier question, that is all I have known of your uncle here until this moment. I hope this explains everything."

It did explain one thing very neatly—perhaps *too* neatly. If Nim was right and Mother had been in the driver's seat all this while, if we were in danger, it would certainly make sense to keep the troops apart as she had—or at least in the dark, with respect to her overall strategy, that is, if they were being orchestrated from behind the scenes, as in a chess game.

Only, my mother didn't play chess.

But I did.

And I clearly knew one thing better than anyone in this room: There was definitely a game going on. But somebody other than my mother was calling the shots. It was my job to find out who.

So while "the group" carried on about my missing mother, trying to put the pieces together so they could unravel her motives and modus, I privately did a bit of unraveling of my own.

I started by revisiting that tidy packet where everything had been wrapped up so neatly. A group of people who'd never met, who had now discovered their common interests here at the Four Seasons. They'd all been called upon by a woman—who was now conveniently missing—to render services, purchase land, employ her daughter, and act as a "front." And that tied the last knot in the parcel.

I stood up and walked over to Sage Livingston. Everyone stopped speaking and turned toward me.

"I figured it out," I told Sage. "I don't know what took me so long. Maybe because my boss, Mr. Boujaron here, led me astray by telling me I played a different role than I actually do. But a new Game has definitely begun. And I've realized that *everyone* my mother invited to her party is a player, including all of us here in this room. But we aren't all on the same side, are we? For instance, I think your mother, Rosemary, is the one who has started this Game again. And despite the fact that Rodo said *I* was, I think she's the White Queen—"

Rodo cut me off. "I said the people at that dinner *believed* you were," he corrected me. "And how could Madame Livingston believe that *you* are something if, as you've just maintained to us, she is that same something herself?"

"It must be," I assured him. "The Livingstons moved to Redlands on the Plateau just after my father's death, when they learned that we were settling there ourselves. Because Rosemary had discovered who my mother really was—"

"No, you're mistaken," said Sage. "We did know who you were as soon as you moved there—that's why Mother asked me to befriend you. But we lived there first. Rosemary assumed you'd come to Colorado for that express purpose—because we were there. After all, as you've just learned, it was *your* mother who secretly arranged to buy land abutting *our* property."

This didn't make sense. That uncomfortable feeling was creeping up once more.

"Why would my mother do that?" I said. "And why did your mother ask you to befriend me?"

Sage looked at me with an expression somewhere between disdain and complete astonishment at my ignorance.

"Just as Rodolfo Boujaron has told you," she said. "Mother has always believed you would be the new White Queen. With your father dead, she hoped she might penetrate the shield at last, break down the defenses. As I said, she knew from the first instant who your mother was, what role she played. And more important, she knew what your mother had *done*."

The feeling had grabbed me by the nape of the neck, like someone yanking me back from the cliff off of which I was about to step. But I couldn't help it. I had to know.

"What *had* my mother done?" I asked her.

Sage glanced at the others, who seemed just as amazed at the course this conversation was taking as I.

"I thought you all must know," she said. "Cat Velis killed my grandfather."

THE QUESTION

Questions are what matters. Questions, and discovering the right ones, are the key to staying on course. . . . The wave of information threatens to obscure strategy, to drown it in details and numbers, calculation and analysis, reaction and tactics. To have strong tactics we must have strong strategy on one side and accurate calculation on the other. Both require seeing into the future.

—GARRY KASPAROV, *How Life Imitates Chess*

I COULD SEE WHY INTELLIGENCE AGENCIES AND spy rings might have a few problems trying to sort out wheat from chaff—not to mention fact from fiction. I felt like I'd just stepped through the mirror into the looking-glass universe and found that everyone here was walking around on his hands.

Sage Livingston, my familiar nemesis ever since our dark grammar school days, had just informed me that her mother, Rosemary, had "sicced" her on me from day one. And why? In order to retaliate against my mother for a highly unlikely homicide and to "plant" someone like me—a purported White Team player from birth—within the evil empire that the Black Team had constructed practically at the Livingstons' front door.

Needless to say, I had a few problems sifting through the mythological debris that seemed to be littering this scenario.

Most obvious among these droppings was that my mother, a born-again recluse, had never, that I'd witnessed or even heard tell of, had truck with any of the

Livingston clan in the whole ten years of her residence in Colorado.

So how could *she* have been pursuing *them* across the board? Far from it.

And as for encouraging daughterly friendships, it seemed to me that would be more of Rosemary's bailiwick. Mother had always disliked Sage just as much I did.

But the biggest drawback to her story was the one with which my uncle was about to take exception. He immediately confronted Sage on her last remark.

"What on earth could possibly bring you to the conclusion that Cat Velis killed your grandfather? She wouldn't harm a fly," Nim snorted with disdain. "I've known Cat since before Alexandra's birth, even since before her marriage! This is the first I've ever heard of such a preposterous presumption."

My sentiments precisely. And Galen and Rodo seemed equally dumbstruck by the notion. We all looked at Sage.

For the first time that I'd ever seen her in the presence of a nearly all-male audience, she seemed at a loss for words, sitting there primly on her satin brocade chair, still toying with that silly diamond tennis bracelet. I noticed it had a little racquet dangling from it, outlined in emeralds. I mean, really.

When it became clear that she would make no reply, Rodo said, "But I am sure that Mademoiselle Sage Livingston did not mean to suggest that Alexandra's mother had harmed anyone on purpose? If such a thing did occur, it was surely an accident or a grave misfortune?"

"Perhaps I've said too much," Sage admitted. "I'm really only a messenger, and the wrong one at that, it seems. After all, as you've just explained, a new Game has begun with new players. That's why my parents had me help Galen try to find Cat when she went missing and why we came here to D.C. to meet with Alexandra. They were so certain that all of you here understood the situation, that you knew about Cat Velis's past actions, that you opposed her plans—most especially Alexandra. After all, everyone knows they've not spoken in years. But now it appears we must have been mistaken . . . "

Sage let her words drift away as she looked around at all of us helplessly. I'd like to say that I'd never seen her look so vulnerable, but the truth is I'd never suspected that the "V-word" even existed in Sage's vocabulary. It was more likely a ruse. And though I resented her inference about my relationship with my mother, I guess, as she said, it wasn't exactly a secret to anyone.

But more important, if a new Game *had* begun, as everyone agreed, and if Sage's mother wasn't the new White Queen—and I wasn't either—then who was it who'd started this new ball rolling? And where was it headed?

I thought it was time to reinsert a few dangling participles.

"I think what Rodo and my uncle were trying to find out," I told her, "was why Rosemary would think my mother responsible for her own father's death, accidental or not. When or where could something like that have happened? After all, Cat doesn't get around much; she's led a pretty insular life—"

"But she got around to Ain Ka'abah," Sage snapped, through narrowed lips.

Come again?

She added, "It's a town in the Atlas Mountains of Algeria. That's where my mother and yours first met, at the mountain home of my grandfather. But it was at his home at La Madrague, a seaport on the Mediterranean coast not far from Algiers, where she killed him."

The room was so hushed it seemed to have been

smothered. You could have heard a pin drop on the thick carpeting. I felt my horror deepening and congealing, as if I were being sucked down to the bottom of a well filled with molasses.

I knew this story, of course, and I recalled exactly where and from whom I'd heard it: from Lily Rad in Colorado. She'd told us that she herself was there in Algeria with my mother. Lily was kidnapped at that seaport by a guy who was after those pieces that the girls had retrieved from the desert. Lily had referred to him as the Old Man of the Mountain.

She'd told us he was the White King!

But your mother, Lily had gone on to recount, *brought reinforcements to my rescue, and coshed him over the head with her heavy satchel of chess pieces.*

Was that how it might have happened? *Could* my mother have killed this man? Could Rosemary Livingston's father really have been the White King?

But there was something else: something about the fellow's name, too, which suddenly seemed important, something that had to do with the events of these past few days. I racked my brain to recall it, but my thoughts were interrupted.

"El-Marad," said the liquid voice that I could never mistake. It was coming from near the door. "That was the name—short for Nimrod, so I've been told—the king of Babylon who built the Tower of Babel."

There, in the open door of my uncle's suite, stood Nokomis Key.

She was looking directly at me.

"Hope you got my note," she told me. "You're a hard babe to find. And believe me, toots, I've really been looking."

She came over and grasped me by the arms to pull me up. As she moved us both, double-time, toward the open doorway, she whispered in my ear, "We've gotta blow this pop stand, and fast, before they figure out *who I am.*"

"We've already guessed who you are," Sage called after her.

She must have satellites for ears, I thought.

But then came another voice—Galen March, who'd hardly spoken a word all this time. "Alexandra, please stop. Both of you," he said with a real sense of urgency. "You mustn't leave yet. Don't you see? Nokomis Key is the new White Queen."

"GOOD LAWDY, MISS CLAWDY!" said Key, as she shoved me through the door.

Once outside in the corridor, before the others could react, she'd yanked the door shut and wedged a bit of metal the size of a credit card into the lock. Tossing her yard-long mass of black satin hair over her shoulder, she turned to me with a grin. "That oughta hold 'em till the rescue posse shows up," she said.

Key knew all the ins and outs of hotels; she had worked her way through college as a sometime chambermaid and porter. But right now she seemed to have nothing but "Out" on her mind. She was motoring me toward the fire escape stairway, puffing like a choo-choo train.

But in my mind, I was still back inside that suite, almost reeling with confusion. What had Galen *meant*?

"Where are you taking me?" I said, attempting unsuccessfully to halt her momentum by digging in my heels.

"I thought that was supposed to be *your* motto—'Theirs not to reason why'?" she quipped. "Just trust me and keep moving. You'll be thrilled that I bailed you out."

"Wherever it is," I said, as she shoved me into the stairwell, "I've only got the clothes on my back. We just left my backpack locked in that room with all my money, my driver's license—"

"We'll get you new ones," she told me. "Where *we're* going, babe, you're gonna require new camouflage, anyway. Don't you get it? Bad folks are lookin' for you, gal."

She'd clattered me down the few more flights of steps to the lobby. Before opening the door, though, she turned to me for an instant.

"Just ignore that White Queen bit of Galen March's," she said, reading my mind. "As far as I'm concerned, Galen's just another 'spy in the ointment.' The guy has a major crush on me. He'd say anything to get my attention."

She might not be far from the truth there, I thought, given the excessive attention Galen had paid *her* at that birthday dinner. But all this did little to address the immediate problem.

I had just left a roomful of people locked upstairs, who'd lured me there and then lied to me in a variety of colorful ways, while tossing disclaimers at one another's stories—stories, I might add, that all appeared to be large soufflés of inflated mythology, sparsely sprinkled with a cherry-picking of facts.

Then, in waltzes Key Almighty, turning everything topsy-turvy once more by high-handedly kidnapping me and jamming the door. If my *previous* abductors hadn't already managed to escape through the ministrations of my uncle's legendary ingenuity, then they could surely have phoned hotel security by now to let them out. They might be hot on our trail at this very moment.

That raised the even *more* immediate problem.

Was there *nobody* I could trust?

I pushed past Key and slammed one hand flat against the storm door to the lobby, while I grabbed the handle and held it firm with my other.

"We're going nowhere until you answer some questions," I informed her. "Why the dramatic surprise entrance to my uncle's suite? What are you doing here, anyway? If you're not a key player, what did you mean up there when you said '*Who I am?*' I need answers. I'm afraid that I really must insist."

Key shrugged and smiled. "And *I'm* afraid that this is a command performance," she told me. "You see, we've been invited to pay a visit to the Queen of Cats."

"ROAD TRIP!" said Key as we drove past the former Thirty-fourth Street residence of her namesake, Francis Scott Key. "Just like the old days!"

After she'd hung a left, in her rented Jeep Cherokee, onto the bridge also bearing his name, she added, "Do you have even the vaguest clue how very difficult it has been to orchestrate and to launch this whole *escape* of yours?"

"Escape? Looks more like an abduction from where *I* sit," I commented drily. "Was all this really necessary? And have you really found my mother?"

"I never lost her," said Key with a private smile. "Who else did you imagine helped her set up that dinner party for her birthday? After all, she couldn't have done all of that all by herself. 'No woman is an island,' as they say."

Of course! I knew *someone* must have helped Mother. At the very least, just to effect that difficult exit.

I'd snapped my head sideways to stare at Key, awaiting more detail. But she was concentrating on the road, still wearing that enigmatic smirk.

"I'll explain everything when we're on our way," she added. "We have plenty of time, a few hours at least, to reach our destination. We're taking the scenic route—since, naturally, we're being followed."

I wanted to check in my side mirror, but I decided to

take her word for it. We were on the George Washington Parkway now, headed south toward the airport. And though I desperately needed to hear what Key had to tell me about Mother and that party, there was just one thing first.

"If someone's tailing us, what about those listening devices they can point at your car as you drive?" I mentioned. "Can't they hear everything we say?"

"Yeah," she said wryly. "Like that cute tennis racket charm that you probably noticed on Ms. Livingston's bracelet. 'In one ear and out the other,' as we always say. Wonder whose ear was picking up on *that* little chat."

Sage's diamond tennis bracelet. Oh Lord, this just went on and on.

"Don't worry about this car, though," said Key. "I had the boys, my usual flight mechanic crew, sweep the car and put a shield on it the moment they'd picked it up for me at the airport. Everything's clean as a whistle; they can't access our innermost thoughts or our talk."

Where had I heard *that* before? But I couldn't spend hours like this, either, locked in a car on the highway without finding out what had really been going on.

"As for your pal Kitty," Key informed me, "there's never a cloud without a silver lining. It's an ill wind that blows nobody good, as they say."

"Meaning?" I prompted.

"Meaning she had a problem, and she figured I was the only one who could help resolve it. So she drew up a guest list, and I herded and corralled the cattle. She wanted to make sure, though, that you would remain just an innocent bystander."

"They're the ones who usually get shot first," I pointed out.

"You did great, though," said Key, undaunted. "You solved all those puzzles in record time; I clocked you. You got into the house less than an hour after you drove out of the Cortez airport in your rental car—just in time for Lily Rad's phone call, informing you that she was lost. We all felt sure that you would phone *me* to bring her home, since the airport where I work is so much closer. We stopped to eat and gave you some extra time to discover the rest. By the time we'd arrived you'd apparently solved the puzzle that your mother and I had left *atop* the piano, since everything *inside* the piano had been removed, and the billiard ball was back in its place in the rack. Even *I* didn't know about that hidden chessboard drawing, though—"

"*You* invented all those puzzles for Mother," I said.

It wasn't a question. It was the only possible answer to what had been bugging me all along. If it hadn't been Nim—and I knew now that it hadn't been—who'd encrypted those puzzles for Mother to communicate with me, who else could have done it but Key? And had there been any doubt in my mind, her recent fax would have erased it.

What a dolt I'd been, even from square one! But at last it started making sense. Everything was starting to fall into place, just like the patterns in a chess game.

Speaking of which—

"Where did you get the idea to set up that game that you stashed inside the piano?" I asked her.

"Apparently, it was Lily's idea to use that specific game," said Key. "She knew it would grab your attention big time. But it was Vartan who provided your mother with the map of exactly *how* we needed to set up the pieces. He seemed to know just where the critical turning point in that last game took place—at least, from your point of view."

Vartan, too? That bastard.

I was sick at heart. I wanted to cry again, but what was the point? And why had they done all this? Why rope me in at such an emotional level by invoking my father's death if Mother really wanted me to remain just an "innocent bystander"? It made absolutely no sense.

"We had no choice," said Key, anticipating my question again. "We all agreed that we had to do it that way—leaving phone messages, planting puzzles and clues of the sort that would mean something specifically to *you.* We even pretended the car broke down so you'd have to give them a ride. Talk about complexity theory! But if we hadn't gone to such ridiculous lengths, you never would have come, you never would have stayed, you never would have agreed to meet with him—now would you?"

Him.

Of course I knew exactly who she meant. And of course, I knew they'd been completely right.

As it was, despite all their chicanery to get me there, I'd still been prepared to bolt from the room the very moment I'd seen Vartan Azov enter the premises, hadn't I? And why not? For ten years, until we'd actually had the chance to speak at length in Colorado, I'd held both him and that bloody game accountable for my father's death.

I had to give some credit to my mother, though, for understanding me better than I understood myself. Both she and Lily Rad must have anticipated exactly what my reaction would be to any suggestion that I meet with Vartan under any pretext they'd invented whatsoever.

But though I now understood their need for manipulation, the obvious question was still hanging in the air.

"If you all wanted to orchestrate a meeting between me and Vartan," I said, "why go to such lengths—not to mention such *distances*—to trick me? What could Vartan Azov possibly have told me that had to be told in the wilds of Colorado instead of New York or even D.C.? And why invite all those others to some kind of trumped-up birthday party? What were they there for? Just camouflage?"

"I'll explain it all in lavish detail, just as soon as we've dropped off this airport rental car," Key said. "We'll be there any minute."

"But we passed National Airport miles back," I told her.

"You know," said Key, "that I *never* fly commercial." She rolled her eyes.

"You flew here yourself?" I said. "But where are we headed, then? Down in this direction there are just military air bases like Fort Belvoir and Quantico. The closest private airstrip in Virginia must be all the way to Manassas."

"There are three of them just across the river from here, in Maryland," she informed me coolly. "I dropped off the plane over there."

"But you've passed the last bridge, too!" I objected. We were almost at Mount Vernon, for God's sakes. "How do you expect to get this car across the river and into Maryland?"

Key let out a tremendous sigh, like the sound of a balloon deflating.

"I thought I *told* you. We're being *fol*-lowed," she explained, as if speaking to a three-year-old child. When I said nothing she added, with a bit more restraint, "So, clearly, I'd planned to ditch the car."

WE PULLED INTO a parking spot at the Mount Vernon ferry landing, between two giant SUVs so tall they looked like they were raised on hoists.

"The better *not* to see us, my dear," Key commented.

She'd twisted her long hair into a loop, tied it with a scrunchy, and stuffed the twist down the back of her safari vest. Then she pulled a canvas bag from the backseat, yanked out two nylon bicycle pullovers, a couple of pairs of dark glasses, and two baseball caps, and she handed one set of everything to me.

Once we'd gussied ourselves up in these disguises, we got out of the car, Key locked up everything carefully, and we went down to the boat.

"Departure in less than five minutes," she told me. "Better not to tip one's hand too early."

We went down the dock and Key handed the ticket guy some prepurchased boarding passes that she pulled from her vest. I noticed she also slipped him the car keys. He wordlessly nodded his acknowledgment, and we went over the gangplank and stepped onto the rocking boat. There were only a few other passengers, and none within earshot.

"You seem to know an awful lot of people," I mentioned to Key. "You trust this ferry caddy to return that expensive car?"

"And that's not all," she said. "For a few more favors, Bub here gets fourteen free flight training hours as a pourboire."

I confess, angry and frustrated as I'd been with her just ten minutes ago, as a born chess player I'd always loved the way Key executed her moves. She'd clearly mapped out this scenario far better than any chess game Lily Rad had ever played, and had anticipated every move and countermove.

That's why Nokomis Key had been my best friend and boon companion ever since grammar school. It was Key who'd taught me early on that I would never have to be afraid as long as I could see far ahead, as long as I knew the lay of the land.

Braves know how to go through the woods alone, even at night, she would tell me. They plan their path, but they don't rehearse their fears.

They'd untied the rope lashing the ferry to the pier

and pulled up the gangplank. We were well out onto the river, when I saw a guy with mirrored glasses come briskly down the boardwalk and say something to the attendant. He looked more than familiar.

The attendant shook his head and pointed upstream across the river, toward Washington, D.C. The man with the shades reached in his jacket and pulled out a phone.

I had that sinking feeling. We were out here in the middle of the river on an open boat, like a crate of eggplants awaiting delivery.

"Secret Service," I mentioned to Key. "We're previously acquainted. I think we should expect a greeting committee on the opposite shore—they must know where this boat is headed. Unless you'd planned for us to get off at midstream and swim?"

"Unnecessary," said Key, "oh, ye of little faith. Just as we go round the point at Piscataway, when we're out of eyesight from either shore, this boat will be making a brief, unscheduled stop to let off two passengers."

"On Piscataway Point?" It was just a preservation wilderness area and wetlands where geese and other waterfowl were under state and federal protection. There weren't even any roads, just foot trails, on the map. "But there's nothing there!" I said.

"There will be something there today," Key assured me. "I think you'll find it rather interesting. It's the former lands and sacred burial grounds of the Piscataway Indians, the first inhabitants of what's now Washington, D.C. The tribes don't actually live there, now that it's federal property, but they'll be there today—and looking forward to our arrival."

THE ORIGINAL INSTRUCTIONS

God gives His Instructions to every creature, according to His plan for the world.

—MATHEW KING, *Noble Red Man*

... we are responsible for following our original instructions—those given by the Creator.

Every component of the universe, in an indigenous conception, has a set of original instructions to follow so that a balanced order can be kept. . . . The people lived in accordance with their original instructions, tempered and ordered by the natural world around them.

—GABRIELLE TAYAC, DAUGHTER OF RED FLAME TAYAC, "Keeping the Original Instructions," *Native Universe*

THIS WAS DEFINITELY THE "SCENIC ROUTE," AS Key had promised. Or had she threatened?

Piscataway was breathtakingly beautiful, even from this distance. Wildfowl of all kinds floated on the current while eagles soared overhead and a few swans sailed in for a watery touchdown. Along the banks, ancient trees clawed the waters with their gnarled roots and thickets of cattails hugged the shoreline.

As we rounded the point, our pilot cut in close to shore, then cut his engine and drifted closer still. A few passengers on deck glanced toward the pilot's cabin with expressions of mild surprise.

Along the shore, I noticed two fishermen wearing battered, tackle-studded hats, sitting on a fallen tree trunk that jutted out from the rocky bank. Their fishing lines trailed out into the water. One of them got to his feet as our boat drifted nearer and started reeling in his line.

Over the megaphone, the pilot said, "Folks, river's pretty calm today, so we're able to drop off a few naturalists here at the wildlife refuge. Only take a minute."

A teenage boy came portside and took up the coil of hawser.

"Now if you peer in the opposite direction," the pilot went on, "just upstream, due north, you'll have a rare view of Jones Point people don't often get to see from this vantage. Right there's where the first, the southernmost stone marker was laid by surveyor Andrew Ellicott and the African American astronomer, Benjamin Banneker, April 15, 1791, the day they began marking out the original Capital City—now Washington, D.C. Those of you interested in Freemasons' history in our nation's capital will want to share with your friends that this stone was set with full Masonic ritual—square, plumb, and level, and sprinkled with corn, oil, and wine—in keeping with their tradition . . ."

He was doing such a great job of pointing the passengers' rapt attention away from their backsides that I'd have been surprised if *anyone* would remember—or had even noticed—the unauthorized passengers he'd landed on Piscataway. I figured Key must have pledged a case of Chivas Regal along with those flight miles.

The waiting fishermen reeled us in with the hawser and helped us clamber onto the giant log; then they tossed the hawser free and the four of us made tracks across the rocky shore for the dense sheltering brush of the shoreline.

"Names are perhaps best left unspoken," said the older of the two fishermen, as he took my hand to help me over the rocks. "You may simply call me Red Cedar—it's my native moniker given me by our moon goddess here—and my assistant, Mr. Tobacco Pouch."

He motioned to the stocky younger fellow, who gave me a crinkly-eyed smile. They both looked sturdy enough to tangle with whatever we might encounter. Key really *did* seem to have a lot of contacts in these parts. But as we followed them into the dense undergrowth, I hadn't a *clue* what was going on.

There was no path that I could see. The forest was so thick with vines and brush and saplings, it seemed impossible that the four of us could beat our way through it, even with machetes. It was like a labyrinth, but one to which Red Cedar seemed to hold the key: The growth seemed miraculously to melt away before him—he didn't even have to touch it—and it closed up again the moment we'd passed through behind him.

Eventually the woods thinned a bit. We found ourselves on a dirt trail with a view of the river in the distance through sun-dappled trees that were just unfurling their spring chartreuse. Here Red Cedar was able to drop back from his lead position. We could all walk side by side on the trail and speak to one another for the first time.

"Piscataway is both a place and a people," Red Cedar told me. "The word means 'Where the Living Waters Blend'—the confluence of many rivers of both water and life. Our people descend from the oldest indigenous peoples, the Lenni Lenape, the grandfathers, going back for more than twelve thousand years. The Anacostan and other local tribes were paying tribute to our first chief, the Tayac, long before the first Europeans arrived."

I must have seemed a bit mystified by the reason for this impromptu, nature-trail anthropology lesson, for he added, "Miss Luna said that you are her friend, that you are in some kind of danger, and that it was therefore of special importance I must tell you something before we reach Moyaone."

"Moyaone?" I said.

"The ossuary fields," he said. Then he added, with a wink and a whisper, "*Where all the bones are buried!*"

At this, he and Tobacco Pouch cackled mightily.

Did he mean a graveyard? Or what exactly was so uproarious about a pile of bones? I glanced toward Key, who was smiling that private smile.

"All the bones and all the *secrets,*" she said. Then to Red Cedar, she suggested, "Before we get there, why don't you tell my friend about the Green Corn Ceremony, the two virgins, and the Feast of the Dead?"

Holy Moly. I knew Key was a bit on the esoteric side, but this was descending deeper into weird-dom by the moment—shades of pagan ritual and virgin sacrifice along the Potomac—or what was that all about?

As I moved through the dappled woods and peered about me, I tried to remind myself that the Secret Service was still hunting us up and down the river, that I had no ID on me, and that no one had a clue where I had gone. Though I knew we were only miles from our nation's capital, it was a strange feeling. Oddly, this mysterious spot felt removed, both in time and space, from everything I knew.

And things were about to get stranger still.

"It has to do with the Original Instructions," Red Cloud was saying. "Everything comes into being along with its own instructions—like a blueprint or a pattern or a set of plans. Water always becomes round, fire is a triangle, many rocks are crystalline, spiders make webs, birds make nests, the analemma of the sun's movement forms a figure eight—"

Key touched him on the arm to move a bit faster, either along the path or along with his tale—or perhaps both.

"So the story of the virgins starts about four hundred years ago," Red Cloud said, "when the English colonists arrived and they set up a place called 'Jamestown,' named after their new king. But even before that, in the 1500s they'd already nabbed a big swath of the land thereabouts, and they'd named it 'Virginia' after James's predecessor, their virgin queen, Elizabeth."

"I'm familiar with the story," I said, trying not to sound too impatient. Where was this headed?

"But you don't know the *whole* story," Red Cedar told me. "About thirty years after those Jamestown colonists, the English had another king, Charles, likely a closet Catholic. He let Lord Baltimore send two boatloads of Catholic settlers and Jesuit priests in ships called the *Ark* and the *Dove*.

"Now, these British had been battling it out for ages over which of the 'true faiths' owned the cross with all of its powers. In a few more years they'd be in a civil war over it, and King Charles himself would be dead. But one thing that all Europeans agreed on, and still do, was the law of discovery: If you discover a place and plant your flag there, then you own it! If there are natives already living there, and you call them barbarians, so much the better. You can convert them by force or you can enslave them by Church edict."

I was familiar with *this* story, too. The land grabs, the broken treaties, the massacred Indian babies, the reservations, the genocide, the Trail of Tears—no love ever lost between indigenous peoples and the crusading conquerors, I thought.

And yet, it was I who was in for a surprise.

"So in short, the Piscataway became converted Catholics," Red Cedar told me, "because the Original Instructions were met by the Feast of the Assumption and the Feast of the Dead."

"Pardon me?" I said, staring across at Key.

"You know," Red Cedar explained, "the Feast of the Dead, when we honor the ancestors in November, is at the same time as in the Catholic calendar when the dead are honored for All Hallows' Eve and All Souls' and All Saints' days. But most important is August fifteenth, the date in the Church calendar when the feast is held that honors the Assumption of the Blessed Virgin Mary into Heaven—that's the date of our ancient Green Corn Ceremony, for the 'first harvest,' which marks the beginning of our new year."

"I gather," I said, "that you're saying the Piscataway converted to the Catholic faith because they could continue to maintain their own beliefs and rituals while paying lip service to the official Church regimen?"

"Not exactly," said Key. "You'll see when we get to the burial grounds. But what Red Cedar's saying—the reason why you needed to meet him and Tobacco Pouch without interference from the troops—is because of the Original Instructions. The Buck Stops Here, as they say—I mean, right here in this very spot."

"Then *let's* stop here," I said, exasperated.

I was getting pretty frustated with the direction this "road trip" of ours was taking. But I'd also halted because we were at the beginning of a long wooden bridge that crossed the vast marshlands we were about to enter just ahead. I hoped it would keep our feet dry, since I only had the one pair of shoes.

I addressed myself to Key. "I don't get it. How does all this religious-ritual-and-ancestor stuff your pal is running off about bear any relation to the immediate problem that you and I are involved in?" I asked her. "What's so important about virgins and corn and dining among the dead?"

Red Cedar clarified: "The Jesuits dubbed the place where they landed 'St. Mary,' " he told me, "and they later named the whole area on this side of the river Mary Land—supposedly after the wife of King Charles, but really after the Virgin Mary, the mother of Jesus. So we now had two virgins facing off across the river from each other—one Protestant and one Catholic! Two virgin islands of Christianity, you might say, afloat in a sea of indigenous peoples—"

Two Virgin Islands. Why did that strike a chime?

Tobacco Pouch had tried on the bridge for size, and it seemed to be high and dry, so we went on, passing over single file again, through the waving sea of high cattails.

But Key, who had something to add, caught up with me. "It was the Potomac tribes in these parts, like the Piscataway, who first launched the 'Two Virgins Theory': that one kernel is not enough. They figured out that if you plant *two* kernels together along the row, it's easier for the corn to pollinate. All part of the Original Instructions. They've been doing it that way since ancient times."

Though Leda the Lesbian would surely go for this philosophy—the idea that two virgin females might equal yin and yang—I was still confused.

But that chime in my head was clanging louder.

And then I knew.

"*You* made up the code for that message Mother left me on the piano," I mentioned softly. "So what *about* those 'Virgin Isles'?"

Key smiled approvingly and nodded.

"That's it," she told me. "That's why we dropped by here, first thing, before anyplace else. 'Virgin Isles' is native code for Washington, D.C. And this spot, right here in Piscataway, is where the Original Instructions were written for our nation's capital."

"I thought that George Washington provided the original instructions for the capital city," I pointed out. "After all, he's the one who bought the land, who hired the folks who laid out the square, with all those moronic-Masonic trappings we've just heard about from your pal, the ferry pilot—"

"Where do you think he *got* those instructions?" Key asked me.

When I said nothing, she pointed across the marshes, out over the river. There, in the far distance, seated high on its green bluff in the brilliant morning sun, lay Mount Vernon, George Washington's home.

"The land for the city was never selected or secured through accident," Red Cedar told me over his shoulder. "It took much secrecy and skilled maneuvering on the president's part. But he knew from the first that this place where we are, Piscataway, was the key to it all. The tradition comes from native belief, but from the Bible, too: They call it the City on the Hill, the High Place. The New Jerusalem. It's all in the Apocalypse—the Book of Revelation of Saint John. The place chosen for the sacred site must be a spot at the confluence of many rivers in order for the power to be invoked."

"What power?" I asked, though I was beginning to get the message.

We left the marsh and had now come out into an open meadow where dandelions and wildflowers were already perking up for spring and birds and insects were chirping, buzzing, humming all around us.

"It's the power we've come here to see," said Key, pointing her arm across the grassland. "That's Moyaone."

As we traversed the meadow, I saw one enormous evergreen tree that dominated the center of the field. If I wasn't mistaken, and I wasn't, the tree was—

"The red cedar," said Key. "A sacred tree. The pith and sap of the trunk are red, like human blood. This one was planted by the last Piscataway chief, Turkey Tayac, whose grave site is also here."

We crossed the meadow and went up to the grave, where a small picture of the Tayac himself, a handsome, bronzed fellow in full feathered regalia, was set into a wooden trail marker plaque. It said that he was buried here, through an Act of Congress, in 1979.

Around it were four tall stakes embedded in the ground, with woven wreaths attached. The tree itself, just beyond, was festooned with red bags that had been tied on with red ribbons—hundreds and hundreds of them.

"Tobacco pouches," said Key. "Tributes to honor the dead."

For the first time all morning, Mr. Tobacco Pouch spoke up. "For your father," he said, handing me a small red cloth pouch that fit in my palm, as he gestured toward the red cedar tree. Key must have clued him in.

I went over to the tree, a bit choked up, and searched a moment before I could locate a branch that was unladen, where I could tie on my gift. Then I inhaled the scent of the tree. What a wonderful tradition: sending smoke rings up to Heaven.

Key had come up behind me. "These spirit posts with the wreaths are here to protect this place from evil," she told me. "They mark the Four Quarters—the four cardinal directions. It all connects together, as you see, right here at this spot."

She meant, of course, the precise layout of Washington, D.C., a city whose very first stone marker had been laid just due north of this place. Some things were definitely coming together—the four corners, four quarters, four directions, the chessboard form of the ancient altars, the ancient rites—

But there was one thing I still really needed to know.

"You told me that the 'Virgin Isles' is a code word for the city of Washington, D.C.," I said to Key and the others. "I can see why George Washington—as the founder of a new country, as a pretty religious guy himself, and maybe even as a Mason—would want to create a fresh new capital city just like the one in the Bible. Why he'd design it this way, bridging the river, to bring the two Christianities together. As you said—two virgin queens, hands across the waters, two kernels of corn in a pod.

"But what I don't get is this: If your mission is to follow the 'Original Instructions,' to go with the natural flow, then what's the point of going over to the enemy? I mean, as you yourselves have just pointed out, all these religions have been battling over their symbols and rites for hundreds of years. How could signing up with that embattled agenda possibly help Mother Nature spin spiderwebs or grow corn? Is this an example of 'If you can't beat 'em, join 'em'?"

Key stopped and looked at me seriously for the first time. "Alexandra, in all these years have I taught you *nothing*?" she said.

Her words struck home. Hadn't Nim asked exactly the same question?

Red Cedar took my arm. "But those *are* the Original Instructions," he told me. "The 'natural order,' as you choose to call it, shows that things only really grow and change from *within*, by achieving a natural balance. Not through external force."

Clearly, my three companions had blanked on a few historic memories of their own. "So you're impregnating the Church with Native rules of order?" I said.

"We are merely demonstrating," said Red Cedar, "that Mother Corn, like Mother Earth, existed long before any other virgins or mothers. And with our help, she will long outsurvive them. We plant corn and harvest as we do, because that's how the corn is happiest and produces the most offspring."

"As they always say," added Key, " 'As ye sow, so shall ye reap.' "

Where had I just heard that?

Tobacco Pouch—who'd been studying the sky—

turned to Key. "He'll be here just now," he told her, motioning across the meadow.

Key glanced at her watch and nodded.

"Who'll be here?" I said, following his gesture.

"Our ride," Key said. "There's a parking strip there, just off the back road. Someone's picking us up for the airport."

I saw a man emerge from a copse of trees at the far side of the meadow, just opposite where we'd entered ourselves.

Even at this great distance, as he came through the unmowed grass, I recognized him at once by his tall, slender form and lanky gait—not to mention that trademark mop of dark curls, blowing in the breeze.

It was Vartan Azov.

THE ASHES

I am ashes where once I was fire,
And the bard in my bosom is dead,
What I loved I now merely admire—
And my heart is as grey as my head.

—Lord Byron,
"To the Countess of Blessington"

It were better to die doing something than nothing.

—Lord Byron,
March 1824

Missolonghi, Greece
Easter Sunday, April 18, 1824

It was raining; it had been raining for days. It seemed the rains would never end.

The Sirocco had arrived from Africa two weeks ago and struck with the terrible force of an unleashed animal, ripping and clawing at the small stone houses along the coast, leaving the rocky shores strewn with odious debris.

Within the Capsali house, where the British and other foreigners were quartered, all was silence just as Drs. Bruno and Millingen had ordered. Even the cannonade, for the traditional Greek celebration of Easter Sunday, had been marched by the militia to a site just beyond the town wall, and the townsfolk were encouraged to follow it, despite the inclement weather.

Now the only sound that could be heard within the

emptied house was the frenzied racket of the unrelenting storm.

Byron lay beneath the covers of his Turkish sofa on the top floor. Even his great Newfoundland, Lyon, lay quietly beside the settee, his head between his paws. And Fletcher the valet stood across the room in silence, pouring water in order to thin the ever-present carafe of brandy.

Byron studied the walls and ceiling of this drawing room, which he'd decorated himself upon his arrival—was it just three months ago?—with trappings from his own private arsenal. This display of suspended swords, pistols, Turkish sabers, rifles, blunderbusses, bayonets, trumpets, and helmets had never failed to impress Byron's boisterous and violent private brigade of Suliote bodyguards, who'd camped out below on the ground floor—that is, until he'd finally paid up the dangerous hooligans and sent them off to the front lines.

Now, as the raging storm battered against the shutters, Byron wished—in one of his rare lucid moments—that he might still possess the strength to stand and cross the room, to throw open the windows to the fury of the storm.

Better to die in the wild embrace of a natural force, he believed, than this slow draining away of one's spark of life with repetitious applications of plasters and leeches. He'd tried his best, at least, to resist all those bleedings. He could never bear the loss of blood. More lives had been lost to the lancet than to the lance—as he'd repeatedly told that incompetent fool, Dr. Bruno.

But by the time that the Greek administrator Mavrocordato's own physician, Luca Vaya, had been able to defy the storm and achieve the beach at Missolonghi, just yesterday, Byron had already suffered the racks of chills and fever for more than a week—ever since that ride, April 9, when the elements had caught up to him, and he'd first taken ill.

And in the end, "Bruno the Butcher" had gotten his way—opening Byron's veins repeatedly to extract pound after pound of blood. Sacred Heaven! The man was worse than a vampire!

Now, with the life force ebbing from Byron moment by moment, he still retained enough awareness to realize that he'd been, in these past days, more than half the time delirious. And he also retained enough of sober consciousness to know that this illness of his was no mere dose of the cold or the chilblains.

It was, in all likelihood, the same "illness" that had seized Percy Shelley.

He was being carefully killed.

Byron understood that if he didn't act quickly, if he didn't reveal what he knew to the one person who needed to know, and who could be trusted, it might well be too late. And all would certainly be lost.

His valet, Fletcher, was now beside his bed, waiting with the bottle of watered cognac that provided Byron's only relief: Fletcher, who in hindsight may have been the wise one from the very beginning. He'd long been reluctant to accompany his master to Greece, and had begged for Byron to reconsider whether his commitment to the cause of Greek independence might not be better served by merely providing financial assets that the patriots required—but without such direct personal involvement. After all, they'd both seen Missolonghi before, just after their visit, thirteen years ago, to Ali Pasha.

But then, nine days ago when Byron had "fallen ill" with this mysterious, unsolvable disease, the normally stoic Fletcher had nearly gone to pieces. The staff of servants, the military men, the doctors all spoke different languages.

"Like the Tower of Babel!" Fletcher had cried, pulling

his hair in frustration. It had required three translations merely to request, on the patient's behalf, a cup of broth with a beaten egg in it.

But at least, thanks to God, Fletcher was here at this moment—and they were, for once, alone. Now, like it or not, the trusted valet must be pressed into one last duty.

Byron touched Fletcher's arm.

"Sire, more brandy?" said the latter, with a countenance so grave and pained that Byron would have laughed—if it hadn't required quite so much effort.

Byron moved his lips, and Fletcher bent his ear to his master.

"My daughter," Byron whispered.

But he instantly regretted having spoken those words.

"You wish me to record a personal letter from you to Lady Byron and to little Ada in London?" asked Fletcher, fearing the worst.

For this kind of exposure could only reflect the last wish of a dying man. The world knew that Byron loathed his wife, and only sent her private communiqués, to which she rarely replied.

But Byron shook his head slightly, among the pillows. He knew that his valet would understand, and that this man who had been his servant for so many years and through so many tribulations, the only one who knew of their true relationship, would reveal this last request to no one.

"Fetch me Haidée," Byron said. "And bring the boy."

IT PAINED HAIDÉE to see her father lying there, so pale and wan, whiter—as Fletcher had warned, just before they saw him—than down beneath the wing of a newborn chick.

Now, as she and Kauri stood before the tattered Turkish bed, where Fletcher had plumped up cushions, she felt like weeping. She had already lost the one man whom she'd believed all her life was her father—Ali Pasha. And now, this father, whom she had known for little more than a year, was draining away before her eyes.

In the year since they'd found each other, as Haidée well knew, Byron had risked everything and exercised every subterfuge to keep her near him while keeping their relationship a secret.

In support of this subterfuge, only months ago, on Byron's thirty-sixth birthday, he told her he'd written a letter to his wife, "Lady B," as he called her, saying he'd found a lovely and lively Greek child, "Hayatée"—just a bit older than their daughter, Ada—who'd been orphaned by the war. He'd like to adopt her and send her to England, where Lady B might look out for her proper education.

Of course, he had never received a word back on the subject. But the spies who opened the mail, as he told Haidée, would believe this pseudo-adoption to be just another of the great lord's well-known foibles.

Haidée's "relationship" with Byron had now been established through rumor, which, in Greece, never lied. And now that he was dying—at a moment when it was imperative that they speak—they both knew it was more important than ever that no one must know the truth of why she'd been brought here.

The Black Queen lay hidden in a cave on an island off the coast of Maino where Byron had once told Trelawney he'd like to be buried—the cave where he'd written *The Corsair.* Only the three of them—Haidée, Kauri, and Byron—knew where to retrieve it. But what good was it now?

For the Greek War of Independence, begun in force three years ago, had now gone from bad to worse. Prince Alexander Ypsilántis—former head of the Philiki

Eteria, the society pledged to free Greece—had led the charge but been renounced and betrayed by his former master, Tsar Alexander I of Russia, and was now rotting in an Austro-Hungarian jail.

The Greek factions were bickering among one another, vying for supremacy, while Byron, perhaps their last hope, lay dying in a squalid room in Missolonghi.

Even worse, Haidée could read the anguish in her father's face, not just from the poison they'd undoubtedly been feeding him, but anguish at leaving this earth, at leaving her, his daughter, with their mission yet undone.

Kauri sat in silence near the bed, with one hand on Lyon's head, while Haidée stood beside her father and took his feeble hand in hers.

"Father, I know how gravely ill you are," she said softly. "But I *must* know the truth. What can our hopes be now, for the salvation of the Black Queen—or the chess service?"

"As you see," whispered Byron, "it was all quite true, everything we feared. The battles and betrayals of Europe will never end until *all* are free. Napoleon betrayed his allies as well as the French people—and even his own ideals, in the end—when he marched into Russia. And Alexander of Russia, in destroying all hope for uniting the Eastern churches against Islam, betrayed those ideals of his grandmother, Catherine the Great. But what use is idealism when the ideals are false ones?"

The poet had leaned back into the pillows, closing his eyes as if he could not go on.

He moved his hand slightly, and Haidée intuitively reached for the cup of *tisane,* a strong infusion of tea that, at Byron's request, Fletcher had made up for his master before departing. Haidée saw that the valet had left a water pipe as well, with the tobacco already burning, to provide the infusion of strength that Byron *himself* would need, to tell what he had to say.

Byron sipped the tea from the cup in Haidée's hand, then Kauri placed the hose from the water pipe between the poet's lips. At last, Byron found the strength to continue.

"Ali Pasha was a man with a great mission," he told them in his weak voice. "It was more than uniting East and West, it was about uniting underlying truths. Meeting him and Vasiliki changed my life, at a time when I was not much older than the two of you. Because of this, I wrote many of my greatest tales of love: the story of Haidée and Don Juan's passion; *The Giaour*—'The Infidel'—of love for Leila by the non-Muslim hero. But *giaour* does not really mean 'infidel.' The oldest meaning—from Persian *gawr*—was a worshipper of fire, a Zoroastrian. Or a Parsee of India, one who worships Agni, the flame.

"It was this that I learned from the pasha and the Bektashis—the underlying flame that is present in all great truths. From your mother, Vasiliki, I learned love."

Byron motioned to them for another strong tea infusion and tobacco to provide the strength he needed. When this was done to his satisfaction, Byron added, "Perhaps I shan't live to see another year, but at least I shall see the dawn tomorrow. Enough time to share with you the secret of the Black Queen that the pasha and Vasiliki, so many years ago, once shared with me. You must know that the Queen now in your possession is not the only one. But it is the *real* one. Lean closer, my child."

Haidée did as he'd asked, and Byron spoke so quietly into her ear that even Kauri had to strain to hear what was said.

THE POET'S TALE

In the town of Kazan in central Russia, sometime in the late 1500s, lived a young girl named Matrona who repeatedly dreamed that the Mother of God had come to her to tell her of an ancient buried icon that possessed tremendous powers. After following the many clues given by the Virgin, the icon was at last located within a demolished house, in the ashes beneath the stove, wrapped in cloth.

It was called the Black Virgin of Kazan. It would become the most famous icon in the history of Russia.

Shortly after its discovery, in 1579, the Bogoroditsa convent was built in Kazan to house the icon—Bogodoritsa meaning "Birth-Giver of God," from Bogomater, Mother of God, the title of all such dark figures connected with the earth.

The Black Virgin of Kazan protected Russia over the past two hundred and fifty years. She accompanied the soldiers who freed Moscow from the Poles in 1612, and even from Napoleon as recently as 1812.

In the 1700s, Peter the Great brought her from Moscow, her second home, to his new city of St. Petersburg. She became patron and protectress of that city.

The moment the Black Queen of Heaven was installed at St. Petersburg in 1715, Peter the Great unfurled his master plan: to drive the Turks from Europe. He declared himself Petrus I, Russo-Graecorum Monarcha—king of Greece and Russia—and vowed to unite the Greek and Russian Orthodox churches. Though he did not succeed in this quest, Peter's ambition would inspire another successor, nearly fifty years later, with similar zeal for the same cause.

She was Tsarina Ekaterina II, Empress of all the Russias, whom we know as Catherine the Great.

In 1762, when Catherine—with the help of her lover, Grigory Orlov—overthrew her husband, Tsar Peter III, in a palace coup, she swiftly joined the Orlov brothers at the Cathedral of Kazan Bogoroditski to officially declare herself empress.

To commemorate the event she had a medallion cast of herself as that other virgin, Athene or Minerva, and she commissioned a copy of the icon of the Black Virgin of Kazan, with a bejeweled *oklad*, a frame cast by master goldsmith Iakov Frolov, which would be hung in the Winter Palace directly above Catherine's bed.

The Russian Church threw its impressive support—the Church owned more than one-third of all Russian land and Russian serfs—behind Catherine's aspirations to drive Islam from the eastern reaches of the continent and unite the two Christian churches. They enthusiastically helped fund exploration, expansion, and warfare: Grigori Shelikov, the "Russian Columbus," established the first Russian colony in Alaska and a trading company in Kamchatka and also mapped eastern Russia, part of western America, and the islands in between.

The Russian Empire had begun to stake its sweeping claim.

Catherine planned that this domain would be ruled by her grandson, Alexander, whom she'd named after the great conqueror of the East.

From the first Russo-Turkish War in 1768, Catherine would secure an important concession—the first toe across the threshold of the great Ottoman Empire: the right under treaty, if a cause should arise, for Russia to protect Christian subjects of the Porte.

Shortly thereafter, in secrecy, Catherine's new favorite, Grigori Potemkin, assisted her in drafting a plan that was breathtaking in scope. They called it the "Greek Project." It was nothing short of the restoration of the entire Byzantine Empire, as it was prior to its conquests by Islam. This would be ruled by Catherine's other grandson, whom she had named after the original founder of the Eastern church: Constantine.

To execute this plan, Potemkin established a military unit of two hundred Greek students, the "Company of

Foreign Believers," to be trained in Russian military technology and expertise, in preparation for a return to their homeland where they would help spearhead the effort to liberate Greece from Turkish rule. This group represented the birth seed of the Etairia ton Philikon, the Society for Greek Independence, which would become so instrumental in everything we do here today.

With her strategy in hand, and some passed pawns planted behind enemy lines, now Catherine's pieces were all in position for a major coup. Or so she believed.

The second Russo-Turkish War, begun in 1787, only two years before the French Revolution, proved even more successful than the first: Potemkin, as commander in chief, secured Russian domination over most of the Black Sea and captured the great Turkish fort, Ismail.

Catherine was about to launch the full "Greek Project," to dismember the Turkish Empire and take Constantinople, when Potemkin—not only Catherine's commander in chief and brilliant political strategist, but some said also her secret husband—while returning from treaty signing, was suddenly seized by a mysterious fever. He died, like a dog, alongside the road to Nikolaiev, in Bessarabia, just north of the Black Sea.

The court at St. Petersburg was in mourning at the news and Catherine was bereft with grief. Her lofty aspirations and all her complex plans seemed to be indefinitely on hold—relegated to the grave along with the mastermind who'd not only helped to conceive them, but had also executed them.

But just at that moment, an old friend from France arrived at the Winter Palace, a friend named Helène de Roque, the Abbess of Montglane. With her, she brought an important piece of the Montglane Service—the chess set that had once belonged to Charlemagne—perhaps the most powerful piece: the Black Queen.

This inspired in Catherine the Great, empress of all

the Russias, the hope that perhaps all her efforts and the anticipated fruits of her "Project" might not be lost after all.

Catherine secured this one chess piece, while keeping a watchful eye on her friend the abbess in an attempt to discover where the other pieces of the service might be found. More than a year would pass before Catherine's son Paul—who loathed her—overheard a conversation between the abbess and his mother, disclosing that the empress Catherine planned to disinherit Paul in favor of his son, Alexander. But when the empress realized that Paul had also learned of the existence of the valuable chess piece hidden in her private vault at the Hermitage, she resolved to take immediate action.

Unbeknownst to anyone, the empress, suspicious of her son Paul's intentions, secretly arranged for the master goldsmith Iakov Frolov—who had made her a perfect copy of the Kazan Black Virgin more than twenty years earlier—to create an equally undetectable copy of the Black Queen.

In desperation, Catherine secretly smuggled the genuine chess piece, through her "Company of Foreign Believers," to the Greek underground. She placed the "perfect" copy in her vault at the Hermitage, where it remained until her death three years later—when Paul found and destroyed his mother's will and became tsar of Russia.

Then he held in his hands, at last, what he believed to be the one thing his mother had always craved most.

But one person knew all.

When Catherine the Great died, and the new tsar Paul found the Queen tucked away in her vault, believing it to be the original, he showed this piece to the Abbess of Montglane just before the State funeral for his mother, in an attempt to elicit, by threats or by force, the abbess's cooperation in finding the others. He showed enough of his hand to convince the abbess that, regardless of what she said or did, she'd be cast into prison. In response, the abbess held out her hand for the chess piece: "That belongs to me," she told Paul.

He refused to hand it to her, but she could see, even from this distance, that something was strange. This appeared in every way to be the same heavy gold carving, caked with uncut gemstones, round and carefully polished like robins' eggs. Indeed, in all respects it was identical to the other: It portrayed a figure dressed in long robes and seated in a small pavilion with draperies drawn back.

But there was just one thing missing.

The Church boasted many stones like these, from Charlemagne's day and earlier, which were not cut with facets, but were polished by hand to the shape of these, or tumbled with fine-grain silicon as pebbles are refined in the sea, leaving a surface of glass that served to enhance either the natural iridescence or the asterism, the inner star of the gem. Throughout the Bible, such stones were described, along with their hidden meanings.

It was because of this that the abbess could substantiate at a glance that this piece was not the same Black Queen that she herself had brought into Russia from France, more than five years ago.

For, in fear that something like this might happen, the abbess had placed her own secret mark on the original, a mark that no one would ever detect but herself. Using the faceted diamond from her abbatial ring, she'd made a small scratch in the shape of a figure eight upon the cabochon fire-ruby just at the base of the pavilion.

A mark that was no longer there!

There was only one way this could be. The tsarina Catherine had somehow created a perfect copy of the Black Queen for the vault, and had somehow disposed of the real one. It was safe from Paul's hands, at least.

The abbess had but one chance. At the empress's funeral, she must pass an encrypted letter to someone in the outside world—through Plato Zubov, the empress's last amour, who, as Paul had just notified her, would soon be sent into exile.

It was her only hope to save the Black Queen.

WHEN BYRON HAD finished this tale, he lay back against the pillows—his skin even whiter than before, due to the lack of blood—and he closed his eyes. It was clear that his energy—what small bit he might have marshaled at the beginning—had completely drained from him. But Haidée knew that time was of the essence.

She reached out to Kauri, who set the water pipe into her hand, along with a small balance with a new measure of shredded tobacco. She lifted the lid and scooped the tobacco onto the coals. When the smoke rose into the pipe, she wafted some of the fumes back to her father.

Byron coughed slightly and opened his eyes. He looked upon his daughter with enormous love and sorrow.

"Father," she said, "I must ask you, how did this information ever reach Ali Pasha, my mother, and the Baba Shemimi, for them to tell you the tale?"

"It reached someone else," said Byron, his voice still reduced to a whisper. "It was the person who invited us all to gather in Rome.

"The next winter after Catherine the Great's death, the war still raged in Europe. The Treaty of Campo Formio was signed, granting France the Ionian islands and several towns along the Albanian coast. Tsar Paul and the British had signed a treaty with the sultan at Constantinople, betraying all that his mother, the empress Catherine, had once promised to Greece.

"Ali Pasha joined forces with France against this nefarious triumvirate. But Ali himself was resolved to play both of these ends against the middle. For by now, he had learned—through Letizia and her friend Shahin—that he held the true Black Queen."

"And what of the Black Queen herself?" asked Haidée, setting aside the water pipe, though in her preoccupation, she still held the small copper balance. "If Kauri and I are to protect her, in whose service must she be placed amid all these betrayals?"

"In the service of Lady Justice," said Byron, with a faint, understanding smile directed toward Kauri.

"Lady Justice?" asked Haidée.

"You are standing closest to her yourself," said her father. "It is she who now holds the Balance in her hands."

THE FLAG

flame . . . <L. *flamma,* flame, blaze, blazing fire, orig. *flagma* √* *flag in flagrare,* burn, blaze: see flagrant

flagrant . . . √* *flag=Gr.* φλεγειν, burn=Skt. √*bhraj,* shine brightly . . . 1. Burning, blazing; hence, shining; glorious

— *The Century Dictionary*

VARTAN WAS LOOKING UNEXPECTEDLY SPECTACULAR, for someone who was a world-class, card-carrying, professional chess nerd.

I couldn't help but recall Key's first comments about him, back in Colorado, as he now crossed the meadow to greet us, the breezes tossing his curls. He was sporting a striped sweater of bright spring colors, sky blue and electric yellow—quite startling here in the wildflower meadow. It almost made me forget for an instant that I was being chased by every dangerous fool on the planet except my aunt Fanny.

I wondered whether Vartan had gotten decked out in this costume just for me.

He came up and greeted Red Cedar and Tobacco Pouch, who had a few private words with Key. Then they shook hands all around and departed by the way we'd come.

Vartan laughed when he noticed I was studying his remarkable sweater. "I'd hoped you would like my pullover," he said, as we started back with Key toward wherever he'd left the car. She walked briskly ahead of us. "I had it made specially. It's the flag of Ukraine. The colors are quite beautiful, I think, but also symbolic.

"The blue is for the sky and the yellow is for grain fields. Grain is everything to us; it carries deep emotional roots. It's often hard to remember that before Stalin created those famines from his enforced collective farming, which killed millions, Kiev had been called the Mother of Russia and that Ukraine was the breadbasket of Europe. There is a wonderful song about America I've heard, which speaks of these same elements of sky and golden meadows of wheat: *'Oh skies so beautiful, with amber fields of waving grain—'* " he tried to sing.

"Yep, we've heard that one," I said. "And if Key here had ever had any clout with her illustrious family, she would have made *that* our national anthem—not the barroom ballad about rockets and bombs by her Sir Francis Scott Namesake."

"Oh, it's just the same," said Vartan as we three continued across the meadow, Key still in the lead. "*Our* national anthem is not so very optimistic either: 'Ukraine Has Not Yet Died.' " Then he added, "But I want you to look at something else, which I have had sewn onto the back of my pullover."

He turned as he walked, to display the embroidered crest stitched on the reverse, also bright yellow and blue, with a sculptured, three-pronged fork in the middle that looked rather Gothic. "The arms of Ukraine," Vartan said. "The crest is of Volodimir, our patron saint, but the trident goes back to before Roman times. Actually, the first one like this was carried by the Indian fire god, Agni. It means rising from the ashes, the eternal flame, 'We have not died' and all that—"

"May I point out," said Key over her shoulder, "that if we don't get this show on the road, PDQ, we might soon be *expecting* to die?"

"I only spoke of it because it's why I wore the

pullover. Because of where we are going right now," Vartan said.

Key had shot him a scathing look. Now she picked up her pace, and Vartan did likewise.

"Whoa," I said, racing to catch up. "You're *not* suggesting that we're going anyplace like the Ukraine?" I wasn't even sure I knew exactly where that was!

"Don't be ridiculous," Key snapped at me over her shoulder.

Her assurance provided me little comfort since, for Key, an average day's outing might involve scaling the side of a glacier with her fingernails. With her in charge, as she seemed to be now, we might be headed almost anywhere. And at this point—having already been waylaid or kidnapped two or three times since breakfast—*nothing* would surprise me.

"No, don't worry," said Vartan, taking my arm when, a little breathlessly, I finally caught up to them. "I'm not even certain myself about our exact destination."

"Then why did you say 'Where we're going'?" I asked.

"We'll all find out soon enough," Key snapped again. "But whether or not we're all going there flying the Ukrainian flag on our chests is a different matter."

"In fact, I really wore this shirt just for you," Vartan told me, ignoring her obvious irritation. "I thought you would like it, because you are part Ukrainian."

What was *that* supposed to mean?

"Kryms'kyy—the Crimea, where your father was born—you know it's part of Ukraine. But there—here is our car at last."

Ours was the only car in the graveled dirt parking area, an inconspicuous gray sedan. When we reached it, Key held out her palm wordlessly and Vartan handed her the key. She opened the rear door for him. When he slid into the backseat, I noted a couple of duffel bags already tucked in there. I got in front on the passenger side, and we hit the road, with Key driving.

These back roads out of the park were dusty and winding; they kept forking in different directions, sometimes with no signs to mark the forks.

Key was taking the blind corners pretty quickly and I started to get more than nervous, hoping she knew where she was going.

But I did know one thing for sure: Right at this moment she was more than miffed.

But what for? Girlish jealousy over Vartan's attentions to me would seem more in keeping with Sage's provenance.

Besides, Vartan Azov, for all his undeniable appeal, definitely wasn't Key's type, as I should know better than anyone. His brains were more of the interior, analytical variety, while Key required someone more connected with the biosphere. Key's idea of an acceptable male was one who could distinguish a sérac from a moraine at a hundred paces, who could tie half a dozen kinds of knots within seconds—in the frozen dark, while wearing mittens—and who traveled nowhere without an extensive selection of pitons, crampons, and carabiners.

So what was this all about? The grim jawline, the tension behind the wheel? I could see that Key was working herself into a silent snit. But with Vartan tucked into the backseat, able to overhear everything that was said in the front, I had to prod my gray cells, trying to come up with a *maxim de communiqué* that he wouldn't understand.

As usual, Key beat me to it.

"Two heads are better than one," she muttered from the side of her mouth. "On the other hand, three's definitely a crowd."

"I thought your motto had always been 'The more, the merrier.' "

"Not today," she said.

After all, Key had had Vartan come all this way through the boondocks to pick us up. Did this mean she now wanted to ditch him?

But looking around at the bleak, deserted landscape, the copses of empty woodland with not one phone line or filling station, I wondered where it might even be possible to set down an unwanted Russian grandmaster who'd proven de trop.

Key pulled off the road into a copse of trees, switched off the engine, and turned to the backseat.

"Where are they?" she demanded of Vartan.

I'm sure my expression revealed as much confusion as did his.

"Where are they watching us from?" she asked, more fiercely. Then she added, "Buster, please don't jerk my chain by playing the ignorant emigré. You must know that I make my *living* by floating in air."

Then Key turned to me.

"Okay, let's just replay this scenario, shall we?" she suggested with complete disgust, ticking off each burst of her fury on a separate outstretched finger. "You and I escape from D.C., just one step ahead of the snapping jaws of guys who—as you inform me—are employed by the Secret Service! We dress in camouflage and get landed in a place that no one else can possibly reach! We go through a swamp and a forest that have been swept clean of observers by the Piscataway elders! We arrange a pickup car via a route that no one can possibly have foreknowledge of! Are we tracking so far?"

She turned to Vartan and poked his chest with her index finger. "Then *this* guy shows up and crosses the open tundra for half a mile, dressed in neon lights like he's trying to get attention in the late-night chorus at the Copa Cabaña!"

She repeated, "Where were they? A plane? A glider? A balloon?"

"You believe I wore this sweater to attract someone's attention?" said Vartan.

"Try another reason on me," she suggested, folding her arms. "And it had better be good. It's at least five miles to the nearest taxi stand, bub."

Vartan stared at her for a moment as if he were tongue-tied. He seemed slightly flushed but Key wasn't budging. Finally, he fixed her with an awkward smile.

"I admit it," he said. "I did it to draw attention."

"So where are they?" she said again.

Vartan pointed at me. "Right there," he said.

Once we'd clocked in to the idea of what he was saying, he added, "I'm very sorry. I thought I explained, I wanted to make some connection for Alexandra about her father and our homeland. I didn't understand about this—camouflage thing. I realize now that it's just like a smothered mate. But I would never wish to place you or Alexandra in any danger. Please believe me."

Key shut her eyes and shook her head, as if she simply *couldn't* believe this complete simpleton.

When she opened them again, Vartan Azov was sitting there in the backseat, topless.

"IF WE HAVE so many failures of understanding, and so early on," Vartan was saying, as Key drove on—and after we'd gotten him to put on another sweater to replace the colorful one he'd peeled off—"it seems that this is going to make the rest of our difficulties even more difficult than they already were to begin with."

Well said and true. But there was one difficulty that *I* certainly wasn't going to have trouble with any longer:

That was the difficulty of trying to imagine Vartan Azov with his shirt off.

I knew what this was. It was called the Drunkard's Curse—being told, when you're well into your cups, that you must try *not* to imagine a purple elephant. Even though you've never seen a purple elephant in your life, you'll never be able to drive the imaginary bugger from your brain.

But as a chess player, I was a master of memory and perception. And I knew that once you've actually *seen* something, as opposed to imagining it—like the two-second flash of a midgame chess position, or the twelve-second one of Vartan Azov's pectorals—then there the image will remain, deposited for eternity in your mental vault. Once seen, it's ineradicable, and try as you may you can never blot it out.

I wanted to kick myself for being a horse's behind.

This Azov fellow: One week ago I wanted to beat him, or beat him up, or destroy him—a healthy, aggressive stance that's saved many a chess player from ruin. But I knew that whatever was between him and me was going to be more than just a duel to the death.

I knew Vartan had been right, back in Colorado, when he'd said that there were too many coincidences in our two lives and that we ought to join forces. But was it really coincidence? After all, if Key was right, it had been my mother who'd gone through all that "loop-de-loop" in the first place, to put him and me together.

I was standing here at the brink of an abyss, not knowing whom I could trust—my mother, my uncle, my boss, my aunt, even my best friend. Then why should I, or would I, ever trust Vartan Azov?

But I did.

I knew now that Vartan Azov was flesh and blood. And not just because he'd failed to keep his sweater on.

He wanted something from me, something that I'd

seen or something I knew, perhaps without even yet realizing, myself, that I knew it. That's why all the chat about Ukraine and colors and symbols and amber waves of grain—

And then, all at once, I *did* know. It all fit together completely.

I turned over my shoulder to where Vartan sat in the backseat. He was looking at me with those fathomless dark purple eyes with the flame ignited at their depths.

And all at once, I knew that he knew exactly what *I* knew.

"Taras Petrossian was more than some typical Russian oligarch and chess devotee, wasn't he?" I said. "He owned a string of chi-chi restaurants, just like Sutalde here in D.C. He was financed by Basil. He had his hand in every pie. And he left it all to *you*."

From the corner of my eye I saw Key's mouth twitch slightly, but she didn't try to stop me. She just kept on driving.

"Yes he did," said Vartan, still looking at me with that intense expression, as if I were a pawn on his board. "At least, all but one thing."

"I know what that thing was," I told him.

I'd racked my mind from the moment I'd stood with Nim on the bridge that night. But hard as I tried to visualize the scenario, there was simply no way I could invent that his mother Tatiana could have gotten back into the courtyard, got inside the treasury—much less into my pocket—to extract the card with the firebird, after my father was killed that day.

But whoever *did* have that card and sent it to Nim, which by his own testimony he had forwarded to my mother, had also sent something else in the same packet.

"The chessboard," I said. "Whoever sent it to my uncle *must* have been there that day at Zagorsk. It had to be Taras Petrossian. That's why they killed him."

"No, Xie," said Vartan. "I sent the chessboard drawing and that card to your uncle myself—just as your mother asked me to do."

He studied me for a moment, as if unsure whether to proceed.

At last, he said, "My stepfather was killed when he sent her the Black Queen."

THE FLIGHT

Flight/Flying. Transcendence; the release of the spirit from the limitations of matter; the release of the spirit of the dead . . . access to a superhuman state. The ability of sages to fly or 'travel on the wind' symbolizes spiritual release and omnipresence.

—J. C. COOPER, *An Illustrated Encyclopaedia of Traditional Symbols*

"PLEASE TRY TO PAY ATTENTION," KEY ADMONished me, as we crossed the tarmac from the tiny air depot to board our waiting plane. "As our teachers in school used to say, 'Some of the information we're about to give you today *will* be appearing on your exam.' "

A critical download of data might come in handy right now, but I wasn't about to prompt it by asking more questions. After this morning's jumble of conflicting reports and information, I'd finally learned to shut up, listen, and keep my opinions to myself.

As we clambered into the plane with the duffel bags from the car, I noticed that I'd never before seen this plane of Key's, a vintage, single-engine Bonanza. I knew that when it came to planes she'd always liked antiques. But her tastes in general had run to rough-and-ready bush planes that could remain airborne at 50 mph.

"New trophy?" I said, once we three were buckled up and we'd begun taxiing.

"Nope," she told me. "The plague of Washington, D.C.: truncated runways. Wherever you land in these parts, you're always trying to put down atop the proverbial postage stamp. This baby's a loaner—heavier, with less float than a high-winged plane, so we can land much shorter. It's fuel-injected, though—very fast—so we'll get there in no time at all."

Nor did I inquire where *there* was. Not that I lacked curiosity, but after that little foray of ours just now on the back roads, it seemed clear enough that, though Key and Vartan might both be draftees on my mother's team, Key still didn't trust him enough to open up and reveal everything she knew.

And I confess, after that bombshell of Vartan's about the Black Queen, the chessboard, and that placard from Zagorsk, I was awaiting a few elaborations myself. So, bereft of options, I decided to follow the flow.

The Bonanza smelled like old leather and damp dog fur. I wondered where she'd dug this relic up. Key revved the engines; the plane vibrated and shuddered down the runway as if thinking over whether it could really make it; but at the last possible moment it got some loft and suddenly took to the skies with surprising ease. Once we'd attained our altitude, and we were clear of heavy sky traffic, Key flipped a few switches and turned to Vartan and me. "Let's let Otto do the driving, shall we, while we continue our little chat?" Otto was bush plane lingo for "Otto-pilot."

I turned to Vartan. "You have our complete attention," I informed him sweetly. "If I'm not mistaken, when we left off in our last episode, your stepfather Taras Petrossian was just embracing the Black Queen."

"I'd like to explain everything that you both want to know," Vartan assured us, "but you must understand it will be a very long story, going back ten years or more. There's no way to say it simply."

"That's okay," Key told him. "What with fuel stops and all, we've got at least twelve hours ahead of us to hear it."

We both stared at her. "That's arriving in *no* time?" I protested.

"I'm a student of Einstein." She shrugged.

"Well, *relatively* speaking," I said, "where are we *relatively* going, then?"

"Jackson Hole, Wyoming," she told me, "to pick up your mom."

JACKSON, AS THE crow flies, was twenty-two hundred miles away. And since airplanes aren't crows, as Key had pointed out, they can't just stop and refuel at the nearest cornfield.

I couldn't believe this.

Last I had heard, my mother had been headed—at least metaphorically—from the Virgin Islands to Washington, D.C. What in God's name was she doing at Jackson Hole? Was she still all right? And which zany was it who'd decided we had to take over half a day to fly there in *this* obsolete rattletrap?

I was wondering, in desperation, why I hadn't thought to bring my parachute—or whether I could bail out at some remote refueling spot and hitch a ride home—when Key interrupted these dire thoughts.

"Divide and conquer, that's what it was all about," she said, by way of minimal explanation. "Your mom may not be much of a chess player, babe, but Cat Velis sure knows how to read the handwriting on the wall. Do you have any *idea* just how long this Game has been under way, how much disruption it caused, before she finally blew the whistle?"

"Whistle?" I said, trying to hang on despite this seeming change of direction.

It was Vartan who intervened. "What Nokomis says is correct," he told me. "Your mother has perhaps understood something important, something absolutely critical, that no one else ever before had thought of in twelve hundred years."

Now I was listening.

"It's . . . I don't know exactly how to say it," Vartan continued. "In all these centuries, as it seems, your mother actually may have been the very first in this Game who has understood the true, the real underlying intention, of the Creator—"

"The *Creator*?" I practically shrieked. Where on earth was this going?

"Vartan means the creator of the *chess set*," said Key with enormous disdain. "His name was al-Jabir ibn Hayyan—remember?"

Sure. I got that.

"And exactly what *was* Mr. Hayyan's 'true underlying intention'?" I managed to choke out. "I mean, of course, according to this theory of my mother's you're both so fond of?"

They looked at me for a very long, drawn-out minute, during which time I could feel the waves of air beneath our wings; I could hear the throb of the single engine humming in hypnotic cadence.

They both seemed to be coming to some unspoken decision.

It was Vartan who broke the ice. "Your mother saw that maybe, all along, the Game has been an illusion. That maybe there *is* no Game—"

"Wait," I cut in. "You're saying that people have been getting killed all this time—have been drafted, or have actually *volunteered* to jump into a Game where they knew that they *might* be killed—just for an *illusion*?"

"People die for illusions every day," said Key, our unremitting *philosophe*.

"But how could so many people think they're involved in some dangerous Game all this time," I said, "if it doesn't exist?"

"Oh, it exists," Vartan assured me. "We are all in it. Everyone always *has* been. And the stakes are very high, just as Lily Rad told us. But that's not what your mother found out."

I was still waiting.

"What your mother discovered," said Key, "is that this 'Game' may be a ruse that leads us entirely in the wrong direction. As long as we're players, we're still inside the box; we're victims of our own myopia; we're black-and-white enemies battling on a board of our own making. We can't see the Big Picture."

A "ruse" that killed my father, I thought.

But aloud, I asked, "So what exactly *is* this 'Big Picture'?"

Key smiled. "The Original Instructions," she said.

MY LIFE JUST SEEMED filled to brimming with new discoveries.

The first of these—and in terms of priorities, perhaps the most urgently in need of addressing—was that we were now flying the first leg of a two-thousand-mile journey in a plane that had no bathroom.

This topic came up rather casually when Key broke out the trail mix and electrolyte drinks to provide sustenance for our trip. She cautioned us not to eat or imbibe too much, though, before approaching our first pit stop near Dubuque, wherever *that* was.

I'll spare the details—only to mention that the logistics seemed to require either the exacting continence that such small-plane pilots are trained for, or else the highly cautious deployment of an empty pickle jar. Since there wasn't even a broom closet on this barge where one might find a shred of privacy, I opted, perforce, for the former, and declined the refreshments.

My second discovery, fortunately, was to prove a bit more rewarding.

It was Vartan's revelation of the real role that had been played by the late Taras Petrossian in this most dangerous, if illusory, Game.

"Taras Petrossian, the man who became my stepfather, was descended from Armenian ancestors who were situated in Krym for generations, and like all Armenians, in the Black Sea region since ancient times," Vartan told us. He added, with a wry smile, "When the USSR fell to pieces ten years ago, this placed my stepfather in an unusual and interesting position—at least, from a chess player's point of view.

"To understand what I mean, you must know a bit of the background of the land I am speaking of: Krym is not only the birthplace of Alexandra's father, but this peninsula, almost an island, and the surrounding world, is also a place of many legends. I think it is no accident that a large part of the story I am about to tell you focuses on this location on the Black Sea."

THE SECOND GRANDMASTER'S TALE

Over the centuries, Krym has changed rulers many times. In the Middle Ages, it was the Golden Horde of Genghis Khan, and the Ottoman Turks ruled it as well. By the fifteenth century Krym had become the largest slave-trading center on the Black Sea. It did not pass into Russian hands until Potemkin captured it for Catherine the Great, during the Russo-Turkish Wars. Then, in the mid-1800s during the Crimean War, it was fought over by Russia, still trying to dismantle the Turkish Empire, versus the British and French—all players in the "Great Game," as it was called. In the following century, Krym was occupied and depopulated by one power or another, through the two world wars. It wasn't until 1954 that

Khrushchev, then Soviet premier, put Krym under the control of Ukraine—which still creates problems today.

Ukrainians can never forget how Stalin created the famine in the thirties, to starve them by the millions, and then killed hundreds of thousands of Crimean Tatars, descendants of Genghis, shipping them to exile in Uzbekistan. Ukrainians dislike Russia, and the Russian majority in Krym dislikes being part of Ukraine.

But *no* one much liked the Armenians. Though they were among the earliest Christians from the time of Eusebius—their ancient churches still exist, mostly boarded up, along the Black Sea coast—they were outsiders to all. In more modern times, they often sided with Russia or Greece against the Islamic Turks, which led to many massacres over the past one hundred years. But during such purges, their brand of Christianity was often left unprotected, even by the Russian, Greek, and Roman churches—resulting in Armenian flight from the region.

But this flight—this diaspora, the Greek word for "scattering the seeds"—had actually begun in ancient times, and plays a most critical role in our tale.

It was this aspect of ancient history that would soon prove of great value to Taras Petrossian, as well as to others, as I shall explain:

The Minni were among the oldest of cultures, early traders who occupied the vast Armenian plateau for thousands of years. The mountainous land drops off toward the north to the Black Sea, and in the south it descends to the Mesopotamian lowlands, where the Minni had moved with ease, over the millennia, down the Tigris and Euphrates into the heart of Babylon, Sumer, and Baghdad.

Three "modern" empires eventually seized this vast plateau land and divided it among themselves. These were the kingdoms of the tsar of Russia, the sultan of Turkey, and the shah of Iran. They met at the center, where rises the seventeen-thousand-foot-high obsidian volcano, Mount Ararat—Koh-i-Noh, the "Mountain of Noah"—the resting place of the Ark, a sacred spot at the very heart of the ancient world, the crossroads from east to west, from north to south.

Taras Petrossian knew this history very well. And he perceived how a powerful ancient legacy might again be invoked to attain even more enormous powers in modern times.

Taras was young—only in his thirties, handsome, intelligent, and ambitious—when, in the 1980s, Mikhail Gorbachev came to power in the Soviet Union, bringing his sweeping policies of glasnost and perestroika like two strong breaths of fresh air. They would soon build into a gust that was strong enough to blow away, like dry leaves before a wind, the rotted and crumbling infrastructure of an aging politburo, along with its decrepit ideas and outworn plans.

The USSR swiftly collapsed into dust—but with no new structure to replace it.

Into this void stepped those who had plans of their own, and who often came professionally well situated—or already equipped with the ill-gotten funds—to carry these out. Gangsters and black marketeers provided prepaid "protection"; impoverished government officials and bankrupted scientists sold trade secrets and weapons-grade materials; the Chechen mafia created the final master blow, in 1992, by defrauding the Bank of Russia of over $325 million.

And there was also another class of opportunists: those nouveau-oligarch entrepreneurs like Taras Petrossian.

Taras Petrossian married my mother when I was nine years old. I had already long made news in the chess tournament arena: WIDOW OF BRAVE RUSSIAN VETERAN REARS PRECOCIOUS CHILD CHESS PRODIGY—that sort of thing.

Petrossian, through funds obtained from his silent partner, Basil Livingston, had established his chain of fashionable restaurants and exclusive clubs around Russia. My stepfather well understood the desperate appetite of Russians for more than food—for a glimpse of real luxury after so many bleak decades of Soviet rule—and he understood how to market to those appetites. He never contradicted those, for instance, who chose to imagine that he himself was descended from that long line of food purveyors to the tsars, and he always made certain that all of his clubs kept icers of their famous caviar at each table.

The themes of these venues were cleverly designed to evoke places where the Armenians had originated or to which they had migrated over the centuries. In St. Petersburg, for example, he opened a costly champagne and wine club that served cuisine from California's Central Valley. In Moscow, the Golden Fleece restaurant served Greek fare, replete with goatskins of retsina, which evoked foods that Jason and the Argonauts might have consumed while crossing the Black Sea from Colchis to Tomis.

But the most sought-after of all these places was the exclusive private Moscow club—its costly membership available by invitation only—called Baghdaddy's. This club alone would have provided Taras Petrossian the resources that he swiftly expended to secure for me, his young stepson, the best chess tutors and trainers money could buy.

This enabled him, as well, to sponsor many tournaments from his own pocket. He did so for reasons that shall soon become clear as I continue.

Baghdaddy's was more than a posh club. It featured Middle Eastern cuisine in an exotic, Orientalist setting of copper trays, camel saddles, and samovars—with a rare chessboard placed beside each divan. At the entrance, a large portrait of the great caliph Harun al-Rashid greeted guests, with this maxim inscribed beneath:

Baghdad, one thousand years ago, the birthplace of competitive chess.

For it is known among devotees of chess history that it was this illustrious Abbasid caliph, al-Rashid—a man who, as it's reputed, could play two simultaneous games of chess blindfolded—who turned the game of chess into an example par excellence of warfare training, thus removing it from the realm of gambling or divination and enhancing its stature within the strictures of the Qur'an against those kinds of things.

The most interesting aspect of this particular club of my stepfather's was his private collection of rare chess pieces he'd gathered from all over the world, which were set into lighted alcoves around the walls. Taras Petrossian let it be known that he was always in the market for more of these, to add to his collection, and that regardless of the cost, he remained always willing to outbid his competitors in the antiquities market.

There was, of course, one chess set in whose pieces he would have been most especially interested. And with the collapse of the Soviet Union, followed by the terrorist attacks of 9/11 and the imminent incursion of American troops into Baghdad—all of these events coming within just a ten-year period—anyone needing a quick infusion of funds and in a position to lay hands on something to barter might have been only too willing to part with a piece of the Montglane Service.

When the government crackdown on private profiteers began, my stepfather quickly disposed of his businesses and fled Russia for London. But it is apparent that when it came to the chess set, he—and perhaps his silent partner—still maintained their same mission. Perhaps they were about to close in on that very objective.

For I believe that just prior to two weeks ago, when Taras Petrossian was killed in London, something they sought had been removed from Baghdad.

WHEN VARTAN FINISHED his story, Key shook her head and smiled.

"I'm afraid I really underestimated you, mister," she told him with a warm pat on his arm. "What a childhood! Raised by a guy who seems to have been so self-obsessed and unscrupulous that he may even have married your mother just in order to get his hands on *you.* You provided the passport for his nefarious mission, to become chess guru to the stars!"

I was sure Vartan would make swift objection to such a long-range potshot, fired by a woman who, after all, hardly knew him and had never met Petrossian. Instead, he merely smiled back at her and said, "It seems I've underestimated you, too."

But I had a bigger question—one that had been bugging me the whole time I listened to Vartan's story, a question that had brought back that pounding of blood behind my eyes, a pounding that was only exacerbated by the constant, humming throb of the Bonanza's engine—though I wasn't sure how I could actually bring myself to ask it. I waited until Key went back to resume the controls from "Otto" and check our bearings. Then I took a deep breath.

"I'm assuming," I said to Vartan, my voice shaking, "that if Petrossian's 'mission'—and Basil Livingston's—was to round up more pieces of the Montglane Service, that would have to include the one that you and my father saw together at Zagorsk?"

Vartan nodded and watched me carefully for a moment. Then he did something entirely unexpected. He took my hand in his and leaned over and kissed me on the forehead as if I were still a little child. I felt the heat of his skin infusing mine at these two contact points, as if we'd been electrically grounded. Then at last, almost reluctantly, he released me.

I was so taken off my guard, I felt my throat growing hard and the tears welling up in my eyes.

"I must tell you all of it," he said in a quiet voice. "After all, that is what we're here for. But do you think you can take this right now?"

I wasn't sure that I could. But I nodded, anyway.

"That tournament in Moscow—the match between you and me—I was just a child myself, so I didn't understand at all then. But from what I've been able to put together, I can think of only one reason why that event was established in the first place: to lure you and your father into Russia. With your mother protecting your father, they could never have gotten him to go back there of his own accord. Do you see?"

I certainly did. I felt like screaming and pulling my hair out. But I knew what he'd said was right on target. And I knew exactly what that meant.

In a way, *I* had killed my father.

If not for my childhood compulsion to become the world's youngest grandmaster—if not for the alluring golden opportunity dangled before us to accomplish that goal—my father would never have returned to his homeland at any cost.

That's what my mother was afraid of.

That's why she'd made me give up chess when he was killed.

"Now that we've learned so much about the Game," Vartan told me, "it must all make perfect sense. Anyone who was a player would surely *know* who your father was—not just the great grandmaster, Aleksandr Solarin, but a major player himself in the Game—and the husband of the Black Queen. My stepfather lured him there to show him that they had that important chess piece, perhaps with the hope that they somehow could strike some kind of bargain . . ."

Vartan paused and looked at me as if he wanted to take me in his arms and comfort me. But his expression was so distraught, it seemed he needed comforting himself.

"Xie, don't you see what this means?" he said. "Your father was sacrificed—but *I* was the bait that was used to lure you both into the trap!"

"No, you weren't," I told him, putting my hand on his arm as Key had done just a moment before. "I *wanted* to beat you; I *wanted* to win; I *wanted* to be the world's youngest grandmaster—just as you did. We were only children, Vartan. How could we possibly have guessed then that it was more than just a game? How would we even know *now*—if Lily hadn't explained it to us?"

"Well, we know very well *now* exactly what it is," he told me. "But *I* certainly should have known even before that. Only a month ago, Taras Petrossian called for me to come to London, though I hadn't seen the man in years, not since he'd emigrated. He wanted me to play in a large tournament he was organizing. By way of incentive to attend, he could not resist reminding me that, if not for his generosity in acquiring coaching and the like during his years as my surrogate parent, my grandmaster title might never have been awarded. I owed him, as he explained to me in no uncertain terms.

"But shortly before the tournament, upon my arrival at the Mayfair Hotel where my stepfather resided, I learned that he had something quite different, something more important, in mind, in the way of that 'payoff.' He asked me to perform him a service. And he showed me a letter he'd received from your mother . . ."

Vartan had paused, for my expression surely said all. I shook my head and motioned for him to go on.

"As I said, Petrossian showed me a letter from Cat Velis. From the gist of her letter, it seems that he possessed several items that had belonged to your late father. He wanted to get them into your mother's hands as quickly as possible. But she didn't want my stepfather to send them to her himself, nor to pass these objects to Lily Rad during the tournament. Either of these alternatives seemed to your mother to be . . . the word she used, I think, was 'imprudent.' She suggested that Petrossian enlist *me,* instead, to send these objects anonymously to Ladislaus Nim."

The chessboard drawing.

The card.

The photo.

Now it was all falling into place. But though Petrossian could have gotten the card from my coat pocket at Zagorsk, how on earth had he ever laid hands on that chessboard drawing, which Nim thought was in the possession of Tatiana, much less that "only photo in existence" of my father's family?

But Vartan hadn't quite finished. "Your mother's letter also invited me to join Lily and Petrossian after the tournament and come to Colorado, which I agreed to do. We could discuss everything there, she said."

He paused and added, "But as you know, my stepfather himself was killed before that London tourney even finished. Lily and I had met privately in London. We were unsure exactly how much to reveal to each other of what your mother had shared with either of us, since Lily hadn't been able to reach her. But we both mistrusted Petrossian and Livingston. And we agreed that Petrossian's involvement, combined with your mother's cryptic party invitations to us all, suggested that your father's death at Zagorsk may not have been an accident. As the only other person who'd been present at Zagorsk when your father died, I privately believed that the items I'd mailed might somehow be involved.

"The moment that Lily and I learned of my stepfather's untimely and suspicious death, we both resolved to leave the tournament at once. And in order to draw less attention to our movements, we agreed to fly to New York and go to Colorado by Lily's private car."

Vartan stopped and regarded me gravely with his dark eyes. "Of course, you know the rest of the story from there," he told me.

Not quite.

Though Vartan might not know how it was that Petrossian had come by the chessboard and those other items in the packet that Mother had arranged for him to send to Nim, there was still one major item that hadn't been accounted for.

"The Black Queen," I said. "You told Key and me, when we were back in Maryland, that it was you yourself who'd sent that chessboard drawing to Nim. Now you've explained how and why. Then you said you believed that Taras Petrossian was killed because he sent the Black Queen to my mother.

"But you'd also told me earlier that the last time you'd seen that piece was ten years ago, inside that glass case in the treasury at Zagorsk. So how did Petrossian get his hands on it? And how—and *why*—would he himself send something that valuable and that dangerous to my mother, when he knew that she was afraid even to have him communicate directly with her?"

"I don't know for certain," said Vartan, "but given the events of these past few days, I have begun to form a very stong suspicion. It occurred to me—odd though it may seem—that Taras Petrossian may *already* have had that chess piece in his possession ten years ago, when we were all at Zagorsk.

"After all, it was *he* who'd arranged to remove our

last game to that remote spot; it was *he* who told me that the chess piece had just been discovered in the cellar of the Hermitage and how famous it was; and it was *he* who said that it had been brought to Zagorsk just in order to display it there for our chess tourney. So why couldn't it also have been Taras Petrossian, the man who'd lured you to Russia, who had placed the chess piece there in that glass case—perhaps in the hope that, when Aleksandr Solarin saw it . . ."

But he stopped, since clearly—as for me—there was no obvious answer as to what Petrossian's objective might have been. Whatever he had hoped might come of all these clever machinations that, as it seemed, had resulted in nothing for anyone—except death.

Vartan rubbed his head of curls to bring the blood back, for even to him it wasn't making sense.

"We've been assuming," he said, picking his way, "that they were all playing on different teams. But what if they weren't? What if my stepfather was trying to contact your parents all along? What if he had always been on their team, but somehow they didn't know it?"

And then I saw it.

And in the same exact moment—so did Vartan.

"I don't know how Petrossian got his hands on that chessboard drawing," I said, "and he could have picked my pocket for the placard—though it's unlikely it would have meant anything to anyone but my father and me. But there's one thing I *do* know. There's only one person on earth who could have given him that photo that you put in the packet and sent to my uncle. I think it's the same person who warned us with that card at Zagorsk."

I took a deep breath and tried to focus on exactly where this was leading. Even Key was listening intently, at this point, from her place at the controls.

"I think," I added, "that the person who gave Taras Petrossian that chess piece in the first place, ten years ago—maybe even the person who helped him to lure us to Moscow—was the same person who gave him that photo, so it could be put in the packet to my mother that you ended up sending to Nim, to make my mother believe in Petrossian's story.

"That person is my grandmother! My father's own mother! You and Key first triggered the idea when you both kept saying that my mother believes there may be no Game, that we may somehow really be on the same team. And if it *was* my grandmother behind all this, it could mean—"

But as Vartan and I looked at each other in astonishment, I couldn't bring myself to face what I'd been about to say. Even after all we'd been forced to face, it was too much to imagine.

"What this means," Key informed us over her shoulder, "is the whole reason your mother's been in hiding. It's the reason she threw that party, the reason that she sent me to fetch you.

"Your father is still alive."

THE CAULDRON

Thus, in nearly all mythologies there is a miraculous vessel. Sometimes it dispenses youth and life, at other times it possesses the power of healing, and occasionally . . . inspiring strength and wisdom are to be found in it. Often, especially as a cooking pot, it effects transformations; by this attribute it achieved exceptional renown as the vas Hermetis *of alchemy.*

—EMMA JUNG AND MARIE-LOUISE VON FRANZ,
The Grail Legend

ALIVE.

Of course.

I felt as if I'd stepped onto an unfamiliar planet whirling across time and space. And from this new perspective, even the craziest and most illogical events of these past few days—impromptu parties, mysterious packages sent from foreign lands, my mother's vanishing act, my abduction by Key—suddenly would all make sense.

Maybe this revelation was the shock that broke the proverbial camel's back. Otherwise, I certainly don't know how it was that I ever got to sleep after that. When I awakened, though, I was completely sacked out, lying in darkness in the back of the fuselage on an improvised bed of duffel bags.

But I wasn't alone.

Beside me was something that was warm. Something breathing.

It took a moment for me to realize that the plane engine was silent. Key was nowhere to be seen. It must be well after midnight, which was when we'd deboarded at our second pit stop near Pierre, South Dakota. That was when Key had announced to us she had to catch a few z's—and that we really all should do so—before heading up over the mountains.

At this moment, I found myself half-sprawled across the firm, prone body of Vartan Azov, who lay with one arm loosely tossed over me from behind, and his face buried in my hair. I thought of disentangling myself from this haphazard embrace, but I realized I might wake him, and I reasoned he probably needed sleep as much as I did.

Also, it felt really good.

What was it with me and Vartan? I had to ask.

And if I waited until Key returned from watering the plane, or whatever she was up to right now, that might afford me a small space to think—minus any vibrating motors or the repeated whiplash of those incoming emotional shocks—with just the peaceful sound of the rhythmic breathing of a snoozing chess player in my ear.

And I knew I had lots of thinking to do—most of it, unfortunately, trying to unravel the twisted skeins of the completely unthinkable. After all, it was only hours ago that I'd learned why my mother had been in hiding, why she'd lured everyone out of the woodwork, and yet kept all of us in the dark all this time—all of us, that is, but Nokomis Key.

But I'd figured it all out somewhere between our first stop today at Moyaone, the ossuary fields at Piscataway, and that first refueling layover of ours in Duluth—four elapsed hours, not bad—when I had finally confronted Key, and she'd admitted to me the role she was actually playing:

That she *was* the White Queen.

"I never said Galen was *wrong* about that," Key had protested when I'd refreshed her memory of her earlier denial in the stairwell at the Four Seasons. "All I said was, Just ignore him! After all, those fools have all had their chance at this Game. Now it's somebody else's turn to turn the tables. That's what your mother and I intend to do."

My mother and Nokomis Key. Though I had trouble visualizing these two joined up in this fashion, if I were to be perfectly honest with myself I'd have to admit that all along, ever since our childhoods, it was Key who had actually been the daughter that my mother had never had.

The Black Queen and the White Queen in cahoots.

I kept hearing a refrain, one of those jingles from *Alice in Wonderland,* something like: *Won't you please be sure to come to tea, with the Red Queen, the White Queen, and me?*

But jingled and jangled though I myself might be, I was grateful beyond words that my mother had decided to "blow the whistle," as Key had told me back on the first leg of our trip, and to join forces, whatever that might entail.

I no longer cared a fig why my mother had apparently cut her connections with my uncle, nor why Key had locked the hotel door on a few who might well be players on the White Team. I'd find out the reason later. Right now I was simply relieved.

Because one thing had finally dawned on me: why Key had worn that ironic smile and why she had made those cryptic remarks about the burial place at Piscataway. And indeed, why we had visited that ossuary field at Moyaone in the first place. *All the bones and all the secrets,* she'd said.

Because I now understood that if my father was alive, as Key said, and if Mother had learned of it, then it was clear that all this time it hadn't been *me* Mother was protecting, nor even herself. It had been my father, all along, who'd been the one in clear and present danger.

And now I also knew why my mother had been so afraid all these years, even before Zagorsk: She was the one who'd put him there. The secrets of the Montglane Service weren't buried with the bones at Piscataway, any more than the pieces were.

They were buried in my father's mind.

Aleksandr Solarin was the only one, of all those who'd ever been involved in this Game, who knew where those pieces were located. If he was alive—and I was sure that Key and my mother must be right about that—then we had to find him before anyone else did.

I only prayed that we wouldn't be too late.

KEY HADN'T BEEN kidding when she'd asked me, back on the parkway, if I had the "vaguest clue" how hard it had been to orchestrate my closet abduction. As the sky seeped lavender, we revved up the little Bonanza and hopped over the Black Hills and Mount Rushmore, headed for the Rockies. And she elaborated a few of those technicalities. She'd come in a plane not licensed to her, and had not filed a flight plan so it would be hard to follow us—or even to guess where we might be headed.

As long as the staff at the private airports knew you, she explained, it wasn't much of a problem. She had only put down for refueling in places where she was sure she could radio ahead for someone she knew to be on-site, even at night, when the airfield staff were gone—like her friend, the mechanic from the Sioux Reservation who'd refueled us last night at Pierre so we could be sure to take off before dawn.

Now, bundled up in our thermal gear that she'd

brought in the duffel bags, we were cruising atop the world.

"Dawn!" Key called down to the mountains. "What an eye-opener! The better to see you with!"

Sailing at fifteen thousand feet over the Rockies in a small plane just after dawn was always breathtaking. The mountains were only a thousand feet beneath us. With the sun rising behind us, gilding our wings, the little plane cut through shreds of pink cloud like a skyborne raptor. We could see everything below in detail—the craggy, purplish rock veined with silver snow; the steep slopes thick with pine and spruce; the brilliant turquoise skies.

Though I'd done mountain trips like this dozens of times with Key, I never got tired of them. Vartan was practically slobbering on the window, looking out at the astonishing view. God's country, the locals called it.

Landing at Jackson Hole four hours later was something else again. Key cut like an arrow through the passes, with mountains looming, almost within spitting distance, on either side. It was always unnerving. Then she dropped to the valley floor with precision. Actually, precision was a prerequisite when landing a plane in the bottomless "Hole."

It was already mid-morning by the time we touched down, so we grabbed the duffels, loaded them in the Land Rover she always kept at the airport, and by unspoken agreement, went to get some chow.

Loading up with eggs and bacon, toast and marmalade, fried potatoes, sliced fruit, juice, and tons of black java, I suddenly realized that this was the first time I had eaten since yesterday's breakfast compliments of my uncle Slava.

I really needed to stop bingeing once a day like this.

"Where's our friend meeting us?" I asked Key when

we'd paid our fare and left the restaurant. "At the condo?"

"You'll see," she replied.

Key kept a pad at the Racquet Club for her stopover flights, so her bush pilots who were headed into the North Country would always have a bath and bed. I'd stayed there myself a few times. It was designed by a custom shipbuilder for maximal use of space and it was comfy and regal at the same time. There were even ball courts of several kinds and a workout room for those who might be athletically obsessed.

My mother wasn't there. Key told us to drop the duffel bags. Then, after sizing up Vartan's height, she pulled three lightweight, thermal jumpsuits from the closet and told us to put them on, along with some waterproof zippered snowbooties, and we went back to the car. She headed up the road without giving us further information.

But after about half an hour, when we'd passed the entrance to Teton Village and Lake Moran, I knew we were running out of what might be called civilization, so I couldn't help but be nervous.

"I thought you said we were headed to pick up my mother, so we could help find my father," I told her. "But this road only leads to Yellowstone National Park."

"Right," Key assured me, with her usual sarcastic glance. "But to pick up your mom, first we have to find her. She's in *hiding,* as you may recall."

ONCE I'D HAD A moment to think things through clearly, I confess, I had to hand it to Key. Her mapping of this mission had been impeccable through and through. I myself couldn't have concocted a better spot where one might have stashed my mother, to ensure minimum visibility, than winter in Yellowstone National

Park. And it *was* winter here, no matter how the official calendar might mislead one into imagining otherwise.

Back in Washington, D.C., early April might be Cherry Blossom Festival and tourist season. But here in northern Wyoming, the twelve-foot-high, red-and-yellow snow marking poles had been placed along the roadside since mid-September. And it might *stay* winter in these parts for another two months yet. Camping wouldn't even begin until June.

The park was always closed to all but Snowcoach and snowmobile traffic—and even those, by reservation only—from November 1 through the middle of May. By next winter, even snowmobiles would be verboten, through a new federal edict, in this, our historic and first-ever national park. Even now, the main road itself—Grand Loop, a 140-mile twisted loop in a figure eight pattern—would be closed throughout much of its northern reaches.

But nothing was completely off-limits to the park rangers and scientific staffers like Key, some of whom conducted their most important research at this time of the year. That was what was so brilliant about her whole clandestine operation, though I confess, I still hadn't seen the Big Picture, as she would put it.

When we reached the park entrance, Key picked up three tickets with her park pass, and we all hopped onto the Snowcoach, a kind of Econoline van with tank treads instead of wheels, and with what looked a lot like water skis stuck to the front to keep us from sinking into the snow.

A number of folks, who seemed to be of the same party, were already on board—all *ooh*-ing and *ahh*-ing as our chatty and informative tour guide pointed out a few of the park's ten thousand geothermal features, "just here to the left and right of us," and peppered everyone like a spray gun with little-known western history involving the early days of the park.

Vartan seemed truly fascinated. But by the time the guide started regaling us with statistics on Old Faithful's burst ratios—how a two-minute eruption of 120 feet meant a shorter interval of maybe fifty-five minutes till the next eruption, while a five-minute eruption averaging 123 feet meant an interval of maybe seventy-eight minutes to the next—I could see people's eyes beginning to glaze over, and Key had gotten that hard, firm set around her mouth.

We jumped off the coach when we reached the Old Faithful Inn. There, Key picked up two snowmobiles that were marked as exclusively reserved for park rangers, as well as three pairs of lightweight snowshoes that could clamp onto our footgear in a pinch if we should break down.

She climbed onto one snowmobile with me just behind her, and Vartan climbed onto the other and followed us. As we headed north, you could hear our guide and the tourists counting loudly: "*Ten, nine, eight, seven, six . . .*"

When we got to the top of the hill, Key pulled off the road for a minute and pointed behind us. Vartan pulled up beside us and looked back as Old Faithful blew his cork and shot steaming water more than a hundred feet into the stark winter sky.

"It explodes, even like this, in the cold?" he asked her in amazement.

"They're heated, many miles below the surface of the earth, to more than six hundred degrees," said Key. "By the time they get back up here again, they don't care *what* the weather's like. It's just a relief to get out-of-doors again."

"What heats them?" said Vartan.

"Aye, there's the rub," Key told him. "We're sitting

atop the biggest volcanic cauldron known to the world. It might shoot off and destroy the entire North American continent just about any millionth year now. We're not sure quite *when* she may blow. And she's not the only one we need to worry about.

"We used to think that Yellowstone Caldera was unique. But now we think it's possible that this cauldron may actually be connected across Idaho to Mount St. Helen's and the Pacific region—to that bigger circle of faults around the Pacific Rim, the Ring of Fire."

Vartan looked at her for a moment. It may have been my imagination, but it was almost as if some silent understanding passed between them, something they were debating whether to share with me.

But in the next instant, the look was gone.

We must have snowmobiled for more than thirty minutes when Key paused again and announced, "We're going off-piste now. It's only a short distance, but we need both snowmobiles so we can put our friend and her gear behind." She paused and added, "If you see any curious grizzlies, turn off the noisy machine, lie down on the snow, and pretend like you're dead."

Yeah. Right.

Key cut into a beautiful woodland, then steered alongside a steaming geyser field that tossed smoky silver into the skies. We sailed past the mudpots that we used to visit here when we were young. They bubbled like a witch's cauldron, popping and hissing with a sound that's impossible to replicate.

Down in the glen just below was one of the small warming shacks scattered through the woods. They usually serve coffee or hot chocolate for skiers and snowshoers, but this one was a bit off the beaten track.

Key pulled out her park ranger two-way radio, and said, "Coming in, over."

And I'll be damned if it wasn't my mother's voice that

replied, over the walkie-talkie, “What kept you so long?”

I HADN’T SEEN MY mother in five years.

And yet she looked exactly as she always had: like someone who has just taken a dip in a pool full of some magical elixir.

As someone, myself, who’d spent her own youth diving into nothing more challenging than a chess game, I suspect it had always been that primal energy of my mother’s, the raw animal power she exuded, that had driven all the men in our lives completely ga-ga over her, and had always placed me, too, in a kind of awe whenever I was in her presence.

But now I was completely thrown for a loop. For the instant we entered the shack, my mother—ignoring Vartan and Key—threw her arms about me in an uncustomary display of emotion, enveloping me in the familiar scent of her hair, that mix of sandalwood and sage, and when she drew away there were actual tears in her eyes. After all I’d learned of my mother that I’d never known these past few days—the lengths to which she’d gone to rescue not just that terrible chess set, but also my father and me—I was ever more experiencing a kind of shock and awe at our being suddenly reunited.

“Thank God you’re all right,” Mother said, embracing me again, more forcefully, as if she could hardly believe it.

“She won’t be for very long,” said Key, “unless we get this pony act on the road, zip-zip. Remember we’ve got a higher calling.”

Mother shook her head as if coming to her senses and let me go. Then turning to Vartan and Key, she embraced them both lightly. “Thanks to you,” she said. “I’m so relieved.”

We helped bring some satchels out of the shack, and Mother boarded the snowmobile behind Key. With a crinkly smile to me, she nodded toward Vartan, who was powering up his own snowmobile. "I'm glad you've come to see eye to eye," she said.

I climbed on behind Vartan and we shot through the woods after Key.

When we were sure the coast was clear, we went back to the main road. In about half an hour we reached the western gate into Idaho, where the barrier was up to halt vehicular traffic into Targhee National Forest. Key stopped her snowmobile and dismounted, collecting Mother's bags.

"What's up?" I asked them both, as Vartan switched off our machine.

"We have a rendezvous with Fate," Key commented. "And she's driving an Aston Martin."

NOTHING COULD BE MORE incongruous than Lily and Zsa-Zsa, ensconced in their fur lap rugs, waiting unobtrusively in that quarter-million-dollar Vanquish in the Targhee parking lot. Luckily, there were no observers around to see them. But how did they get here, with the forest shut down for winter? Key's sidekicks must include every park ranger on the planet, I thought.

The girls had exited the car to greet us, while Key began loading Mother's bags into the back. Zsa-Zsa, reaching out from Lily's arms, gave me a big wet kiss. I wiped it off on my sleeve. Lily went over to embrace my mother.

"I was so worried," Lily said. "I'd been waiting at that ghastly motel, with no word in *days*. But everything appears to have gone all right so far—at least we're all present and accounted for." She turned to Key. "So when will we all get going?"

"And *where* will we 'all get going'?" I asked her.

I seemed to have remained the only one in the dark.

"I'm not sure you really want to know," Key informed me, "but I'll tell you anyway. As I said, this hasn't been easy to orchestrate, but we've got it all mapped. We worked out the plan as much as we could, once we were alone in Denver. Then Vartan and I flew back East to round you up. So right now, we three will return to Jackson Hole as if we'd just been out snowmobiling, and we'll have a good dinner there tonight. We'll crash at my place and catch the first flight out in the morning. Your mom and Lily will drive. They'll meet us at the other end. I'm afraid that the closest rendezvous spot we could all agree on was Anchorage—"

"*Anchorage!?*" I cried. "I thought we were going to find my father. Do you mean to tell me he's in *Alaska*?"

Key gave me that look. "I *mentioned* that you might prefer not to know," she said. "But no, that's not where we're going. That's where Cat and Lily will pick your father up on our return. In fact, for security purposes, your mother and I are the only ones who know precisely where your father is—and in my case, only because I'm the one who had to figure out how to get him back from there."

I waited for her other shoe to drop. But it was my mother who dropped it.

"As to where *there* is," said Cat, "I believe that the region is generally known as the Ring of Fire."

RING OF FIRE

Nothing so resembles a living creature as fire does.
—PLUTARCH

The [alchemical] operation begins with fire and ends with fire.
—IBN BISHRUN

The fire which enlightens is the fire which consumes.
—HENRI-FRÉDÉRIC AMIEL

All things change to fire and fire, exhausted, falls back into all things.
—HERACLITUS

"ALASKA'S ALEUTIAN TRENCH," KEY TOLD US, SOMEtime between the appetizer and the soup course. "It divides the Pacific Ocean and the Bering Sea. It was once a part of Russia, back in Catherine the Great's day. It's called the Ring of Fire because it boasts the largest collection of active volcanoes in the world. I'm on a first-name basis with most of them—Pavlof, Shishaldin, Pogromini, Tulik, Korovin, Tanaga, Kanaga, Kiska—there's even a new young caldera that I discovered myself, which I'm trying to get dubbed 'Modern Millie.' "

And she added, "These are a big part of my dissertation that I'm doing on calorimetry—James Clerk Maxwell, Jean-Baptiste-Joseph Fourier, *The Analytic Theory of Heat*, and all of that. But as you know, what has always interested me most is observing the behavior of heat under extreme pressure."

I tried not to notice when Vartan glanced quickly up

at me, then back at his soup. But I couldn't help wondering if, on the plane, he'd also felt that electric current surge beween us when he touched me. I confess, it was pretty hard for *me* to forget.

We'd taken this small private dining room here at the Inn at the Hole, where Key knew the management. This enabled us, she explained, to stuff ourselves at leisure while still retaining the seclusion we needed to speak of what tomorrow would bring. And tomorrow already sounded like a doozy, starting off with the charter flight to Seattle and Anchorage that Key told us she'd arranged for us at dawn.

"But you said that my father's not in Alaska," I reminded her. "So what does this Ring of Fire have to do with the place where we're actually going?"

"It's the Yellow Brick Road," she told me. "I'll explain once our grub's been served."

Key and Vartan had agreed to share the crispy, whole roast duck, large enough for two, stuffed with foie gras, a specialty of the house, while I opted for prime rib, the one dish that Rodo never prepared at Sutalde.

As our courses rolled on, though, from soup to salad, I couldn't help thinking about all that I'd left locked up back in that hotel suite in Georgetown—my uncle Slava, my boss, and probably any hope that I might once have had of a future career.

Well, tomorrow was another day, as Ms. Scarlett Key O'Hara would indubitably say at such a moment—and, even had I wanted to, there wasn't much I could do about all that now, when I found myself relegated to the role of a lowly pawn-in-the-dark, shoved into center board by Key and Cat, that unlikely pairing of Queens.

I could scarcely wait.

Once we felt we'd made a good dent in our meals, we ordered a bottle of Poire William and a lemon soufflé to go with it. That would keep the waiters occupied for a good twenty or thirty minutes, we reasoned, waiting around for our egg whites to rise.

As soon as we were sure we were alone, Key said to me, "As you know, your mom has tried to keep you out of the loop as long as she could, for your own safety—on the theory that ignorance is bliss.

"But she has now empowered me to tell both of you everything that I know about what's happened, about where we're headed tomorrow, as well as what we will have signed on board to do once we get there. After my story, if anyone wants to bail out, please feel free to do so. But I don't think it's likely that you will. This involves us all in ways that have even surprised me, as you'll see."

Key pushed her salad plate away and put the duck platter closer to Vartan. Then plucking up her slender glass of Verdicchio, she began her tale.

THE WHITE QUEEN'S TALE

Ten years ago, when Alexandra's father was shot in Russia, when he was believed by all to be dead, Cat realized something had happened almost worse than losing her husband: that although she'd been sure all these years that the Game had been ended for good and all, another round must now have begun.

But how could that be?

The pieces had been buried, and only Alexander Solarin knew their locations. The players from the last round, thirty years earlier, had all retired from the playing field, or else they were dead.

So who could have begun it? Unfortunately, she didn't need to wait long to find out.

After the "tragic death" at Zagorsk, the U.S. embassy had arranged for little Alexandra to be escorted from Moscow back to America under diplomatic protection, and they also made arrangements to transfer her father's remains on the same plane.

The coffin, of course, was empty.

The Russian who was assisting in this coordination, as we now know, was Taras Petrossian. Coordinating on behalf of the American embassy was a reclusive millionaire. His name was Galen March.

As soon as Alexandra was home safely with her mother in New York, Galen contacted Cat on his own. When they met, he told her at once that he was involved in the Game, which had indeed begun again with the death of her husband—and that he himself had brought an important message for Cat's ears only. But she must agree not to stop him until he had communicated all that he'd come to say.

To this, Cat agreed, for his words supported her own earlier suspicions about the Game.

Galen minced no words. He revealed to Cat that Solarin was not dead, but had been so badly injured that for the moment it appeared he might as well be.

In the pandemonium following the shooting at Zagorsk, Solarin's ravaged body, comatose and losing blood, was privately removed from the site through the cooperation of the same man who had organized the chess tournament, Taras Petrossian. And it was given into the custody of the woman who'd actually orchestrated the event from behind the scenes: Alexander Solarin's mother, Tatiana.

Cat was naturally in shock at hearing all this. She demanded that Galen immediately reveal how he'd come to know such things. How had Solarin's mother managed to survive, when her own sons believed her long dead? Cat insisted on learning where her husband had been taken. She wanted to go to Russia and find Solarin at once, regardless how grave the danger.

"I will agree to all this, and I shall help you even a

great deal more," Galen March assured her. "But first, as you agreed yourself, you must hear the rest of what I've come to tell you."

Tatiana Solarin, Galen went on, had for decades awaited a chance to contact her long-lost son—indeed, even from the very moment that the prior Game had ended, when, as Lily told us, Minnie simply walked off and disappeared from the board, leaving Cat holding the pieces, along with the bag.

But though a fresh start was now possible, Tatiana knew she needed to create a complex strategy in order to bring her grandmaster son back into Russia, as she must, and back into the Game. She sought a way to unite herself not only with Solarin, but with his wife, Cat, who was now the Black Queen. This was part of her larger strategy.

But Tatiana's first opportunity came only when the Berlin Wall collapsed and the Soviet Union disintegrated. At that time an event occurred of a sort that she'd scarcely thought to imagine: Alexander Solarin's young daughter Alexandra had grown to become a major chess contender. If he would not come to Russia for himself, he would surely come for *her.*

Galen March pledged himself to help Tatiana any way he could in this mission—in a very real sense, she was chosen for it—and for a most critical reason.

Tatiana herself was now the new White Queen.

"THIS WAS ACTUALLY Alexandra's grandmother?" said Vartan in amazement.

But Key merely nodded, for our soufflé had just arrived.

After all had been set up, and the waiters had taken Key's card for *l'addition* and departed, she cut into the soufflé and was just about to answer Vartan.

But first, I had one or two questions of my own.

"How could *Tatiana* be the White Queen when Galen told me that *you* are—and you even agreed with him? Who *is* this guy Galen, anyway? You're telling me he's been playing footsie with my mother for more than ten *years* and I didn't know about it? Please come clean."

"I've had a little time to pick Galen March's brains myself by now," Key told me. "It would seem he's been a behind-the-scenes player for quite a while. When I put his story together with what your mom had already told me, it all made sense.

"But let me finish with New York. As soon as Galen had revealed this scenario to Cat, she knew that you, her little daughter, might be in danger, too. And she knew exactly who *from*—certainly not from your own grandmother, babe—and even from *where*. Somebody was buying up tons of land near your ancestral home in Four Corners—"

"The Botany Club," I said, and Key merely nodded.

Now it all made sense.

Why we'd moved to Colorado in the first place.

Why she'd convinced Nim to buy the ranch next door under Galen's name.

Why Mother's party, with all those specific players, had had to take place right there, at the Octagon.

What it meant.

The chessboard is the key.

My God.

"Rosemary Livingston *was* the White Queen," I said, "but she betrayed her own team for personal revenge. She arranged to have my father shot at Zagorsk when she knew the White Team planned to meet with him there. She wanted to get even with my mother over her father El-Marad's death. So they must have . . . *fired* her somehow and replaced her with Tatiana. And now with *you*. She still doesn't know it. That's why she and her cronies were trying so hard to find out whether *I* was the new White Queen!"

Key smiled a bitter little smile of acknowledgment. "Now you're cookin' with gas, my friend," she said. "But there's a whole lot more you need to know about the players. For instance, you asked about Galen.

"It appears that back in the 1950s Tatiana was captured by the Soviets. They locked her away in a Gulag, while her little son Aleksandr was put in an orphanage by his 'grandmother,' the never-aging Minnie Renselaas, and Tatiana's Greek husband and her other son Ladislaus escaped to America with some of the chess pieces. It was Galen who found out where Tatiana had been taken. He convinced Minnie that the KGB would never release her unless they'd been given an offer they couldn't refuse. Minnie swapped the drawing of the chessboard, which we now possess, for Tatiana's freedom. But now that some of the family had escaped with some pieces, it was clear that Tatiana would never be safe unless she went completely undercover. Galen gave her the Black Queen himself, the one you saw at Zagorsk. Then he hid Tatiana in a place where no one would ever think to look. Except for that brief foray to Zagorsk with the Queen, she's been holed up there for nigh on fifty years."

Key paused and added, "That's the place where we're headed tomorrow. Your dad is there."

"But first you said Seattle and Alaska," I protested, "then something about the Ring of Fire. And what was all that Yellow Brick Road stuff?"

"No," said Vartan suddenly, speaking for the first time in all this.

I glanced over at him. His face was set in granite.

"I'm afraid that it's a 'yes' for tomorrow morning," said Key.

"Absolutely no," said Vartan. "The place you're

speaking of is more than a thousand miles long, and the worst place on earth. Thick fog and snow all the summer, winds of one hundred twenty kilometers per hour, waves of thirteen meters high—that's more than forty feet!"

"As they say," Key said, "there's no such thing as bad weather—only bad clothing."

"Yes, all right, perhaps you may fly high *above* it," Vartan told her. "But not *across* it or *through* it, as you are proposing."

"Where's *it*?" I asked.

"I've looked at everything, I assure you," Key said in exasperation. "It's the only way to get there without attracting the attention of the entire U.S. Navy and Coast Guard, and alerting every Russian submarine under the Arctic Circle. But as I said, it's still not too late to bow out yourselves, if you're so inclined."

"Where's *there*?" I repeated.

Vartan shot me a dark look.

"She proposes to fly a small private plane—tomorrow, illegally—into Kamchatka, Russia," he said. "And then somehow—should we live that long ourselves, which is quite unlikely—she proposes that we shall bring your father back."

♔

"YOU AIN'T JUST TOOTIN' HAY. We may need that," said Key, when Vartan pulled out some cash, handed it to the waiter, tucked the whole bottle of our costly pear brandy beneath his arm, and headed out the door.

"We Ukrainians can't drink like the Russians," Vartan informed her. "Even so, I hope to get very drunk tonight."

"Now there's a plan," she agreed, following him. "Too bad I can't join you. I have to catch a plane in the morning."

Back at the condo, we quickly went through the closets and packed the duffels we'd brought with plenty of the lightweight thermal gear we found.

"Better to be safe than sorry," said Key.

No kidding.

The condo was not only designed by a shipbuilder, it even looked like a ship inside: the long, skinny mirrored bathroom built like a galley with a large, step-in shower where the stove would be; the single bedroom like a small stateroom; the high walls of the main room crosshatched with long strips of oak in a herringbone pattern, and with drop-down beds built into the wall.

Key said she hoped we didn't mind, but since she was the one who'd soon be doing all the work behind the stick, she would require a good, solid night of shut-eye. So she was relegating to herself the full-sized bed in the private bedroom, and letting Vartan and me camp out on the two bunk beds in the "ship's" main hold.

When she'd gone off to hit the sack and had closed the bedroom door behind her, Vartan smiled. "Do you usually prefer to be on the top or on the bottom?" he asked, gesturing to the two bunk beds.

"Don't you think we ought to save that question until we know each other a bit better?" I asked, with a laugh.

"You know," he said, more seriously, "if we are in fact going where your friend Nokomis *says* we are going tomorrow, then I think I should mention that tonight may be the very last night you and I shall ever have to spend together—or indeed, to spend anywhere on earth. This route she has chosen is the very worst on the planet. She's either the world's best pilot, or completely mad. And of course, we are both mad to go with her."

"Do we have a choice?" I said.

Vartan shrugged and shook his head in resignation. "Then, may a man who is certainly about to die quite soon hope to be granted one last wish?" he said, in a tone that seemed to contain not even a sliver of irony.

"A wish?" I said.

My heart was pounding. But what could he possibly wish for—at least, that *I* had in mind—when Key was asleep in just the next room, and he knew very well that we all had to be ready to hit the skies before dawn?

Vartan whipped out the bottle of Poire William, along with a small shot glass that looked suspiciously like one from the restaurant. Then, carrying these in one hand, he took me by the arm and headed for the bathroom. "I find that I've suddenly been overcome," he informed me, "by a passionate desire to discover more about the thermal properties of exactly how heat behaves under enormous pressure. If we let the shower run for a very long while—just how hot do you think we can make it?"

He shut the bathroom door behind him and leaned against it. He poured a drink, took a sip, handed it to me, and set the bottle down. Then, never taking his eyes from me for a moment, he reached over and turned on the shower. I was almost speechless.

Almost—but not quite.

"It could get pretty hot in here," I agreed. "Are you sure you want to learn that much about burning calories tonight? I mean, with this important mission in front of us, just ahead?"

"I believe we've both absorbed the rules of this Game pretty well by now," said Vartan, bending toward me. "It seems that there is *nothing* more important than understanding the true properties of fire. Perhaps we should learn more about precisely what those are."

He touched his finger to the lip of the glass in my hand, then touched the liquid to my lips, where the brandy burned. Then he put his lips to mine, and I felt that current of heat moving through me again. The room was filling with steam.

Vartan looked at me, still not smiling. "I believe we've achieved the right temperature to engage in any experiment we should care to undertake," he suggested. "But let's not forget, when it comes to alchemy, timing is everything."

He drew me to him and we kissed again. I could feel the heat through my jumpsuit—but not for long. Vartan unzipped the thin mylar and peeled it from me. Then he began removing my clothes. By the time he got to his own haberdashery, my heart was beating so hard that I thought I might black out from an oversupply of blood—not all of it headed, I must confess, to my brain.

"I want to show you something really beautiful," Vartan told me, as soon as he'd undressed.

Good God.

He took me to the long mirrored wall, wiped away a large circle of steam, stood behind me, and pointed at the mirror. As the steam began to enfold our images in fog once more, I looked into Vartan's eyes in the mirror.

God, I could think of nothing else but wanting him.

When I found my voice at last, I said, "*You're* really beautiful."

He laughed. "I was speaking about *you*, Xie," he told me. "I wanted you to see yourself for a moment as I see you."

We watched as our images vanished again back into the steam. Then he turned me to face him.

"But whatever we do right now, tonight," he said, "and even if we both get badly burned, I may assure you of one thing. We shall *definitely* be following the Original Instructions—just as they were written."

SHOCK AND AWE

But here we must at once draw a distinction between three things . . . the military power, the country, *and* the will of the enemy. *The military power must be destroyed. . . . The country must be conquered. . . . But even when both of these things are done, still the War . . . cannot be considered at an end as long as the will of the enemy is not subdued also.*

—CARL VON CLAUSEWITZ, *On War*, first published in 1832

War against desert Nomads can never be pressed home: their answer to overwhelming force is wide dispersal and guerrilla tactics. An army cannot break them any more than a fist can a pillow.

—E.W. BOVILL, *The Golden Trade of the Moors*

IF I KEPT HANGING AROUND WITH NOKOMIS *LA magnifica*, I was going to get pretty used to lying around on duffel bags. Our prop jet "charter flight" to Anchorage was a cargo plane with no seats in the back.

"Best I could arrange in a pinch," Key told us.

I was feeling pretty pinched myself, what with the piles of boxes roped down with only fishnet cordons at every side. I hoped our ballast wouldn't shift.

The flight was uneventful but long, long, long. Three thousand miles from Jackson to Anchorage, with the one stopover in Seattle to unload, reload, and refuel—both us and the plane—twelve hours in all. But I was damned sure at this point that *no* one would ever dream, even wildly, of following us on this boondoggle.

We touched down at Anchorage International Airport just before dawn. Vartan and I were sound asleep among the cargo and didn't even feel the landing gear grinding down. Key got us rousted and told us to grab the bags; this was becoming a habit with her. Key thanked our pilots, and just outside on the landing strip we hopped a cargo van bearing a sign that read LAKE HOOD.

As we rattled over the tarmac, Key said, "We could have taken off from a smaller, much more private locale. I picked this spot not just because it's the most convenient to our proposed venue"—she raised one brow to Vartan—"but because Lake Hood is the largest and busiest float plane harbor anyplace in the world. It's equipped for any manner of flight we might have tried. They dug a channel during the war, back in the forties, to connect Lake Hood and Lake Spinnard. By the seventies they had a twenty-two-hundred-foot paved runway and multiple extra tie-down channels so the craft won't blow away, and they can handle anything that lands, whether with wheels, standard or amphibious floats, or even ski planes in winter. And you know, depending on what the weather report was for today, skis might have come in handy!

"I radioed ahead," she added, "to have Becky all saddled up for us—pontooned and ready to run."

"Becky?" I said. "I thought you preferred Ophelia."

Key turned to clarify for Vartan. "De Havilland makes the best bush planes in the world. They like to name them after animals like 'Chipmunk,' 'Caribou'—my plane back in the Tetons is Ophelia Otter. And Becky, whom you're about to meet, is a Beaver, which is the ubiquitous and definitive bush plane. Any airport where you land—even with Lear Jets and Citations on the strip—the pilots always walk up to this one instead." She added, "All the more reason to take off from a spot like Lake Hood, where we'll be just one of the 'Madding Crowd.' "

Whatever else you could say about her, Key thought of everything.

But there was one thing that *I* hadn't thought of until her comment.

"Pontoons?" I said. "I thought last night you'd implied that we'd be island-hopping today."

"Yeah," said Key, with just a dash of Vartan's grimness. "I agree, that *is* how everybody usually gets around in those parts—one-hour hops, squishing down on those fat tundra tires. That's how I usually do it myself. But as I told you, this whole scenario has taken more than the optimal round of thinking and planning. And at the end of *our* Yellow Brick Road, I'm afraid, we'll be splashing down in water."

THE SUN WAS WELL above the horizon at Lake Hood by the time Key had overseen the fueling and checked all her gauges and spare tanks; she'd had us don our life vests and weighed in the three of us and our gear so she could do her final fuel calculations.

When we were at last unlashed from the tie-down and putt-putting out to the channel to await our clearance for takeoff, I could see the foamy water below as it churned over our floats. Key finally turned and explained. "Sorry about my fuel obsession, but it's all that private pilots like me ever think about, it's a matter of life and death. Over the past sixty years plenty of fuel-starved planes have been recovered from the rocks where we're going. Even though there are a half-dozen airports or landing strips scattered along this chain, they can't all refuel directly by the water, some are inland. Betsy here has got three fuel tanks, plus her tip tanks—the fuel in the wingtips—but that's still only one hundred and thirty-five gallons. In four hours, we'll be flying off the fuel from our second and final wingtip, and Becky's tummy will be starting to growl for its lunch."

"What then?" asked Vartan, clearly trying to suppress an "I told you so."

"What *then*?" said Key. "Well, there's good news and there's bad news. In anticipation that we might not be able to refuel exactly when and where we want, I brought as much extra one-hundred-octane low-lead fuel as I could, in five-gallon jerry cans. I've refueled that way far out at sea. It's not too hard—you stand on the float to do it."

"What's the bad news?" I said.

"First, of course," said Key, "you have to find a spot that's calm enough to land the plane."

DESPITE ALL THE DIRE implications, imprecations, and impracticalities of these past twenty-four hours, once we were aloft and headed west-by-southwest, I was glad just to be up in the air and *doing* something. For the first time—having overcome the awe I felt at the sight of my mother and absorbed the shock of learning that my father was alive—I was able to focus on the astonishing idea that we were actually going to find him.

Maybe that's why I was less grim than Vartan and Key about our prospects for this trek—indeed, I felt almost ebullient. This feeling was enhanced by the fact that I really loved these bush planes. Somehow, flimsy as they might seem from the outside, once you were actually up in the air they felt safer than being trapped within one of those big, clunky jumbo jets.

Becky the Beaver herself was very airy inside, and full of light. The back of her fuselage was designed like a minivan made to seat seven; the backseats, Key said, could be removed just by loosening two bolts, and there was a sling seat in the far back that could be raised from the floor if needed. Key had left all the seats because she wasn't sure what shape my father might be in for the return flight, if in fact there was one.

We'd already refueled twice by the time we'd passed through the Shelikof Strait and reached the end of the peninsula where the Aleutians begin. We were still cruising at an altitude so low that I could see the massed flocks of seabirds swirling along the coastline to our right, and in the distance just beyond, glittering fields of light resembled sparkling nets of diamonds that were cast upon the surface of the open sea.

Vartan finally looked up from the map he'd been studying obsessively ever since takeoff. Even he seemed captivated by the moving view just beneath us, and as he took me by the hand, it seemed he may have lost some of his Slavic pessimism about the trip, as well. But as Key would say, appearances can be deceiving.

"It's really beautiful," Vartan told Key, in a tone I couldn't peg. "I don't think I've ever seen a wild place quite like this one. And we've just passed Unimak Island, so we've only perhaps a thousand miles remaining until we reach Russian waters and the peninsula."

Key shot him a sideways glance.

He added, "By my calculation, at the rate we are going, that is another ten hours and two or three more refuelings. Perhaps that leaves us enough time that you, as our pilot, might even consider sharing with us precisely where we are going. Not that it matters so much, since neither Alexandra nor I can fly this plane. If anything happens to *you*, we'll never arrive there, anyway."

Key took a deep breath and let out a very long sigh. She reached over and switched on Otto, to captain the ship on his own. Then she turned to us.

"Okay, kids, I fess up," she said. "We're headed for a romp in my own personal sandbox. Grandmaster Azov here will likely have heard of the place. It's called—pardon my Russian—Klyuchevskaya Sopka."

"Where's that?" I asked.

"Alexandra's father is at Klyuchi?" said Vartan, releasing my hand. "But how is it possible we could ever get there from here, ourselves?"

"Where's *there*?" I repeated, feeling very much like an addlepated parrot.

"We don't get *there,*" Key went on as if I'd never spoken. "We'll wait on the water with the plane. My colleagues and I have already established our own shortwave connection, for professional reasons, and their camp is right near the Klyuchi Sopka base. They'll bring Solarin to us, along the river to the inlet, and they'll refuel the plane from there. You *do* understand now, I hope, the reason why our precautions have been an absolute necessity. This was the only way to get to the spot—though we can, and will, depart by a different route."

"This is remarkable," said Vartan. Turning to me, he added, "I'm sorry. I seem to have underestimated your friend Nokomis once more. In her profession, she must know this place as well, if not better, than anyone."

I was tempted to say *What place?* but he finally clued me in.

"The Klyuchi Group is famous," he told me. "It is surely the most highly active concentration of volcanoes in Russia, perhaps in all of northern Asia, and Klyuchevskaya Sopka itself is the highest peak, nearly five thousand meters—more than fifteen thousand feet. This volcano erupted in August 1993, only shortly before we were all at Zagorsk that day in September. But if your father had been taken to that region at that exact moment, it would have been highly dangerous, when it was still pouring lava and shooting rocks into the sky."

"According to Cat's sources on what happened," said

Key, "Solarin was first hidden among the Koryak peoples of Kamchatka, but he was healed by the famous Chukchi shamans from farther north. The geyser fields of the Kamchatka Peninsula are the second largest in the world after Yellowstone and, like ours, they're reputed to have important curative properties. According to our sources, Solarin wasn't moved farther north, to near the volcanologists' camp, until only months ago, when they believed he'd recovered enough to travel and when Cat could finally arrange for the three of us to go and get him out of there."

"So," I said, "these knowledgeable *sources* of yours would be . . . ?"

"Well, your grandmother Tatiana, for one," said Key, as if that were obvious to anyone. "And of course there was Galen March."

THAT NAME AGAIN. Galen March. Why did everyone keep dropping it as if he were the very height of fashion instead of perhaps the heart of a deadly, conspiratorial plot where no one seemed able to sort out right from wrong?

I was about to pursue Mr. Charlemagne's role with a renewed vengeance when suddenly we all heard a frightening, unidentified *thunk* against the side of the plane.

Key snapped to at once and seized her pilot's job back from Otto. But I definitely feared that we might have flunked a major intelligence test in having yakked as long as we had without paying more attention to our surroundings.

The steel-gray soup that had suddenly closed around us looked pretty menacing. "I'm going down," said Key.

"Shouldn't we try to climb above this?" asked Vartan.

"Unlikely that we *could,*" said Key. "But I need to drop down and read the water terrain to see how viable it is that we could land *and* take off again if we need to. Plus, for all we know this fog may go up three or four thousand feet. We don't want to be caught up there with our tongues hanging out if there's a williwaw coming in. It might slap us into the side of a volcano."

"Williwaw?" I said.

Key gave me the grim grimace. "Unique to these isles. It's a freaky air current of gale force, like what our friend here was mentioning earlier, that can suck a 747 out of the skies or flip an aircraft carrier upside down and slap it onto the rocks like chewing gum. They say we lost more planes and ships to williwaws in the Aleutians during World War II than to the Japanese."

Lovely.

The *thunks* were pattering against the plane now like so many marbles, and Becky was descending as if she were flouncing down a steep flight of steps.

"What if you can't *see* the water?" Vartan asked tensely.

"The radar altimeter's good within twenty feet," Key said. "But eyeballs *are* every experienced bush pilot's positioning system of choice. And that's the chief advantage of making this trip in Becky: We can go under the curtain, even if the visibility's only thirty feet. She's slow—so it's true she may take a long time to get us where we're going—but she can still remain airborne at fifty miles an hour. On skis, we can even land these babies on an ice floe or the side of a glacier. Of course, those aren't usually *moving* surfaces."

The charcoal fog suddenly opened up beneath us and we could see the water's surface less than a hundred feet below, whipping and frothing against a gravelly shore.

"Shit," said Key. "Well, this may be our last best chance, so I'm setting her down. I don't want to take the risk we might dunk in the water. Even with life vests and the inflatable dinghy we won't last long—the water temp in these parts is thirty degrees. Just wish I could see anything along here, so we could lash her down."

Vartan was looking at his map again. "Is this one of the 'Islands of Four Mountains'?" he asked Key. "It says one of them is six thousand feet."

She glanced at her GPS reading and nodded as her eyes lit up. "Chuginadak," she replied. "And beyond it, the Carlisle volcano that created the birthplace of the Aleut peoples—the place where the mummy caves still are."

"Then," said Vartan, "this inlet between them, it's protected by the mountains?"

VARTAN WAS BEING a better sport about all this than I'd imagined. Despite our water-repellent thermal gear, we got pretty wet standing in thigh-deep water to lash Becky among the rocks in a safe enough spot. We toweled off as best we could once we were back inside the plane, and we all donned whatever dry clothes we could dig out.

The storm—a *mild* one, according to Key—only lasted six hours. All the while we were locked in a cabin with screaming winds, fifteen-foot waves, pelting pebbles, sand, tundra grass all howling to get inside. But it gave us the chance to rethink. If we doubled back to an island we'd just passed, we could top off our fuel tanks again at Nikolski airstrip near the water. And living under the volcano like this had given Key the chance to agree that if we found ourselves in another jam, she might condescend to blow our cover—at least long enough to roust a volcanologist or a wildlife botanist on her radio for an assist.

"Why didn't I think of this place in the first place?" Key was asking herself aloud, just after we'd taken off from Nikolski early on Saturday morning.

It was the only village in these parts, as Vartan and I had just learned, to have survived intact under the Alaska Native Claims Settlement Act for restoration of land. And Key, being an obvious descendant of *some* tribe or other, had appeared here just before dawn, descending from the skies in latent stardust like some rare, long-lost native bird that had surprised everyone by itself surviving extinction.

Not only were we lavished with breakfast and gifts by the locals—eel fritters and small, hand-painted totem poles, carved with our own distinctive totem animals—but Key also was given a hand-drawn map showing all the hidden inlets with private, waterside refueling spots—open only to local native trappers, hunters, and fishermen—from here up to Attu, at the end of the island chain.

Now *she* was ebullient, and Vartan actually hugged her just before we took off.

Five hours and our second and final fuel stop later came the trickiest leg of our trip: Attu, just this side of the international date line from Russian waters, which would be crawling with navy and coast guard, patrol ships and submarines, floating satellite monitors and radar, all of it constantly scanning the sea or pointed at the sky.

But as Key pointed out, like the infant Zeus in his suspended hammock, nobody ever looked for something that touched the boundaries of neither earth nor sky. So she switched off our GPS and radar to enhance our invisibility, then dropped our altitude to sixty feet above sea level. We sliced through that illusory membrane that only *appears* to separate east from west, water from sky.

It was two o'clock on Saturday, April 12, when we left America behind and crossed the international date line. Then all at once, it was noon on Sunday, April 13, and the waters and sky we were sailing between were now Russian.

Vartan looked at me in amazement. "You do realize what we've done?" he said. "If they bring down this plane and capture us, I'll be shot for treason and you'll both be captured as American spies."

"Oh, why all this pessimism?" said Key. "We're as good as there."

She was undoubtedly still giddy from euphoria over this morning's tribal conspiracy granting her secret navigational paths over water and land, for she added, "What totems did they give you two? I got raven and beaver, which I guess is the closest you could get to how Becky Beaver and I arrived and departed this morning: the magic bird from the moon, and the animal that knows the best escape routes from the pond! And what about our smuggled traitor?"

Vartan pulled the little animal totems he'd been given from his pocket. "Mine are the bear and the wolf," he said.

"The insignia of a natural-born chess master," said Key approvingly. "The bear hibernates in his cave and spends half his life in silence, meditation, and introspection. Wolf comes from the dog star, Sirius, worshipped by many cultures. Even if he's a lone wolf, he's still the teacher of concerted and concentrated effort, of how to focus on what the pack's trying to achieve."

I looked at my carved totems, a whale and an eagle painted in four colors, bright red, yellow, teal, and black. "The eagle's the thunderbird, right?" I asked Key. "But what's the whale?"

"The thunderbird is also the firebird, or the lightning," said Key. "He signifies balance because he soars high and touches Great Spirit, but he also brings heaven's fire and energy down to earth in the service of man."

Vartan said, "They're very good at this, aren't they, this assignment of totems? My wolf and Alexandra's firebird—these are the two animals that come to the rescue of Prince Ivan in our famous Russian folktale, and they restore him to life." He smiled at me, adding to Key, "And what of Alexandra's whale?"

"Ah, that's the most mysterious totem of them all," Key told him, still watching ahead as we soared across the wide, open waters of the Pacific. "The whale's an ancient mammal with an encoded genetic memory. Nobody knows how long he's traveled down there alone, deep beneath the surface we're skimming across right now, tucked away on the ocean floor like an enormous library of ancient genetic wisdom. Like the drumbeat of the shaman. Like a heartbeat carrying the oldest knowledge of the ancient wisdom . . ."

She glanced at Vartan and me with a mischievous grin, as if she knew what we both were thinking.

"Like the Original Instructions?" Vartan suggested, smiling back.

"Whatever the instructions may be," said Key, "it seems we're just about to find out."

She gestured toward the sea spread before us. On the horizon lay a long green coast with high white mountains just beyond. Key added, "I believe the appropriate aphorism would be 'Land ho.' "

RETURN OF THE EIGHT

The soul is bound by the City of Eight that resides in the mind, intellect and ego, and consists of the arising of the five subtle elements of sensory perception.

— *The Stanzas on Vibration*
(Translated by Mark S. G. Dyczkowski)

What is that intermediate universe? It is the . . . world, fully objective and real, where everything existing in the sensory world has its analogue, but not perceptible by the senses, is the world that is designated [in Islam] as the eighth climate.

—HENRI CORBIN, *Swedenborg and Esoteric Islam*

All things are eight.

—THOMAS TAYLOR, quoting a Pythagorean maxim

UST KAMCHATSK
KAMCHTKAN PENINSULA

A light snow sifted through the filtered sunlight above the river. The day was beautiful.

Aleksandr Solarin knew who he was. He was able to remember some of what lay behind him and had learned much more about what might lie just ahead.

He also knew that this might be the last time he would see this view, the river he'd come from, rushing down from the high valley, those glittering obsidian mountains, capped with snow, steaming their rosy and dangerous fumes into the sky.

He stood beside his mother, Tatiana, aboard his ship

that lay at anchor here in the bay, and here he awaited his future, the future that was soon to take him to another world, a world and a future where she would not go with him. He'd lost her once, when a boy—that scene he remembered so vividly. That night, the rain, his father, his brother, his grandmother—and the three chess pieces. He remembered it all as if an enormous light shone on every instant and every detail.

And he remembered playing chess. He could feel the cool, smooth touch of the pieces; he could visualize the board. He could remember games he'd played, so many of them. That's what he was, that's what he had always been: a chess player.

But there was another game, a different game—a kind of secret game, almost like a map—where the pawns and the pieces were all hidden, not on the board, where one had to have some special kind of vision, some trick of memory, to be able to look beneath the surface and see them. He had even begun in his mind to be able to make out where some of them were . . .

But there was one thing he could never see. That day when it happened. Whenever he thought of it the explosion returned in force. The pain.

And what of his daughter? Alexandra, her name was, Tatiana had told him. And what of his wife? He would soon see them both. Then surely he would know.

But there was one thing he did know.

They were an important part of his pain.

KEY NEVER FAILED to amaze me.

It was nearly four hundred miles from Kamchatsky to our departure point in Chukotskiy to cross the Bering Sea, but bad as our rusty, battered trawler looked, Key said it would make it in under six hours.

We'd found the trawler—a former dragnet fishing vessel converted to marine observation—lying at anchor awaiting us in the Ust Kamchatsky harbor, moored at such an angle that it blocked any view of Becky Beaver from within the port when she came putt-putting from where we'd touched down just outside, and we slipped right into the open bay of the ship, where they used to bring in their netted hauls of fish.

"I seem to observe," Key informed me, "that you're starting to believe what I first told you, about what a bitch this little junket was for me to orchestrate. Even though glasnost may have been tossed out with the bathwater in these parts—and even if there's no honor among thieves, as they say—I can tell you that cooperation among wildlife researchers, volcanologists, and native peoples has reached an all-time high, not to mention insane levels of complexity and risk. If I ever again volunteer to help reunite a family like yours, just shoot me in the foot, so I'll have some recovery time to give it a second thought."

I confess, now that I was really about to see my father, I was having many of the same reservations. My heart felt as if it were shuddering like Becky's engine. I knew nothing of his condition, how ill he had been all this time, how much or little he might have recovered. Would he even remember me? Vartan and Key, reading my mind, had each placed a hand on my shoulders as we went up on deck together.

There, at the far end, stood the tall blond woman, her hair shot with a few wisps of silver, whom I now could recognize as the grandmother I'd never met. And beside her stood the man whom I'd believed that, over all these past ten years, I'd never see again.

My father was watching the three of us as we approached along the flat deck. Even from here, perhaps thirty feet away, I could see how much weight he'd lost, the strong, clean lines of his face and jaw against the dark, open collar of his pea jacket. As we came nearer, I couldn't help observing that his pale, shaggy hair, though it tumbled over his forehead, barely concealed the scar.

When we three arrived, his silvery-green eyes, the color of bottle glass, focused just upon me.

I started to cry.

My father opened his arms and I walked into them without a word.

"Xie," he said, as if remembering something crucial he thought he'd forgotten forever, "Xie, Xie, Xie."

WHERE CHUKOTSKIY POLUOSTROV, the Chukchi Peninsula, juts out between the Chukchi and the Bering seas, if you look due west across the Bering Strait you'll find you're so close that a cat could spit and it would hit the good old U.S. of A.

Our trawler was headed for a reconnaissance mission with Chukchi marine biologists who were concerned about declining cormorant populations on the northern and eastern shores. We five were just along for the ride. Tatiana would return with the Kamchatkans and reunite with Chukchi shamans after we and our plane had been dropped at a suitable locale where we could take off without too much fanfare. Once we were over U.S. waters, said Key, we'd refuel at Kotzebue in Alaska for our flight with my father back to Anchorage.

Twilight came fast at this time of year. We sat on the trawler deck around a small brazier that Key's cronies had set out for us. We drank kvass, we roasted potatoes, and we braised chunks of marinated reindeer meat, the staple diet in these parts, on wooden skewers that we set among the coals. My father had his arm wrapped tightly about my shoulders. He looked down at me from time to time to be sure I was still there beside him—almost as if he feared I would fly off into the night sky like a bird.

My gorgeous grandmother, Tatiana, seemed both exotic and ageless, with her high cheekbones, her costume of embroidered, fringed reindeer skin, and that silvery blond hair shimmering in the firelight before us. But she could only speak to us in broken English with a thick Slavic accent, so Vartan offered to help in the translation. She took the floor to tell us what we'd all been waiting so long to hear.

"I was captured in Krym one night in autumn of 1953 and taken by boat to the Gulag. One cannot imagine it—many died on those boats, deprived of water and food and even heat—and had it been winter when I was transported, I might have frozen to death, just like thousands of others. The forced labor camp system in all has killed tens of millions.

"I do not know how long I remained in the Gulag camp, eating slops, drinking filthy water, working the permafrost soil to help build roads until my hands were raw and bleeding. Less than a year. But I was lucky, for my escape was bought. And more fortunate still—for although the local Kamchatkan and Koryak tribes, along with their children, had been slaughtered in the past when they were found to be harboring 'political prisoners' like me, I was given shelter among a group farther north. They themselves had been hunted almost into extinction. Most of those who remained were women—the Chukchi shamans. It is they who saved Sascha's life, as well. The man who arranged for our salvation calls himself 'Galen March.' "

Once he'd finished the translation for us, Vartan asked her, "Calls himself?"

"If you spell it the Gaelic way," I explained, "it's an

acronym for Charlemagne." But then to Tatiana, I added, "I don't understand. How could Galen have rescued you, too—fifty years ago—when the man I met can't be more than in his early thirties?"

Vartan translated.

Then Tatiana turned to me and replied in her limited English, "No, he is older. His name is not Charlemagne, not Galen March. I give you something from him that explains all—how you say? All things."

She reached into her reindeer robes and extracted a small packet. She handed it to Vartan and motioned for him to give it to me.

"He writes this for you, who is the next Black Queen, and—"

I had felt my father's arm tightening about me, almost trembling, as he cut in on her. "What do you mean?" he demanded.

Tatiana shook her head and spoke quickly to Vartan in another language I didn't recognize—perhaps Ukrainian. After a moment he nodded, but when he looked back to me he wore an expression I couldn't read.

"What Tatiana insists I tell you, Xie," Vartan said, "is that this packet from Galen is important for all of us to read right now, and most especially critical for you and me. She says that Galen March is the White King but won't be for long—it seems he hopes to replace himself with *me*. But the crux of the matter, she says, is *why* he's leaving. He can't accomplish the mission at all, she says—only *we* can."

Vartan looked at all three of us, seeming very confused. Then he turned his eyes to my father. "Perhaps this will mean little to you, sir, until more of your memory has returned," Vartan told him. "But your mother, Tatiana, says that the man we are speaking of, Galen March, is actually your ancestor. He's the son of Minnie

Renselaas, the nun called Mireille. And his name is Charlot de Remy."

"YOUR MOTHER MUST have known all along," said Key. "That's the only explanation of why she would trust Galen that way from the moment she first met him, why she'd agree to move back to Four Corners, with him as backup should the need arise. I guess the need *did* arise when she learned that your father was able to remember things. It might have put all of you in danger if 'someone we know' found out where he was and got their hands on him before *we* did. That's when she decided she had to move Galen physically into place as a buffer in Colorado, and why she got Vartan and me aboard the train as well.

"It also makes sense why Cat would want to keep you and your uncle and Lily Rad in the dark about what she knew and her plans, until the last possible moment. They were players the last time around and this was a brand-new ball game. Besides, all three of you are such risk-taking chess players, just like your father, she was likely afraid one of you might go off on your own like a cannon. So she arranged it all herself. She's a tough chick, that babe."

Durn tootin', I thought.

It was agreed to be simpler if Vartan and I read Galen's packet of papers first, and we could fill in the others afterward as needed. So we sat alone in the light of the brazier, unfolded the packet, and read the tale of Charlot de Remy.

THE WHITE KING'S TALE

I was not yet seven years old when I returned from Egypt to London along with my mentor, Shahin, who had raised me as more than a father—truly as both father and mother—from my infancy. It was foretold that I would be the one to solve the mystery, and my mother, Mireille, believed this. The Game had seized possession of her own life at the time when, even before I was born, it had taken the life of her closest companion, her beloved cousin Valentine.

Shahin and I, arrived in London from Egypt, learned that during our absence my mother had spent months in Paris with my father, from whom she'd received seven pieces of the service captured from the White Team—with the promise of even more if my father could obtain them.

As the fruit of this rare meeting that occurred between my parents, we learned that my mother, just before our arrival from Egypt, had given birth to my little sister, Charlotte. For four years, as Charlotte grew into a healthy child, my mother, Shahin, and I labored over the papers of Isaac Newton in the Cambridge rooms overlooking the kitchen gardens that had once been his. It was there that I made a discovery: The secret everyone had fought over for centuries was more than transmutation of base metals, it was the very secret of immortality—*al-Iksir,* the Arabs called it—the elixir of life. But I did not yet know all.

I was ten years old and Charlotte was already four when we first met our father, Charles-Maurice Talleyrand, at the baths of Bourbon-l'Archambault. My mother, resolved to finish the Game that so possessed her, had brought us with her to help collect on Father's promise to secure more of the pieces.

After that night at the baths of Bourbon, when I was ten, I would not see my father for another twenty years. Though he'd prevailed upon my mother to let him raise little Charlotte as his own adopted daughter—with which Mother concurred—she could not yet part with me. I was the prophet who was foretold, she said. I was born beneath the eyes of the goddess in the desert. I was the one who would solve the mystery of the Montglane Service.

And in this one truth, she was right.

For nearly twenty years, we labored, first in London and then in Grenoble, but for years we made little progress beyond that initial discovery of what we believed the secret actually was.

At Grenoble was the Académie Delphinale, of which Jean-Baptiste Joseph Fourier, author of *The Analytic Theory of Heat,* had been an instrumental founder. It was Fourier whom Shahin and I had spent so much time with during our foray into Egypt in Napoleon's campaign, when I was just a child, an expedition that had brought back a stone from Rosetta that required as much time to decipher as our project on the Montglane Service had consumed—and would soon be connected to it in a most important way.

By 1822, Fourier himself was already famous for the great works he'd written on the many scientific discoveries still pouring out of Egypt. He had personally sponsored at the academy of Grenoble one young man who had a great facility with ancient languages, and whom we came to know extremely well. His name was Jean-François Champollion.

On September 14 of 1822, Jean-François flew through the streets to his brother's offices and cried, "*Je tiens l'affaire!*" After nearly twenty years of work himself on the problem, almost since his own boyhood, he was the first to unravel the mystery of the Rosetta Stone. The key to the secret was a single word: *Thoth.*

My mother was filled with excitement. For Thoth, it is well known, was the great god of Egypt whom the Romans equated with Mercury and the Greeks with Hermes, father of Alchemy. The land of Egypt itself, in ancient times, was called al-Khem. We were certain, all of us including Fourier himself, that Jean-François had found the key to more than the Egyptian transcriptions, that he had found the key to the ancient mysteries, one of which, the Montglane Service, my mother held in her hands.

I myself felt that we were at the brink of a great discovery, a discovery in which I played the very role that my mother believed I was born for. But try as I might, I could not quite yet touch it.

At my mother's instigation, therefore, I left Fourier and Champollion to the advancement of their great scientific breakthrough, and my mother and Shahin with the Service itself. And I went alone into the desert to seek the ancient scriptures on those ever more ancient rocks where I'd been born.

My mother felt certain in her belief that the only way to end the Game, for once and all, was for one team, even one person, to collect enough of the pieces to solve the puzzle, to create the formula, and to drink it.

In this belief, she was grievously mistaken.

This mistake would prove to destroy her life.

As well as my own.

WHEN VARTAN AND I had come this far in the manuscript, he put his hand over mine on the page. "We shall continue this story in a moment," he told me softly. "But I believe that you and I likely already know the answer to what it is that this man believes has destroyed *his* life, if not his mother's. And to why it seemed so critical that he's done as he has, and that he has written this for *us*."

I looked up into Vartan's dark eyes in the reddish light of the coals. And I knew he was right.

"Because he's still alive," I said.

Vartan nodded slowly and said, "And the one he loves is not."

CITY OF FIRE

At the end of the world, the world shall be judged by fire, and all these things that God made of nothing shall by fire be reduced to ashes, from which ashes the Phoenix is to produce her young. . . . After the conflagration, there shall be formed a new heaven and a new earth, and the new man will be more noble in his glorified state.

—Basil Valentinus, *The Golden Tripod*

God gave Noah the rainbow sign,
No more water, the fire next time!

—James Baldwin, *The Fire Next Time*

You've got to bang a few rocks together to create fire.

—Garry Kasparov, *How Life Imitates Chess*

It was indeed a long and winding road, but a glorious one, back to that shining City on the Hill that I called home.

First, Key, as usual, had prearranged (with Lily, this gig's designated driver) for all of us to rendezvous at a more private venue than Lake Hood, a small private seaplane base on a lake slightly north of Anchorage: a place where people might not even know what a limited-edition Aston Martin was, much less a place where it might attract attention. But how *did* they get that car here all the way from Wyoming, over thousands of miles of rough tundra?

"Let me guess," I said to Lily, "you and my mother shared 24/7 shifts up the Alcan Highway singing

'Night and Day.' Or just how in hell did you get here?"

"My usual technique," said Lily, brushing the lacquered tips of her fingers to her lacquered thumbnail in the timeless gesture signifying *moolah*. "Naturally, once I had examined our proposed terrain, I knew that private car ferries over water would have to be my route of preference."

But then a hush fell as Vartan helped my father from the plane and my father got a glimpse of my mother for the first time in ten years. Even Ms. Zsa-Zsa was silent.

Of course, we all know the basics of how each of us has arrived here on the planet: A sperm dances with an egg. Some think God provides the spark that triggers the process, others view it as more of a chemical thing. But what we were seeing before us was something completely different, and we all knew it. Now I was glad that Vartan had made us two stand before that steamy mirror so I could see myself as he saw me. Right now, seeing my own parents look upon each other for the first time in ten years, I understood that I was actually witnessing how I myself had even come to be here.

However you looked at it, it was some kind of miracle.

My father's hands were in my mother's hair, and as their lips met, their bodies seemed to flow together, to meld into each other. We all watched them for a very long time.

Key, at my side, whispered, "They must have read *all* the Instructions." She paused to consider, and added, "Or maybe they even wrote the book."

I could feel tears welling up again. If this became any more of a habit I'd have to start carrying a hanky.

As they continued their embrace, my father slowly extended his arm toward us. Lily said to me, "I think he wants *you*."

When I went over to them, he wrapped his arm around me and my mother did likewise, so we were all wrapped together in a bundle. But before I could get embarrassed that this might be getting a bit too goopy, Father said something he'd struggled to explain to me during our flight. "It was my fault, Alexandra. I can see it now. It's the only time I ever opposed Cat over anything. But I want you to know that I didn't do it for *you*—I did it for myself."

Though he was speaking to me, he never took his eyes from my mother's face.

"Once here in America, when I found that I would have to exchange one of the two things I loved for the other—to abandon chess in order to have the life that I'd chosen with Cat—it was so difficult. Too difficult. But when I knew that my daughter could play, that she *wanted* to play the game"—he turned those silvery green eyes upon me; *my* eyes, I realized—"I knew that you, my daughter, Xie, could be my surrogate," he said. "In a way, I used you, like one of those parents pushing forward their child—how do you call them?"

"*Stage* mothers," my mother said, with a light laugh, breaking up the Slavic angst a bit. She put her hand on my father's head and pushed his hair back from the dark purple scar that could never be removed from our lives. With a sad smile, she told him, "But you've paid for your crime, I think."

Then Mother turned to me. "I don't want to replace your father as your Svengali," she said, "but there *is* that other Game that we need to discuss, and I'm afraid we must do it right now. I've had little time to discover just how much you know. But you *were* able to decipher all the messages I left you, weren't you? Especially the first one?"

"The chessboard is the key," I said.

Then she did the oddest thing. She released my father,

put her arms around me in a crushing embrace, and said in my ear, "Whatever happens, that's my gift to you."

Then she let me go, and she beckoned for the others to join us.

"Lily has a place on the water, on Vancouver Island," she told us. "We are going there for a while—the three of us. And Zsa-Zsa." She scruffled the dog's head and Zsa-Zsa wriggled in Lily's arms. "Nokomis has agreed to fly us there from here and to have Lily's car shipped back east. For the time being, only this group will know where we are, until we are sure of my husband's condition. And Lily will contact Nim about it, in person, as soon as she returns to New York."

Then Mother looked at Vartan and me. "How much have you read of Galen's papers?"

"All of them," said Vartan. "How he helped to rescue the girl, how he obtained from her the true Black Queen of the Sufis, how he used it to help his mother solve the formula, and how, in the end, he drank the elixir himself. When combined with the story that Lily had already told us about Mireille, Charlot's mother, it was truly awful. To live forever, always at risk and in fear. And to understand that you will be forever alone with the knowledge that you, yourself, have created—"

"But there's more," my mother cut in. "I've just given Xie the key to all the rest. If you do replace Galen as White King, and if Alexandra agrees to take my place, then perhaps at last you two will be the ones who'll be able to provide the solution to those who will understand the appropriate thing to do with it."

To me she said, "Just remember one thing, my love: the card that Tatiana Solarin gave you so long ago in Russia. On one side lies freedom. On the other lies eternity. The choice is everything." Then, as Key routed the others onto the plane, Mother said to us with a smile, her eyes a bit misty, "But both of you *will* know where to find me, should you have any questions about the instructions."

TAIL WINDS FROM west to east cut our flying time like crazy. Three hours to Seattle and four and a half from there to D.C. So even though we lost three hours in time zone translation, it was just closing on dinnertime Monday night—one week after "that night in Baghdad"—when Vartan and I walked into my apartment.

He dropped the one duffel bag with our belongings on the floor and folded me into his arms. "I don't care *what* happens by tomorrow," he murmured into my hair. "Tonight we start our serious home studies on those instructions your parents were showing us. That looked like something I really want to learn."

"Dinner first," I said. "I don't know what food is here, but I don't want you collapsing from hunger when we're just getting started on our homework."

I went off to the kitchen and pulled down some cans and boxes of pasta. "It's spaghetti," I said as I leaned out the door.

Vartan was standing in the living room, looking down at the chessboard that Nim had left set up there on my round oak table.

"Have you ever had regrets about that last game?" he asked. He looked up at me. "Oh, I don't of course mean regrets about your father, or of all that came after. I mean regrets that you and I never were given the chance to play that game at all."

"Did I regret it? Bitterly," I said with a smile. "That game was my one last opportunity to churn you into creamed buttermilk."

"Then let's do it," he suggested.

"Do what?"

"Let's play it now," Vartan said. "I know that you're

out of practice, but it might do you some good to play just this once."

He plucked the white and black queens from the board and mixed them behind his back. Then he held out his two fists to me, the queens concealed inside.

"This is crazy," I said.

But I tapped his right hand, feeling myself a little tingly all over.

When he opened it, the white queen sat on his palm. Vartan handed her to me. Then he seated himself at the far side of the table, where the black pieces were, and set his queen in situ. "Your move," Vartan said, gesturing for me to take my place in the chair opposite.

The moment I'd taken my seat and I'd set the white queen in her place on the board, it was as if something clicked to life inside of me. I forgot that I hadn't sat before a chessboard in more than ten years. I felt energy flooding through me, crackling with potentialities, my brain calibrating just like Key's Fourier transform and Maxwellian equations, and calculating those infinitely rolling waves of heat and light and sound and lasers and high infrared vibrations that no one could see or hear.

I picked up the knight and put it on d4.

I was still looking at the board some moments later when I realized that Vartan hadn't yet made his opening move. I looked up and saw that he was watching me with a strange expression I couldn't fathom.

"Your move," I pointed out.

"Maybe this was a poor idea," he told me.

"No, it was a good one," I said, feeling thoroughly juiced. "Go on, go ahead."

"Alexandra," he said, "I've been playing in competition all these past ten years, you know. My ELO is far above twenty-six hundred. You simply can't defeat me with the King's Indian, if that's what you think."

It had always been my favorite, so neither of us needed him to add, *You couldn't last time, either.*

"I don't care whether or how I defeat you," I told him. *I lied.* "But if you prefer, just reply with a different defense." I couldn't believe we were *discussing* this instead of playing.

"I'm afraid I don't even know *how* to lose," Vartan said with an apologetic smile, as if he'd just realized what he was doing. "Far less how to lose graciously. You know that I can't simply *throw* this, even if I wanted to, just to make you feel good."

"Fine—you can throw a tantrum instead, when I beat you," I said. "Just play."

With some reluctance he moved his knight out, and we were on.

In fact, on his next move he did adopt another defense than expected—he played pawn to e6! The *Queen's* Indian! I tried not to show my excitement. For this was exactly what my father and I had planned and hoped and strategized and rehearsed for, when I was to play White at Zagorsk!

And since every possible reply to this defense had been etched into my brain, ever since my childhood, I was well prepared to pull out my big guns, should anyone ever have used it against me. Vartan had told me back in Wyoming that timing was everything, hadn't he?

Well, now was the time.

Life imitates art. Reality imitates chess.

On the ninth move, I threw my wrench into Vartan's machinery. I slid out my knight's pawn g2 to g4.

Vartan looked up at me in surprise and let out a short laugh. He'd clearly forgotten that this was supposed to be a serious game. "You never played that move in your life," he said. "Who do you think you are—a little Kasparov?"

"No," I said, keeping my poker face in place. "I'm a little Solarin. And I believe it's your move."

He shook his head, still laughing—but now, for once, he was paying more attention to the board than to me.

Chess is an interesting game that never stops providing lessons in how the human mind works. I knew, for instance, that Vartan had the advantage of a brain jam-packed with ten years of variations that I'd never even heard of. In those ten years, he had played against the best players in the field, and more often than not he'd won.

But weak though my position against his might be in these respects, I knew that right now I held the advantage of surprise. When Vartan first sat down to this chessboard he thought he was playing against that traumatized, twelve-year-old chess dropout he'd fallen in love with—and whom he hoped not to harm emotionally any further than he could help. But with one unanticipated pawn move, he'd suddenly discovered that he was playing a game that—if he didn't start paying sharp attention, and quickly—he might actually lose.

It felt great.

But I knew I had to deep-six all my euphoria or I'd never make it through this game. After all—and I'd bet my bippy on it, as Key would say—with Vartan's encyclopedic memory storage and vast experience—called "tacit knowing" in chess—he could instantly recall all the variations on that last move of mine, same as any others. But it's known that masters tend to focus on what is abnormal but then to recall what is normal. So I'd have to fool with his mind, muck up that carefully honed intuition.

I had only one trick tucked up my sleeve that might yet save me, one that my father had given me, a technique that he'd shared with no one as far as I knew. And I knew it was something that was hardly part of the normal toolbox of standard chess training. For years, I'd actually been afraid to deploy it, because of my so-called *Amaurosis Scacchistica,* which had even overcome me during tournament play. Indeed, I'd wondered if it wasn't this technique of my father's itself that might've *caused* my chess blindness because of how it sometimes turned everything topsy-turvy.

Everyone knows, my father had told me ever since I was small, *that if one of your positions is threatened, you have two choices of a response: either to defend or to attack. But there is another option no one ever thinks of: to ask the pieces for their own opinion of the situation that they find themselves in.*

This made enormous sense to a child. He meant that, although each *position* you find yourself in might have its strong or weak points in terms of attack or defense of the overall board, when it came to the *pieces,* the situation was completely different. For a chess piece, such strengths and weaknesses are part and parcel of its very nature, of its persona. They are its modus operandi, both the freedom and the limitations of how that piece moves around within its seemingly closed black-and-white world.

Once my father had pointed this out, I could quickly see, for instance, that when a queen was threatening a knight, the knight couldn't threaten the queen back. Or when a rook is attacking a bishop, the bishop's in no position to attack the rook. Even the queen, the most powerful piece on the board, can't afford to pause very long on an oblique square that's smack in the oncoming path of a lowly pawn, or she'll get nailed. Each piece's weakness—in terms of its natural limitations, of how it could be trapped or attacked—was also its strength when it was attacking someone else.

What my father liked was to find situations where you could exploit these innate traits in concert, in an aggressive all-out tactical bombardment—a true revelation to a fearless six-year-old child, and one that I hoped I could use today. I'd always been more of a close-in, hand-to-hand tactical player anyway. And I knew—just in order to *tie* with Vartan Azov—I definitely needed a few more surprises.

AFTER WHAT SEEMED a *very* long time, I glanced up. Vartan was looking at me with a strange expression.

"Astonishing," he said. "But why haven't you said it?"

"Why haven't you moved?" I wanted to know.

"All right," he agreed. "So I shall then make the only move that's open to me."

Vartan reached out with one long fingertip and toppled his king. "You failed to mention that you had me in checkmate," he told me.

I stared at the board. It took me a full fifteen seconds to find it.

"You didn't see it?" he asked in amazement.

I was in a kind of giddy shock. "I guess I need a little more coaching before I jump back into the big time," I admitted.

"Then how did you do it?" he asked.

"It's a strange technique of looking at the game that my father taught me when I was little," I said. "But it seems sometimes to backfire, once it gets inside *my* synapses."

"Whatever it is," Vartan said with a widening grin, "I think you had better teach this 'technique' to *me*. It's the only time in my life that I never really saw it coming."

"I didn't either," I confessed. "And when I lost that last game to you in Moscow, it was the same thing—*Amaurosis Scacchistica*. I've never wanted to discuss it with anyone, but I admit that wasn't the first time it happened."

"Xie, listen to me," Vartan said, coming around the table to take my hands. He pulled me to my feet. "Every player knows that chess blindness can strike anybody, anywhere, and at any time. Each time it happens, you curse yourself. But it's a mistake ever to believe that it's some special curse from the gods that was reserved just for *you*. You had already left the game before you were able to discover that on your own.

"Now," he told me, "I want you to look at this board. What you did just now was very strong, and not just an accident. Maybe not a sophisticated strategy either. In fact, I've never seen it before. It was more a case of tactics flying everywhere, like bits of shrapnel. But it took me completely off guard." He paused till he got my complete attention. Then he added, "And you *won*."

"But if I don't recall *how*—" I began.

"Go on," he said. "That's why I want you to sit here and study it as long as it takes you, to reconstruct everything till you *know* how you got there. Otherwise, it'll be like falling from a horse. If you don't remount at once, you become afraid to ride."

I'd been afraid to ride for more than ten years of accumulated fear and guilt, ever since Zagorsk, and maybe even earlier. But I did know that Vartan was right about this: I would always be left lying in the dust behind that fleeing horse until I really knew.

Vartan smiled and kissed the tip of my nose. "I'll make us dinner," he said. "Tell me when you've got the answer. I don't wish to distract you just at the critical moment in your deciphering. But I can safely promise that once you've solved it you can expect a handsome reward. A grandmaster will sleep in your bed and do delightful things to you all night long."

He was halfway to the kitchen when he turned and added, "You *have* got a bed, haven't you?"

VARTAN FLIPPED THROUGH the pile of paper, my reconstruction of our game, as he wolfed down the spaghetti he'd prepared for us in my woefully wanting kitchen. But he never complained, even about his own cooking.

I watched his face from across the table. From time to time, he nodded. Once or twice, he laughed out loud. Finally he looked up at me.

"Your father was some kind of self-created genius," he said. "I assure you that he never got any of *these* ideas you have just thrust upon me from that long term of sentence that he'd endured, as a boy, at the 'Palace of Young Pioneers.' You got these blitz techniques from him? But it's like something Philidor might have invented, only using pieces instead of pawns." He paused and added, "Why did you never use any of this on me before today? Ah yes, your *'Amaurosis.'* "

Then he looked at me as if he'd just had a true revelation. "Or perhaps it's we two who have *both* been blind," he said.

"Blind about what?" I asked.

"Where is that card that Tatiana gave you at Zagorsk?"

When I retrieved it from the trouser pocket where I'd left it, he flipped it back and forth to look at both sides. Then he stared at me. *"Je tiens l'affaire,"* he said, like Champollion finding the key to the hieroglyphic. "You see it? That's why it says here 'Beware the Fire.' The Phoenix is the fire, the eternity that your mother spoke of—the perpetual death and rebirth in ashes and flame. But the firebird doesn't die in fire or ashes or anything.

Her magical feathers bring us eternal light. I think that's the freedom your mother meant. And the choice. And it would explain what she's discovered about the chess set itself—why neither Mireille nor Galen could attain the true meaning, nor could your mother by helping either of them. They'd already drunk the elixir—for whatever their individual motives might have been. They'd exploited the service toward their own ends, but not for the original purpose of the designer."

"You mean, it's like a built-in fail-safe mechanism," I said, in amazement, "and that al-Jabir had designed it so that *no* one who used the Service for personal gain would then be able to access its higher powers."

Great solution, I thought. But it still seemed to leave that same old problem facing us.

"So what *are* those higher powers?" I said.

"Your mother told me that she'd given *you* the key to all the rest," said Vartan. "What did she tell you?"

"Nothing, really," I said. "She only asked if I'd understood all of *her* messages that she'd left for me in Colorado—especially the first one: *The chessboard is the key.* She told me that that message had been for me, her special gift."

"How could it be her special gift," said Vartan, "when we all saw that drawing of the chessboard, just as she surely knew we would? It must have been *another* chessboard she was speaking of as the key."

I stared down at the board that still sat there before us on the table, that checkmate still in place on its surface. Vartan's eyes followed mine.

"I found it inside Mother's piano in Colorado," I said. "It was set up with our last Moscow game, yours and mine, just at the place where I fumbled. Key told me you'd sent Mother the position yourself—"

But Vartan was already removing our spaghetti plates

and wineglasses from the table and sweeping the pawns and pieces to one side.

Then he turned to me and said, "It has to be in here—not hidden in the pieces. She said the board."

I looked at Vartan and I could feel my heart pounding. He was examining the board closely with his fingertips, just as he had with that desk in Colorado. I had to stop this. I'd never before felt so afraid of my own future.

"Vartan," I said, "what if we end up just like all those others? After all, you and I are both natural-born competitors even since our childhoods. Just now in that game, I only wanted to defeat you. I didn't think even once about sex or passion or love. What if it grabs us? What if, like them, it turns out that we just can't stop playing the Game, even against each other?"

Vartan looked up at me and after a moment he smiled. It took me by surprise—it was truly radiant. He reached over and took me by the wrist, turning my hand up to kiss the place where my pulse was beating harder than usual. "Chess will certainly be the only 'game' we shall ever play against each other, Xie," he said. "And all these other games must be stopped, too."

"I know," I said. I leaned my forehead down on his hand that still held my wrist. I was too exhausted to think.

He rested his other hand on my hair for a moment, then pulled me back to face him. "As for how we'll 'end up,' " he said, "I think it will be a bit more like your parents. That is, if we are very, very lucky. But every chess player knows Thomas Jefferson's famous line, 'I'm a great believer in luck and I find the harder I work, the more I have of it.'

"Now let's go to work," he added. "And let's hope we get lucky."

He took my hand and he placed it on the chessboard. Then, with his hand resting over mine, he slid my fingertip beneath his own until I heard a *click*. He lifted my hand from the board, where a section of the surface had popped open. Inside was a single sheet of paper in a loose plastic wrapper. Vartan extracted it and passed it to me so we could both study it.

It was a tiny drawing of a chessboard. I could see that many of the pawns and pieces were connected to little lines that were then drawn out to the side of the page, where a set of different numbers was written above each line. I counted; there were twenty-six lines in all—the exact number of pieces Lily told us that my mother had captured herself, in the last round of the Game. Some of them seemed to be clustered in sets, like bunches of twigs.

"These numbers," said Vartan, "they must be some kind of geodesic coordinates, perhaps the area on a map where each of their pieces has been hidden. So one of two things must be true: Either your father was not the only one who knew this information, or else he had taken a decision to write it down, after all, despite the risk." He added, "But numbers like these would provide us no more than a general idea, not the specific location."

"Except maybe this one here," I said, for I'd noticed something. "Look, there's an asterisk printed beside these numbers."

We traced that line back to the chessboard illustration to see which piece these coordinates might be connected to.

It led to the Black Queen.

Vartan flipped the page over. On the reverse side was a small map of a spot that looked all too familiar, with a tiny arrow at the bottom, pointing north, that seemed to suggest: *Start here*. By now I could hear my heart pounding so loudly in my ears that it was deafening. I gripped Vartan by the arm.

"You mean you actually recognize where this place is?" said Vartan.

"It's right here in Washington, D.C.," I told him, trying hard to swallow. "And given which chess piece the line was pointing to on the flip side, it must be in this very spot, right here inside the District itself, where Mother hid the true Black Queen!"

A familiar voice from across the room said, "I couldn't help but overhear, my dear."

The hair on my neck stood up!

Vartan had jumped to his feet, the chessboard drawing still clutched in his hand. "Who in God's name is *that*?" he hissed at me.

There in the open doorway—much to my horror and distress—stood my boss, Rodolfo Boujaron.

"THERE, THERE," SAID RODO, "please resume your seats once more. I did not mean to *déranger* you both when it seems you were just about to finish with your meal."

Nonetheless, he came into the room and put out his hand to Vartan. "Boujaron here," he said, "Alexandra's employer."

Vartan had surreptitiously dropped the map into my lap as he stepped forward and shook hands with Rodo. "Vartan Azov," he said. "A friend of Alexandra's from childhood."

"Oh, a great deal more than that by now, I'm quite sure," said Rodo. "As you'll recall, I did overhear you. I didn't intend to pry in upon your private conversation. But I'm afraid, Alexandra, that you *did* leave your cell phone in the sofa cushions when you last departed. Galen and I and our compatriots were merely using it to monitor those who might come into this place searching for things in your absence. You see, only your mother knew where she had hidden her list, and she trusted only you to retrieve it. But with that manner of yours these past few days—in and out of here, knocking about exactly like a bocce ball—well, we did all feel that one cannot be too careful in these most difficult times. As I am certain you will both agree."

He went over and pulled the phone from between the cushions where Nim had left it, opened the window, and flung it out into the canal far below.

So I'd been caught with my phone down again. What in God's name was *wrong* with me? I felt ill at the thought of everything he must already have overheard—not least, of course, some of those intimate musings between Vartan and me.

But at this point, I figured it would seem silly to act naive and say, "*List? What list?*" So instead I opted for, "Who's all this '*we*'? *What* 'compatriots'?"

"Those men up at Euskal Herria," Rodo assured us, taking a seat at the table and motioning for us to do the same. "They like to dress up in berets and red sashes and pretend they are Basques, though, as it proves, trained dervishes *can* be trained to do the high kicks in the *Jota* quite well."

He'd whipped out a flask from his pocket and extracted some shot glasses from his other one. "Basque cherry brandy." He filled the glasses and handed them around. Then he added, "You'll enjoy it."

Being plenty ready for a drink, I tasted the brandy. It was wonderful, tart and fruity, and it went down my throat like liquid fire. "The Basque brigade are actually dervishes?" I said, though already I was beginning to get the message.

"They've been waiting a very long time, the Sufis, from the time of al-Jabir," Rodo said. "My people in the

Pyrenees have worked with theirs for more than twelve hundred years. That motto over my kitchen door about Basque mathematics—*4+3=1*—you know, these numbers also add up to *eight,* a game your mother knows very well. That moment, ten years ago, when Galen told her the truth behind your father's death and the schism created in the White Team by it, she came directly to me."

"Schism?" said Vartan. "You mean the one Rosemary Livingston created?"

"In a sense, it was she who triggered it," Rodo told us. "When her father was killed, she was yet a mere child. The first time that Rosemary, as a child, met your mother, it appears that Cat handed her a small White Queen from a pegboard chess set—which deceived her father, El-Marad, into believing Cat was a White player, though he quickly learned otherwise. From the moment you began to play chess yourself, though Rosemary was never completely certain what part you were to play, she began to move in as a predator stalks its prey. She's still quite young for such a ruthless player, though no one knew quite how ruthless she could be.

"When Galen March, along with Tatiana Solarin, his descendant whom he'd rescued, realized that the only way to bring the pieces together, at least in the manner that was originally intended by al-Jabir, was to bring the *players* together, they knew that their best chance in this was to bring Tatiana's son Aleksandr, and through him, his wife, Cat, back into the Game. Taras Petrossian was the instrument through which they executed this plan. Once they knew that a final chess game would definitely take place at Zagorsk, they brought the Black Queen there to be put on display. No one realized that this was the very opportunity Rosemary and Basil were seeking: They turned the tables, had Solarin shot before he could depart with this information, and seized the Black Queen for themselves."

"So," said Vartan, "you are saying that my stepfather, Petrossian, was not involved in their plot?"

"Difficult to know," said Rodo. "All we *do* know is that he helped save the life of Alexandra's father by removing him from there. But Petrossian was forced to flee Russia shortly thereafter, though it appears that Livingston continued to support at least one of his chess tourneys in London, at any rate."

"Then," I asked Rodo, "if the Livingstons stole the Black Queen at Zagorsk, where were they hiding it all this time? How did Petrossian obtain it, so he could get it into the hands of my mother?"

"Galen March smuggled it to Petrossian to send to your mother," said Rodo. "That's why your mother arranged her birthday *boum* in Colorado the very moment she learned that Petrossian had been killed. She was desperate. She had to draw all the players away from the place where the piece was now hidden until she could contact *you* somehow. But what of that *Washington Post* that I left on your doorstep a week ago? Your mother wanted us to alert you, but with no fanfare, when Baghdad was entered. She felt sure you'd make the connection for yourself. But then when we overheard your conversation with your uncle, we realized we'd overlooked something mentioned there in the paper—the covey of Russian diplomats that was strafed when departing Baghdad. The Livingstons knew they'd been betrayed by someone, but not by whom. Galen and I made copies of the paper to send to those who needed this very vital piece of information—"

He paused, for he could see that I now had found the answer to almost all my questions.

"Of course!" I cried. "Rosemary hid the Black Queen in Baghdad! That secret room at the Baghdad airport!

Basil's Russian connections! Their party here at Sutalde last Monday with all those oil magnates—they must have set it up the moment they learned that the Queen was already missing from Baghdad, that Galen might have taken it, that it might already be in my mother's hands." But I had to laugh at my next thought. "Rosemary must have done a pretty fast U-turn from here to Colorado and back again, if she thought that my mother was somehow, somewhere, going to pass that hot chess piece on to *me*!"

But then came the sobering recognition of exactly what that must mean.

"If Rosemary had my father killed at Zagorsk so she could grab the Queen and prevent him from passing information about its very existence to anyone," I said, "and if ten years later, once she'd learned of Petrossian's betrayal, she had him killed for exactly the same reason—to prevent him from telling anyone at the chess tourney where he'd sent the Queen until she herself could arrive at that destination—"

I looked at Vartan. From the grimness of his expression, and the fact that we both knew the parts of the puzzle I myself was holding—the drawing of the board and the location of the pieces, starting with the Black Queen—I probably didn't have to state the obvious.

I'm next.

Rodo saved me the breath anyway. "You are safe for the time," he said calmly, pouring us all a splash more brandy, as if any danger were far from this room and a thing of the past. "The moment that your prankster friend Nokomis sealed us four into that hotel suite, Nim was headed for the door, phone in hand, to dial security and to try to break open the lock, when Galen March stopped him in both endeavors, putting a hand on his arm. That's when Galen told us."

"Told you?" said Vartan.

"That this had all been planned by Alexandra's mother," Rodo continued. "He'd already said that Key was the new White Queen. He said that this was, as people say, a new ball game, but one with completely new rules. That Alexandra had a drawing of the board and would soon have knowledge of the location of the pieces, as well."

"He said what?" I gasped, as I saw Vartan flinch from the corner of my eye.

This was worse than my worst imagining! Mr. Galen "Holy Roman Emperor" March had set me up royally. And there was something else, wasn't there? I racked my brain to reconstruct the context inside that room at the Four Seasons, at the instant when I'd left it: my uncle Slava, Galen, and Rodo . . .

And Sage Livingston.

Sage Livingston sitting there toying with her tennis bracelet.

"Sage's bracelet was bugged all that time!" I told Rodo.

"*Mais bien sûr,*" he said with his enduring sangfroid. "How else could your mother have protected you all these years—have communicated what she wanted the Livingstons to believe—without Sage's unwitting assistance?"

"Her unwitting assistance?" I said.

I was horrified. Sage's mother had pressed her to befriend me, and my mother had used her, among other things, to cut the real estate deal that had moved Galen March to center board in Colorado. And what did Rodo mean by "all these years"? Had Sage already been running this Mata Hari racket in grammar school?

"That is why Galen was upset earlier," Rodo went on. "When your mother suddenly vanished and Galen couldn't contact her, he planned, along with Nokomis Key, to meet with you and your uncle privately and reveal everything. When Sage continued to attach herself to him like so much chewing gum to the bottom of a shoe, he sought my help. But at the Four Seasons, when he saw you drag Sage into the locker room to interrogate her privately, he became alarmed and returned down the stairs of the club. He was afraid that, without intending to, you might reveal something to her, or she to you, which could find other ears outside and ruin everything. At last, when Nokomis arrived and saw Sage there, she took matters into her own hands. Galen felt that his only solution was to draw Sage's attention—and that of the ever-present Livingston security guards—back toward the Game. And away from that mystery that your family were protecting."

Now at least I could guess how the eavesdropping "Secret Service" had gotten on our tails so fast, until Key ditched them crossing the river. But if the Livingston clan were out there somewhere with even that much data, my own life wasn't worth a plugged farthing.

"How can you claim that I'm 'safe for the time'?" I refreshed Rodo's comment. "Exactly where is this motley crew of villains right at this moment?"

Rodo said, "Once we were rid of Sage, Galen revealed the truth about Solarin; then he and Nim were able to form a plan to protect you. I was empowered to share this as soon as you both returned tonight. Your uncle has managed to spare you the effort of dealing any further with the Livingstons. Ladislaus Nim is, after all, one of the world's great computer technocrats. Once he'd grasped the situation, as I understand it, he ensured that, through cooperative antiterrorist channels, the Livingstons' funds in a variety of countries were instantly frozen pending criminal investigations: in London, the investigation into the assassination of a former Russian citizen living on British soil. An arrest order has also been served, of course, over a certain Colorado oil and uranium baron's complicity with the former regime in Baghdad."

Rodo glanced at his watch. "As for where the Livingstons are at this precise moment—since there is only one country likely to refuse to cooperate with such extradition proceedings—just now I should imagine they are somewhere in the air above Arkhangel'sk, headed for St. Petersburg or Moscow."

Vartan slammed his hand on the table in frustration. "You all believe that merely by seizing the Livingstons' assets and exiling them to Russia, that will protect Alexandra?"

"Only one thing will protect her," Rodo told him. "The truth."

Then he turned to me.

"Cat was more realistic," he added. "She knew what was required to save you. She sent you to me only when she understood that it was a kitchen, not a chessboard, where you should go to learn the lessons required of an alchemist. And she realized that we all need some kind of a chariot driver to pull our forces together, like those horses of Socrates, one pulling toward heaven, one toward the earth, like the battle of spirit and matter. You see it all around us: people flying airplanes out of the skies and crashing into buildings because they hate the material world and want to destroy it before they depart it; other people despising the spiritual so much that they want to bomb it into their idea of normality. That's not what we would call being 'well-balanced.' "

Until this moment, I'd had no idea that Rodo had any thoughts on this—or on any other such subject—though I wasn't sure where this "opposites must attract" theme was exactly leading. But then I recalled what he'd said about Charlemagne and the Montglane fortress.

I asked, "Is that why you said my mother's and my birthdays are important? Because April 4 and October 4 are opposite in the calendar?"

Rodo beamed a smile at both Vartan and me. He said, "That's how the process takes place: April 4 lies between the first spring zodiac signs, *le Bélier* and *Taureau,* the Ram and the Bull, when the seeds of the Great Work are shown to be sown in every alchemy book. The harvest is six months later, between Libra the Balance and Scorpio—symbolized in its lower aspect by the scorpion, but in its higher aspect by an eagle or firebird. These two poles are described by the Indian proverb, *Jaisi Karni, Vaise Bharni*—our results are the fruits of our actions. *As ye sow, so shall ye reap.* That's what *The Books of the Balance* of al-Jabir ibn Hayyan are all about: Sowing seed and harvesting means finding the balance. Alchemists call this process the Great Work."

Rodo added, "The man we call Galen March—you've read his papers, so you know—was the first in one thousand years to solve the first phase of this puzzle."

I looked at him and said, "He's played so important a role in all of this. But what's become of Galen now?"

"*En retraite* for a while, just like your mother," said Rodo. "He sent you both this."

He handed me a packet, similar to the one Tatiana had given us but smaller. "You may read it when I've gone tonight. I believe it will come in useful in your quest tomorrow. And perhaps even longer."

I was filled with questions, but when Rodo got to his feet, so did Vartan and I.

Rodo said, "Since Cat has led you to the first of the hidden pieces, right here in D.C., I can guess—even without seeing that map you've hidden from me—just *where* you two may be doing your reaping tomorrow." When he got to the door, he turned back over his shoulder to us. "Both of you together, that's perfect. It's the secret, you know," he told us. "The marriage of black and white, of spirit and matter—it's been known since ancient times as 'the Alchemical Marriage'—the only way the world will survive."

I felt my face turn more than a little pink. I couldn't even look at Vartan.

Then Rodo was out the door and into the night.

We sat back down and I poured us each another splash of the cherry brandy as Vartan slashed open Charlot's letter packet and he read it aloud for me.

THE ALCHEMIST'S TALE

It was the year 1830 when I discovered the secret of making the formula, just as it had been prophesied.

I was in the south, living at Grenoble, when France once more fell into the throes of a revolution that began, as always, in Paris. Our country was again in turmoil, just as it had been at the time of my conception so long ago—when my mother, Mireille, had run the barricades to flee to Corsica with the Bonapartes, and my father, Maurice Talleyrand, had fled to England and then to America.

But in this revolution, things would soon prove to be far different.

By July of 1830, our restored Bourbon monarch Charles X—after six years in power, having revoked civil liberties and disbanded the national guard—had infuriated the people once more by dismissing the magistrates and closing all independent newspapers. That July, when the king quit Paris to go on a hunting trip at one of his country estates, the bourgeoisie and the masses of Paris called upon the Marquis de La Fayette, the only noble of the old guard who seemed still to believe that the restoration of our liberties was plausible, and they charged him to reconstitute a new national guard in the name of the people and to scour the countrysides of France for additional troops and munitions. Then, in swift succession, the people appointed the duc d'Orléans regent of France, voted to restore the constitutional monarchy, and sent a missive to King Charles demanding that he resign his crown.

But as for I myself, living in happiness at Grenoble, none of these politics meant anything. As I foresaw things, it seemed that my life was only just beginning.

For at age thirty-seven—the exact age that my father was when he had first met my mother—I was filled with joy, I was on the brink of complete fulfillment. My vision had returned along with my powers. And, as if fate itself had intervened, things were coming together in a most extraordinary way.

Most astonishing of all, I was deeply in love. Haidée—now twenty years of age, and more ravishingly beautiful than when I'd first met her—was now my wife and was expecting our first child. I was certain in my confidence that we would soon possess that idyllic life and love that my father had so craved and yearned for during all his own. And I had a great secret that I'd kept, even from Haidée, as a surprise. If I completed this great work, for which I knew I'd been born and destined, impossible as it might seem, Haidée's love and my own might even survive the grave.

All seemed perfect.

Through my mother's efforts, we now possessed the drawing of the chessboard and the bejeweled cloth that covered it, both of which the Abbess of Montglane had rescued for us, and we had the seven chess pieces that were once captured by my stepmother, Mme. Catherine Grand. We also held the Black Queen that had been given to Talleyrand by Alexander of Russia, which—thanks to the abbess's last communiqué to Letizia Bonaparte and Shahin—we now knew was only a copy that had been made by Tsar Alexander's grandmother, Catherine the Great. My mother, with Shahin and Kauri, were still off in quest of the other pieces, as they had been for some time.

But I also possessed the *real* Black Queen—minus one emerald—that had been protected for so many decades by the Bektashis and Ali Pasha. This Haidée and I, with Kauri's help, had rescued from where Byron had hidden it upon a rocky, deserted isle off the coast of Maino.

Each afternoon now at Grenoble I spent in our laboratory with Jean-Baptiste Joseph Fourier, the great scientist whom I'd known since my childhood in Egypt. His protégé, Jean-François Champollion, had recently made a tour, at the Duke of Tuscany's expense, of those Egyptian antiquities already scattered throughout collections of Europe, and only last year Champollion had returned from a second tour of Egypt itself, from whence he'd brought us back vital information.

Therefore, despite the limited number of pieces in our hands at this moment, I foresaw that I was now on the very brink of the great discovery that had so long eluded me—the secret of eternal life.

Then, toward the end of July, La Fayette sent a young man to us in Grenoble in support of the coup d'état that was still under way in Paris. This emissary was the son of a great deceased military commander, General Thomas Dumas, who, under Napoleon, had been general in chief of the army of the western Basque Pyrenees.

The son, twenty-eight-year-old Alexandre Dumas, now a popular playwright in Paris, cut a romantic, Byronic figure with his exotic Creole features and mass of cotton-wool hair, his jacket of military cut dashingly offset with a long, flowing foulard about his throat. He'd purportedly been sent hither by La Fayette to bring back magazines of weapons, powder, and shot from the south. But in fact, he was sent to bring back information.

The scientist Monsieur Fourier had long been world-famous as the author of *The Analytic Theory of Heat,* which over the years had already led to better designs for cannon and other gunpowder weapons. But his old friend and ally La Fayette, it seems, had somehow got wind of another project. The general, visualizing France at the dawn of a renewed hope for a restored republic or a constitutional monarchy, himself held new hope for a different sort of breakthrough—one having nothing to do with warfare or its materials—a discovery that had been spoken of since time immemorial.

La Fayette's young emissary Alexandre, however, did not expect what he found when he came to Grenoble. How could he? No one could know what the future was destined, quite soon, to bring to all of us—no one, that is, except myself.

But there was one thing my vision still could not encompass.

Haidée herself.

"Haidée!" the youthful Dumas exclaimed the moment he met my extremely beautiful and very pregnant wife. "*Ma foi!* An adorable name! Are there, then, really women who bear the name Haidée anywhere but in Byron's poems?"

In short, he was besotted by her charms, as anyone might be, and not only those who were admirers of her father's verses! Alexandre spent days, weeks, doting upon my lovely Haidée and hanging upon her every word. She shared her life with him. They grew to love each other as friends.

Little more than a month elapsed after Alexandre's arrival, before Fourier—an aging revolutionary himself of sixty-two—felt we must share with Alexandre our secret, all of it, including Byron's involvement, to take back and share in turn with La Fayette.

We were so close to the truth.

We had completed the first stage—the Philosopher's Stone, as it was known in alchemy—the reddish powder that led to everything else, as I had believed since I was ten years old. This would create the perfect human being, perhaps the first step in manifesting the perfect civilization that the chess set was designed to create. We had wrapped the stone in beeswax and gathered the heavy water at just the right time of the year.

I knew the time had arrived. I stood on the threshold of extending my perfect present into an infinitely perfect future.

I took the powder.

I drank.

Then something went horribly wrong.

I looked up. Haidée was standing in the laboratory doorway, one hand to her heart. Her silvery eyes were large and luminous. Beside her, clutching her hand in his, was the very last person I expected to see: Kauri.

"No!" my wife cried.

"It is too late," said Kauri.

His expression of awful anguish I shall never forget. I stared at the two of them across the room. It seemed an infinity before I could bring myself to speak. "What have I done?" I said in a choked voice, as the horror of my private action slowly began to dawn.

"You have destroyed all hope," Haidée whispered.

Before I could realize what she meant, her eyes rolled back and she fainted. Kauri caught her in his arms to lower her to the ground, and I raced across the laboratory to assist him. But no sooner had I got there than the potion overcame me. Overcome by dizziness, I sat on the floor beside the silent form of my prostrate bride. Kauri, in his long robes, hunkered beside us.

"No one ever imagined you would do this," he told me gravely. "You were the one who was foretold, as even my father knew. He believed that you and your mother—White King and Black Queen—might accomplish the task that *The Books of the Balance* calls for. But now, I fear, the most we can hope for is to scatter the pieces—to protect them by again hiding at least those that we have until someone else appears who can stop this Game. But you yourself cannot solve it, now that you've drunk, now that you have succumbed to the hunger within that overpowers reason. It must be someone who is prepared to protect them for an eternity, if necessary, without any hope of reaping the rewards of the service for themselves."

"An eternity?" I said, confused. "You mean, if Haidée drinks the elixir as I've done, we'll have to wander the earth forever, protecting these pieces until someone else comes along who can find the deeper answer to the mystery?"

"Not Haidée," Kauri told me. "She will never drink. From the moment that she accepted this commission, when we were only children, she has taken no action that served herself, or even those she loved. All has been in service of that higher mission for which the Service itself was originally intended."

I looked at him as the horror overwhelmed me. My dizziness was almost nauseating. What had I done?

"Would you even wish it upon her," Kauri asked me softly, "this future that you face yourself? Or will you place this in Allah's hands?"

Whether it was Allah or fate or kismet, the choice would not be mine to make. For within less than one month, my mother and Shahin returned under urgent request.

My son, Alexandre Dumas de Remy, was born.

And three days later, Haidée died.

The rest, you know.

WHEN HE'D FINISHED READING THIS, Vartan set the letter down gently as if he might bruise the past somehow. He looked at me.

I was still slightly in shock.

"God, what an awful thing," I said, "to find at your happiest moment that you've actually created a formula for tragedy. But he's spent a very long lifetime trying to atone for that mistake."

"That's why Mireille drank it herself, of course," Vartan said. "That's what Lily told us from the very beginning in Colorado—that this was what Minnie had said in her letter to your mother, that it caused misery and suffering. Your mother called it an obsession, that it had ruined the lives of everyone Minnie had known or touched. But most of all it was her own son, by driving him for thirty years, ever since his childhood, toward solving the wrong formula."

I shook my head and hugged Vartan. "If I were you I'd be very careful," I told him. "You may be getting mixed up with the wrong chick here—after all, I seem to be related to all these obsessive people. Maybe these compulsions have been genetically transmitted."

"Then our children might get these?" said Vartan with a grin. "I propose, then, that the sooner we try to find out the better." He ruffled my hair.

He picked up the spaghetti plates and I carried our glasses to the kitchen. When we'd washed up, he turned to me with the most beautiful smile.

"*Jaisi Karni, Vaise Bharni,*" he said. "I'll have to remember that—'Results are the fruits of our actions.' " He glanced at his watch. "It's nearly midnight; if we want to follow that map of your mother's, we should be up and going by dawn, leaving us only six hours. Exactly how many seeds do you think we can sow tonight, before we have to get up and start reaping?"

"Quite a few," I told him. "As I recall, the place where we're going doesn't even open until two in the afternoon."

THE BOOK OF BALANCE

Opposite pairs working in harmony: this has become a theme of our quest to perfect decision-making. Calculation and evaluation. Patience and opportunism, intuition and analysis, style and objectivity . . . strategy and tactics, planning and reaction. Success comes from balancing these forces and harnessing their inherent power.

—GARRY KASPAROV, *How Life Imitates Chess*

VARTAN AND I, AS SEASONED CHESS PLAYERS, HAD effectively utilized our time within the constraints allotted by both our biological and chronological clocks. We had fourteen hours until our appointment with destiny—of which we spent seven "fruitfully," as Rodo had recommended—and the only thing competitive about it was which of us could give the other more pleasure.

When I finally awakened, the sun was well up and Vartan's curly head was lying on my breast. I could still feel the warmth of his hands from last night, his lips moving over my body. But when I finally roused him from sleep, we still weren't any readier to see dawn than Romeo and Juliet were after *their* first night out. He groaned, kissed my stomach, and rolled out of bed just after I did.

When we were finally bathed and changed and had wolfed down a bit of dry cereal, some yogurt, and coffee, I grabbed my mother's valuable list of chess coordinates, shoved it into an empty backpack from my coatrack, and we went downstairs.

Obviously, when Mother had said we could contact

her for "further instructions," she hadn't been talking about something as sensitive as what she had transferred into my hands under this multilayered cover. When it came to the Black Queen and the number of folks still seeking her and the other pieces, it was clear that Vartan and I must be on our own.

"You say you know this place," said Vartan, "so how exactly do we get there?"

"We walk," I said. "Oddly enough, it's not far from here."

"But how could that be?" he objected. "You said it was high up on a hill, and we are now coming from the lowest place—the river."

"Well, the city's not laid out in your usual fashion," I said as we trekked straight uphill through the steep, serpentine, and crisscrossed streets of Georgetown. "People always believe that Washington, D.C., was built in some kind of swamp—many books say it's true. But there's never been any swampland around here—just some cattail marshes that they dredged to build the Washington Monument. In fact, it's much more like that sacred 'City on the Hill' that Galen and the Piscataway were talking about—the high place, the altar, the sanctum, the temple of man. The hill that we're climbing up now was one of the original land grants given out by the British in these parts—maybe even the first one—named after a famous battle at the Rock of Dumbarton in Scotland. The place we're now headed—where the arrow points on my mother's map, about twelve blocks from here—is called Dumbarton Oaks."

"I know it, of course," said Vartan, which came as something of a surprise to *moi.* He added, "It's famous. Everybody in Europe and around the world must know it. It's where, before the end of World War II, the first meeting was held—with the United States, the UK, the USSR, and the Republic of China—the conference that first created the United Nations. The meeting just after that one was held at Yalta, in Krym, near where your father was born."

When he saw my blank expression, Vartan looked at me oddly, as if Americans' ignorance of great historical events in their own backyards might prove contagious. He said, "But how will we get in? Isn't such a place under close security?"

"It's open to the public most days at two P.M.," I told him.

By the time we reached the top of Thirty-first, where it dead-ends into R Street, across the way the big iron gates of Dumbarton Oaks were already open. The broad drive swept uphill between the massive oak trees up to the steeper steps leading to the mansion. Just inside the gates to the right, at the small ticket carrel, we got a map of the sixteen-acre park and a brochure that told some of the place's history, which I handed to Vartan.

"Why would your mother hide something in so well-known a spot where she might have been observed?" he whispered to me.

"I'm not sure it's actually *here,*" I told him. "Her map just shows an arrow pointing toward the gates and leading into the grounds. That suggests to me that whatever Mother left here, it would be somewhere within the park instead of the house or any other buildings."

"Possibly not," said Vartan, who'd noticed something in his brochure. "Why don't you have a look at this picture?"

On the inside flap of the brochure was the illustration of a colorful tapestry with the figure of a woman surrounded by what looked like cherubs and angels, all wearing halos. The woman at the center seemed to be handing out Christmas gifts to the crowd. Beneath her was a caption in Greek.

"Hestia Polyolbos," said Vartan, translating, *"Full of Blessings."*

"Hestia?" I said.

"She is the most ancient Greek goddess, it seems," said Vartan, "the goddess of fire. She's almost as ancient as Agni in India. They say here that this tapestry is very rare—early Byzantine made in Egypt in the fourth century and a masterpiece of this collection—but that it's even rarer because Hestia is almost never depicted at all. Like Yahweh, she's only ever appeared as the fire itself. She's the *'focus'*—that means the hearth of a house, or more important, of a *city.*"

He glanced up at me with a significant look.

"Okay," I agreed. "Then let's go inside first and have a look."

The mansion, the *orangerie,* and the Byzantine room were completely deserted. Though it was already afternoon, we appeared to be early birds.

Our first glimpse of the wool tapestry was astonishing. It was about six feet high by four feet wide and oozing surreal colors: not only red, blue, gold, and yellow, but greens of every hue from dark to light, saffron, pumpkin, teal, and midnight blue. Surely this beautiful ancient queen was connected with the Queen that *we* sought, but how?

Vartan read aloud from the larger catalog nearby: *Young men, praise Hestia, the most ancient of goddesses*—that was the invocation to her prayer. It seems this is an icon that was used in worship, like that Russian Black Virgin of Kazan that we read about. They say Hestia was the tutelary goddess in every *prytaneum*—that's the hearth where the eternal flame burned at the heart of every city throughout the ancient Greek world.

"The form of this tapestry, it says—this layout with all the eight figures, six putti, and two attendants staring right out of the frame at some midpoint toward the viewer—is not Greek, but far older. It comes from ancient pagan Babylon, Egypt, and India. And there's something else here written in Greek—let me see."

I couldn't take my eyes from the enormous tapestry with its fresh flowers floating in the background, the beautiful Queen of Fire, covered in extravagant jewels—just like the Montglane Service. How was she connected? Her two attendants at either side looked like angels. The male held some sort of parchment scroll in his hand, while the female to the right held a book with a Greek word on the cover. The gifts that Hestia was passing out to the cherubs around her looked like wreaths that also had words written inside.

As if he'd read my mind, Vartan translated, "The wreaths are the gifts of the fire—those are the 'blessings'—wealth, mirth, praise, abundance, merit, progress. Her hearth at the *prytaneum* is where the communal banquets were held; she was the patroness of cooks! At the Panathenaia, the great festival of Athene, there were torch races where they carried the eternal flame from her hearth to rejuvenate the city. But wait—she's connected with Hermes, too. As goddess of the hearth, Hestia represents the interior, the strength of the city, *civitas*. Hermes is the god of travel, strangers, nomads, the circulation of wealth." He looked at me. "She's the square and he's the circle—matter and spirit."

"And," I reminded him, "Galen's story said that Hermes himself, who was called Thoth in Egypt, was also the Greek god of alchemy."

"And Hestia, as the fire herself," said Vartan, "is the source of all the transformations that take place in that process, regardless of where they happen. It says everything in this tapestry is symbolic. But the symbols your mother is referring to she would want to mean something specifically to *you*."

"You're right," I told him. "The key my mother was pointing at *has* to be in this image somewhere."

But if just for me, why did Rodo say he'd guessed where we might be going? I studied the tapestry before me and racked my brain, trying to think of all we had learned in just one week about everything connected with the fire and with what it must have meant to al-Jabir, a man who, twelve hundred years ago, had created a chess set that contained the ancient wisdom of all time—which, if used for one's own ends alone, could be dangerous to yourself and to others, and yet, in the larger scheme, might be so beneficial to all.

Hestia was looking out of the tapestry, straight at me. Her eyes were a strange, blue-green color, not Egyptian at all. They seemed to see inside my soul. She seemed to be asking *me* an important question, instead of my asking her. I listened for a moment.

And then I knew.

The chessboard is the key.

As ye sow, so shall ye reap.

I grabbed Vartan by the hand. "Let's go," I said. And we left the building.

"What is it?" he whispered behind me, as he tried to keep up with my stiff pace.

I took him back down near the gates where we'd come in, where I'd noticed a narrow stone path that seemed to disappear between some boxwoods. Now I found it and dragged Vartan between them and behind me, down a long path that led around the perimeter of the acreage. When I was sure we were well away from any possible eavesdroppers—though all was so silent it seemed there was no one within miles—I stopped and turned to him. "Vartan, it isn't *where* or *what* that we're supposed to be looking for. It's *how.*"

"How?" he said, with a mystified expression.

"Did that tapestry of Hestia remind you of anything?" I asked him. "I mean the layout of it."

Vartan glanced at the small image on his brochure.

"There are *eight* figures surrounding her," he said, glancing back at me.

"I mean the chessboard," I told him. "It wasn't the chessboard drawing by the abbess or the chessboard in my apartment—it was all three—but especially *this* one. What if you took this little chessboard drawing of my mother's here in my backpack and you placed it smack in the middle of the tapestry—right in Hestia's lap?" When he stared at me, I added, "I think that Mother either moved the pieces, or else she had them buried from the very beginning in keeping with the theme of that tapestry. How many bunches of lines on our map? Six. How many cherubim—or whatever they are—on that tapestry? Six. How many gifts are the little boys receiving from Hestia? Six."

"Six-six-six," said Vartan. "The Number of the Beast."

The other part of my mother's original coded message.

"The first gift she gives on the tapestry that you translated from Greek was 'wealth,' " I added to Vartan. "And the first chess piece where Mother put a star and an arrow to here was the Black Queen, represented by Hestia herself here at center board. What better place to hide the most precious piece of all for that higher order than here—the birthplace of the United Nations, the wealth of nations, so to speak."

"Then there must be another pointer in this park to help us find the real Queen," said Vartan.

"Right," I agreed, sounding more confident than I felt about actually finding what I thought we were looking for. But where else could it be?

Behind the mansion, steep stone steps descended the back of the mountain. The landscaping within the sixteen-acre park was beautiful and mysterious, like a secret garden. Each time we emerged from an arch, a wall of huge bushes, or turned a corner, a surprise of the landscape greeted us—sometimes a high, splashing fountain, at others a vista spread before us of an orchard, a vineyard, or a pool. At last we came through an arcade with high trellised walls that had ancient fig trees trained up the sides, twisting thirty feet toward the sky. When we passed through the last arch of this arcade, I knew I'd found what I'd been looking for.

Before us spread an enormous pool of swirling gravelly waters that resembled a wide, babbling brook, but so shallow you could cross it almost without wetting your feet. The bottom was made of thousands of round, smooth pebbles set into the concrete in a wavy design. At the far end were enormous fountains of galloping metallic horses that seemed to be rising from the sea, spraying their lacy waters high into the sky.

Vartan and I walked to the river's opposite end and we looked across the vast expanse toward the fountains. From this perspective, those wavy patterns of stones beneath the shallow waters merged, like an optical illusion, to form a design that must be exactly what we were looking for: an enormous sheaf of wheat that seemed to be waving in a hidden breeze just beneath the rippling surface of the water.

Vartan and I stood for a moment without speaking, then he touched my arm and gestured down toward where we stood. Just at our feet, carved into the rock at the edge of the pool, was a motto:

Quod Severis Metes
As ye sow, so shall ye reap

The top of the sheaf of wheat was pointing toward the frothing sea horses across the pool—due north: the same compass direction that pointed away from Piscataway and Mount Vernon—toward the very top point of Washington, D.C.

"*How,*" said Vartan, taking my hand and looking down into my eyes. "You mean, it's not just the Queen or where she is located that we are seeking. The secret is *how* we sow and reap. Maybe, how they were planted and how we collect them?"

I nodded.

"Then I think I know where your mother is pointing us with this wheat sheaf—and where we are going," said Vartan. Whipping out his more detailed map of D.C., he pointed it out. "We get there down a path that runs just beside this park and underneath it, very steep—Dumbarton Oaks Park, it looks like a large wilderness." He looked up at me with a smile. "It's a very *long* path, too, called Lovers' Lane—designed for our alchemical project, no doubt. So if we find nothing while we're down there, perhaps we can resume some of our previous agricultural undertakings of last night."

For now, no comment, though the cherry blossoms in the orchard we were passing through *were* saturating the air with their heavy, sensual scent that I tried to ignore.

We went out the gates to the left and headed down Lovers' Lane. Dark trees smothered the sky here, and thick leaves from autumn still covered the earthy path. But in the meadow on the far side of the stone wall, we caught glimpses between the trees of jonquils, snowdrops, and starflowers already popping their heads up in the fresh spring grass.

At the bottom of the hill, where a tumbling creek ran along the road, our footpath forked in three directions.

"One goes up to the Naval Observatory, the highest point in Washington," Vartan said, studying his D.C.

map. "The lower one goes to some river. Here it is—it's Rock Creek, one of the lowest points, perhaps?"

Rock Creek was the third river—with the Potomac and Anacostia—that divided the city into a Pythagorean Y, as we'd learned from Key's pals, the Piscataway, and Galen's journals.

"If it's balance we're looking for," I said, "looks like it's the middle path." After about half an hour, we came onto a bluff that looked out upon everything—the rippling creek far below, the high rock that the observatory and the vice president's house resided on. In the distance an enormous arched stone bridge rose high above the river in the afternoon light, like a Roman aqueduct left in the middle of nowhere. This was the end of our road.

Here where we stood, ancient trees grew out of these even more ancient cliffs above us. Their twisted roots clawed for purchase in the rocky soil. Everything here was cast in deep shadow except one beam of western light that came through a wedge in the rock behind us, leaving a small pool of sunshine on the forest floor. Standing at this spot, with babbling waters far beneath us, birds warbling in the newly greening spring trees, it seemed that *civitas* was thousands of miles away.

Then I noticed that Vartan was looking down at me. Unexpectedly, and without a word, he folded me into his arms and kissed me. I could feel that same warm, glowing current of energy surge through me as before. He drew me away, and said, "I only thought to remind us that the purpose of our mission has to do with alchemy and human beings—not just with saving civilization."

"At this moment," I agreed, "I'm wishing that civilization could fend for itself for an hour or two, so I could get something else off my mind."

He ruffled my hair.

"But this *has* to be the spot," I added. "We can see

everything above and below. We're at the end of the road."

I looked around for another clue. But I saw none.

Then I let my eyes move slowly over the cliff that rose behind us. It wasn't actually a cliff—more of a retaining wall of enormous, ancient boulders. The afternoon sun was just about to move below the V in the rock wall and what little light we had right here would vanish.

Then something struck me.

"Vartan," I said quickly, "the book that al-Jabir wrote—*The Books of the Balance*—the deep secrets behind it, the keys to the ancient path, are supposed to be hidden in the chess set, right? Just as my mother's message to us is hidden in that tapestry?"

"Yes," said Vartan.

"In the tapestry," I said, "the book that the angel is holding in her hand—just like the 'gifts' that Hestia was handing out—that book also had a word printed on it, didn't it?"

"Phos," said Vartan. "It means 'light.' "

We both looked up at the steep wall of hewn stone, where the sun was dipping down.

"Can you climb?" I asked him.

Vartan shook his head.

"Well, I can," I told him. "So I guess this message was intended just for me."

LESS THAN ONE HOUR LATER, we were sitting at a table in the upper room at Sutalde, just Vartan and I, beside the wall of windows overlooking the western sun gilding the bridge and the river. I had three broken fingernails and I was nursing a scuffed knee, but otherwise I was none the worse for wear for walking up the side of a cliff.

Beside us on a third chair was my backpack that I'd

lowered to Vartan from its cache on high. It still contained that list of map coordinates of the buried pieces, but now also the mailing tube with the abbess's chessboard drawing that we'd stopped to pick up from my post office on our way back down the hill.

Between us on the table sat a breathing decanter of Châteauneuf du Pape with two wineglasses, and beside them, the heavy figure about six inches high, all encrusted with jewels, minus one emerald: the Black Queen.

And something else I'd found up there in the rock, sealed in a waterproof container. Vartan drew closer so we could study it together. It was a book written in Latin, clearly a copy of the original, with interesting illustrations, though these, too, Vartan said, may have been added at a later date. It was apparently a medieval translation of an older book in Arabic.

The Books of the Balance.

The owner's inscription on the inside flap merely read: *Charlot.*

"*Do not let yourself be hampered by any doubt,*" Vartan was translating it for me. "*One introduces fire and applies it to the degree necessary, without however allowing that thing to be consumed by the fire—which would add to its depredation. In this way, the body which is submitted to the action of fire reaches equilibrium and attains the desired state.*"

Vartan turned to me. "Al-Jabir does discuss how to make the elixir," he said. "But his emphasis seems to be always on equilibrium, balance among the four elements, earth, air, water, and fire, the balance within ourselves, and also that between us and the natural world. I do not understand why this idea is dangerous." He added, "Do you think your mother left you this book because she wishes for you not only to find the pieces, but also to solve this problem?"

"I'm sure she does," I said, pouring the wine into our glasses. "But how can I think that far ahead? One week ago I was estranged from my mother and I thought my father was dead. I believed that you were my worst enemy and that I was a sous-chef with a predictable, regimented life who could no longer play chess even if her life depended on it. Now it appears that my life *may* depend on it. But I can't predict anything even ten minutes ahead. Everything that I once thought I knew has been turned on its head. I don't know *what* to think anymore."

"*I* know what to think," said Vartan with a smile. "And so do you."

Closing the book, he took me by both my hands and pressed his lips to my hair, ever so gently. When he drew away, he said, "How could you ever have faced your future until you'd resolved your past? Was it your fault that those 'resolutions' turned out to be that all those things you'd always thought were true were actually only illusions?"

"But after all that," I said, "what can I believe now?"

Vartan said, "It seems, as Rodo told us last night, that when it comes to this ancient wisdom, it isn't enough to believe. One has to find out the truth. I think that is the message of this book your mother left you, the message al-Jabir hid in the chess set twelve hundred years ago."

"But what exactly *is* that message?" I asked in frustration. "Let's say that we've gathered all the pieces and put them together. What will we know then that nobody else knows now?"

"Why don't we put together some of the parts that we already have right now, and try to find out?" Vartan suggested, passing me my backpack.

I pulled out the cylinder tube that I'd mailed to myself, with the abbess's chessboard illustration, and handed it over for Vartan to open. Then I delved deeper into my pack to extract my mother's little sketch in plastic, with its list of map coordinates, which I'd stuffed in there just before we'd left my apartment, and then my fingertip snagged on something cold and sharp at the bottom of the pack.

I froze.

I was afraid that I knew exactly what it was. Even before I pulled it out my heart was thudding.

It was a diamond tennis bracelet.

With an emerald-lined racquet attached.

I sat there, the bracelet dangling from the tip of my finger. Vartan glanced up and saw it. He looked at it for a moment, then at me, and I nodded. I felt ill. *How did this get here? How long had it been here?*

I now realized that this was the very backpack I'd left behind—five days ago, along with my down parka—in my uncle's suite at the Four Seasons. But how had this satchel wound up hanging innocently on the coatrack inside my apartment, with Sage Livingston's "wired" tennis bracelet concealed at the bottom of the pack?

And how long had that damned bracelet been in our vicinity?

"Ah," came Sage's affected voice from the doorway across the room, "here we all are, together again. And I see you've found my bracelet. I *wondered* where I had accidentally dropped it."

She stepped inside and shut the door behind her, then crossed the room through the forest of tables and extended her hand for the keepsake. I let it slip from my fingertip into my glass of Châteauneuf du Pape.

"That wasn't very nice," said Sage, looking at her jewels through the murk in the bottom of my wineglass.

How long had she been listening? How much did she know? I had to assume the worst. Even if she didn't know that my father was alive, at the very least she now knew the contents, and their value, of everything lying exposed upon this table.

I got to my feet to face her head-on, and Vartan did likewise.

But then I glanced down.

In Sage's hand there was suddenly a small, pearl-handled revolver.

Oh Lord. And I'd thought *Key* was the only one addicted to hovering on the edge.

"You're not going to shoot us," I told Sage.

"Not unless you insist," she said. Her face seemed to have been stripped from a Mount Rushmore of condescension. Then she clicked off the gun's safety and added, "But if they hear a shot from in here, my colleagues who are waiting just outside may not possess those same reservations."

Damn. The thug factor. I had to think of something. But my only thought was, what was she even *doing* here?

"I thought you and your folks had gone off together on a long trip?" I said.

"They left without me," she told me, then added, "They aren't necessary now. That's what *I* was chosen for. This contingency was already planned for, you know, practically since I was born."

As she held the gun loosely in one hand, she studied the nails of her other as if it had been entirely too many minutes since yesterday's manicure. I was waiting for the other shoe to drop, when she looked up at Vartan and me and added, "Apparently, neither of you has even the vaguest conception of *who I am*."

Those words again.

But this time—suddenly—I did know.

Slowly, the horror seeped down through my brain like red wine or blood, forming a veil just behind my eyes, staining my vision of the room around me, of Vartan, of

Sage standing there with that gun in her hand, ready at any moment to call her security detachment from just outside.

She didn't require their aid in order to decimate *me.* I'd already been blindsided again. Nor did I need a gun in my face to put all of this into perspective.

Hadn't I already sensed, during that powwow at my uncle's suite, that somebody *else* behind the scenes was calling some secret shots? Why hadn't I seen, even then, that it wasn't Rosemary or Basil—that it had been Sage, herself, all along?

Practically since I was born, she'd said.

How right that was.

Hadn't it been Sage, even when we both were children, who'd tried not to befriend me, as I'd imagined then, but rather to bring me within her sphere of control, her circle of influence, affluence, and power?

Again, it was Sage who'd swiftly broken up her social camp in Denver, moved her high-society operations to D.C.—almost the moment I'd arrived there myself. Though I never saw her during most of those years, how did I know whether *she'd* been watching *me*? It was Sage, too, who'd somehow intruded herself into the midst of the Sky Ranch transaction, despite the fact that, realistically, she could hardly pose as a realtor.

What else had she posed as?

When it came down to it, no one ever seemed to notice much about Sage except her looks, her superficial style. She was always ensconced in a cloud of social comportment, camouflaged by her entourage. But I suddenly recognized that, like a spider in its web of intrigue, Sage had actually been at the middle of everything, everywhere, and with everyone. Indeed, it wasn't just the bugging device she'd planted in my backpack that gave her access to everyone's thoughts and deeds. She'd been privy to *every* private chat.

At my mother's private *boum* in Four Corners.

At the Brown Palace in Denver with Lily and Vartan.

At the Four Seasons in D.C. with Nim, Rodo, and Galen.

I suddenly recalled her comment there, about my relations with my mother: *It seems we were mistaken.*

Now I saw that it was this vacuous, socialite stance that drew attention away from her true role. And now I understood exactly what role had been intended as hers from birth.

I said, "You're *the* Sage Livingston."

She smiled coldly, one eyebrow raised in appreciation of my acuity.

Vartan shot me a sideways glance.

I turned to him and explained. "I mean *the* 'Wise Living Stone.' In Charlot's story he called it the Philosopher's Stone, the powder that produces the Elixir of Life. When Sage said she'd been chosen from birth, that's what she meant—that she was raised from birth to succeed her mother as White Queen. Her parents believed they had regained control of the White Team and the Game after they killed my father and held the chess piece. But somebody else took the reins away without them realizing it. They didn't know about Galen March and Tatiana—or about your stepfather switching camps. They never understood the real purpose the Service was intended for."

Sage let out an unladylike snort that drew me up sharply. I noticed that the gun, held in a tighter grip than before, was now pointed at a part of my body that I'd like to keep on ticking.

She said, "The real purpose of the Service is *power.* It has never been anything else. It's completely naive to think otherwise, regardless of what those fools you've been listening to may have tried to lead you into believing. I may not be a star chess player, as the two of you are, but I do know what I'm speaking of. After all, throughout my life I've been suckled at the nipple of power—real power, *world* power, power that neither of you could even begin to imagine—and I haven't yet been weaned of it . . ."

Et cetera.

As Sage ranted on about how she'd been born and bred to suck power through a straw, I was getting more and more frightened by the moment. I could feel Vartan's tension even from here. It must have been as clear to him as it was to me that Ms. "Philosophia de Stone" here had lost what little bit of a mind she might once have moderately possessed. But neither of us seemed able to figure out how to make a spring for her at ten paces—or even to interrupt her tirade.

And it was becoming even clearer that, for those who were addicted to power, even relative *proximity* to this miserable chess set was like offering them an instant megalomaniac pill. Indeed, Sage seemed to have swallowed a bottleful just prior to her arrival here today.

Furthermore, I realized it was only a matter of time before our girl Sage might suddenly stop worrying about whether pulling the trigger would spoil her bright new manicure. I knew we had to get out of here, and fast. And that we must take our coordinates with us.

But how?

I glanced toward Vartan. His eyes were still on Sage as if he were calculating exactly the same thing. The massive chess queen sat exposed between us upon the table, but even if we grabbed it to use as a weapon, we couldn't throw it faster than a bullet could reach us. And even if we could overpower her, we could hardly hope to escape those professional hirelings outside with the aid of just that little pearl-handled gun. I had to come up with something. I wasn't sure I could break through

Sage's "diatribe on suckling" long enough to reason with her, but anything was worth a try.

"Sage," I cut in, "even assuming that you *can* collect all these chess pieces, what will you do with them? You're not the only one looking for them, you know. Where would you go? Where can you hide?"

Sage looked momentarily stunned, as if perhaps she'd never thought that far ahead in designing her castle in the air. I was about to press my point, but the phone on the maître d's desk near the front door began ringing. Sage kept the gun pointed at me as she took a few steps back amid the tables for a wider view.

Then I noticed the other sound. A soft sound. Something familiar passing just nearby, though it did take a moment before I recognized it myself.

The *whish* of Rollerblades over stone.

It seemed to be moving stealthily past us toward the front, hidden behind that long, high rack that traversed the length of the room, displaying Rodo's collection of ceramic cider jugs. But even with the relentless din of the phone up there, how long would it be before Leda passed close enough to Sage that she would hear it, too?

From the corner of my eye I could see Vartan start to inch his way forward. Sage swung the gun toward him and he halted.

Just then, as Key would say, all hell broke loose. An awful lot of cider was about to hit the fan.

It all happened in a matter of seconds.

A gallon jug of *Sagardoa* flew out of a large pigeonhole and exploded on the stone floor at Sage's feet, splattering cider everywhere. Instinctively attempting to preserve her six-hundred-dollar shoes, Sage skittered backward, but as Vartan made to spring at her she halted him again with the pointed gun. At the same moment, another jug flew off the top of the rack, right at her head. Sage quickly ducked behind a nearby table as the jug hurtled by and crashed to the floor beside her.

The avalanche of cider pots moved along the line. *Sagardoa* jugs were flying from high pigeonholes as Sage—crouched behind the table, her elbow braced like a sharpshooter's—shot them out of the air like clay pigeons. She took a few potshots at the rack, too, trying to nail her hidden adversary.

At the first shot, Vartan had dragged me down behind our table and toppled it over, spilling the contents—book, valuable papers, chess queen, and Châteauneuf du Pape—upon the stone floor. We hunkered behind it. The crashes and gunshots continued as the phone kept ringing at the far end of the room.

Vartan expressed my thoughts. "I don't know who our savior is behind that wine rack, but he won't hold her off much longer. We must find a way to get at her."

I peered out from behind the loose tablecloth. The place reeked of fermented apple mash.

Sage, in her relatively protected position, controlling center board, had managed to reload faster than Annie Oakley. I prayed that she ran out of bullets before Leda ran out of cider. But even if so, I hadn't much hope, since her heavies outside, on hearing this commotion, would be crashing in here at any instant.

Suddenly, the phone stopped ringing. A deafening silence filled the room. No crashes. No gunshots.

My God, was it all over?

Vartan and I peered over the tabletop just in time to see the door of the restaurant burst open. Sage, on her feet, her profile to us, had turned with a smug little smile to greet her cronies. But instead a blur of white trousers, red sashes, and black berets charged through the door into the room, Rodo leading the pack with his ponytail flying, his phone in his hand, and Eremon just behind him.

In astonishment, Sage's eyes narrowed, and she leveled her gun at them from across the room.

But around the corner of the cider rack, intervening between Sage and her target, sailed what appeared to be a large copper soup tureen on wheels, three feet across and held like a shield. It was barreling between the tables right at Sage. Leda launched the kettle aloft just as Sage fired the gun in her direction. The tureen descended, taking Sage down like a bowling pin—but I saw that Leda was knocked off her pins, too, and sitting on the ground. Had she been hit?

While Vartan and the others raced to grab the gun and decommission Sage, I scrambled to make sure Leda was okay, but Eremon beat me to it. He gracefully helped Leda to her feet and gestured to the leaking cider bottle in the rack across the room that the bullet had actually hit. While Vartan secured the gun, a couple of Basque Brigadeers pulled Sage up, yanked off their waist sashes, and bound her hand and foot. Then, as she writhed in furious indignation, still babbling, they dragged her out the door.

Rodo smiled in relief when he saw that we were all okay. I retrieved the diamond bracelet from the mess of broken glass and wine puddles on the floor and handed it to Eremon. He shook his head and tossed it far out the door into the canal.

Rodo was telling me, "When the *Cygne* was coming here to work, she noticed some people she recognized, under the wisteria pergola at Key Park. It was La Livingston, who'd come to have me help find you the other day at your uncle's, and the security men from the morning before the private *boum* at Sutalde. The *Cygne* thought it was suspicious, seeing them together right there, just near your house. So when she got here to work she phoned Eremon and me. We thought it was suspicious, too. By the time you arrived here, she was downstairs preparing the fires for tonight and we were already en route. But she phoned again on my cell phone after she heard the entry of another person up here, crept upstairs, and saw that you were in real danger. She told us your friend was threatening you with a gun and those men were posted outside. We laid our plan—that the moment we had disarmed the men out there, I would ring the house phone in here. That would be the Swan's signal to create a distraction inside—to divert La Livingston so she wouldn't shoot you before we could come through the door."

"The Swan 'diverted' her all right," I agreed, hugging Leda in thanks. "And not a moment too soon. Sage was getting an itchy trigger finger, and I was afraid we might inadvertently scratch it. But how did you disarm those guys outside?"

Eremon said, "They were derailed by a few *Jota* moves that they were certainly not expecting. E.B. has lost none of his high kicks. These men have now been turned over to Homeland Security of the U.S. government, which is holding them for bearing illegal firearms within the District and for impersonating Secret Service agents."

"But Sage Livingston?" Vartan asked Rodo. "She seems mad. And with rather the opposite goal of the one you were espousing to the two of us just last night. What can become of someone like her, who was raised to destroy everything in her path?"

Leda said, "I recommend a *very* lengthy shift at some feminist lesbian spiritual retreat in some *very* remote part of the Pyrenees. Think we can arrange it?"

"I'm certain that we could," said Rodo. "But there is someone we know who especially wishes to take charge of Sage's case. I should say, *two* someones, for their own different reasons. *Quod Severis Metes*. I believe, if you think of this, you will understand who they are. For now, you know the combination to my safe. When you've finished with those materials, don't leave them lying about there on the floor, do as you've done in the past." He winked.

With that, Rodo was out the door, snapping instructions in Basque left and right, all the way across the footbridge.

Eremon was on his knees, *tsk-tsk*-ing as he checked out Leda's scruffed legs and bruises from her fall. He stood, put his arm around her shoulders, and accompanied her to the cellar, to "help with the heavy logs," as he said. I thought there might be hope for something a bit more alchemical there yet.

Vartan and I returned to our place beside the windows where the setting sun now licked the tops of the high-rise buildings across the river, and we started putting away our valuable, dangerous, wine-splashed stash. "The combination to his safe?" he said.

"Basque mathematics," I told him.

I knew that Rodo didn't have a safe, but he did have a P.O. box up the street, just like mine. The number was 431. He was hinting that the safest route was to get the stuff out of here by mail again, as I'd done before, and worry about the rest later.

I was about to slip *The Books of the Balance* back into its container when Vartan put his hand on my arm. Looking at me with those dark purple eyes, he said, "You know, I thought she really might kill you."

"I don't think she wanted to kill me," I told him. "But she was so completely crazed at losing, in just one day, all her wealth, connections, her access to power—everything she's ever believed she wanted."

"*Believed?*" said Vartan. "She sounded to me quite convinced."

I shook my head, for I thought maybe I'd finally gotten the message.

Vartan said, "But who is it who will 'take charge of the case' of a person like her, as Boujaron said? Sage was raised to believe she is something like a god. Who could imagine anybody who would want to deal with such a person?"

"I don't need to imagine," I told him. "I already know. It's my mother and my aunt Lily who will help her."

Vartan stared at me across the table. "But *why*?" he said.

"My mother—even if it *was* in self-defense, or in defense of Lily Rad—did kill Rosemary's father. And Rosemary was sure that she'd killed *my* father—tit for tat. It appears that Sage herself was raised to be like a tracer bullet, a heat-seeking missile looking for a place to explode. Or to *implode*. She almost did it right here in this room."

Vartan said, "This might explain your mother wanting to help Sage—maybe a kind of atonement. But what of Lily Rad? She never even knew of the Livingstons' connection with your mother."

"But," I pointed out, "Lily *did* know that her own father was the Black King and her mother the White Queen. She knew the devastation that had swept her own life because of it. She's known what it feels like to be a pawn within your own family."

This was what my mother had saved me from.

The Game.

And now I knew exactly what I must do.

I said to Vartan, "This book, *The Books of the Balance,* and the secret that al-Jabir hid in the chess set have been waiting more than twelve hundred years for someone to come along and release them from the bottle. I think we're it. I think it's time."

We stood there beside the wall of windows overlooking the canal, filled with the beautiful rosy flamingo flame of the sunset, and Vartan put his arms around me from behind. I opened the wine-spattered book that was still in my hand. Vartan looked over my shoulder as I flipped through the pages until I came to the small illustration of a matrix of three-by-three squares with a number printed in each. They looked familiar.

4	9	2
3	5	7
8	1	6

"What does it say, just underneath here?" I asked Vartan.

He translated, "*The most ancient Magic Square, which is represented here, existed thousands of years ago in India, and in Babylonia under the Chaldean Oracles.*" Vartan paused to add, "This seems to be some medieval commentator speaking, not al-Jabir himself."

He went on. "*In China, this square was used to lay out the eight provinces of the land with the emperor living at center. It was sacred because each number had esoteric significance; also, each row, column, and diagonal adds up to 15, which, if added in turn, reduces to the number 6.*"

"Six-six-six," I said, glancing up over my shoulder at Vartan.

He released me from behind, and together we took the book closer to the window, where he continued.

"However, it was al-Jabir ibn Hayyan, the father of Islamic alchemy, who made this square renowned, in The Books of the Balance, *for its other important properties of 'correct proportions' that lead to balance. If the four squares in the southwest corner are carved out as shown, they add to 17, providing the series 1:3:5:8 of perfect Pythagorean musical ratios by which, according to Jabir, 'everything in the world exists.' The remaining numbers in this magic grid—4, 9, 2, 7, 6—add up to 28, which is the number of 'mansions' or stations of the moon, and also of letters in the Arabic alphabet. These are the numbers most important to al-Jabir: 17 adds to 8, the esoteric path, which provides the larger 'Magic Square of Mercury' made of 8 by 8 squares. This is also the layout of a gaming board with 28 squares around the outside—the exoteric or outer path."*

"The chessboard is the key," I told Vartan. "Just as my mother said."

Vartan nodded. "But there is more: *Al-Jabir invested this ancient wisdom in the symbol of Mercury. Mercury is the only both astronomical symbol of 'above' and alchemical symbol of 'below' that contains all three important sigils for both: the circle representing sun and the crescent representing moon or spirit, and the cross or 'plus' sign, representing the four aspects of matter: four directions, four corners, four elements, four aspects—fire, earth, water, air—hot, cold, wet, dry . . ."*

"Put them together," I said, "and you have Basque mathematics—'four-plus-three-equals-one.' The square of earth *plus* the triangle of spirit equals 'One.' Unity. Wasn't that the first gift of Hestia on the tapestry?"

"It was wealth," said Vartan.

"Wealth," I said, "like the 'Commonwealth of Virginia,' *wealth* or *weal,* it means *'whole'*—whole, healthy, holistic, holy. It all means 'Unity.' *'In order to form a more perfect Union.'* That's what George Washington, Tom Jefferson, Ben Franklin, what all of them wanted—the marriage of heaven and earth, those 'spacious skies and amber waves of grain.' What al-Jabir had already built into the Service of the *Tarik'at. That's* the illumination they were all looking for, that New City on the Hill. Not *possessing* power. *Creating* balance."

He said, "That's what you meant earlier, when you said what you thought the message was? When you said it's not *when* or *where,* it's *how?*"

"Right," I said. "It's not a *thing,* where once you've grabbed it and deployed it, you'll get nuclear weapons, power over others, eternal life. What al-Jabir set down in the chess set is actually a *process.* That's why he called it the Service of the *Tarik'at*—The Key to the Secret *Way.* These *are* the Original Instructions—like trail markers on a path, just as the Sufis and shamans and Piscataway have been saying all along. And if we put all those pieces together and follow those instructions, nothing is impossible. We can set ourselves and the world onto a better path—a 'way' of illumination and joy. My parents have risked their lives to save this chess set so that it could be used for that higher purpose."

During this, Vartan had set down the book. Now he took me into his arms once again.

"In my case, Xie, if truth is what we're looking for—the truth is that I'll do whatever you believe is right. The truth is that I love you."

"I love you back," I said.

And I knew that—though we would certainly recover the pieces—at this moment I didn't care what else any of the others wanted, I didn't care about the Game, what it had cost people in the past, or how it might profit us all in the future. I didn't care what roles others might have chosen for Vartan and me to play, White King or Black Queen. It didn't matter what they dubbed us, because I knew that Vartan and I were the real thing—the alchemical marriage everyone had been looking for these past twelve hundred years, yet couldn't see when they found it right before them. We ourselves *were* the Original Instructions.

And for the first time in my life, I felt as if all those ropes that had bound me for so long had been completely cut free, that I could soar into the skies like a bird.

A firebird, bringing light.

ACKNOWLEDGMENTS

THE COURSE OF A TRUE BOOK NEVER DID RUN smooth.

As a novelist who would never recognize a smooth path if she saw one, I find that often when you stub your toe against a rock, beneath it you find a pot of gold you'd never have discovered had you been rushing along smoothly, as originally planned. Here I thank as many as possible of those pots of gold who've provided passion for their work, surprises, and more fascinating knowledge than I ever expected I could squeeze into one novel.

These are listed in alphabetical order by topic.

ALBANIA: Thanks to Auron Tare, director, Albanian National Trust, for our five-year discussion and research on Ali Pasha, Vasiliki, Haidée, Haji Bektash Veli, and the Bektashi Sufi order, the secret weapon that Byron procured for the Pasha; his colleague Professor Irakli Kocollari, for a last-moment synopsis and translation of his landmark book *The Secret Police of Ali Pascha,* based on original archival sources; Doug Wicklund, senior curator, National Firearms Museum of the NRA, for running to earth the Kentucky repeating·rifle, the likely candidate for the "secret weapon" Byron sent Ali.

AVIATION, ALEUTIANS: Thanks to Barbara Fey—friend of thirty years, member of the Explorers Club and of the Silver Wings Fraternity (those who've flown more than fifty years), who has solo-flown the North Atlantic, Africa, Central America, and the Middle East and has helicopter-skied the Himalayas—for the Bonanza and all the technical and fascinating eyewitness input about areas I've flown through but have never really seen, and for finding me Drew Chitiea—bush pilot extraordinaire and trainer of National Outdoor Leadership School (whose mother, Joan, ran the Iditerod at age sixty-six)—who convinced me it should be Becky Beaver, not the Otter, and gave me all the great technical, fuel and refueling, and flight and landing info in which Key is so well-versed; Cooper Wright, who works in Attu for detailed maps and descriptions of flying in the Aleutians and for the great Brian Garfield book *The Thousand-Mile War,* which describes the weather conditions in World War II.

BAGHDAD: Special thanks to Jim Wilkinson, chief of staff of the U.S. Treasury, for casually mentioning over lunch one day—just when I thought I was in the home stretch of writing this book—that he'd learned to play chess in Baghdad while he was serving as one of the advance group into Iraq in March 2003. What others think of as serendipity, we in fiction regard as the research writing on the wall. Jim's valuable input was a critical turning point both for my heroine and for her author. Thanks also for those e-mail addresses!

BASQUES: Thanks to the wonderful Patxi del Campo, former president, World Congress of Music Therapy, for making me familiar with the Basque Pyrenees and a people I thought I already knew; to Agustin Ibarrola, for painting all those trees in the forest of Oma; to Aitziber Legarza, for feeding and housing us; to my late great friend Carmen Varela, for making me spend so much time in northern Spain.

CHESS: Thanks to Dr. Nathan Divinsky, past president of FIDE Canada, for finding the chess game upon which this book is based (played by a fourteen-year-old Russian, later world champion) and also for having found that previous game (accurate to the period) played by Rothschild in my book *A Calculated Risk;* Marilyn Yalom, for conversations about her book *Birth of the Chess Queen;* Dan Heisman, for being a big support in connecting me with recent goings-on within the chess world—and, when *Amaurosis Scriptio* (writer's blindness) kept me in the dark about one of my characters—for introducing me to Alisa Melekhina (twelve years old at the time) who helped give me rare insight into a child chess competitor's perspective on what it feels like to play international competition chess.

COOKING: Thanks to the late Kim Young, who won the right to be a chef in Talleyrand's kitchen at a charity auction (she appears as "the young Kimberly") and who became a lifelong friend—sending me gobs of notes on historic kitchens she visited from Brighton to Curacao; Ian Kelly, for chats about his book *Cooking for Kings* and his fascinating one-man play on Talleyrand's chef Carême; William Rubel, for his excellent presentation at the French embassy in D.C., his advice on open-hearth cooking, and his marvelous book, *The Magic of Fire,* the best treatment I know of in English of the topic; and my friend Anthony Lanier for renovating Georgetown's Cady's Alley, creating a great restaurant and a club there that (by serendipity) looks so much like the secret basement of Sutalde.

INDIANS (Native Americans): Thanks to the former head of the Inter-Tribal Council and my friend of nearly twenty years Adam Fortunate Eagle, for introducing me to indigenous reality for the first time; Rick West, founding director of the National Museum of the American Indian (NMAI) and his wife, Mary Beth, for connecting me with the D.C. area tribes; Karenne Wood, director, Virginia Indian Heritage Trail, for helping to refresh ten thousand years of pre-European history here in Virginia;

and Gabrielle Tayac (daughter of Red Flame, granddaughter of Turkey Tayac), for walking the ancient ossuary fields of Piscataway with me and for introducing me through her writings and our conversations to Mathew King, *Noble Red Man,* and to the Original Instructions.

ISLAM, MIDDLE EAST, FAR EAST: Thanks to Professor Fathali Moghaddam of Georgetown University for our many discussions, his helpful insights, and prepublication papers and books on pre- and post-9/11 terrorist psychology in these regions of the world; the director of the Middle East and Africa Division of the Library of Congress, Mary Jane Deeb (also my fellow novelist and friend), for getting me my first LOC library card and helping me dig out all of Byron's collected correspondence and a glut of other great stuff; and to Subhash Kak, for his assistance over the years on all things Kashmiri, and especially for *The Astronomical Code in the RgVeda,* his connection between Indian cosmology, and fire altars.

MATHEMATICS, MYTHOLOGY, AND ARCHETYPES: Thanks to Michael Schneider, for the *Beginner's Guide to Constructing the Universe* and his subsequent workbooks (if I'd had these as a child, I'd be a mathematician today) and especially for finding for me the Islamic phoenixes that fit into the "Breath of God" tilings in Iran; Magda Kerenyi, for giving me so much "mythological help" over the years and for her many insights into the thoughts of her late husband, the great mythographer Carl Kerenyi; Stephen Karcher, of *Eranos I-Ching* fame, for information on deep east-west connections and divination; Vicki Noble, for providing me data from three years of her extensive travels and research into female shamanism, especially in eastern Russia; Professor Bruce MacLennan of the University of Tennessee, who has never failed, these past twenty years, to help convert *any* mathematical puzzle I come up with, regardless of how obtuse or esoteric, into something that will work credibly within a novel; and especially my friend David Fideler, author of *Jesus Christ Sun of God*, for telling me so many years ago that 888 (my favorite number) is the Greek gematria (secret numeric decoding) for the name of Jesus, just as 666 is the gematria for mankind; and my friend Ernest McClain, for *The Pythagorean Plato* and *The Myth of Invariance* exploring the harmonics of such numbers in the names of the ancient gods of Egypt and Greece.

MEMORY AND PERCEPTION: First, thanks to Dr. Beulah McNab of the Netherlands, for sending me, in 1996, de Groot & Gobet's *Perception and Memory in Chess*, still the definitive study, which opened my mind to how chess players think differently than we mere mortals; thanks also to Galen Rowell, the late, great mountaineer and photographer, for his (August 1999) insights, in a private letter, into a similar intuitive process in rock climbing; and thanks especially to my mate, Dr. Karl Pribram, for explaining (often under duress) what we know of memory and perception through brain research and how past and future interconnect in our thought processes.

RUSSIA: Thanks to Elina Igaunis for helping all of us Americans to escape from the monks at Zagorsk (and for lending us sweaters in the subzero "Women's Summer"); and to Richard Pritzker many (mixed) thanks for choosing that Moscow restaurant where, while sipping margaritas, we witnessed an underworld-mob stabbing. Thanks to artist Yuri Gorbachev, for my magical "Bird of Heaven" painting, and to his art dealer, Dennis Easter, for the Russian icon and the David Coomler *Russian Icon* book. And very special thanks to the late Aleksandr Romanovitch Luria and Professor Eugene Sokolov, for together taking Karl Pribram to the first Soviet Palekh Art Exhibition—at Moscow in 1955—and for presenting him with the boxed set of prints of the lacquered art that inspired the first scene of this book.

VOLCANOES AND GEYSERS: Thanks to the Yellowstone Society and all the park rangers and historians for updates on everything from mudpots to volcanoes in my old stomping grounds; the Geyser Observation and Study Association (GOSA) and Frith Maier for research and the film of the Kamchatka geysers; and especially to Stephen J. Pyne for his wonderful and definitive series of books on the history of fire that kept on inspiring this book, and to my friend of twenty years Professor Scott Rice of San Jose State University for introducing us.

THE REST: As Nokomis Key would say, if I ever loaded my plate with food that I left uneaten, "Your eyes are bigger than your stomach."

Most of the fascinating research that people have provided me with more than generously over these past many years was, due to the exigencies of plot, unfortunately destined to be relegated to the cutting-room floor, at least for this book.

Thomas Jefferson's Poplar Forest: Director Lynne Beebe, archaeologists Travis MacDonald and Barbara Heath for decades of research assistance.

Thomas Jefferson's Monticello: Foundation president Daniel P. Jordan; William L. Beiswanger, Robert H. Smith Director of Restoration; Peter J. Hatch, director of Gardens and Grounds; Andrew J. O'Shaughnessy, Saunders Director of the Robert H. Smith International Center for Jefferson Studies; Gabriele Rausse, associate director of Gardens and Grounds; Jack S. Robertson, foundation librarian; Mary Scott-Fleming, director of Adult Programs; Leni Sorenson, African-American Research Historian; Susan R. Stein, Richard Gilder Senior Curator and vice president for museum; and especially to Lucia "Cinder" Stanton, Shannon Senior Research

Historian, for her many years of research and assistance.

United States Capitol Historic Society: Thanks to all the foundation people for assistance over the years, and especially to Steven Livengood for extensive background and a great tour of the Capitol.

Virginia Foundation for the Humanities: Thanks to President Robert Vaughan; Susan Coleman, director, VA Center of the Book; and Nancy Coble Damon and Kevin McFadden of VA Book.

Esoteric architecture, astrology, freemasonry, and design of D.C.: Thanks over many years to authors Robert Lomas and Christopher Knight; astrologers Steve Nelson, Kelley Hunter, and Caroline Casey; and to esoteric architecture experts Alvin Holm and Rachel Fletcher.

Dumbarton Oaks: Thanks to Stephen Zwirn, assistant curator, Byzantine Collection; and Paul Friedlander for *Documents of a Dying Paganism* on the Hestia Tapestry.

Thanks to Edward Lawler Jr., historian of the Independence Hall Association, for his extensive efforts at the President's House in Philadelphia, which led to saving from obscurity and extinction the slave quarters where Washington's chef Hercules, Oney Judge, and others lived.

Historian, for her many years of research and assistance.

United States Capitol Historical Society: Thanks to all the dedicated people for assistance over the years, and especially to Steve [illegible] for [illegible] background [illegible].

Virginia Foundation for the Humanities: Thanks to President Robert Vaughan, [illegible], and [illegible] of the Book, and Nancy Coble Damon and Kevin McFadden of VaBook!

[illegible] D.C.: Thank you over many years to [illegible] Loomis and [illegible] Stephen Keller, [illegible] Keller, Harper and Caroline [illegible] experts [illegible].

Dr. [illegible] Carron [illegible]: Thanks [illegible] and Paul [illegible] [illegible].

[illegible] Edward [illegible] [illegible] Washington [illegible] [illegible].

PUBLISHING NOTE

IN THE 1980S, I WAS LIVING IN A SIX-HUNDRED-square-foot tree house in Sausalito, California. Above a sea of acacia trees I had a wraparound view of San Francisco Bay, with Tiburon and Angel Island in the distance; eucalyptus trees grew through my front deck; my landlord's terraced orchid gardens lay on the hill behind me; a thirty-foot-high hedge of night-blooming jasmine bordered the steep drive. That's where I wrote *The Eight,* at night and on weekends, on my vintage IBM Selectric typewriter (which I still have in my memorabilia cupboard), while working days at the Bank of America.

I kept asking my friends, "Don't you think this is the perfect setting for writing a swashbuckling bestseller?" Likely they thought that it was an ideal spot for writing a book that no one would ever buy or read.

But my original literary agent, Frederick Hill, recognized the moment he read *The Eight* that there were no other books like it. With two interwoven stories set two hundred years apart; sixty-four characters, all pieces in the chess game that was the plot; tales-within-a-tale; Sherlock Holmesian encryption; magic puzzles like Dr. Matrix, *The Eight* looked more like an intergalactic map of relationships in the universe than a novel. But fortunately, Fred also knew that the publishing team at Ballantine Books, the premier paperback publisher in

America, had been looking for a literary property to launch its first-ever hardcover line of books. They wanted something unique—neither standard "literary" nor standard "bestseller" fare, something that couldn't easily be pigeonholed.

The Ballantine team members with this vision were: president Susan Peterson; VP of marketing Clare Ferraro; and editor in chief Robert Wyatt. They acquired *The Eight*, half completed, in 1987. On March 15, 1988, my editor, Ann LaFarge, and I completed the edit. The book was presented at the American Booksellers Association convention in May. We were all surprised by its instant reception, how everyone embraced it as if they'd discovered it on their own. In swift succession, translation rights were acquired by eleven countries; the Book-of-the-Month Club selected the book, author interviews were conducted by *Publishers Weekly* and the *Today* show—all before the book had even been published here in the United States.

Still, no one knew how to describe it. It was reviewed as a mystery, science fiction/fantasy, romance, thriller, adventure, literary, esoteric, and/or historical novel. As author, I was called the female Umberto Eco, Alexandre Dumas, Charles Dickens, and/or Steven Spielberg. Over the years *The Eight* has been a bestseller in forty or fifty countries and has been translated into more than thirty languages—largely, to judge from reader opinion, *because* it is unique.

Readers often asked when I would reprise the plot and characters. But given the interwoven nature of the plot, the kinds of surprises and secrets revealed in *The Eight* about the characters and the chess set, I thought the only way for the book to remain unique was *not* to make it into a sequel or a series. But my book, it seems, had a mind of its own; it wasn't yet through telling its story.

As events in real life unfolded following 2001, as they

involved more of the elements of my first novel's plot—oil, the Middle East, terrorism, Arabs, Berbers, Russians, the KGB, chess—I knew that I had to revisit the part of the world where the Montglane Service had originally been "invented" by al-Jabir in *The Eight:* Baghdad.

In 2006, my literary agents, Simon Lipskar in America and Andrew Nurnberg abroad, together convinced me to write the first three chapters of what I'd told them I was planning for the plot and characters in the sequel to *The Eight.* And the Ballantine team that "lit the match" that brought *The Fire* to life were: Random House Publishing Group president Gina Centrello; publisher Libby McGuire; and the wonderful Kimberly Hovey, who began twenty years ago as my original publicist for *The Eight,* who has been publicity director for my other Ballantine books over the years, and who is now Ballantine's director of marketing.

Finally, I'd especially like to credit my editor, Mark Tavani, for yanking the rug out from under me, in July of 2007, by telling me that I could not just "rest on my backstory" (as we say in fiction) but that I must dive deeper and soar higher.

So I did.

[illegible]

[illegible] more of the [illegible] of my [illegible] of [illegible] the Middle [illegible] [illegible] Bugs [illegible] the ACF [illegible] they had [illegible] part [illegible] where the Mongol [illegible] [illegible] by [illegible] The Fight [illegible]

In 2000 my literary agent [illegible] and Andrew [illegible] about [illegible] convinced me to write [illegible] stories of what I'd [illegible] fight [illegible] too

The Fight [illegible] that the [illegible] were Kamumi Honga [illegible] called Cima [illegible] and [illegible] However [illegible] years ago as my original [illegible] for [illegible] who has been [illegible] directly [illegible] other [illegible] books over the years and [illegible] the [illegible] of this book.

Thanks [illegible] editor [illegible] for [illegible] in [illegible] of 2002, [illegible] me that I could not just [illegible] back [illegible] that [illegible] consecutive [illegible] together.

[illegible] and